GRAND CENTRAL
PUBLISHING

October 2015

Dear Reader,

I think it is safe to say this is author Noah Hawley's moment. This year alone he won every top media award for his work as writer and creator of the TV show <u>Fargo</u>: the Emmy, the Golden Globe, the PGA, the Peabody, the Critics' Choice and a PEN award. And now, he has written BEFORE THE FALL, a book I think should be, deserves to be, and can be, <u>the</u> summer read...possibly <u>the</u> read of the entire year. Not only is it unputdownable, but it is smart. And it has been bought outright by Sony...with Noah writing the screenplay.

BEFORE THE FALL opens with this line—"A private plane sits on a runway in Martha's Vineyard, forward stairs deployed"—and immediately sucks you right in with a plot of survival and intrigue, driven by characters whose secrets and back stories will not let you go.

I urge you to start reading immediately. And I promise you, once you begin, you won't want to stop.

Best,

Deb Futter
Vice President, Editor-in-Chief

BEFORE
THE
FALL

BEFORE

THE

FALL

NOAH HAWLEY

GRAND CENTRAL
PUBLISHING

NEW YORK   BOSTON

Grand Central Publishing
Hachette Book Group
1290 Avenue of the Americas
New York, NY 10104

HachetteBookGroup.com

Printed in the United States of America

RRD-C

First Edition: May 2016

10 9 8 7 6 5 4 3 2 1

Grand Central Publishing is a division of Hachette Book Group, Inc.
The Grand Central Publishing name and logo is a trademark of Hachette Book Group, Inc.

The Hachette Speakers Bureau provides a wide range of authors for speaking events. To find out more, go to www.hachettespeakersbureau.com or call (866) 376-6591.

The publisher is not responsible for websites (or their content) that are not owned by the publisher.

Library of Congress Cataloging-in-Publication Data is available upon request.

ISBN 978-1-4555-6178-0 (hardcover)
ISBN 978-1-4555-6614-3 (large print)

For Kyle

BEFORE
THE
FALL

A PRIVATE PLANE sits on a runway in Martha's Vineyard, forward stairs deployed. It is a nine-seat OSPRY 45XR, built in 2001 in Wichita, Kansas. Whose plane it is is hard to say with real certainty. The ownership of record is a Dutch holding company with a Cayman Island mailing address, but the logo on the fuselage says GULLWING AIR. The pilot, James Melody, is British. Charlie Busch, the first officer, is from Odessa, Texas. The flight attendant, Emma Lightner, was born in Mannheim, Germany, to an American air force lieutenant and his teenage wife. They moved to San Diego when she was nine.

Everyone has their path. The choices they've made. How any two people end up in the same place at the same time is a mystery. You get on an elevator with a dozen strangers. You ride a bus, wait in line for the bathroom. It happens every day. To try to predict the places we'll go and the people we'll meet would be pointless.

A soft halogen glow emanates from the louvered forward hatch. Nothing like the harsh fluorescent glare you find in commercial planes. Two weeks from now, in a *New York Magazine* interview, Scott Burroughs will say that the thing that surprised him most about his first trip on a private jet was not the legroom or the full bar, but how personalized the decor felt, as if, at a certain income level, air travel is just another form of staying home.

1

It is a balmy night on the Vineyard, eighty-six degrees with light winds out of the southwest. The scheduled time of departure is ten p.m. For the last three hours, a heavy coastal fog has built over the sound, tendrils of dense white creeping slowly across the floodlit tarmac.

The Bateman family is the first to arrive in their island Range Rover: father David, mother Maggie, and their two children, Rachel and JJ. It's late August and Maggie and the kids have been on the Vineyard for the month, with David flying out from New York on the weekends. It's hard for him to get away any more than that, though he wishes he could. David is in the entertainment business, which is what people in his line of work call television news these days. A Roman circus of information and opinions.

He is a tall man in his with an intimidating phone voice. Strangers, upon meeting him, are often struck by the size of his hands. His son, JJ, has fallen asleep in the car, and as the others start toward the plane David leans into the back and gently lifts JJ from the car seat, supporting his weight with one arm. The boy instinctively throws his arms around his father's neck, his face slack from slumber. The warmth of his breath sends a chill down David's spine. He can feel the bones of his son's hips in his palm, the spill of legs against his side. At four, JJ is old enough to know that people die, but still too young to realize that that one day he will be one of them. David and Maggie call him their perpetual motion machine, because really it's just nonstop all day long. At three, JJ's primary means of communication was to roar like a dinosaur. Now he is the king of the interruption, questioning every word they say with seemingly endless patience until he's answered or shut down.

David kicks the car door closed with his foot, his son's weight pulling him off balance. He is holding his phone to his ear with his free hand.

"Tell him if he says a word about any of this," he says quietly, so as not to wake the boy, "we'll sue him biblically until he thinks lawyers are falling outta the sky like frogs."

At fifty-six, David wears a hard layer of fat around his frame like a bulletproof vest. He has a strong chin and a good head of hair. In the 1990s David built a name for himself running political campaigns—governors, senators, and one two-term president—but he retired in 2000 to run a lobbying firm on K Street. Two years later, an aging billionaire approached him with the idea of starting a twenty-four-hour news network. Thirteen years and thirteen billion in corporate revenue later, David has a top-floor office with bomb-resistant glass and access to the corporate jet.

He doesn't get to see the kids enough. David and Maggie both agree on this, though they fight about it regularly. Which is to say, she raises the issue and he gets defensive, even though, at heart, he feels the same. But then isn't that what marriage is, two people fighting for land rights to the same six inches?

Now, on the tarmac, a gust of wind blows up. David, still on the phone, glances over at Maggie and smiles, and the smile says *I'm glad to be here with you.* It says *I love you.* But it also says, *I know I'm in the middle of another work call and I need you to give me a break about it.* It says, *What matters is that I'm here, and that we're all together.*

It is a smile of apology, but there is also some steel in it.

Maggie smiles back, but hers is more perfunctory, sadder. The truth is, she can no longer control whether she forgives him or not.

They've been married less than ten years. Maggie is thirty-six, a former preschool teacher, the pretty one boys fantasize about before they even understand what that means—a breast fixation shared by toddler and teen. Miss Maggie, as they called her, was cheerful and loving. She came in early every morning at six thirty to straighten up. She stayed late to write progress reports and work on her lesson plan. Miss Maggie was a twenty-six-year-old girl from Piedmont, California, who loved teaching. Loved it. She was the first adult any of these three-year-olds had met who took them seriously, who listened to what they had to say and made them feel grown.

Fate, if you would call it that, brought Maggie and David together

3

in a ballroom at the Waldorf Astoria one Thursday night in early spring 2005. The ball was a black-tie fund-raiser for an educational fund. Maggie was there with a friend. David was on the board. She was the humble beauty in a floral dress with blue finger paint smeared on the small curve inside her right knee. He was the heavyweight charm shark in a two-button suit. She wasn't the youngest woman at the party, or even the prettiest, but she was the only one with chalk in her purse, the only one who could build a papier-mâché volcano and owned a striped *Cat in the Hat* stovepipe hat she would wear to work every year on Dr. Seuss's birthday. In other words, she was everything David had ever wanted in a wife. He excused himself and made his approach, smiling a cap-toothed smile.

In retrospect, she never had a chance.

Ten years later they have two children and a town house on Gracie Square. Rachel, nine years old, goes to Brearley with a hundred other girls. Maggie, retired from teaching now, stays home with JJ, which makes her unusual among women of her station—the carefree house-wives of workaholic millionaires. When she strolls her son to the park in the morning, Maggie is the only stay-at-home mother in the playground. All the other kids arrive in European-designed strollers pushed by island ladies on cell phones.

Now, on the airport runway, Maggie feels a chill run through her and pulls her summer cardigan tighter. The tendrils of fog have become a slow roiling surf, drafting with glacial patience across the tarmac.

"Are you sure it's okay to fly in this?" she asks her husband's back. He has reached the top of the stairs, where Emma Lightner, their flight attendant, wearing a trim blue skirt suit, greets him with a smile.

"It'll be fine, Mom," says Rachel, nine, walking behind her mother. "It's not like they need to see to fly a plane."

"No, I know."

"They have instruments."

Maggie gives her daughter a supportive smile. Rachel is wearing her green backpack—*Hunger Games*, Barbies, and iPad inside—and as she walks, it bumps rhythmically against the small of her back. Such a big girl. Even at nine there are signs of the woman she'll become. A professor who waits patiently as you figure out your own mistakes. The smartest person in the room, in other words, but not a show-off, never a show-off, with a good heart and musical laughter. The question is, are these qualities she was born with, or qualities seeded inside her by what happened? The true crime of her youth? Somewhere online the entire saga is recorded in words and pictures—archived news footage on YouTube, hundreds of man-hours of beat reporting all stored in the great collective memory of ones and zeros. A *New Yorker* writer wanted to do a book last year, but David quashed it quietly. Rachel is only a child, after all. Sometimes, when Maggie thinks about what could have gone wrong, she worries her heart will crack.

Instinctively, she glances over at the Range Rover, where Gil is getting their bags. Gil is their shadow, a big Israeli who never takes off his jacket. He is what people in their income bracket call *domestic security*. Six foot two, 190 pounds. There is a reason he never takes off his jacket, a reason that doesn't get discussed in polite circles. This is Gil's third year with the Bateman family. Before Gil there was Misha, and before Misha came the strike team of humorless men in suits, the ones with automatic weapons in the trunk of their car. In her schoolteacher days, Maggie would have scoffed at this kind of military intrusion into family life. She would have called it narcissistic to think that money made you a target for violence. But that was before the events of July 2008, before her daughter's kidnapping and the agonizing three days it took to get her back.

On the jet's stairs, Rachel spins and gives a mock royal wave to the empty runway. She is wearing blue fleece over her dress, her hair in a bowed ponytail. Any evidence that Rachel has been damaged by those three days remains mostly hidden—a fear of small spaces, a certain trepidation around strange men. But then Rachel has always been

5

a happy kid, a bubbly trickster with a sly smile, and though she can't understand how, Maggie is thankful every day that her kid hasn't lost that.

"Good evening, Mrs. Bateman," says Emma as Maggie reaches the top of the airplane stairs.

"Hi, thanks," says Maggie reflexively. She feels the usual need to apologize for their wealth, not her husband's necessarily, but her own, the sheer implausibility of it. She was a preschool teacher not so long ago, living in a six-story walk-up with two mean girls, like Cinderella.

"Is Scott here yet?" she asks.

"No, ma'am. You're the first to arrive. I've pulled a bottle of pinot gris. Would you like a glass?"

"Not right now. Thanks."

Inside, the jet is a statement of subdued luxury, contoured walls ribbed with sleek ash paneling. The seats are gray leather and laid out casually in pairs, as if to suggest you might enjoy the flight more with a partner. The cabin has a moneyed hush, like the inside of a presidential library. Though she's flown this way many times, Maggie still can't get over the indulgence of it. An entire airplane just for them.

David lays their son in his seat, covers him with a blanket. He is on another call already, this one clearly serious. Maggie can tell by the grim set of David's jaw. Below him the boy stirs in his seat but doesn't wake.

Rachel stops by the cockpit to talk to the pilots. It is something she does everywhere she goes, seeks out the local authority and grills them for information. Maggie spots Gil at the cockpit door, keeping the nine-year-old in sight. In addition to a handgun, he carries a Taser and plastic handcuffs. He is the quietest man Maggie has ever met.

Phone to his ear, David gives his wife's shoulder a squeeze.

"Excited to get back?" he asks, covering the mouthpiece with his other hand.

"Mixed," she says. "It's so nice out here."

"You could stay. I mean, we have that thing next weekend, but otherwise, why not?"

"No," she says. "The kids have school, and I've got the museum board thing on Thursday."

She smiles at him.

"I didn't sleep that well," she says. "I'm just tired."

David's eyes go to something over Maggie's shoulder. He frowns.

Maggie turns. Ben and Sarah Kipling stand at the top of the stairs. They're a wealthy couple, more David's friends than hers. All the same, Sarah squeals when she sees Maggie.

"Darling," she says, throwing open her arms.

Sarah gives Maggie a hug, the flight attendant standing awkwardly behind them, holding a tray of drinks.

"I love your dress," says Sarah.

Ben maneuvers past his wife and charges David, shaking his hand vigorously. He is a partner at one of the big four Wall Street firms, a blue-eyed shark in a tailored blue button-down shirt and a pair of belted white shorts.

"Did you see the fucking game?" he says. "How does he not catch that ball?"

"Don't get me started," says David.

"I mean, I could have caught that fucking ball and I've got French toast hands."

The two men stand toe-to-toe, mock posturing, two big bucks locking horns for the sheer love of battle.

"He lost it in the lights," David tells him, then feels his phone buzz. He looks at it, frowns, types a reply. Ben glances quickly over his shoulder, his expression sobering. The women are busy chatting. He leans in closer.

"We need to talk, buddy."

David shakes him off, still typing.

"Not now."

"I've been calling you," Kipling says. He starts to say more, but Emma is there with drinks.

"Glenlivet on the rocks, if I'm not mistaken," she says, handing Ben a glass.

"You're a doll," Ben says, and knocks back half the scotch in one gulp.

"Just water for me," David says as she lifts a glass of vodka from the tray.

"Of course," she says, smiling. "I'll be right back."

A few feet away, Sarah Kipling has already run out of small talk. She gives Maggie's arm a squeeze.

"How are you," she says, earnestly, and for the second time.

"No, I'm good," says Maggie. "I just—travel days, you know. I'll be happy when we're home."

"I know. I mean, I love the beach, but honestly? I get so bored. How many sunsets can you watch and not want to just, I don't know, go to Barneys?"

Maggie glances nervously at the open hatch. Sarah catches the look.

"Waiting for someone?"

"No. I mean, I think we'll be one more, but—"

Her daughter saves her from having to say more.

"Mom," says Rachel from her seat. "Don't forget, tomorrow is Tamara's party. We still have to get a gift."

"Okay," says Maggie, distracted. "Let's go to Dragonfly in the morning."

Looking past her daughter, Maggie sees David and Ben huddled together, talking. David doesn't look happy. She could ask him about it later, but her husband has been so standoffish lately, and the last thing she wants is a fight.

The flight attendant glides past her and hands David his water.

"Lime?" she says.

David shakes his head. Ben rubs his bald spot nervously. He glances at the cockpit.

"Are we waiting for somebody?" he says. "Let's get this show on the road."

"One more person," says Emma, looking at her list. "Scott Burroughs?"

Ben glances at David. "Who?"

David shrugs. "Maggie has a friend," he says.

"He's not a friend," Maggie says, overhearing. "I mean, the kids know him. We ran into him yesterday at the market. He said he had to go to New York, so I invited him to join us. I think he's a painter."

She looks at her husband.

"I showed you some of his work."

David checks his watch.

"You told him ten o'clock?" he says.

She nods.

"Well," he says, sitting, "five more minutes and he'll have to catch the ferry like everyone else."

Through a round portal window, Maggie sees the captain standing on the tarmac examining the wing. He stares up at the smooth aluminum, then walks slowly toward the plane.

Behind her, JJ shifts in slumber, his mouth slack. Maggie rearranges the blanket over him, then gives his forehead a kiss. He always looks so worried when he sleeps, she thinks.

Over the chair back she sees the captain reenter the plane. He comes over to shake hands, a man quarterback-tall with a military build.

"Gentlemen," he says, "ladies. Welcome. Should be a short flight. Some light winds, but otherwise the ride'll be pretty smooth."

"I saw you outside the plane," says Maggie.

"Routine visual inspection," he tells her. "I do it before every flight. The plane looks good."

"What about the fog?" asks Maggie.

Her daughter rolls her eyes.

"Fog isn't a factor with a sophisticated piece of machinery like this," the pilot tells them. "A few hundred feet above sea level and we're past it."

"I'm gonna eat some of this cheese then," says Ben. "Should we put on some music maybe? Or the TV? I think Boston's playing the Cubs."

Emma goes to find the game on the in-flight entertainment system, and there is a long moment of settling in as they take their seats and stow their belongings. Up front, the pilots run through their pre-flight instrument check.

David's phone buzzes again. He checks it, frowns.

"All right," says David, getting antsy. "I think that's all the time we've got for the painter."

He nods to Emma, who crosses to close the main cabin door. In the cockpit, as if by telepathy, the pilot starts the engines. The front door is almost closed when they hear a man's voice yell, "*Wait!*"

The plane shakes as their final passenger climbs the gangway stairs. Despite herself, Maggie feels herself flush, a thrum of anticipation starting in her belly. And then he is there, Scott Burroughs, mid-forties, looking flushed and out of breath. His hair is shaggy and starting to gray, but his face is smooth. There are worn gouache splotches on his white Keds, faded white and summer blue. He has a dirty green duffel bag over one shoulder. In his bearing there is still the flush of youth, but the lines around his eyes are deep and earned.

"Sorry," he says. "The cab took forever. I ended up taking a bus."

"Well, you made it," says David nodding to the copilot to close the door. "That's what matters."

"Can I take your bag, sir?" says Emma.

"What?" says Scott, startled momentarily by the stealthy way she has moved next to him. "No. I got it."

She points him to an empty seat. As he walks to it, he takes in the interior of the plane for the first time.

"Well, hell," he says.

"Ben Kipling," says Ben, rising to shake Scott's hand.

"Yeah," says Scott, "Scott Burroughs."

He sees Maggie.

"Hey," he says, giving her a wide, warm grin. "Thanks again for this."

Maggie smiles back, flushed.

"It's nothing," she says. "We had room."

Scott falls into a seat next to Sarah. Before he even has his seat belt on, Emma is handing him a glass of wine.

"Oh," he says. "No, thank you. I don't—some water maybe?"

Emma smiles, withdraws.

Scott looks over at Sarah.

"You could get used to this, huh?"

"Truer words have never been spoken," says Kipling.

The engines surge, and Maggie feels the plane start to move. Captain Melody's voice comes over the speakers.

"Ladies and gentlemen, please prepare for takeoff," he says.

Maggie looks over at her two kids, Rachel sitting with one leg folded under her, scrolling through songs on her phone, and little JJ hunched in slumber, slack-faced with childish oblivion.

As she does at a thousand random moments out of every day, Maggie feels a swell of motherly love, ballooning and desperate. They are her life, these children. Her identity. She reaches once more to readjust her son's blanket, and as she does there is that moment of weightlessness as the plane's wheels leave the ground. This act of impossible hope, this routine suspension of the physical laws that hold men down, inspires and terrifies her. Flying. They are flying. And as they rise up through the foggy white, talking and laughing, serenaded by the songs of 1950s crooners and the white noise of the long at bat, none of them has any idea that sixteen minutes from now their plane will crash into the sea.

1.

WHEN HE WAS six, Scott Burroughs took a trip to San Francisco with his family. They spent three days at a motel near the beach: Scott, his parents, and his sister, June, who would later drown in Lake Michigan. San Francisco was foggy and cold that weekend, wide avenues rolling like tongue tricks down to the water. Scott remembers his father ordering crab legs at a restaurant, and how, when they came, they were monstrous, the size of tree branches. As if the crabs should be eating them instead of the other way around.

On the last day of their trip Scott's dad got them on a bus down to Fisherman's Wharf. Scott—in faded corduroys and a striped T-shirt—knelt on the sloped plastic seat and watched as the flat wide stucco of the Sunset District turned to concrete hills and wide-plank Victorians lining the serious incline. They went to the Ripley's Believe It or Not Museum and had their caricatures drawn—a family of four comically oversize heads bobbling side by side on unicycles. Afterward, they stopped and watched the seals splay themselves on salt-soaked docks. Scott's mother pointed at flurries of white-winged gulls with wonder in her eyes. They were landlocked people. To Scott, it was if they had taken a spaceship to a distant planet.

For lunch they ate corn dogs and drank Coke out of comically large plastic cups. Entering Aquatic Park, they found a crowd had gathered.

There were dozens of people looking north and pointing toward Alcatraz.

The bay was slate gray that day, the hills of Marin framing the now defunct prison island like the shoulders of a guard. To their left the Golden Gate Bridge was a hazy, burnt-orange giant, suspension towers headless in the late-morning fog.

Out on the water Scott could see a mass of small boats circling.

"Was there an escape?" Scott's father asked aloud to no one.

Scott's mother frowned and pulled out a brochure. As far as she knew, she said, the prison was closed. The island was just for tourists now.

Scott's father tapped the man next to him on the shoulder.

"What are we looking at?" he asked.

"He's swimming over from Alcatraz," the man said.

"Who?"

"The exercise guy. What's it? Jack LaLanne. It's some kind of stunt. He's handcuffed and pulling a goddamn boat."

"What do you mean, pulling a boat?"

"There's a rope. This is off the radio. See that boat there. The big one. He's gotta drag that thing all the way over here."

The guy shook his head, like all of a sudden the world had gone insane on him.

Scott climbed to a higher step where he could see over all the adults. There was indeed a large boat out on the water, bow pointed toward shore. It was surrounded by a fleet of smaller boats. A woman leaned down and tapped Scott's arm.

"Here," she said, smiling, "take a look."

She handed Scott a small pair of binoculars. Through the lenses he could just make out a man in the water, wearing a beige swim cap. His shoulders were bare. He swam in surging forward lunges, like a mermaid.

"The current is nuts right there," the man told Scott's father. "Not to mention the damn water is, like, fifty-eight degrees. There's a reason nobody ever escaped from Alcatraz. Plus, you got the sharks. I give the guy one shot in five."

Through the binoculars Scott could see that the motorboats surrounding the swimmer were filled with men in uniforms. They were carrying rifles and staring down into the chop.

In the water the swimmer lifted his arms from the surf and surged forward. He was bound at the wrists, focused on the shore. His breathing was steady. If he was aware of the deputies or the risk of shark attack, he didn't show it. Jack LaLanne, the fittest man on earth. His sixtieth birthday was in five days. Sixty. The age where anyone with sense slows down, puts up their feet, and let a few things slide, but, as Scott would later learn, Jack's discipline transcended age. He was a tool constructed to complete a task, an overcoming machine. Around his waist, the rope was like a tentacle trying to pull him down into the cold, black deep, but he paid it no mind, as if by ignoring the weight he was pulling he could take away its power. Jack was used to it anyway, this rope. At home he tied himself to the side of the pool and swam in place for half an hour a day. This was in addition to ninety minutes of weight lifting and thirty minutes of running. Looking at himself in the mirror afterward, Jack didn't see a mortal man. He saw a being of pure energy.

He had done this swim before too, back in 1955. Alcatraz was still a prison then, a cold rock of penitence and punition. Jack was forty-one, a young buck already famous for being fit. He had the TV show and the gyms. Every week he stood in simple black and white wearing his trademark jumpsuit, tailored skintight, his biceps bulging. Every so often without warning he would drop to the floor and punctuate his advice with a hundred fingertip push-ups.

Fruits and vegetables, he'd say. Protein, exercise.

On NBC, Mondays at eight, Jack gave away the secrets of eternal life. All you had to do was listen. Towing the boat now, he remembered that first swim. They said it couldn't be done, a two-mile swim against strong ocean currents in fifty-degree water, but Jack did it in just under an hour. Now nineteen years later he was back, hands tied, legs bound, a thousand-pound boat chained to his waist.

In his mind there was no boat. There was no current. There were no sharks.

There was only his will.

"Ask the guys who are doing serious triathlons," he would later say, "if there are any limits to what can be done. The limit is right here [in your head]. You've got to get physically fit between the ears. Muscles don't know anything. They have to be taught."

Jack was the puny kid with the pimples who gorged himself on sweets, the pup who went sugar-mad one day and tried to kill his brother with an ax. Then came the epiphany, the burning bush resolve. In a flash it came to him. He would unlock his body's full potential. He would remake himself entirely, and by doing so change the world.

And so chubby sugar-brained Jack invented exercise. He became the hero who could do a thousand jumping jacks and a thousand chin-ups in ninety minutes. The muscle that trained itself to finish 1,033 push-ups in twenty minutes by climbing a twenty-five-foot rope with 140 pounds of weight strapped to his belt.

Everywhere he went, people came up to him on the street. It was the early days of television. He was part scientist, part magician, part god.

"I can't die," Jack told people. "It would ruin my image."

Now, in the water, he lunged forward using the flopping butterfly stroke that he'd invented. The shore was in sight, news cameras massing by the water. The crowd had grown. They spilled over the horseshoe steps. Jack's wife, Elizabeth, was among them, a former water ballerina who had chain-smoked and lived on donuts before she met Jack. "There he is," someone said, pointing. A sixty-year-old man pulling a boat.

Handcuffed. Shackled. He was Houdini, except he wasn't trying to escape. If Jack had his way he would be chained to this boat forever.

They'd add a new one every day until he was pulling the whole world behind him. Until he was carrying all of us on his back into a future where human potential was limitless.

Age is a state of mind, he told people. That was the secret. He would finish this swim and bound from the surf. He would leap into the air, like a boxer after a knockout. Maybe he'd even drop and knock off a hundred push-ups. He felt that good. At Jack's age, most men were stooped over, whining about their backs. They were nervous about the end. But not Jack. When he turned seventy he would swim for seventy hours pulling seventy boats filled with seventy people. When he turned a hundred they would rename the country after him. He would wake every morning with a boner of steel until the end of time.

On shore, Scott stood on tiptoes and stared out at the water. His parents were forgotten. The lunch he hadn't liked. There was nothing on earth now except the scene before him. The boy watched as the man in the swim cap struggled against the tide. Stroke after stroke, muscle against nature, willpower in defiance of witless primal forces. The crowd was on its feet, urging the swimmer on, stroke by stroke, inch by inch, until Jack LaLanne was walking out of the surf, newsmen wading out to meet him. He was breathing hard, lips turning blue, but he was smiling. The newsmen untied his wrists, pulled the rope from his waist. The crowd was going crazy. Elizabeth waded out into the waves, and Jack lifted her into the air as if she were nothing.

The waterfront was electrified. People felt like they were witnessing a miracle. For a long time after, they would find themselves believing that anything was possible. They would go through their day feeling elevated.

And Scott Burroughs, six years old, standing on the top step of the bleachers, found himself undone by a strange surge. There was a swelling in his chest, a feeling—elation? wonder?—that made him want to weep. Even at his young age he knew that he had witnessed something unquantifiable, some grand facet of nature that was more than animal. To do what this man had done—to strap weight to his body, bind his limbs, and swim two miles through freezing water—was something Superman would do. Was it possible? Was this Superman?

"Hell," said his father, ruffling Scott's hair. "That was really something. Wasn't that something?"

But Scott had no words. He just nodded, his eyes fixed on the strong man in the surf, who had picked a news reporter up over his head and was mock-throwing him out into the water.

"I see this guy on TV all the time," his dad said, "but I thought it was just a joke. With the puffed-up muscles. But man."

He shook his head from wonder.

"Is that Superman?" Scott asked.

"What? No. That's—I mean, just a guy."

Just a guy. Like Scott's dad or Uncle Jake, mustached and potbellied. Like Mr. Branch, his gym teacher with the Afro. Scott couldn't believe it. Was it possible? Could anyone be Superman if they just put their mind to it? If they were willing to do what it took? *Whatever* it took?

Two days later, when they got back to Indianapolis, Scott Burroughs signed up for swim class.

WAVES

HE SURFACES, SHOUTING. It is night. The salt water burns his eyes. Heat singes his lungs. There is no moon, just a diffusion of moonlight through the burly fog, wave caps churning midnight blue in front of him. Around him eerie orange flames lick the froth.

The water is on fire, he thinks, kicking away instinctively.

And then, after a moment of shock and disorientation:

The plane has crashed.

Scott thinks this, but not in words. In his brain are images and sounds. A sudden downward pitch. The panicked stench of burning metal. Screams. A woman bleeding from the head, broken glass glittering against her skin. And how everything that wasn't tied down seemed to float for an endless moment as time slowed. A wine bottle, a woman's purse, a little girl's iPhone. Plates of food hovering in midair, spinning gently, entrées still in place, and then the screech of metal on metal and the barrel roll of Scott's world ripping itself to pieces.

A wave smacks him in the face, and he kicks his feet to try to get higher in the water. His shoes are dragging him down, so he loses them, then forces his way out of his salt-soaked chinos. He shivers in the cold Atlantic current, treading water, legs scissoring, arms pushing the ocean away in hard swirls. The waves are quilted with froth,

21

not the hard triangles of children's drawings, but fractals of water, tiny waves stacking into larger ones. Out in the open water they come at him from all directions, like a pack of wolves testing his defenses. The dying fire animates them, gives them faces of sinister intent. Scott treads his way into a 360-degree turn. Around him he sees humps of jagged wreckage bobbing, pieces of fuselage, a stretch of wing. The floating gasoline has already dissipated or burned down. Soon everything will be dark. Fighting panic, Scott tries to assess the situation. The fact that it's August is in his favor. Right now the temperature of the Atlantic is maybe sixty-five degrees, cold enough for hypothermia, but warm enough to give him time to reach shore, if that's possible. If he's even close.

"Hey!" he shouts, turning himself in the water. "I'm here! I'm alive!"

There have to be other survivors, he thinks. How can a plane crash and only one person survive? He thinks about the woman sitting next to him, the banker's chatty wife. He thinks about Maggie with her summer smile.

He thinks about the children. Fuck. There were children. Two, yes? A boy and a girl. How old? The girl was bigger. Ten maybe? But the boy was small, a toddler still.

"Hello!" he shouts, with added urgency, swimming now toward the biggest piece of wreckage. It looks like part of a wing. When he reaches it, the metal is hot to the touch and he kicks away hard, not wanting to get swept onto it by the waves and burned.

Did the plane break up on impact? he wonders. Or did it crack open on the way down, spilling passengers?

It seems impossible that he doesn't know, but the data stream of memory is clogged with indecipherable fragments, pictures with no order, and right now he has no time to try to clarify anything.

Squinting in the dark, Scott feels himself rising suddenly on a heavy wave. He struggles to stay on top of it, realizing he can no longer avoid the obvious.

Straining to stay afloat, he feels something in his left shoulder pop. The ache he endured post-crash becomes a knife that cuts through him whenever he raises his left arm above his head. Kicking his legs, he tries to stretch the pain away, like you would a cramp, but it's clear something in the socket is torn or broken. He will have to be careful. He still has partial motion—can manage a decent breaststroke—but if the shoulder gets worse he could find himself a one-armed man, adrift, injured, a tiny fish in the saltwater belly of a whale.

It occurs to him then that he may be bleeding.

And that's when the word *sharks* enters his mind.

For a moment there is nothing but pure animal panic. Higher reason evaporates. His heart rate soars, legs kicking wildly. He swallows salt water and starts to cough.

Stop, he tells himself. *Slow down. If you panic right now, you will die.*

He forces himself to be calm, rotating slowly to try to get his bearings. If he could see stars, he thinks, he could orient himself. But the fog is too thick. Should he swim east or west? Back toward the Vineyard or toward the mainland? And yet how will he even know which is which? The island he has come from floats like an ice cube in a soup bowl. At this distance, if Scott's trajectory is off by even a few degrees he could easily swim right past it and never even realize.

Better, he thinks, to make for the long arm of the coast. If he keeps his stroke even, Scott thinks, rests occasionally, and doesn't panic, he will hit land eventually. He is a swimmer, after all, no stranger to the sea.

You can do this, he tells himself. The thought give him a surge of confidence. He knows from riding the ferry that Martha's Vineyard is seven miles from Cape Cod. But their plane was headed to JFK, which means it would have flown south over the open water toward Long Island. How far did they travel? How far are they from shore? Can Scott swim ten miles with one good arm? Twenty?

He is a land mammal adrift in the open sea.

. . .

The plane will have sent a distress signal, he tells himself. The Coast Guard is on its way. But even as he thinks this, he realizes that the last flame has gone out, and the debris field is scattering with the current.

To keep himself from panicking, Scott thinks of Jack. Jack, the Greek god in his swim trunks, grinning, arms flexed into rippling towers, shoulders hunched forward, lats popped out. The crab. That's what they called it. *Snapping a crab.* Scott kept his poster on the wall throughout his childhood. He had it there to remind himself that anything was possible. You could be an explorer or an astronaut. You could sail the seven seas, climb the tallest mountain. All you had to do was believe.

. . .

Under water, Scott folds himself in half, peeling off his wet socks and flexing his toes against the cool deep. His left shoulder is starting to tighten up on him. He rests it as much as he can, pulling his weight with the right, settling for fifteen minutes at a time into a child's dog paddle. Once more, he recognizes the sheer impossibility of what he must do, choose a direction at random and swim for who knows how many miles against strong ocean currents with only one working arm. Panic's cousin, despair, threatens to settle in, but he shakes it off.

His tongue is already starting to feel dry in his mouth. Dehydration is another thing he will have to worry about, if he's out here long enough. Around him the wind is picking up, roughing the seas. *If I'm going to do this*, Scott decides, *I need to start swimming now*. Once more he looks for a break in the fog, but there is none, so he closes his eyes for a moment. He tries to feel *west*, to divine it like the iron filling feels the magnet.

Behind you, he thinks.

He opens his eyes, takes a deep breath.

He is about to take his first stroke when he hears the noise. At first he thinks it's gulls, a high-pitched ululation that rises and falls. But then the sea lifts Scott a few feet, and at the wave's peak he realizes with a shock what he's hearing.

Crying.

Somewhere a child is crying.

He spins, trying to pinpoint the sound, but the waves rise and fall unevenly, creating bounces and echoes.

"Hey," he calls. "Hey, I'm here!"

The crying stops.

"Hey," he shouts, kicking against the undercurrent, "where are you?"

He looks for the wreckage, but whatever pieces haven't sunk have floated off in any number of directions. Scott strains to hear, to find the child.

"Hey!" he yells again. "I'm here. Where are you?"

For a moment there is just the sound of the waves, and Scott starts to wonder if maybe it was gulls he heard. But then a child's voice comes, sharp and surprisingly close.

"Help!"

Scott lunges toward the sound. He is no longer alone, no longer a solitary man engaged in an act of self-preservation. Now he is responsible for the life of another. He thinks of his sister who drowned in Lake Michigan when she was sixteen, and he swims.

He finds the child clinging to a seat cushion thirty feet away. It is the boy. He can't be more than four.

"Hey," says Scott when he reaches him. "Hey, sweetie."

His voice catches in his throat as he touches the boy's shoulder, and he realizes he is crying.

"I'm here," he says. "I've got you."

The seat cushion doubles as a flotation device with arm straps and a cinch belt, but it is designed for an adult, so Scott has a hard time getting it to stay on the boy, who is shivering from the cold.

"I threw up," the boy says.

Scott wipes his mouth gently.

"That's okay. You're okay. Just a little seasick."

"Where are we?" the little boy asks.

"We're in the ocean," Scott tells him. "There was a plane crash and we're in the ocean, but I'm going to swim to shore."

"Don't leave me," the boy says, panic in his voice.

"No, no," says Scott. "Of course not. I'm taking you with me. We're just going to—I have to get this thing to stay on you. And then I'll—you'll lie on top and I'll pull you behind me. How does that sound?"

The boy nods, and Scott gets to work. It's hard with only one working arm, but after a few torturous moments he manages to tie the flotation device straps into a weave. He slips the boy into the harness and studies the results. It's not as tight as he'd like, but it should keep the boy above the water.

"Okay," says Scott, "I need you to hold on tight and I'm going to pull you to shore. Can you—do you know how to swim?"

The kid nods.

"Good," says Scott. "So if you fall off the cushion I want you to kick real hard and paddle with your arms, okay?"

"Dog and cat," says the boy.

"That's right. Dog and cat with your hands, just like Mommy taught you."

"My daddy."

"Sure. Just like Daddy taught you, okay?"

The boy nods. Scott sees his fear.

"Do you know what a hero is?" Scott asks him.

"He fights the bad guys," the boy says.

"That's right. The hero fights the bad guys. And he never gives up, right?"

"No."

"Well, I need you to be the hero now, okay? Just pretend the waves are the bad guys and we're gonna swim through them. And we can't give up. We won't. We'll just keep swimming until we reach land, okay?"

The boy nods. Wincing, Scott loops his left arm through one of the straps. His shoulder is screaming now. Each swell that lifts them adds to his sense of disorientation.

"Okay," he says. "Let's do this."

Scott closes his eyes and tries once again to feel which way to swim. *Behind you*, he thinks. *The shore is behind you.*

He rotates carefully around the boy in the water and starts to kick, but just as he does moonlight breaks through the fog. A patch of starry black is briefly visible overhead. Scott searches desperately for constellations he recognizes, the gap closing quickly. Then he spots Andromeda, and then the Big Dipper, and with it the North Star.

It's the other way, he realizes with a sickening vertigo.

For a moment Scott feels an overwhelming urge to vomit. Had the sky not cleared, then he and the boy would have set out into the Atlantic deep, the East Coast receding behind them with every kick, until exhaustion overtook them and they sank without a trace.

"Change of plans," he tells the boy, trying to keep his voice light. "Let's go the other way."

"Okay."

"Okay. That's good."

Scott kicks them into position. The farthest he has ever swum is fifteen miles, but that was when he was nineteen, and he had trained for months. Plus the race was in a lake with no current. And both of his arms worked. Now it's night, and the water temperature is dropping, and he will have to fight the strong Atlantic current for who knows how many miles.

If I survive this, he thinks, *I'm going to send Jack LaLanne's widow a fruit basket.*

The thought is so ridiculous that, bobbing in the water, Scott starts to laugh, and for a moment can't stop. He thinks of himself standing at the counter of Edible Arrangements, filling out the card.

With deepest affection—Scott.

"Stop," says the boy, afraid suddenly that his survival is in the hands of a crazy person.

"Okay," says Scott, trying to reassure the boy. "It's okay. Just a joke I thought of. We're going now."

It takes him a few minutes to find his stroke, a modified breast-stroke, pulling water more with the right hand than the left, legs kicking hard. It is a noisy mess, his left shoulder a bag of broken glass. A gnawing worry settles into his gut. They will drown, both of them. They will both be lost to the deep. But then somehow a rhythm presents itself, and he begins to lose himself in the repetition. Arm up and in, legs scissoring. He swims into the endless deep, ocean spray in his face. It's hard to keep track of time. What time did the plane take off? Ten p.m.? How much time has passed? Thirty minutes? An hour? How long until the sun comes up? Eight hours? Nine?

Around him the sea is pockmarked and ever changing. Swimming, he tries not to think about the great tracts of open water. He tries not picture the depth of the ocean or how the Atlantic in August is the birthplace of massive storm fronts, hurricanes that form in the cold troughs of undersea gorges, weather patterns colliding, temperature and moisture forming huge pockets of low pressure. Global forces conspiring, barbarian hordes with clubs and war paint who charge shrieking into the fray, and instantly the sky thickens, blackens, an ominous gale of lightning strikes, huge claps of thunder like the screams of battle, and the sea, which moments ago was calm, turns to hell on earth.

Scott swims in the fragile calm, trying to empty his mind.

Something brushes against his leg.

He freezes, starts to sink, then has to kick his legs to stay afloat.

Shark, he thinks.

You have to stay still.

But if he stops moving he'll drown.

He rolls over onto his back, breathing deeply to inflate his chest. He has never been more aware of his tenuous place on the food chain. Every instinct in his body screams at him not to turn his back on the deep, but he does. He floats in the sea as calmly as he can, rising and falling with the tide.

"What are we doing?" the boy asks.

"Resting," Scott tells him. "Let's be real quiet now, okay? Don't move. Try to keep your feet out of the water."

The boy is silent. They rise and fall with the swells. Scott's primal reptilian brain orders him to flee. But he ignores it. A shark can smell a drop of blood in a million gallons of water. If either Scott or the boy is bleeding they're done. But if not and they stay completely still the shark (if it was a shark) should leave them alone.

He takes the boy's hand.

"Where's my sister?" the boy whispers.

"I don't know," Scott whispers back. "The plane went down. We got separated."

A long beat.

"Maybe she's okay," Scott whispers. "Maybe your parents have her, and they're floating someplace else. Or maybe they've already been rescued."

After a long silence the boy says:

"I don't think so."

They float for a while with this thought. Overhead the fog begins to dissipate. It starts slowly, the clearing, first a hint of sky peeking through, then stars appear, and finally the crescent moon, and just like that the ocean around them becomes a sequined dress. From his back, Scott finds the North Star, confirms that they're going in the right direction. He looks over at the boy, eyes wide with fear. For the first time Scott can see his tiny face, the furrowed brow and bowed mouth.

"Hi," says Scott, water lapping at his ears.

The boy's expression is flat, serious.

"Hi," he says back.

"Are we rested?" Scott asks.

The boy nods.

"Okay," says Scott, turning over. "Let's go home."

He rights himself and starts to swim, certain that at any moment he will feel a strike from below, the razor grip of a steam-shovel mouth, but it doesn't come, and after a while he puts the shark out of his mind. He wills them forward, stroke after stroke, his legs moving behind him in figure eights, his right arm lunging and pulling, lunging and pulling. To keep his mind busy, he thinks of other liquids he would rather be swimming in; milk, soup, bourbon. An ocean of bourbon.

He considers his life, but the details seem meaningless now. His ambitions. The rent that is due every month. The woman who has left him. He thinks of his work, brushstrokes on canvas. It is the ocean he is painting tonight, stroke by stroke, like Harold and his purple crayon, drawing a balloon as he falls.

Floating in the North Atlantic, Scott realizes that he has never been more clear about who he is, his purpose. It's so obvious. He was put on this earth to conquer this ocean, to save this boy. Fate brought him to that beach in San Francisco forty-one years ago. It delivered to him a golden god, shackled at the wrists, battling the ocean winds. Fate gave Scott the urge to swim, to join first his junior high swim team, then his high school and college crews. It pushed him to swim practice every morning at five, before the sun was up, lap after lap in the chlorinated blue, the applause of the other boys' splashing, the *kree* of the coach's whistle. Fate led him to water, but it was *will* that drove him to victory in three state championships, will that pushed him to a first-place medal in the men's two-hundred-meter freestyle in high school.

He came to love the pressure in his ears when he dove down to the pool's apple-smooth bottom. He dreamed of it at night, floating like a buoy in the blue. And when he started painting in college, blue was the first color he bought.

He is starting to get thirsty when the boy says:

"What's that?"

Scott lifts his head from the water. The boy is pointing at something to their right. Scott looks over. In the moonlight Scott sees a hulking black wave creeping silently toward them, growing taller, gathering strength. Scott measures it instantly at twenty-five feet, a monster bearing down. Its humped head sparkles in the moonlight. A lightning bolt of panic hits him. There is no time to think. Scott turns and starts swimming toward it. He has maybe thirty seconds to close the gap. His left shoulder screams at him, but he ignores it. The boy is crying now, sensing that death is near, but there isn't time to comfort him.

"Deep breath," Scott yells. "Take a deep breath now."

The wave is too big, too fast. It is on them before Scott can get a good breath himself.

He pulls the boy from the flotation device and dives.

Something in his left shoulder pops. He ignores it. The boy struggles against him, against the madman dragging him down to his death. Scott grips him tighter and kicks. He is a bullet, a cannonball streaking down through the water, diving under a wall of death. The pressure increases. His heart pounds, his lungs tick—swollen with air.

As the wave passes overhead, Scott is certain he has failed. He feels himself being sucked back up to the surface in a maelstrom of undertow. The wave will chew them up, he realizes, rip them apart. He kicks harder, holding the boy to his chest, fighting for every inch. Overhead the wave crests and topples into the sea behind them—twenty-five feet of ocean falling like a hammer, millions of gallons of angry surge—and the updraft is replaced in an instant by a churning rinse cycle.

They are spun and dragged. Down becomes up. Pressure threatens to rip them apart, man from boy, but Scott holds on. His lungs are screaming now. His eyes are burning from the salt. In his arms the boy has stopped struggling. The ocean is pure blackness, no sign of the stars or moon. Scott releases the air in his lungs and feels the bubbles cascade downward across his chin and arms. With all his strength he flips them over and kicks for the surface.

He emerges, coughing, his lungs half full of water. He screams them clear. The boy is limp in his arms, his head lying inert against Scott's shoulder. Scott turns the boy until his back is against Scott's chest, and then, with all his strength, compresses the boy's lungs in rhythm until he too is coughing up salt water.

The seat cushion is gone, chewed up by the wave. Scott holds the boy with his good arm. Cold and exhaustion threaten to overwhelm him. For a time it's all he can do just to keep them afloat.

"That was a big bad guy," the boy says finally.

For a moment Scott doesn't understand the words, but then it comes back to him. He told the boy that the waves were bad guys and they were the heroes.

So brave, Scott thinks, amazed.

"I could really go for a cheeseburger," he says, in the calm between waves. "What about you?"

"Pie," the boy says after a moment.

"What kind?"

"All of them."

Scott laughs. He cannot believe that he is still alive. He feels giddy for a moment, his body thrumming with energy. For the second time tonight he has faced certain death and lived. He looks for the North Star.

"How much longer?" the boy wants to know.

"It's not far," Scott tells him, though the truth is they could still be miles from shore.

"I'm cold," says the boy, his teeth chattering.

Scott hugs him.

"Me too. Hold on, okay?"

He maneuvers the boy onto his back, working to stay above the spray. The boy hugs Scott's neck, his breath loud in Scott's ear.

"Finish strong," Scott says, as much for himself as the boy.

He gives one more look to the sky, then starts to swim. He uses a sidestroke now, scissoring his legs, one ear submerged in the salty murk. His movements are clumsier, jerky. He can't seem to find a rhythm. Both of them are shivering, their core temperature falling with every passing second. It is just a matter of time. Soon his pulse and respiration will slow, even as his heart rate increases. Hypothermia will quicken its pace. A massive heart attack is not out of the question. The body needs warmth to operate. Without it, his major organs will start to fail.

Don't give up.

Never give up.

He swims without pause, teeth chattering, refusing to surrender. The weight of the boy threatens to sink him, but he kicks harder with his rubbery legs. Around him the sea is bruise purple and midnight blue, the cold white of the wave caps glimmering in the moonlight. The skin of his legs has started to chafe in the spots where they rub together, the salt doing its insidious damage. His lips are cracked and dry. Above them, seagulls chatter and glide like vultures waiting for the end. They mock him with their cries, and in his mind he tells them all to go to hell. There are things in the sea that are impossibly old, astonishingly large, great undersea rivers pulling warm water up from the Gulf of Mexico. The Atlantic Ocean is a nexus of highways, of undersea flyovers and bypasses. And there, like a speck on a dot on a flea, is Scott Burroughs, shoulder screaming as he fights for his life.

After what feels like hours, the boy shouts a single word.

"Land."

For a moment Scott isn't sure the boy actually spoke. It must be a dream. But then the boy repeats the word, pointing.

"Land."

It seems like a mistake, like the boy has mixed up the word for survival with the word for something else. Scott lifts his head, half blind with exhaustion. Behind them, the sun is starting to rise, a gentle pinkening to the sky. At first Scott thinks the landmass ahead of them is just some low-hanging clouds on the horizon, but then he realizes that he is the one who's moving.

Land. Miles of it. Open beach curving toward a rocky point. Streets and houses. Cities.

Salvation.

Scott resists the urge to celebrate. There is still a mile to go at least, a hard mile against riptides and undertow. His legs are quivering, his left arm numb. And yet he can't help but feel a surge of elation.

He did it. He saved them.

How is that possible?

. . .

Thirty minutes later a graying man in his underwear stumbles out of the surf, carrying a four-year-old boy. They collapse together onto the sand. The sun is up now, thin white clouds framed against a deep Mediterranean blue. The temperature is somewhere around sixty-eight degrees, gulls hanging weightless in the breeze. The man lies panting, a heaving torso ringed with useless rubber limbs. Now that they're here he cannot move another inch. He is done.

Curled up against his chest, the boy is crying softly.

"It's okay," Scott tells him. "We're safe now. We're gonna be okay."

There is an empty lifeguard station a few feet away. The sign on the back reads MONTAUK STATE BEACH.

New York. He swam all the way to New York.

Scott smiles, a smile of pure, joyous *fuck you*.

Well, hell, he thinks.

It's going to be beautiful day.

A WALLEYED FISHERMAN drives them to the hospital. The three crowd together on the worn bench seat of his pickup, bouncing on battered shocks. Scott is pantless and shoeless, without money or ID. Both he and the boy are racked with bone-deep chills. They have been in sixty-degree water for almost eight hours. Hypothermia has made them slow-witted and mute.

The fisherman speaks to them eloquently in Spanish about Jesus Christ. The radio is on, mostly static. Beneath their feet wind whistles into the cabin through a rust hole in the floor. Scott pulls the boy to him and tries to warm him through friction, rubbing the child's arms and back vigorously with his one good hand. On the beach, Scott told the fisherman in his limited Spanish that the boy was his son. It seemed easier than trying to explain the truth, that they are strangers drawn together by a freak accident.

Scott's left arm is completely useless now. Pain knifes through his body with every pothole, leaving him dizzy and nauseous.

You're okay, he tells himself, repeating the words over and over. *You made it.* But deep down he still can't believe they survived.

"*Gracias*," he stutters as the pickup pulls into the crescent driveway of the Montauk hospital emergency room. Scott bucks the door open with his good shoulder and climbs down, every muscle in his body

35

numb with exhaustion. The morning fog is gone, and the warm sun on his back and legs feels almost religious. Scott helps the boy jump down. Together they limp into the emergency room.

The waiting area is mostly empty. In the corner, a middle-aged man holds an icepack to his head, water dripping off his wrist onto the linoleum floor. On the other side of the room an elderly couple holds hands, their heads close together. From time to time the woman coughs into a balled-up Kleenex she keeps clutched tightly in her left hand.

An intake nurse sits behind glass. Scott limps over to her, the boy holding on to his shirttails.

"Hi," he says.

The nurse gives him a quick once-over. Her name tag reads MELANIE. Scott tries to imagine what he must look like. All he can think of is Wile E. Coyote after an ACME rocket has exploded in his face.

"We were in a plane crash," he says.

The words out loud are astonishing. The intake nurse squints at him.

"I'm sorry."

"A plane from Martha's Vineyard. A private plane. We crashed into the sea. I think we're hypothermic, and my—I can't move my left arm. The collarbone may be broken."

The nurse is still trying to work through it.

"You crashed in the sea."

"We swam—I swam—I think it was ten miles. Maybe fifteen. We just came ashore maybe an hour ago. A fisherman drove us here."

The words are making him dizzy, his lungs shutting down.

"Look," he says, "do you think we could get some help? At least the boy. He's only four."

The nurse looks at the boy, damp, shivering.

"Is he your son?"

"If I say *yes* will you get us a doctor?"

The nurse sniffles.

"There's no need to get surly."

Scott feels his jaw clenching.

"There is actually every need. We were in a fucking plane crash. Get the damn doctor."

She stands, uncertain.

Scott glances over at the ceiling-mounted television. The sound is down, but onscreen are images of search-and-rescue boats on the ocean. A banner headline reads, PRIVATE PLANE FEARED LOST.

"There," says Scott, pointing, "that's us. Will you believe me now?"

The nurse looks at the TV, images of fractured wreckage bobbing in the sea. Her reaction is instantaneous, as if Scott has produced a passport at the border crossing after pantomiming a frantic search.

She pushes the intercom button.

"Code Orange," she says. "I need all available doctors to intake immediately."

The cramping in Scott's leg is beyond critical. He is dehydrated, potassium-deficient, like a marathoner who has failed to give his body the nutrition it demands.

"Just," he says, buckling to the floor, "one would do, probably."

He lies on the cool linoleum looking up at the boy. The boy's face is sober, worried. Scott tries to smile reassuringly, but even his lips are exhausted. In an instant they are surrounded by hospital personnel, voices shouting. Scott feels himself being lifted onto a gurney. The boy's hand slips away.

"No!" the boy shouts. He is screaming, thrashing. A doctor is talking to him, trying to make the boy understand that they will take care of him, that nothing bad will happen. It doesn't matter. Scott struggles to sit up.

"Kid," he says, louder and louder until the boy looks at him. "It's okay. I'm here."

He climbs down off the gurney, his legs rubbery, barely able to stand.

"Sir," a nurse says, "you have to lie down."

"I'm fine," Scott tells the doctors. "Help him."

To the boy he says: "I'm here. I'm not going anywhere."

The boy's eyes, in daylight, are startlingly blue. After a moment he nods. Scott, feeling light-headed, turns to the doctor.

"We should do this fast," he says, "if it's not too much trouble."

The doctor nods. He is young and smart. You can see it in his eyes.

"Fine," he says, "But I'm getting you a wheelchair."

Scott nods. A nurse wheels over the chair and he falls into it.

"Are you his father?" she asks him as they roll to the exam room.

"No," Scott tells her. "We just met."

Inside the exam bay, the doctor gives the boy a quick once-over, checking for fractures, light in the eyes, *follow my finger.*

"We need to start an IV," he tells Scott. "He's severely dehydrated."

"Hey, buddy," Scott tells the boy, "the doctor needs to put a needle in your arm, okay? They need to give you some fluids, and, uh, vitamins."

"No needles," the boy says, fear in his eyes. He is one wrong word away from losing his mind.

"I don't like them either," says Scott, "but you know what? I'll get one too, okay? We'll do it together. How about that?"

The boy thinks about this. It seems fair. He nods.

"Okay, good," says Scott. "Let's—hold my hand and we'll—don't look, okay?"

Scott turns to the doctor.

"Can you do us together?" he asks.

The doctor nods, issues orders. The nurses ready the needles and hang IV bags on metal arms.

"Look at me," Scott tells the boy when the time comes.

The boy's eyes are blue saucers. He flinches when the needle goes in. His eyes tear up and his bottom lip quivers, but he doesn't cry.

"You're my hero," Scott tells him. "My absolute hero."

Scott can feel the fluids entering his system. Almost immediately the urge to pass out dissipates.

"I'm going to give you both a mild sedative," the doctor says. "Your bodies have been working overtime just to stay warm. You need to downshift."

"I'm fine," Scott says. "Do him first."

The doctor sees there's no point in arguing. A needle is inserted into the boy's IV line.

"You're going to rest a little bit," Scott tells him. "I'll be right here. I may go outside for a minute, but I'll come back. Okay?"

The boy nods. Scott touches the crown of his head. He remembers when he was nine and he fell out of a tree and broke his leg. How he was brave through the whole thing, but when his dad showed up at the hospital Scott started bawling. And now this boy's parents are most likely dead. No one is going to walk through the door and give him permission to fall apart.

"That's good," he tells the boy as his little eyes start to flutter shut. "You're doing so good."

After the boy is asleep, Scott is wheeled into a separate exam room. They lay him on a gurney and cut off his shirt. His shoulder feels like an engine that has seized.

"How are you feeling?" the doctor asks him. He is maybe thirty-eight with smile lines around his eyes.

"You know," says Scott, "things are starting to turn around."

The doctor does a surface exam, checking for obvious cuts or bruises.

"Did you really swim all that way in the dark?"

Scott nods.

"Do you remember anything?"

"I'm a little fuzzy on details," Scott tells him.

The doctor checks his eyes.

"Hit your head?"

"I think so. On the plane before we crashed..."

The penlight blinds him for a moment. The doctor clucks.

"Eye response looks good. I don't think you have a concussion."

Scott exhales.

"I don't think I could have done that—swim all night—with a concussion."

The doctor considers this.

"You're probably right."

As he warms up and his fluids are replaced, things start to come back to Scott, the world at large, the concept of countries and citizens, of daily life, the Internet, television. He thinks of his three-legged dog, staying with a neighbor, how close she came to never eating another under-the-table meatball again. Scott's eyes fill with tears. He shakes them off.

"What's the news saying?" he asks.

"Not much. They say the plane took off around ten o'clock last night. Air traffic control had it on their radar for maybe fifteen minutes, then it just disappeared. No mayday. Nothing. They were hoping the radio was broken and you made an emergency landing someplace. But then a fishing boat spotted a piece of the wing."

For a moment Scott is back in the ocean, treading water in the inky deep, surrounded by orange flames.

"Any other... survivors?" he asks.

The doctor shakes his head. He is focused on Scott's shoulder.

"Does this hurt," he says, gently lifting Scott's arm.

The pain is instantaneous. Scott yells.

"Let's get an X-ray and a CAT scan," the doctor tells the nurse.

He turns to Scott.

"I ordered a CAT scan for the boy too," he says. "I want to make sure there's no internal bleeding."

He lays a hand on Scott's arm.

"You saved his life," he says. "You know that, right?"

For the second time, Scott fights back tears. He is unable, for a long moment, to say anything.

"I'm going to call the police," the doctor tells him. "Let them know you're here. If you need anything, anything, tell the nurse. I'll be back to check on you in a few."

Scott nods.

"Thanks," he says.

The doctor stares at Scott for a moment longer, then shakes his head.

"Goddamn," he says, smiling.

. . .

The next hour is filled with tests. Flush with warm fluids, Scott's body temperature returns to normal. They give him Vicodin for the pain, and he floats for a while in twilight oblivion. It turns out his shoulder is dislocated, not broken. The procedure to pop it back into place is an epic lightning strike of violence followed immediately by a cessation of pain so intense it's as if the damage has been erased from his body retroactively.

At Scott's insistence, they put him in the boy's room. Normally, children stay in a separate wing, but an exception is made given the circumstances. The boy is awake now, eating Jell-O, when they wheel Scott inside.

"Any good?" Scott wants to know.

"Green," the boy says, frowning.

Scott's bed is by the window. He has never felt anything as comfortable as these scratchy hospital sheets. Across the street there are trees and houses. Cars drive past, windshields flashing. In the bike lane, a woman jogs against traffic. In a nearby yard, a man in a blue ball cap push-mows his lawn.

It seems impossible, but life goes on.

"You slept, huh?" says Scott.

The boy shrugs.

"Is my mommy here yet?" he says.

Scott tries to keep his face neutral.

"No," Scott tells him. "They've called your—I guess you have an aunt and uncle in Connecticut. They're on their way."

The boy smiles.

"Ellie," he says.

"You like her?"

"She's funny," the boy says.

"Funny is good," says Scott, his eyelids fluttering. *Exhausted* doesn't describe the kind of heavy-metal gravity pulling at his bones right now. "I'm going to sleep for a bit, if that's okay."

If the boy thinks otherwise, Scott never hears it. He is asleep before the kid can answer.

. . .

He sleeps for a while, a dreamless slumber, like a castle dungeon. When he wakes the boy's bed is empty. Scott panics. He is half out of bed when the bathroom door opens and the boy comes out wheeling his IV stand.

"I had to tinkle," he says.

A nurse comes in to check Scott's blood pressure. She's brought a stuffed animal for the boy, a brown bear with a red heart in its paws. He takes it with a happy sound and immediately starts to play.

"Kids," the nurse says, shaking her head.

Scott nods. Now that he's slept he is anxious to get more details about the crash. He asks the nurse if he can get out of bed. She nods, but tells him not to go far.

"I'll be back, buddy, okay?"

The boy nods, playing with his bear.

Scott puts a thin cotton robe over his hospital gown and walks his IV stand down the hall to the empty patient lounge. It's a narrow interior room with particleboard chairs. Scott finds a news channel on TV, turns up the volume.

"...the plane was an OSPRY, manufactured in Kansas. On board were David Bateman, president of ALC News, and his family. Also confirmed now as passengers are Ben Kipling and his wife, Sarah. Kipling was a senior partner at Wyatt, Hathoway, the financial giant. Again, the plane is believed to have gone down in the Atlantic Ocean off the coast of New York sometime after ten p.m. last night."

Scott stares at the footage, helicopter shots of gray ocean swells. Coast Guard boats and rubbernecking weekend sailors. Even though he knows the wreckage would have drifted, maybe even a hundred miles by now, he can't help but thinking that he was down there not that long ago, an abandoned buoy bobbing in the dark.

"Reports are coming in now," says the anchor, "that Ben Kipling may have been under investigation by the SEC, and that charges were forthcoming. The scope and source of the investigation aren't yet clear. More on this story as it develops."

A photo of Ben Kipling appears on the screen, younger and with more hair. Scott remembers the eyebrows. He realizes that everyone else on that plane except he and the boy exist now only in the past tense. The thought makes the hair on his neck flutter and stand, and for a moment he thinks he may pass out. Then there is a knock on the door. Scott looks up. He sees a group of men in suits hovering in the hallway.

"Mr. Burroughs," says the knocker. He is in his early fifties, an African American man with graying hair.

"I'm Gus Franklin with the National Transportation Safety Board."

Scott starts to stand. A reflex of social protocol.

"No, please," says Gus. "You've been through a lot."

Scott settles back onto the sofa, pulling the cotton robe closed over his legs.

"I was just—watching it on TV," he says. "The rescue. Salvage? I'm not sure what to call it. I think I'm still in shock."

"Of course," says Gus. He looks around the small room.

"Let's—I'm gonna say four people max in this room," he tells his cohorts. "Otherwise, it's gonna get a little claustrophobic."

There is a quick conference. Ultimately, they agree on six, Gus and two others (one man and one woman) in the room; two more in the doorway. Gus sits beside Scott on the sofa. The woman is to the left of the television. A trim, bearded man to her right. They are, for want of a better word, nerds. The woman has a ponytail and glasses. The man sports an eight-dollar haircut and a JCPenney suit. The two men in the doorway are more serious, well dressed, military haircuts.

"As I said," says Gus, "I'm with the NTSB. Tracy's with the FAA and Frank is with OSPRY. And in the doorway is Special Agent O'Brien from the FBI and Barry Hex from the SEC."

"The SEC," says Scott. "I just saw something about that on the TV."

Hex chews gum silently.

"If you feel up to it, Mr. Burroughs," says Gus, "we'd like to ask you some questions about the flight, who was on it, and the circumstances leading up to the crash."

"Assuming it was a crash," says O'Brien. "And not an act of terrorism."

Gus ignores this.

"Here's what I know," he tells Scott. "As of now we've found no other survivors. Nor have we recovered any bodies. A few pieces of wreckage were found floating about twenty-nine miles off the coast of Long Island. We're examining them now."

He leans forward, placing his hands on his knees.

"You've been through a lot, so if you want to stop just say so."

Scott nods.

"Somebody said the boy's aunt and uncle are coming from Connecticut," he says. "Do we know when they'll get here?"

Gus looks at O'Brien, who ducks out of the room.

"We're checking that for you," says Gus. He pulls a file folder from his briefcase. "So the first thing I need to do is confirm how many people were on the flight."

"Don't you have, I mean, an itinerary?" Scott asks.

"Private jets file flight plans, but their passenger rosters are pretty unreliable."

He looks over his paperwork.

"Am I right in saying your name is Scott Burroughs?"

"Yes."

"Do you mind giving me your Social Security number? For our records."

Scott recites the number. Gus writes it down.

"Thanks," he says. "That helps. There are sixteen Scott Burroughs in the tristate area. We weren't sure exactly which one we were dealing with."

He offers Scott a smile. Scott tries to work up an encouraging response.

"From what we've been able to piece together," Gus tells him, "the flight was crewed by a captain, a first officer, and a flight attendant. Would you recognize the names if I said them?"

Scott shakes his head. Gus makes a note.

"Passenger-wise," says Gus, "we know that David Bateman chartered the flight and that he and his family—wife Maggie and two children, Rachel and JJ—were on board."

Scott thinks of the smile Maggie gave him when he boarded. Warm and welcoming. A woman he knew in passing, small talk at the market—*How are you? How are the kids?*—the occasional conversation about his work. That she is dead right now at the bottom of the Atlantic makes him want to throw up.

"And finally," says Gus, "in addition to yourself, we believe that Ben Kipling and his wife, Sarah, were on board. Can you confirm that?"

"Yes," says Scott. "I met them when I got on the plane."

"Describe Mr. Kipling for me, please," asks Hex, the agent with the SEC.

"Uh, maybe five-eleven, gray hair. He had, uh, very prominent eyebrows. I remember that. And his wife was very chatty."

Hex looks at O'Brien, nods.

"And just so we're clear," says Gus. "Why were you on the plane?"

Scott looks at their faces. They are detectives scrambling for facts, filling in missing pieces. A plane has crashed. Was it mechanical failure? Human error? Who can be blamed? Who is liable?

"I was—" says Scott, then starts again, "—I met Maggie, Mrs. Bateman, on the island a few weeks ago. At the farmers market. I would—I went there every morning for coffee and a bialy. And she would come in with the kids. But sometimes alone. And we started talking one day."

"Were you sleeping with her?" asks O'Brien.

Scott thinks about this.

"I wasn't," he says. "Not that it's relevant."

"Let us decide what's relevant," O'Brien says.

"Sure," says Scott, "though maybe you can explain to me how the sexual interactions of a passenger in a plane crash are relevant to your—what is this?—investigation."

Gus nods quickly three times. They are getting off course. Every second wasted takes them farther from the truth.

"Back to the point," he says.

Scott holds O'Brien's eye for a long antagonistic moment, then continues.

"I ran into Maggie again Sunday morning. I told her I had to go to New York for a few days. She invited me to fly with them."

"And why were you going to New York?"

"I'm a painter. I've been—I live on the Vineyard and I was going in to meet with my rep and talk to some galleries about doing a show. My plan was to take the ferry to the mainland. But Maggie invited me, and, well, a private plane. The whole thing seemed very—I almost didn't go."

"But you did."

Scott nods.

"At the last minute. I threw some things together. They were actually closing the doors when I ran up."

"Lucky for the boy you made it," says Leslie from the FAA.

Scott thinks about it. Was it lucky? Is there anything lucky about surviving a tragedy?

"Did Mr. Kipling seem agitated to you?" Hex interjects, clearly impatient. He has his own investigation and it has little to do with Scott.

Gus shakes him off.

"Let's do this in order," he says. "I'm leading this—it's my investigation."

He turns to Scott.

"The airport log says the plane took off at ten oh six."

"Sounds right," says Scott. "I didn't look at my phone."

"Can you describe the takeoff?"

"It was—smooth. I mean, it was my first private jet."

He looks at Frank, the OSPRY rep.

"Very nice," he says. "Except for the crashing, I mean."

Frank looks stricken.

"So you don't remember anything unusual?" Gus asks. "Any sounds or jostling out of the ordinary?"

Scott thinks back. It happened so fast. Before he could even get his seat belt on they were taxiing. And Sarah Kipling was talking to him, asking him about his work and how he knew Maggie. And the girl was on her iPhone, listening to music or playing a game. The boy was sleeping. And Kipling was—*what was he doing?*

"I don't think so," he says. "I remember—you felt the force of it more. The power. I guess that's what a jet is. But then we were off the ground and rising. Most of the shades were closed and it was very light in the cabin. There was a baseball game on the TV."

"Boston played last night," says O'Brien.

"Dworkin," says Frank in a knowing way, and the two feds in the doorway smile.

"I don't know what that means," Scott says, "but I also remember music. Something jazzy. Sinatra maybe?"

"And did there come a time when something unusual happened?" Gus asks.

"Well, we fell into the ocean," says Scott.

Gus nods.

"And how exactly did that happen?"

"Well—I mean—it's hard to remember exactly," Scott tells him. "The plane turned suddenly, pitched, and I—"

"Take your time," says Gus.

Scott thinks back. The takeoff, the offered glass of wine. Images flash through his mind, an astronaut's vertigo, a blare of sounds. Metal shrieking. The disorienting whirl. Like a movie negative that has been cut and reassembled at random. It is the job of the human brain to assemble all the input of our world—sights, sounds, smells—into a coherent narrative. This is what memory is, a carefully calibrated story that we make up about our past. But what happens when those details crumble? Hailstones on a tin roof. Fireflies firing at random. What happens when your life can't be translated into a linear narrative?

"There was banging," he says. "I think. Some kind of—I want to say concussion."

"Like an explosion?" asks the man from OSPRY, hopefully.

"No. I mean, I don't think so. It was more like—a knocking and then—at the same time the plane kind of—dropped."

Gus thinks about saying something then, a follow-up question, but doesn't.

In his mind, Scott hears a scream. Not of terror, but an involuntary expulsion, a reflexive vocal reaction to something unexpected. It is the sound fear makes when it first appears, the sudden, visceral realization that you are not safe, that this activity you are engaged in is deeply, deeply risky. Your body makes the sound and immediately you break out in a cold sweat. Your sphincter clenches. Your mind, which up until this moment has been moving along at pedestrian speeds, suddenly races forward, running for its life. Fight or flight. It is the moment when the intellect fails and something primal, animal takes over.

With a sudden prickling certainty, Scott realizes that the scream came from him. And then blackness. His face pales. Gus leans in.

"Do you want to stop?"

Scott exhales.

"No. It's fine."

Gus asks an aide to bring Scott a soda from the machine. While they're waiting Gus lays out the facts he's managed to assemble.

"According to our radar," he says, "the plane was in the air for fifteen minutes, forty-one seconds. It reached an altitude of twelve thousand feet, then began to descend rapidly."

Sweat is dripping down Scott's back. Images are coming back to him, memories.

"Things were—*flying* is the wrong word," he says. "Around. Stuff. I remember my duffel bag. It just kind of levitated off the floor, just calmly floated up in the air like a magic trick, and then, just as I reached for it, it just—took off, just disappeared. And we were spinning, and I hit my head, I guess."

"Do you know if the plane broke up in the air?" Leslie from the FAA asks him. "Or was the pilot able to make a landing."

Scott tries to remember, but it's just flashes. He shakes his head.

Gus nods.

"Okay," he says. "Let's stop there."

"Hold on," says O'Brien. "I still have questions."

Gus stands.

"Later," he says. "Right now I think Mr. Burroughs needs to rest."

The others stand. This time Scott gets to his feet. His legs are shaking.

Gus offers his hand.

"Get some sleep," he says. "I saw two news vans pull up outside as we were coming in. This is going to be a story, and you're going to be at the center of it."

Scott can't for the life of him figure out what he's talking about.

"What do you mean?" he says.

"We'll try to shield your identity as long as possible," Gus tells him.

"Your name wasn't on the passenger roster, which helps. But the press is going to want to know how the boy made it to shore. Who saved him. Because that's a story. You're a hero now, Mr. Burroughs. Try to wrap your mind around that—what it means. Plus, the boy's father, Bateman, was a big deal. And Kipling—well, you'll see—this is a very messy situation."

He extends his hand. Scott shakes it.

"I've seen a lot of things in my day," says Gus, "but this—"

He shakes his head.

"You're a hell of a swimmer, Mr. Burroughs."

Scott feels numb. Gus herds the other agents out of the room with his hands.

"We'll talk again," he says.

After they're gone Scott sways on his feet inside the empty lounge. His left arm is in a polyurethane sling. The room is buzzing with silence. He takes a deep breath, lets it out. He is alive. This time yesterday he was eating lunch on his back porch and staring out at the yard, egg salad and iced tea. The three-legged dog was lying in the grass licking her elbow. There were phone calls to make, clothes to pack.

Now everything has changed.

He wheels his IV over to the window, looks out. In the parking lot he sees six news vans, satellite dishes deployed. A crowd is gathering. How many times has the world been interrupted by the cable buzz of special reports? Political scandals, spree killings, celebrity intercourse caught on tape. Talking heads with their perfect teeth ripping apart the still-warm body? Now it is his turn. Now he is the story, the bug under the microscope. To Scott, watching through tempered glass, they are an enemy army massing at the gates. He stands in his turret watching them assemble their siege engines and sharpen their swords.

All that matters, he thinks, is that the boy be saved from that.

A nurse knocks on the door of the lounge. Scott turns.

"Okay," she tells him. "Time to rest."

Scott nods. He remembers the moment from last night when the fog first cleared, and the North Star became visible. A distant point of light that brought with it absolute certainty about which direction they should go.

Standing there, studying his reflection in the glass, Scott wonders if he will ever have that kind of clarity again. He takes a last look at the growing mob, then turns and walks back to his room.

List of the Dead

David Bateman, 56
Margaret Bateman, 36
Rachel Bateman, 9
Gil Baruch, 48
Ben Kipling, 52
Sarah Kipling, 50
James Melody, 50
Emma Lightner, 25
Charlie Busch, 30

DAVID BATEMAN

APRIL 2, 1959–AUGUST 26, 2015

IT WAS THE chronic chaos that made it interesting. The way a story could spark from a cinder and race through a news cycle, changing speed and direction, growing wilder, devouring everything in its path. Political gaffes, school shootings, crises of national and international import. News, in other words. On the tenth floor of the ALC Building the newsmen rooted for fires, both literal and metaphoric, betting money on them like a back-alley dice game.

Anyone who could guess the length of a scandal down to the hour got a salad spinner, David used to say. Cunningham would give you the watch off his wrist if you could predict a politician's apology word for word before it happened. Napoleon offered sex with his wife to any reporter who could get a White House press secretary to curse into an open mike. They spent hours establishing the ground rules on that one—what constituted a curse? *Fuck*, sure. *Shit* or *twat*. But what about *damn*? Was *hell* enough?

"*Hell* will get you a handjob," Napoleon told them, feet stacked up on his desk, left over right, but when Cindy Bainbridge got Ari Fleischer to say it, Napoleon told her it didn't count because she was a girl.

If you were lucky, what started as a brush fire—a governor's name found on the client list of a call-girl ring, for example—quickly became a raging inferno, exploding in backdraft share points and swal-

53

lowing all the oxygen out of the broadcast market. David used to remind them constantly that Watergate started with a simple B&E.

"What was Whitewater, after all," he'd say, "but a bush-league, Podunk land scandal?"

They were twenty-first-century newsmen, prisoners of the cycle. History had taught them to dig for scandal in the fringes of every fact. Everyone was dirty. Nothing was simple except for the message.

ALC News, with a staff of fifteen thousand and a viewership that hovered around two million a day, was founded in 2002 with a hundred-million-dollar investment by an English billionaire. David Bateman was its architect, its founding father. In the trenches they called him The Chairman. But really what he was was a general, like George S. Patton who stood unflinchingly as machine-gun fire strafed the dirt between his legs.

David had worked on both sides of the political scandal racket in his day. First, in his role as a political consultant running to stay ahead of the gaffes and missteps of his candidates, and then, after he retired from politics, in constructing an upstart twenty-four-hour news network. That was thirteen years ago. Thirteen years of outrage and messaging, of jeering chyrons and knock-down, drag-out war; 4,745 days of constant signal; 113,880 hours of sports and punditry and weather; 6,832,800 minutes of tick-tock air to fill with words and pictures and sound. The sheer, endless volume of it was daunting sometimes. Hour after hour stretching out to eternity.

What saved them was that they were no longer slaves to the events they covered. No longer held hostage by the action or inaction of others. This was the Big Idea that David had brought to the table in constructing the network, his masterstroke. Sitting down for lunch with the billionaire all those years ago, he laid it out simply.

"All these other networks," he said, "they *react* to the news. Chase after it. We're going to Make The News."

What that meant, he said, was that unlike CNN or MSNBC, ALC would have a point of view, an agenda. Sure, there would still be random of acts of God to cover, celebrity deaths and sex scandals. But that was just gravy. The meat and potatoes of their business would come from shaping the events of the day to fit the message of their network.

The billionaire loved this idea, of controlling the news, as David knew he would. He was a billionaire, after all, and billionaires get to be billionaires by taking control. After coffee they settled it with a handshake.

"How soon can you be up and running?" he asked David.

"Give me seventy-five million and I'll be on the air in eighteen months."

"I'll give you a hundred. Be on in six."

And they were. Six months of frantic building, of stealing anchors from other networks, of logo design and theme music composition. David found Bill Cunningham throwing snark on a second-tier newsmagazine show. Bill was an angry white guy with a withering wit. David saw past the small time of the program. He had a vision of what the guy could become with the right platform, a godhead from Easter Island, a touchstone. There was a point of view there that David felt just might personify their brand.

"Brains aren't something they hand out in Ivy League schools," Cunningham told David when they met for breakfast that first time. "We're all born with them. And what I can't stand is this elitist attitude that we're all, none of us, smart enough to run our own country."

"You're doing a rant now," David told him.

"Where'd you go to college anyway?" Cunningham asked him, ready to pounce.

"Saint Mary's Landscaping Academy."

"Seriously. I went to Stonybrook. State school. And when I got out, none of those fucks from Harvard or Yale would give me the time of day. And pussy? Forget it. I had to sleep with Jersey girls for six years until I got my first on-air."

They were in a Cuban-Chinese place on Eighth Avenue, eating

eggs and drinking paint-brown coffee. Cunningham was a big guy, tall with a deliberate loom. He liked to get in your face, to unpack his suitcase and move in.

"What do you think of TV news?" David asked him.

"Shit," said Cunningham, chewing. "This pretend impartiality, like they don't take sides, but look at what they're reporting. Look at who the heroes are. The working stiff? No way. The churchgoing family man who works a double so his kid can go to college? It's a joke. We got a guy in the White House getting blowjobs from those guys' daughters. But the president's a Rhodes Scholar so I guess that makes it okay. They call it objective. I call it bias, pure and simple."

The waiter came and left the check, an old striped carbon sheet torn from a pocket-size pad. David still has it, framed on the wall of his office, one corner discolored by coffee. As far as the world was concerned Bill Cunningham was a washed-up, second-rate Maury Povich, but David saw the truth. Cunningham was a star, not because he was better than you or me, but because he *was* you or me. He was the raging voice of common sense, the sane man in an insane world. Once Bill was on board, the rest of the pieces fell into place.

Because at the end of the day, Cunningham was right, and David knew it. TV newsmen tried so hard to appear objective when the truth was, they were anything but. CNN, ABC, CBS, they sold the news like groceries in a supermarket, something for everyone. But people didn't want just information. They wanted to know what it meant. They wanted perspective. They needed something to react against. I agree or I don't agree. And if a viewer didn't agree more than half of the time, was David's philosophy, they turned the channel.

David's idea was to turn the news into a club of the like-minded. The first adopters would be the ones who'd been preaching his philosophy for years. And right behind them would be the people who had been searching their whole lives for someone to say out loud what they'd always felt in their hearts. And once you had those two groups, the curious and the undecided would follow in droves.

This deceptively simple reconfiguration of the business model turned out to bring a sea change to the industry. But for David, it was simply a way to relieve the stress of waiting. Because what is the news business, really, except the work of hypochondriacs? Anxious men and women who inflate and investigate every tic and cough, hoping that this time it might be the big one. Wait and worry. Well, David had no interest in waiting, and he had never been one to worry.

He grew up in Michigan, the son of an autoworker at a GM plant, David Bateman Sr., who never took a sick day, never skipped a shift. David's dad once counted the cars he'd built over the thirty-four years he worked the rear suspension line. The number he came up with was 94,610. To him that was proof of a life well lived. You got paid to do a job and you did it. David Sr. never had more than a high school diploma. He treated everyone he met with respect, even the Harvard management types who toured the plant every few months, sluicing down from the curved driveways of Dearborn to slaps the backs of the common man.

David was an only child, the first in his family to go to college. But in an act of allegiance to his father, he declined the invitation to go to Harvard (full scholarship) in order to attend the University of Michigan. It was there that he discovered a love for politics. Ronald Reagan was in the White House that year, and David saw something in his folksy manner and steely gaze that inspired him. David ran for class president his sophomore year and lost, then ran again the next year and lost worse. He had neither a politician's face nor charm, but he had ideas, strategy. He saw the moves like billboards in the far distance, heard the messages in his head. He knew how to win. He just couldn't do it himself. It was then that David Bateman realized that if he wanted a career in politics, it would have to be behind the scenes.

Twenty years and thirty-eight state and national elections later, David Bateman had earned a reputation as a kingmaker. He had turned his love of the game into a highly profitable consulting business whose clients included a cable news network that had hired David to help them revamp their election coverage.

It was this combination of items on his résumé that led, one day in March 2002, to the birth of a movement.

DAVID WOKE BEFORE dawn. It was programmed into him now after twenty years on the campaign trail. Marty always said, *You snooze you lose*, and it was true. Campaigns weren't beauty contests. They were about endurance, the long, ugly blood sport of gathering votes. Rarely was there a first-round knockout. It was usually about who was still standing in the fifteenth, shrugging body blows from rubbery legs. It's what separated the something from the something else, David liked to say. And so he learned to go without sleep. Four hours a night was all he required now. In a pinch he could get by with twenty minutes every eight hours.

The wall-size windows in his bedroom across from the bed framed the first glow of sunlight. He lay on his back, looking out, as downstairs the coffee was making itself. Outside he could see the towers of the Roosevelt Island tramway. Their bedroom—his and Maggie's—faced the East River. Glass as thick as an unabridged copy of *War and Peace* blocked the endless roar of the FDR Drive. It was bulletproof, along with all the other windows in the town house. The billionaire had paid for the installation after 9/11.

"Can't afford to lose you to some jihadi cabdriver with a shoulder rocket," he told David.

Today was Friday, August 24. Maggie and the kids were out at the

Vineyard, had been all month, leaving David to pad the marble bathroom floors alone. Downstairs he could hear the housekeeper making breakfast. After a shower, he stopped at the kids' rooms, as he did every morning, and stared at their perfectly made beds. The decor in Rachel's room combined scientific gadgetry and horse worship. JJ's was all about cars. Like all children, they tended toward chaos, a juvenile disorder the house staff erased systematically, often in real time. Now, staring at the sterile, vacuumed order, David found himself wanting to mess things up, to make his son's room look more like a kid's and less like a museum of childhood. So he went over to a toy bin and kicked it over with his foot.

There, he thought. *That's better.*

He would leave a note for the maid. When the children left town she was to leave their rooms as she found them. He would tape them off like a crime scene if he had to, anything to make the house feel more alive.

He called Maggie from the kitchen. The clock on the stove read 6:14 a.m.

"We've been up for an hour," she said. "Rachel's reading. JJ is seeing what happens when you pour dish soap in the toilet."

Her voice muffled as she covered the mouthpiece.

"Sweetie," she yelled. "That is not what we call a good choice."

In New York, David mimed drinking and the housekeeper brought him more coffee. His wife came back on the line. David could hear the frazzled energy she got in her voice when she spent too long parenting by herself. Every year he tried to get her to bring Maria, the au pair, with them to the island, but his wife always refused. Summer vacation was for them, she said, family time. Otherwise, Rachel and JJ would grow up calling the nanny *Mommy*, like all the other kids in their neighborhood.

"It's super foggy out," his wife said.

"Did you get the thing I sent?" he asked.

"Yes," she said, sounding pleased. "Where did you find them?"

"The Kiplings. They know a guy who travels the world collecting old-world clippings. Apples from the eighteen hundreds. Peach trees no one's seen since McKinley was president. We had that fruit salad at their place last summer."

"Right," she said. "That was yummy. Were they—is it silly to ask?—were they expensive? This seems like something that you'd hear on the news is the price of a new car."

"A Vespa, maybe," he said.

It was just like her to ask price, as if part of her still couldn't fathom their net worth, its implications.

"I didn't even know there was such a thing as a Danish plum," she said.

"Me either. Who knew the world of fruit could be so exotic?"

She laughed. When things were good between them, there was an easiness. A rhythm of give-and-take that came from living in the moment, from burying old grudges. Some mornings when he called, David could tell that she had dreamed about him in the night. It was something she did from time to time. Often she told him afterward, biting off her words, unable to look him in the eye. In the dream he was always a monster who scorned and abandoned her. The conversations that followed were chilly and brief.

"Well, we're going to plant the trees this morning," Maggie told him. "It'll give us a project for the day."

They made small talk for another ten minutes—what his day looked like, what time he thought he'd be out tonight. All the while his phone chimed, breaking news, schedule changes, crises to be managed. The sound of other people's panic reduced to a steady electronic hum. Meanwhile the kids buzzed in and out of Maggie's end of the line like yellow jackets scouting a picnic. He liked hearing them in the background, the melee of them. It was what set his generation apart from his father's. David wanted his children to have a childhood. A real childhood. He worked hard so that they could play. For David's father, childhood had been a luxury his kids could not afford. Play was considered a gateway drug to idleness and poverty. Life, Dad said, was a Hail Mary. You only got one shot at it, and if you didn't train every day—with wind sprints and grass drills—you would blow it.

As a result, David had been burdened with chores at an early age. At five, he was cleaning the trash cans. By seven he was doing all their laundry. The rule in their house was that homework was done and chores were completed before a single ball was thrown, before a bike was ridden or army men were dumped from the Folgers can.

You don't become a man by accident, his father told him. It was a belief that David shared, though his was a milder version. In David's mind, the training for adulthood began in the double digits. At ten, he reasoned, it was time to start thinking about growing up. To take the soft-serve lessons about discipline and responsibility that had been fed to you in your youth, and cement them into rules for a healthy and productive life. Until then you were a child, so act accordingly.

"Daddy," said Rachel, "will you bring my red sneakers? They're in my closet."

He walked into her room and got them while they were talking so he wouldn't forget.

"I'm putting them in my bag," he told her.

"It's me again," said Maggie. "Next year I think you should come out here with us for the whole month."

"Me too," he said immediately. Every year they had the same conversation. Every year he said the same thing. *I will.* And then he didn't.

"It's just the fucking news," she said. "There'll be more tomorrow. Besides, haven't you trained them all by now?"

"I promise," he said, "next year I'll be there more." Because it was easier to say yes than to dicker through the real-world probabilities, lay out all the mitigating factors, and try to manage her expectations.

Never fight tomorrow's fight today, was his motto.

"Liar," she said, but with a smile in her voice.

"I love you," he told her. "I'll see you tonight."

. . .

The town car was downstairs waiting for him. Two security contractors from the agency rode up in the elevator to get him. They slept in shifts in one of the first-floor guest rooms.

"Morning, boys," said David, shrugging on his jacket.

They took him out together, two big men with Sig Sauers under their coats, eyes scanning the street for signs of threat. Every day David got hate mail, apoplectic letters about God knows what, sometimes even care packages of human shit. It was the price he paid for choosing a side, he reasoned, for having an opinion about politics and war.

Fuck you and your God, they said.

They threatened his life, his family, threats he had learned to take seriously.

In the town car he thought about Rachel, the three days she was missing. Ransom calls, the living room filled with FBI agents and private security, Maggie crying in the back bedroom. It was a miracle they got her back, a miracle that he knew would never happen twice. So they lived with the constant surveillance, the advance team. Safety first, he told his children. Then fun. Then learning. It was a joke between them.

He was driven cross-town through the stop-and-go. Every two seconds his phone blorped. North Korea was test-firing missiles into the Sea of Japan again. A Tallahassee policeman was in a coma after a car stop shooting. Nude cell phone photos of a Hollywood starlet sent to an NFL running back had just dropped. If you weren't careful it could feel like a tidal wave bearing down, all this eventfulness. But David saw it for what it was, and understood his own role. He was a sorting machine, boxing the news by category and priority, forwarding tips to various departments. He wrote one-word replies and hit SEND. *Bullshit* or *Weak* or *More*. He had answered thirty-three emails and returned sixteen phone calls by the time the car pulled up in front of the ALC Building on Sixth Avenue, which was light for a Friday.

A security man opened the back door for him. David stepped out into the bustle. Outside, the air was the temperature and consistency of a patty melt. He was wearing a steel-gray suit with a white shirt and a red tie. Sometimes in the mornings he liked to veer away from the front door at the last second and wander off to find a second breakfast. It kept the security guys on their toes. But today he had things to do if he was going to make it to the airport by three.

David's office was on the fifty-eighth floor. He came off the elevator at a fast clip, eyes focused on his office door. People got out of the way when he walked. They ducked into cubicles. They turned and fled. It wasn't the man so much as the office. Or maybe it was the suit. The faces around him seemed to get younger every day, David thought, segment producers and executive administrators, online nerds with soul patches and artisanal coffee, smug with the knowledge that they were the future. Everyone in this business was building a legacy. Some were ideologues, others were opportunists, but they were all there because ALC was the number one cable news network in the country, and David Bateman was the reason.

Lydia Cox, his secretary, was already at her desk. She had been with David since 1995, a fifty-nine-year-old woman who had never married, but had never owned a cat. Lydia was thin. Her hair was short, and she carried a certain old-school Brooklyn chutzpah that, like a once thriving Indian tribe, had long since been driven from the borough by hostile gentrifiers from across the sea.

"You've got the Sellers call in ten minutes," she reminded him first thing.

David didn't slow. He went in to his desk, took off his jacket, and hung it on the back of his chair. Lydia had put his schedule on the seat. He picked it up, frowned. Starting the day with Sellers—the increasingly unpopular LA bureau chief—was like starting the day with a colonoscopy.

"Hasn't somebody stabbed this guy yet?" he said.

"No," said Lydia, following him in. "But last year you did buy a burial plot in his name and send him a picture of it for Christmas."

David smiled. As far as he was concerned there weren't enough moments like that in life.

"Push it to Monday," he told her.

"He's called twice already. *Don't you dare let him blow this off*, was the gist."

"Too late."

There was a hot cup of coffee on David's desk. He pointed to it.

"For me?"

"No," she said, shaking her head. "It's the pope's."

Bill Cunningham appeared in the doorway behind her. He was in jeans, a T-shirt, and his trademark red suspenders.

"Hey," he said. "Got a sec?"

Lydia turned to go. As Bill stepped aside to let her pass, David noticed Krista Brewer hovering behind him. She looked worried.

"Sure," said David. "What's up."

They came in. Bill closed the door behind them, which wasn't something he normally did. Cunningham was a performance artist. His whole shtick was built on a rant against secret backroom meetings. In other words, nothing he did was ever private. Instead he preferred to go into David's office twice a week and yell his head off. About what didn't matter. It was a show of force, like a military exercise. So the closed door was a concern.

"Bill," said David, "did you just close the door?"

He looked at Krista, Bill's executive producer. She seemed a little green. Bill dropped onto the sofa. He had the wingspan of a pterodactyl. He sat, as he always did, with his knees spread wide so you could see how big his balls were.

"First of all," he said, "it's not as bad as you think."

"No," said Krista. "It's worse."

"Two days of bullshit," said Bill. "Maybe the lawyers get involved. Maybe."

David got up and looked out the window. He found the best thing you could do with a showman like Bill was not look at him.

"Whose lawyers?" he asked. "Yours or mine?"

"Goddammit, Bill," said Krista turning on the anchor. "This isn't a rule you broke, *Don't spit in church*. It's a law. Several laws probably."

David watched the traffic go by on Fifth Avenue.

"I'm going to the airport at three," he said. "Do you think we'll have reached the point by then, or are we going to have to finish this by phone?"

He turned and looked at them. Krista's arms were crossed defiantly. *Bill's gotta say it*, was her body language. Messengers get killed for delivering bad news, and Krista wasn't going to lose her job for another one of Cunningham's dumb mistakes. Bill, meanwhile, had an angry smile on his face like a cop after a shooting he'll swear on the stand was justified.

"Krista," said David.

"He tapped people's phones," she said.

The words hung there, a crisis point, but not yet a full-blown crisis.

"People," David echoed cautiously, the word bitter on his tongue.

Krista looked at Bill.

"Bill has this guy," she said.

"Namor," said Bill. "You remember Namor. Former Navy SEAL, former Pentagon intel."

David shook his head. In the last few years Bill had taken to surrounding himself with a bunch of Gordon Liddy kooks.

"Sure you do," Bill said. "Well, we're drinking one night. This is maybe a year ago. And we're talking about Moskewitz, you remember the congressman who liked smelling black girls' feet? Well, Namor is laughing and he says wouldn't it be great if we had those phone calls on tape? Broadcast gold, right? A Jewish congressman telling some black chick how he wants to smell her feet? And so I say, yes, that would be good. And whatever, we order couple more seven-and-sevens and Namor says, *You know . . .*"

Bill paused for dramatic effect. He couldn't help it. It was in his nature to perform.

"... *You know* ... it's not hard. This is Namor. In fact, he says, it's a fucking cinch. Because everything goes through a server. Everyone has email, cell phones. They've got voice mail passwords and text messaging user names. And that shit is all accessible. It's crackable. Hell, if you know somebody's phone number you can just clone their phone, so every time they get a call ..."

"No," said David, feeling a hot flush climb up his spine from his asshole.

"Whatever," said Bill. "It's two guys in a bar at one in the morning. It's just bullshit cocksmanship. But then he said, pick a name. Somebody whose phone calls you want to hear. So I say, *Obama*. And he says, *That's the White House. Not possible. Pick somebody else. Lower down.* So I say, Kellerman—you know, that piece-of-shit liberal reactionary on CNN. And he says *Done.*"

David found himself in his chair, though he couldn't remember sitting. And Krista was looking at him like, *It gets worse.*

"Bill," said David, shaking his head, his hands up. "Stop. I can't hear this. You should be talking to a lawyer."

"That's what I told him," said Krista.

Cunningham waved them off like they were a couple of Pakistani orphans at an Islamabad bazaar.

"I didn't do anything," he said. "Picked a name. And who cares anyway? We're two drunks at a bar. So I go home, forget about the whole thing. A week later, Namor comes to the office. He wants to show me something. So we go into my office and he takes out a Zip drive, puts it in my computer. It's got all these audio files on it. Fucking Kellerman, right? Talking to his mother, his dry cleaner. But also to his producer about cutting some bits from a story to make it skew a different way."

David felt a moment of vertigo.

"Is that how you ..." he said.

"Shit yes. We found the original footage and ran the piece. You loved that story."

David was standing again, fists clenched.

"When I thought it was journalism," he said. "Not..."

Bill laughed, shaking his head with wonder at his own inventiveness.

"I gotta play these tapes for you. It's classic."

David came around the desk.

"Stop talking."

"Where are you going?" Bill asked.

"Don't say another fucking word to anyone," David told him, "either of you," and walked out of his office.

Lydia was at her desk.

"I've got Sellers on line two," she said.

David didn't stop, didn't turn. He walked through rows of cubicles, sweat dripping down his sides. This could be the end of them. He knew it in his bones, didn't even have to hear the rest of the story.

"Move," he yelled at a group of crew cuts in short-sleeved shirts. They scattered like rabbits.

Mind racing, David reached the elevator bank, pushed the button, then, without waiting, kicked open the door to the stairs, went down a floor. He stalked the halls like a spree killer with an assault rifle, found Liebling in the conference room, sitting with sixteen other lawyers.

"Out," said David. "Everybody."

They scrambled, these nameless suits with their law degrees, the door hitting the last one on the heels. Sitting there, Don Liebling had a bemused look on his face. He was their in-house counsel, mid-fifties and Pilates fit.

"Jesus, Bateman," he said.

David paced.

"Cunningham," was all he could say for a moment.

"Shit," said Liebling. "What did that wet dick do now?"

"I only heard some of it," David said. "I cut him off before I could become an accessory after the fact."

Liebling frowned.

"Tell me there isn't a dead hooker in a hotel room somewhere."

"I wish," David said. "A dead hooker would be easy compared to this."

Looking up, he saw an airplane high above the Empire State Building. For a moment his need to be on it, going somewhere, anywhere, was overwhelming. He dropped into a leather chair, ran his hand through his hair.

"The fucktard tapped Kellerman's phone. Probably others. I got the feeling he was going to start listing victims, like a serial killer, so I left."

Liebling smoothed his tie.

"When you say *tapped his phone...*"

"He has a guy. Some intel consultant who said he could get Bill access to anybody's email or phone."

"Jesus."

David leaned back in the chair and looked up at the ceiling.

"You have to talk to him."

Liebling nodded.

"He needs his own lawyer," he said. "I think he uses Franken. I'll call."

David tapped his fingers on the tabletop. He felt old.

"I mean, what if it was congressman or senators?" he asked. "My God. It's bad enough he's spying on the competition."

Liebling thought about that. David closed his eyes and pictured Rachel and JJ digging holes in the backyard, planting old-world apple trees. He should have taken the month off, should be there with them right now, flip-flops on, a Bloody Mary in hand, laughing every time his son said, *What's up, chicken butt?*

"Could this sink us?" he asked, eyes still shut.

Liebling equivocated with his head.

"It sinks him. That's for sure."

"But it hurts us?"

"Without a doubt," said Liebling. "A thing like this. There could be congressional hearings. At the very least you've got the FBI up your ass for two years. They'll talk about pulling our broadcast license."

David thought about this.

"Do I resign?"

"Why? You didn't know anything. Did you?"

"It doesn't matter. A thing like this. If I didn't know, I should have." He shook his head.

"Fucking Bill."

But it wasn't Bill's fault, thought David. It was his. Cunningham was David's gift to the world, the angry white man people invited into their living rooms to call bullshit at the world, to rail against a system that robbed us of everything we felt we deserved—the third-world countries that were taking our jobs. The politicians who were raising our taxes. Bill Cunningham, Mr. Straight Talk, Mr. Divine Righteousness, who sat in our living rooms and shared our pain, who told us what we wanted to hear, which was that the reason we were losing out in life was not that we were losers, but that someone was reaching into our pockets, our companies, our country and talking what was rightfully ours.

Bill Cunningham was the voice of ALC News and he had gone insane. He was Kurtz in the jungle, and David should have realized, should have pulled him back, but the ratings were too good, and the shots Bill was taking at the enemy were direct hits. They were the number one network, and that meant everything. Was Bill a diva? Absolutely. But divas can be handled. Lunatics on the other hand.

"I've gotta call Roger," he said, meaning the billionaire. Meaning his boss. *The* boss.

"And say what?" said Liebling.

"That this thing is coming. That it's out there, and he should get ready. You need to find Bill and pull him into a room and beat him with a sock full of oranges. Get Franken here. Get the truth, and then protect us from it."

"Does he go on tonight?"

David thought about this.

"No. He's sick. He has the flu."

"He won't like that."

"Tell him the alternative is he goes to jail or we break his kneecaps. Call Hancock. We put it out there this morning that Bill's sick. On Monday we run a *Best Of* week. I don't want this guy on my air again."

"He won't go quietly."

"No," said David. "He won't."

INJURIES

AT NIGHT, WHEN Scott dreams, he dreams of the shark, sleek-muscled and greedy. He wakes thirsty. The hospital is an ecosystem of beeps and hums. Outside, the sun is just coming up. He looks over at the boy, still asleep. The television is on at low volume, white noise haunting their sleep. The screen is split into fifths, a news crawl snaking across the floor. Onscreen, the search for survivors continues. It appears the navy has brought in divers and deep-sea submersibles to try to find the underwater wreckage, to recover the bodies of the dead. Scott watches as men in black wet suits step from the deck of a Coast Guard cutter and vanish into the sea.

"They're calling it an accident," Bill Cunningham is saying from the screen's largest box, a tall man with dramatic hair, thumbing his suspenders. "But you and I know—there are no accidents. Planes don't just fall out the sky, the same way that our president didn't just forget that Congress was on vacation when he made that hack Rodriguez a judge."

Cunningham is smoky-eyed, his tie askew. He has been on the air for nine hours now delivering a marathon eulogy for his dead leader.

"The David Bateman I knew," he says, "—my boss, my friend— couldn't be killed by mechanical failure or pilot error. He was an avenging angel. An American hero. And this reporter believes that

72

what we're talking about here is nothing less than an act of terrorism, if not by foreign nationals, then by certain elements of the liberal media. Planes don't just crash, people. This was sabotage. This was a shoulder-fired rocket from a speedboat. This was a jihadi in a suicide vest on board the aircraft, possibly one of the crew. Murder, my friends, by the enemies of freedom. Nine dead, including a nine-year-old girl. Nine. A girl who had already suffered tragedy in her life. A girl I held in my arms at birth, whose diaper I changed. We should be fueling up the fighter jets. SEAL teams should be jumping from high-altitude planes and sharking up from submarines. A great patriot is dead, the godfather of freedom in the West. And we will get to the bottom of things."

Scott turns down the volume. The boy stirs but does not wake. In sleep he is not yet an orphan. In sleep his parents are still alive, his sister. They kiss him on the cheeks and tickle his ribs. In sleep it is last week and he is running through the sand, holding a squirmy green crab by the claw. He is drinking orange soda through a straw and eating curly fries, his brown hair bleached by the sun, freckles splashed across his face. And when he wakes up there will be that moment when all the dreams are real, when the love he carries up with him is enough to keep the truth at bay, but then the moment will end. The boy will see Scott's face, or a nurse will come in, and just like that he will be an orphan again. This time forever.

Scott turns and looks out the window. They are meant to be discharged today, Scott and the boy, expelled from the looped loud-speaker of hospital life, BP checked every half hour, temperature taken, meals delivered. The boy's aunt and uncle arrived last night, red-eyed and somber. The aunt is Maggie's younger sister, Eleanor. She sleeps now in a hard-backed chair beside the boy's bed. Eleanor is in her early thirties and pretty, a massage therapist from Croton-on-Hudson, upstate. Her husband, the boy's uncle, is a writer, squirrelly about eye contact, the kind of knucklehead who grows a beard in summer. Scott doesn't have a good feeling about him.

It has been thirty-two hours since the crash, a heartbeat and a lifetime. Scott has yet to bathe, his skin still salty from the sea. His left arm is in a sling. He has no ID, no pants. And yet, despite this, his idea is still to head into the city later as planned. There are meetings on the books. Career connections to be made. Scott's friend Magnus has offered to drive out to Montauk and get him. Lying there, Scott thinks it will be good to see him, a friendly face. They are not close really, he and Magnus, nothing like brothers, more like drinking buddies, but Magnus is both unflappable and relentlessly positive, which is why Scott thought to call him last night. It was essential that he avoid talking to anyone who might cry. Keep things casual. That was his goal. In fact, after he'd finished telling Magnus—who didn't own a TV—what had happened, Magnus said *weird*, and then suggested they should grab a beer.

Looking over, Scott sees that the boy is awake now, staring at him unblinking.

"Hey, buddy," says Scott quietly, so as not to wake the aunt. "You sleep okay?"

The boy nods.

"Want me to put on some cartoons?"

Another nod. Scott finds the remote, turns channels until he finds something animated.

"Sponge Bob?" Scott asks.

The boy nods again. He hasn't spoken a word since yesterday afternoon. In the first few hours after they reached shore it was possible to get a few words out of him, how he was feeling, if he needed anything. But then, like a wound swelling shut, he stopped speaking. And now he is mute.

Scott spies a box of powdery rubber exam gloves on the table. As the boy watches, he pulls one out.

"Uh-oh," he says, then quietly fakes the big buildup to a sneeze. With the *achoo* he hangs the glove from his left nostril. The boy smiles.

The aunt wakes, stretches. She is a beautiful woman with a blunt bang haircut, like a person who makes up for driving an expensive car by never washing it. Scott watches her face as she regains full consciousness, as she realizes where she is and what has happened. For a moment he sees her threaten to collapse under the weight of it, but then she sees the boy and forces a smile.

"Hey," she says, smoothing the hair back from his face.

She looks up at the TV, and then at Scott.

"Morning," he says.

She brushes her own hair off her face, checks to make sure her clothes are on properly.

"Sorry," she says. "I guess I fell asleep."

It doesn't feel like a comment that deserves a response, so Scott just nods. Eleanor looks around.

"Have you seen...Doug? My husband?"

"I think he went to get some coffee," Scott tells her.

"Good," she says, looking relieved. "That's good."

"You two been married a long time?" Scott asks her.

"No. Just, uh, seventy-one days."

"But who's counting," says Scott.

Eleanor flushes.

"He's a sweet guy," she says. "I think he's just a little overwhelmed right now."

Scott glances at the boy, who has stopped watching the TV and is studying Scott and his aunt. The idea that *Doug* is overwhelmed given what they've been through is mystifying.

"Did the boy's father have any family?" Scott asks. "Your brother-in-law?"

"David?" she says. "No. I mean, his parents are dead, and he's, I mean I guess he was an only child."

"What about your parents?"

"My, uh, mom is still around. She lives in Portland. I think she's flying in today."

Scott nods.

"And you guys live in Woodstock?"

"Croton," she says. "It's about forty minutes outside the city."

Scott thinks about this, a small house in a wooded glen, easy chairs on a porch. It could be good for the boy. Then again, it could be disastrous, the isolation of the woods, the glowering drunken writer, like Jack Nicholson in the winter mountains.

"Has he ever been there?" Scott asks, nodding toward the boy.

She purses her lips.

"I'm sorry," she says, "but why are you asking me all these questions?"

"Well," says Scott, "I guess I'm just curious as to what's going to happen to him now. I'm invested, you could say."

Eleanor nods. She looks scared, not of Scott, but of life, what her life is about to become.

"We'll be fine," she says, rubbing the boy's head. "Right?"

He doesn't answer, his eyes focused on Scott. There is a challenge in them, a plea. Scott blinks first, then turns and looks out the window. Doug comes in. He's holding a cup of coffee and wearing a misbuttoned cardigan over a checked lumberjack shirt. Seeing him, Eleanor looks relieved.

"Is that for me?" she asks, pointing.

For a moment Doug looks confused, then he realizes she means the coffee.

"Uh, sure," he says, and hands it to her. Scott can tell from the way she holds it that the cup is almost empty. He sees her face get sad. Doug comes around the boy's bed and stands near his wife. Scott can smell alcohol on his clothes.

"How's the patient?" Doug asks.

"He's good," says Eleanor. "Got some sleep."

Studying Doug's back, Scott wonders how much money the boy stands to inherit from his parents. Five million? Fifty? His father ran a TV empire and flew in private planes. There will be riches, real estate. Sniffling, Doug hikes up his pants with both hands. He pulls a small toy car from his pocket. It still has the price tag on it.

"Here you go, slugger," he says. "Got this for you."

There are a lot of sharks in the sea, thinks Scott, watching the boy take the car.

Dr. Glabman enters, eyeglasses perched on top of his head. He has a bright-yellow banana sticking out of his lab coat pocket.

"Ready to go home?" he asks.

They get dressed. The hospital gives Scott a pair of blue surgical scrubs to wear. He puts them on one-handed, wincing as the nurse maneuvers his fragile left arm into the sleeve. When he comes out of the bathroom the boy is already dressed and sitting in a wheelchair.

"I'm giving you the name of a child psychiatrist," the doctor tells Eleanor, out of earshot of the boy. "He specializes in post-traumatic cases."

"We actually don't live in the city," says Doug.

Eleanor shushes him with a look.

"Of course," she says, taking the business card from the doctor. "I'll call this afternoon."

Scott crosses to the boy, kneels on the floor in front of him.

"You be good," he says.

The boy shakes his head, tears in his eyes.

"I'll see you," Scott tells him. "I'm giving your aunt my phone number. So you can call. Okay?"

The boy won't look at him.

Scott touches his tiny arm for a moment, unsure what to do next. He has never had a child, never been an uncle or a godfather. He's not even sure they speak the same language. After a moment Scott straightens and hands Eleanor a piece of paper with his phone number.

"Obviously, call anytime," he says. "Not that I know what I can do to help. But if he wants to talk, or you..."

Doug takes the number from his wife. He folds it up and jams it in his back pocket.

"Sounds good, man," he says.

Scott stands for a minute, looking at Eleanor, then at the boy, and finally at Doug. It feels like an important moment, like one of those critical junctures in life when you're supposed to say something or do something, but you don't know what. Only later does it hit you. Later, the thing you should have said will be as clear as day, but right now it's just a nagging feeling, a clenched jaw and low nausea.

"Okay," he says finally and walks to the door, thinking he will just go. That that's the best thing. To let the boy be with his family. But then as he steps into the hall he feels two small arms grab his leg, and he turns to see the boy holding on to him.

The hall is full of people, patients and visitors, doctors and nurses. Scott puts a hand on the boy's head, then bends and picks him up. The boy's arms encircle his neck, and he hugs hard enough to cut off Scott's air. Scott blinks away tears.

"Don't forget," he tells the boy. "You're my hero."

He lets the boy hug himself out, then carries him back to the wheelchair. Scott can feel Eleanor and Doug watching him, but he keeps his eyes on the boy.

"Never give up," he tells him.

Then Scott turns and walks off down the hall.

. . .

In the early years, when he was deep in a painting, Scott felt like he was underwater. There was that same pressure between the ears, the same muted silence. Colors were sharper. Light rippled and bent. He had his first group show at twenty-six, his first solo show at thirty. Every dime he could scrabble together was spent on canvas and paint. Somewhere along the way he stopped swimming. There were galleries to commandeer and women to fuck and he was a tall, green-eyed flirt with a contagious smile. Which meant there was always a girl to buy him breakfast or put a roof over his head, at least for a few nights. At the time this almost made up for the fact that his

work was good, not great. Looking at it, you could see he had potential, a unique voice, but something was missing. Years passed. The
big solo shows and high-profile museum acquisitions never happened.
The German biennials and genius grants, the invitations to paint and
teach abroad. He turned thirty, thirty-five. One night, after several
cocktails at his third gallery opening of the week to celebrate an artist
five years younger than himself, it occurred to Scott that he would
never became the overnight success he thought he'd be, the enfant
terrible, the downtown superstar. The heady exhilaration of artistic
possibility had become elusive and frightening. He was a minor artist.
That's all he'd ever be. The parties were still good. The women were
still beautiful, but Scott felt uglier. As the rootlessness of youth was replaced by middle-aged self-involvement, his affairs turned quick and
dirty. He drank to forget. Alone in his studio, Scott took to staring at
the canvas for hours waiting for images to appear.

Nothing ever came.

He woke one day up and found he was a forty-year-old man with
twenty years of booze and debauchery ballooning his middle and
weathering his face. He had been engaged once and then not, had
sobered and fallen from the wagon. He had been young once and
limitless, and then somehow his life became a foregone conclusion.
An *almost was*, not even a *has been*. Scott could see the obituary. Scott
Burroughs, a talented rakish charmer who had never lived up to his
promise, who had long since crossed the line from fun-loving and
mysterious to boorish and sad. But who was he kidding? Even the
obituary was a fantasy. He was a nobody. His death would warrant
nothing.

Then, after a weeklong party at the Hamptons house of a much
more successful painter, Scott found himself lying facedown on the
living room floor. He was forty-six years old. It was barely dawn. He
staggered to his feet and out onto the patio. His head was pounding
and his mouth tasted like a radial tire. He squinted in the glare of sudden sunlight, his hand rising to shield his face. The truth about him,

his failure, came back as a throbbing head pain. And then, as his eyes adjusted, he lowered his hand and found himself staring into the famous artist's swimming pool.

It was there that the artist and his girlfriend found Scott an hour later, naked and swimming laps, his chest on fire, his muscles aching. They yelled at him to come for a drink with them. But Scott waved them off. He felt alive again. The moment he entered the water it was like he was eighteen again and winning a gold medal at the national championship. He was sixteen, executing a perfect underwater pivot. He was twelve and getting up before dawn to slice the blue.

He swam backward through time, lap after lap, until he was six years old and watching Jack LaLanne tow a thousand-pound boat through San Francisco Bay, until that feeling returned—that deep boy certainty:

Anything is possible.

Everything is gettable.

You just have to want it badly enough.

Scott wasn't old, it turned out. He wasn't finished. He had just given up.

Thirty minutes later he climbed out of the pool and, without drying off, put on his clothes and went back to the city. For the next six months he swam three miles a day. He threw away the booze and the cigarettes. He cut out red meat and dessert. He bought canvas after canvas, covering every available surface with an expectant white primer. He was a boxer training for a fight, a cellist practicing for a concert. His body was his instrument, battered like Johnny Cash's guitar, splintered and raw, but he was going to turn it into a Stradivarius.

He was a disaster survivor in that he had survived the disaster that was his life. And so that's what he painted. That summer he rented a small house on Martha's Vineyard and holed up. Once again the only thing that mattered was the work, except now he realized that the work was him. *There is no separating yourself from the things you make*, he thought. *If you are a cesspool, what else can your work be except shit?*

He got a three-legged dog and cooked her spaghetti and meatballs. Every day was the same. An ocean swim. Coffee and a pastry at the farmers market. Then hours of open time in his studio, brushstrokes and paint, lines and color. What he saw when he finished was too exciting to say out loud. He had made the great leap forward, and knowing this he became strangely terrified. The work became his secret, a treasure chest hidden in the rocky ground.

Only recently had he come out of hiding, first by attending a few dinner parties on the island, and then by allowing a Soho gallery to include a new piece in their 1990s retrospective. The piece had garnered a lot of attention. It was bought by an important collector. Scott's phone started ringing. A few of the bigger reps came out and toured the studio. It was happening. Everything he had worked toward, a life's pursuit about to be realized. All he had to do was grab the ring.

So he got on a plane.

A DOZEN NEWS vans are parked outside the hospital, camera crews assembled and waiting. Police barricades have been erected, half a dozen uniformed officers keeping things orderly. Scott spies on the scene from the hospital lobby, hiding behind a potted ficus. This is where Magnus finds him.

"Jesus, man," he says. "You don't do anything half-assed, do you?"

They man-hug. Magnus is a part-time painter and full-time ladies' man, with just a trace of Irish lilt in his voice.

"Thanks for doing this," Scott tells him.

"No worries, brother."

Magnus gives Scott the once-over.

"You look like shite."

"I feel like shite," Scott says.

Magnus holds up a duffel bag.

"I brought some skivvies," he says, "a fetching frock and some panties. You want to change?"

Scott looks over Magnus's shoulder. Outside, the crowd is growing. They are there to see him, to get a glimpse, a sound bite from the man who swam for eight hours through the midnight Atlantic with a four-year-old boy on his back. He closes his eyes and pictures what will happen once he is dressed, once he steps through those doors, the spotlight and questions, his own face on TV. The circus of it, the blood frenzy.

There are no accidents, he thinks.

To Scott's left is a long hall and a door that reads LOCKER ROOM.

"I've got a better idea," Scott says. "But it involves you breaking the law."

Magnus smiles.

"Just one?"

Ten minutes later, Scott and Magnus walk out a side door. They are both in scrubs now, wearing white lab coats, two doctors going home at the end of a long shift. Scott holds Magnus's cell phone to his ear, talking to the dial tone. The ruse works. They reach Magnus's car, a seen-better-days Saab, with a sun-bleached fabric roof. Inside, Scott reaffixes the sling over his left shoulder.

"Just so you know," Magnus tells him, "we're definitely wearing these out to the bar later. Ladies love a medical man."

As they drive out past the press line, Scott shields his face with the phone. He thinks about the boy, hunched over and tiny in his wheelchair, an orphan now and forever. Scott has no doubt that his aunt loves him, no doubt that the money he inherits from his parents will insulate him from anything close to ruin. But will it be enough? Can the boy grow up to be normal, or will he be forever broken by what has happened?

I should have gotten the aunt's number, Scott thinks. But as he does, he wonders what he would do with it. Scott has no right to force his way into their lives. And even if he did, what does he have to offer? The boy is only four, and Scott is a single man approaching fifty, a no-torious womanizer and recovered alcoholic, a struggling artist who's never been able to keep a single lasting relationship. He is nobody's role model. Nobody's hero.

They take the LIE toward the city. Scott rolls down the window and feels the wind on his face. Squinting into the sun, he can half convince himself that the events of the last thirty-six hours were just a dream. That there was no private plane, no crash, no epic swim or harrowing hospital stay. With the right combination of cocktails and professional victories he could erase it all. But even as he thinks this, Scott knows it's bullshit. The trauma he suffered is part of his DNA now. He is a soldier after an epic battle, one he will inevitably return to fifty years from now on his deathbed.

Magnus lives in Long Island City, in a condemned shoe factory that's been converted into lofts. Before the crash, Scott's plan was to stay there for a few days and commute into the city. But now, changing lanes, Magnus tells Scott that things have changed.

"I've got strict fecking instructions," he says. "To take you to the West Village. You're moving up in the world."

"Strict instructions from who?" Scott wants to know.

"A new friend," says Magnus. "That's all I can say at this moment."

"Pull over," Scott tells him in a hard voice.

Magnus gives Scott a double eyebrow lift, smiles.

Scott reaches for his door handle.

"Chill, boyo," says Magnus, swerving slightly. "I can see you're in no mood for mystery."

"Just tell me where we're going?"

"Leslie's," says Magnus.

"Who's Leslie?"

"Geez, did you crack your head in the crash. Leslie Mueller? The Mueller Gallery?"

Scott is at a loss.

"Why would we go to the Mueller Gallery?"

"Not the gallery, you tosser. Her house. She's a billionaire, yeah? Daughter of that tech geezer who made that gizmo in the 'nineties. Well, after you called me I maybe shot my mouth off a bit about how I was coming to get you and how you and me were gonna hit the town, get some ladies' numbers—you being a shit-you-not hero and all—and I guess she heard, 'cause she called me. Says she saw what you did on the news. Says her door is open. She's got a guest suite on the third floor."

"No."

"Don't be stupid, amigo. This is Leslie Mueller. This is the difference between selling a painting for three thousand dollars and selling one for three hundred thousand. Or three million."

"No."

"Perfect. I hear you. But think about *my* career for a minute. This is Leslie fucking Mueller. My last show was at a crab shack in Cleveland. At least let's go for dinner, let her rub up against that giant hero boner of yours, commission a few pieces. Maybe throw in a good word for your boyo. Then we make excuses."

Scott turns to look out the window. In the car next to them a couple is arguing, a man and woman in their twenties, dressed for work. The man is behind the wheel, and but he isn't looking at the road. His head is turned and he is waving one hand angrily. In response, the woman holds an open lipstick, half applied, and jabs it in the man's direction, her face lemoned with distaste. Looking at them, Scott has a sudden flash of memory. He is back on the flight, seat belt on. Up front, at the open cockpit door, the young flight attendant—what was her name?—is arguing with one of the pilots. Her back is to Scott, but the pilot's face is visible over her shoulder. It is ugly and dark, and as Scott watches the pilot grabs the girl's arm tightly. She pulls away.

In the memory, Scott feels the seat belt clasp in his hand. His feet are flat under him, his quads tensed as if he is about to stand. Why? To go to her aid?

It comes in a flash and then it's gone. An image that could be from a movie, but feels like his life. Did that happen? Was there some kind of fight?

In the next lane the furious driver turns and spits out the window, but the window is up. A frothy rope of spit runs down the curved glass, and then Magnus speeds up and the couple is gone.

Scott sees a gas station ahead.

"Can you pull in here?" Scott asks. "I want to get a pack of gum."

Magnus digs around in the center console.

"I've got some Juicy Fruit somewhere."

"Something mint," Scott says. "Just pull over."

Magnus turns in without signaling, parks around the side.

"I'll just be a second," Scott tells him.

"Get me a Coke."

Scott realizes he's wearing scrubs.

"Lend me a twenty," he says.

Magnus thinks about this.

"Okay, but promise we're going to Mueller's. I bet she's got scotch in her cabinets that was bottled before the fecking *Titanic*."

Scott looks him in the eye.

"Promise."

Magnus pulls a crumpled bill from his pocket.

"And some chips," he says.

Scott closes the passenger door. He is wearing disposable flip-flops.

"Be right back," he says, and walks into the gas station convenience store. There is a heavyset woman behind the counter.

"Back door?" Scott asks her.

She points.

Scott walks down a short hall, past the restrooms. He pushes open a heavy fire door and stands squinting in the sun. There is a chain-link fence a few feet away, and behind that the start of a residential neighborhood. Scott puts the twenty in his front pocket. He tries to climb the fence one-handed, but the sling gets in the way so he ditches it. A few moments later he is on the other side, walking through a vacant lot, his flip-flops slapping against his heels. It is late August, and the air is thick and broiled. He pictures Magnus behind the wheel. He will have turned on the radio, found an oldies station. Right now he's probably singing along with Queen, arching his neck on the high notes.

Around Scott, the neighborhood is lower-class, cars on blocks in driveways, aboveground pools sloshing in backyards. He is a man in hospital scrubs and flip-flops walking through the midday heat. A mental patient for all anybody knows.

Thirty minutes later he finds a fried chicken joint, goes inside. It's just a counter and stove with a couple of chairs in front.

"You got a phone I could use?" he asks the Dominican guy behind the counter.

"Gotta order something," the guy tells him.

Scott orders a bucket of thighs and a ginger ale. The clerk points to a phone on the wall in the kitchen. Scott takes a business card from his pocket and dials. A man answers on the second ring.

"NTSB."

"Gus Franklin, please," says Scott.

"Speaking."

"It's Scott Burroughs. From the hospital."

"Mr. Burroughs, how are you?"

"Fine. Look. I'm—I want to help—with the search. The rescue. Whatever."

There is silence on the other end of the line.

"I'm told you checked out of the hospital," says Gus, "somehow without being seen by the press."

Scott thinks about this.

"I dressed up like a doctor," he says, "and went out the back door."

Gus laughs.

"Very clever. Listen. I've got divers in the water searching for the fuselage, but it's slow going, and this is a high-profile case. Is there anything you can tell us, anything else you can remember about the crash, what happened before?"

"It's coming back," Scott tells him. "Still just fragments, but—Let me help with the search. Maybe being out there—maybe it'll shake something loose."

Gus thinks about this.

"Where are you?"

"Well," says Scott, "let me ask you this—how do you feel about chicken thighs?

PAINTING #1

THE FIRST THING that catches your eye is the light, or rather two lights angled toward a single focal point, becoming a figure-eight flare at the center of the canvas. It is big, this painting, eight feet long and five feet high, the once white tarpaulin transformed into a smoky gray glitter. Or maybe what you see first is calamity, two dark rectangles slicing the frame, jackknifed, their metallic skeletons glowing in the moonlight. There are flames on the edge of picture, as if the story doesn't end just because the painting stops, and people who view the image have been known to walk to the far edges looking for more information, microscoping the framing wood for even a hint of added drama.

The lights that flare out the center of the image are the headlights of an Amtrak passenger train, its caboose having come to rest almost perpendicular to the twisted iron track that bends and waves below it. The first passenger car has disconnected from the caboose and now makes the trunk of a T, having maintained its forward momentum and smashed the engine dead center, bending its bread-box contours into a vague V.

As with any bright light, the headlight glare here obscures much of the image, but upon further examination a viewer might discover a single passenger—in this case a young woman—dressed in a black skirt and torn white blouse, her hair tousled across her face, matted by blood. She is wandering shoeless through the jagged wreckage, and if you squint past the illusion of light you can see that her eyes are wide and searching. She is the victim of disaster, a survivor of heat and impact, cantilevered from her resting position into an impossible parabola of unexpected torture, her once placid world—gently rocking, click clack, click clack—now a screeching twist of metal.

What is she looking for, this woman? Is it merely a way out? A clear and sensible path to safety? Or has she lost something? Someone? In that moment, when gentle rocking turned into a cannonball ricochet, did she go from wife and mother, from sister or girlfriend, from daughter or paramour to refugee? A fulfilled and happy *we* to a stunned and grieving *I*?

And so, even as other paintings call to you, you can't help but stand there and help her look.

STORM CLOUDS

THE LIFE VEST is so tight it's hard to breathe, but Scott reaches up and pulls the straps again. It is an unconscious gesture. One he's been doing every few moments since they got on the helicopter. Gus Franklin sits across from him, studying his face. Beside him is Petty Officer Berkman in an orange jumpsuit and glassy black helmet. They are in a Coast Guard MH-65C Dolphin racing over the wave caps of the Atlantic. In the distance Scott can just make out the cliffs of Martha's Vineyard. Home. But this is not where they're going. Not yet. Sneeze, the three-legged dog, will have to wait. Scott thinks of her now, a white mutt with one black eye. An eater of horse shit, a connoisseur of long grass, who lost her back right leg to cancer last year and was climbing stairs again within two days. Scott checked in with his neighbor after he got off the phone with Gus this morning. The dog was fine, his neighbor told him. She was lying on the porch panting at the sun. Scott thanked her again for watching the dog. He said he should be home in a couple of days.

"Take your time," his neighbor said. "You've been through a lot. And good for you. What you did for that boy. Good for you."

He thinks of the dog now, missing a limb. *If she can bounce back, why can't I?*

The helicopter bucks through chunky air, each drop like a hand slapping a jar, trying to dislodge the last peanut. Except in this case Scott is the peanut. He grips his seat with his right hand, his left arm still in a sling. The trip from the coast takes twenty minutes. Looking out the window at the miles of ocean, Scott can't believe how far he swam.

Scott was at the barbecue joint sipping water for an hour before Gus arrived. He drove up in a white sedan—*company car*, he told Scott—and entered the restaurant with a change of clothes in hand.

"I took a guess at the size," he said and threw the clothes to Scott.

"I'm sure they'll be great. Thanks," said Scott and went into the bathroom to change. Cargo pants and a sweatshirt. The pants were too big in the waist and the sweatshirt too tight in the shoulders—the dislocated shoulder made changing clothes a challenge—but at least he felt like a normal person again. He washed his hands and pushed the scrubs deep into the garbage.

On the helicopter, Gus points out the starboard side. Scott follows his finger to the Coast Guard Cutter *Willow*, a gleaming white ship anchored in the sea below.

"You ever been on a helicopter before?" Gus yells.

Scott shakes his head. He is a painter. Who would bring a painter on a helicopter? But then again, that's what he thought about private planes, and look how that turned out.

Looking down, Scott sees the cutter has company. Half a dozen ships are spread out on the ocean. The plane, they believe, has crashed into an especially deep part of the sea. The *something* trench. That means, Gus tells him, it may take weeks to locate the submerged wreckage.

"This is a joint search-and-recovery operation," Gus says. "We've got ships from the navy, the Coast Guard, and the NOAA."

"The what?"

"National Oceanic and Atmospheric Administration."

Gus smiles.

"Sea nerds," he says, "with multibeam and side scan sonar. Also the air force lent us a couple of HC-130s, and we've got thirty navy divers and twenty from the Massachusetts State Police ready to go into the water if and when we find the wreckage."

Scott thinks about this.

"Is that normal when a small plane goes down?" he asks.

"No," says Gus. "Definitely a VIP package. This is what happens when the president of the United States makes a phone call."

The helicopter banks right and circles the cutter. The only thing keeping Scott from falling out the open door and into the sea is his seat belt.

"You said there was wreckage on the surface when you came up," yells Gus.

"What?"

"Wreckage in the sea."

Scott nods. "There were flames on the water."

"Jet fuel," says Gus. "Which means the fuel tanks ruptured. It's lucky you weren't burned."

Scott nods, remembering.

"I saw," he says, "I don't know, part of a wing? Maybe some other debris. It was dark."

Gus nods. The helicopter drops with another quick jerk. Scott's stomach is in his throat.

"A fishing boat found pieces of wing near Philbin Beach yesterday morning," Gus tells him. "A metal tray from the galley, a headrest, toilet seat. It's clear we're not looking for an intact aircraft. Sounds like the whole thing came apart. We may see more wash up in the next few days, depending on the current. The question is, did it break up on impact or in midair?"

"Sorry. I wish I could say more. But, like I said, at a certain point I hit my head."

Scott looks out at the ocean, endless miles of open water as far as his eye can see. For the first time he thinks, *Maybe it was good that it was dark*. If he had been able to see the vastness around him, the epic emptiness, he may never have made it.

Across from him, Gus eats almonds from a ziplock bag. Where the average person appreciates the beauty of surf and waves, Gus, an engineer, sees only practical design. Gravity, plus ocean current, plus wind. Poetry to the common man is a unicorn viewed from the corner of an eye—an unexpected glimpse of the intangible. To an engineer, only the ingenuity of pragmatic solutions is poetic. Function over form. It's not a question of optimism or pessimism, a glass half full or half empty.

To an engineer, the glass is simply too big.

This was how the world looked to Gus Franklin as a young man. Raised in Stuyvesant Village by a trash collector father and a stay-at-home mom, Gus—the only black kid in his AP calculus class—graduated summa cum laude at Fordham. He saw beauty not in nature, but in the elegant design of Roman aqueducts and microchips. To his mind, every problem on earth could be fixed by repairing or replacing a part. Or—if the operational flaw was more insidious—then you tore the whole system apart and started again.

Which is what he did to his marriage after his wife spit in his face and stormed out the door on a rainy night in 1999. *Don't you feel anything*, she'd shouted moments earlier. And Gus frowned and thought about the question—not because the answer was no, but because he so clearly did have feelings. They just weren't the feelings she wanted.

So he shrugged. And she spit and stormed out.

To say his wife was emotional would be an understatement. Belinda was the least engineer-minded person Gus had ever meant—she once said the fact that flowers had Latin names *robbed them of their mystery*. This, he decided (spit running down his jaw), was the fatal error in his marriage that could not be fixed. They were incompatible, a square peg in a round hole. Instead, his life required a systemic redesign, in this case a divorce.

He had tried in the lonely year of their marriage to apply practical solutions to irrational problems. She thought he worked too much—but in truth he worked less than most of his colleagues, so the term *too much* seemed misplaced. She wanted children right away, but he believed they should wait until his career was more established, meaning his pay had increased, resulting in an expanded living allowance, ergo a bigger apartment—in finite terms: one with room for children.

So Gus sat with her one Saturday and walked her through a PowerPoint presentation on the topic—complete with bar graphs and spreadsheets—which concluded with an equation proving that their perfect moment of conception (assuming, of course, a set of givens—his hierarchical advancement, graduated income, et cetera) would be September 2002, three years in the future. Belinda called him an unfeeling robot. He told her that robots, by definition, were unfeeling (at least currently), but he was clearly not a robot. He had feelings. They just didn't control him the way they controlled her.

Their divorce proved much simpler than their marriage, mostly because she hired an attorney driven by a bottom-line desire for monetary gain—that is, someone with a clear and rational goal. And so Gus Franklin went back to being a solitary human being, who—as he had projected in his PowerPoint presentation—advanced quickly, rising up the ranks at Boeing, and then accepting a lead investigative role at the NTSB, where he had been for the last eleven years.

And yet, over the years, Gus found his engineer's brain evolving. His previously narrow view of the world—as a machine that operated with dynamic mechanical functionality—blossomed and grew. Much of the change had to do with his new job as an investigator of large-scale transportation disasters—which exposed him to death and the urgency of human grief on a regular basis. As he had told his ex-wife, he was not a robot. He felt love. He understood the pain of loss. It was just that as a young man those factors seemed controllable, as if grief were simply a failure of the intellect to manage the body's subsystems.

But then his father was diagnosed with leukemia in 2003. He passed away in 2009, and Gus's mother died of an aneurysm a year later. The void their deaths created proved to be beyond the practical comprehension of an engineer. The machine he believed himself to be broke down, and Gus found himself immersed in an experience he had witnessed for years in his job with the NTSB, but never truly understood. Grief. Death was not an intellectual conceit. It was an existential black hole, an animal riddle, both problem and solution, and the grief it inspired could not be fixed or bypassed like a faulty relay, but only endured.

And so now, at fifty-one, Gus Franklin finds himself leaving simple intelligence behind and approaching something that can only be described as wisdom, defined in this case by an ability to understand the factual and practical pieces of an event, but also appreciate its full human import. A plane crash is not simply the sum total of time line + mechanical elements + human elements. It is an incalculable tragedy, one that shows us the ultimate finiteness of human control over the universe, and the humbling power of collective death.

So when the phone rang that night in late August, Gus did what he always did. He snapped to attention and put the engineer part of himself to work. But he also took the time to think about the victims— crew members and civilians, and worse: two small children with their whole lives ahead of them—and to reflect on the hardship and loss that would be endured by those they left behind.

First though, came the facts. A private jet—*make? model? year built? service history?*—had gone missing—*departing airport? destination airport? last radio transmission? radar data? weather conditions?* Other planes in the area had been contacted—*any sightings?*—as had other airports—*has the flight been diverted or contacted another tower?* But no one had seen or heard from the flight since the precise second that ATC at Teterboro lost track of it.

A daisy chain of phone calls were made, a Go Team assembled. In daylight, telephones rang in offices and cars. In the middle hours of the night, they rang in bedrooms, shattering sleep.

By the time he was in the car, a passenger manifest had been assembled. Projections were made—*this much fuel x maximum speed = our potential search radius*. At his command the Coast Guard and navy were contacted, helicopters and frigates deployed. And so, by the time Gus reached Teterboro, a nautical search was already under way, everyone still hoping for a radio malfunction and a safe landing somewhere off the grid, but knowing better.

It would be twenty-two hours before the first wreckage was found.

FOR ALL THE drama of its descent, the helicopter lands gently, like a toe testing the water. Petty Officer Berkman slides opens the door and they jump out, rotors rotating overhead. Ahead, Scott can see dozens of seamen and technicians at their posts.

"How long after we went missing—" he starts to say, but before he can finish, Gus is already answering.

"I'll be honest. ATC at Teterboro fucked up. For six minutes after your flight dropped off radar, nobody noticed. Now, that's a dog's age in flight control time. It opens up a huge search grid in every direction. Because maybe the plane crashed instantly, or maybe it just dropped below radar and flew on. Over water anything below eleven hundred feet is off radar, so a plane could easily drop below that and keep going. Then there's *what if the plane changed direction?* Where should we look? So the controller realizes the plane is missing and first he tries to raise it on the radio. That's ninety seconds. Then he starts calling other planes in the area to see—maybe they have a visual. Because maybe your plane just has an antenna problem or the radio's broke. But he can't find anyone who sees your plane. So he calls the Coast Guard and says, *I've got a plane off radar for eight minutes. Last location was this, heading in so-and-so direction at such-and-such speed.* And the Coast Guard scrambles a ship and launches a helicopter."

"And when did they call you?"

"Your flight went into the water at approximately ten eighteen p.m. on Sunday. By eleven thirty I was on my way to Teterboro with the Go Team."

An air force HC-130 plane roars past above him. Scott ducks reflexively, covering his head. The plane is a lumbering beast with four propellers.

"He's listening for transponder signals," says Gus, of the plane. "Basically, what we're doing is using all these ships, helicopters, and planes to do a visual search in an ever-expanding grid. And we're bouncing sonar off the seabed, looking for wreckage. We want to recover everything we can, but especially the plane's black box. Because that plus the cockpit voice recorder will tell us second by second what happened aboard the plane."

Scott watches the plane bank and maneuver into a new search approach.

"And there wasn't any radio contact?" he asks. "No mayday? Nothing."

Gus pockets his notebook.

"The last thing the pilot said was *thank you, tower,* approximately thirty seconds before takeoff."

The ship rises on the back of a wave. Scott grabs the rail to steady himself. In the distance he can see the NOAA ship moving slowly.

"So I landed at Teterboro at eleven forty-six," says Gus, "and downloaded the facts from ATC. I've got a private plane with no flight plan and an unknown number of passengers missing over water for an hour and twenty minutes."

"They didn't file a flight plan?"

"It's not mandatory for private flights within the US, and there was a passenger roster, but it was just for the family. So crew plus four. But then I hear from Martha's Vineyard that they think at least seven were on board, so now I have to figure out who else was on the plane, and did that have anything to do with what happened—which at this point we still don't know what that is—did you change course, fly to Jamaica? Or land at a different airport in New York or Massachusetts?"

"I was swimming at that point, me and the boy."

"Yes, you were. And by now there are three Coast Guard helicopters in the air, and maybe even one from the navy, because five minutes before I walk into ATC I get a call from my boss who got a call from his boss saying David Bateman is a very important person—which I know—and the president is already monitoring the situation—which means no fuckups under any circumstances—and there's an FBI team meeting me and potentially someone high up in Homeland Security."

"And when did you find out about Kipling?"

"So the SEC calls me while I'm in the air between Teterboro and Martha's Vineyard and says they had a tap on Ben Kipling's phone and they think he was on the flight. Which means, in addition to the FBI and Homeland Security, I've got two agents from the SEC joining the team and now I'm gonna need a bigger helicopter."

"Why are you telling me this?" Scott asks.

"You asked."

"And is that why you brought me out here? Because I asked?"

Gus thinks about that, human truth versus strategic truth.

"You said it might help you remember," he says.

Scott shakes his head.

"No. I know I'm not supposed to be here. This isn't how you work."

Gus thinks about that.

"Do you know how many people survive most plane crashes? None. Maybe being here will help you remember something. Or maybe I'm just tired of going to funerals. Maybe I wanted you to know that I appreciate what you did."

"Don't say *for the boy*."

"Why not? You saved his life."

"I . . . was swimming. He called out. Anybody would have done what I did."

"They might have tried."

Scott looks out over the water, chewing his lip.

"So because I was on the high school swim team I'm some kind of hero?"

"No. You're a hero because you acted heroically. And I brought you out here because that means something to me. To all of us."

Scott tries to remember the last time he ate.

"Hey, what did he mean?"

"Who?"

"In the hospital. When the guy from the feds said Boston played last night. The guy from OSPRY said something about baseball."

"Right. Dworkin's at-bat. He's a catcher for the Red Sox."

"And?"

"And on Sunday night he broke the record for the longest at-bat in baseball history."

"So?"

Gus smiles.

"He did it while you were in the air. Twenty-two pitches in just over eighteen minutes starting the moment you took off and ending within seconds of the crash."

"You're kidding."

"No. Longest at-bat in baseball history, and it lasted the exact length of your flight."

Scott looks out at the water. Heavy gray clouds are massing on the horizon. He remembers a game being on, that something remarkable seemed to be happening—at least the two other guys on board were getting worked up about it. *Take a look at this, hon*, and *Can you believe this fucking guy?* But Scott was never one for sports and he barely looked over. Now, though, hearing the story—the coincidence of it—he feels the hair on the back of his neck stand. Two things happen at the same time. By mentioning them together they become connected. Convergence. It's one of those things that *feels* meaning-ful, but isn't. At least he doesn't think it is? How could it be? A batter in Boston fouling pitches into the stands while a small plane struggles through low coastal fog. How many millions of other activities begin and end at the same time? How many other "facts" converge in just the right way, creating symbolic connectivity?

"Early reports on the pilot and copilot look clean," says Gus. "Melody was a twenty-three-year veteran who flew with GullWing for eleven years. No black marks, no citations or complaints. Kind of an interesting childhood, though, raised by a single mom who took him to live with a doomsday cult when he was little."

"Like a Jim Jones Guyana cult?" asks Scott.

"Unclear," says Gus. "We're doing some digging, but most likely it's just a detail."

"And the other one?" asks Scott. "The copilot?"

"A little bit more of a story there," says Gus. "And obviously none of this is to be repeated, but you'll probably see a lot of it in the press. Charles Busch was Logan Birch's nephew. The senator. Grew up in Texas. Did some time in the National Guard. Sounds like he was kind of a playboy. A couple of citations, mostly for appearance—showing up to work unshaven. Probably partied too hard the night before. But no red flags. We're talking to the airline, trying to get a clearer pic-ture."

James Melody and Charles Busch. Scott never even saw the copilot, has only a vague memory of Captain Melody. He tries to commit the details to memory. These are the people who died. Each had a life, a story.

Around them the sea has turned choppy. The Coast Guard cutter ramps and banks.

"Looks like a storm is coming," says Scott.

Gus holds the rail and stares out at the horizon.

"Unless it's a class four hurricane," he says, "we don't abandon the search."

. . .

Scott has a cup of tea inside while Gus manages the search. There is a TV on in the galley, pictures of the ship he is on from a news helicopter, the search in progress live. Scott feels like he's in one of those mirrored rooms, his image reflecting off into infinity. Two sailors on break drink coffee and watch themselves on TV.

The image of the search party is replaced by a talking head—Bill Cunningham in red suspenders.

"—watching the search as it progresses. Then at four p.m. don't miss a special broadcast, *Are Our Skies Safe?* And look—I've held my tongue long enough—but this whole thing smells more than a little fishy to me. 'Cause if this plane really did crash, then where are the *bodies*? If David Bateman and his family are really—dead—then why haven't we seen the—and now I'm hearing, and ALC broke this story just hours after the event, that Ben Kipling, the notorious money manager rumored to be on board the flight—that Kipling was about to be indicted by the SEC for trading with the enemy. That's right, folks, for investing money illegally obtained from countries like Iran and North Korea. And what if this disaster was an enemy nation tying up loose ends. Muzzle this Kipling traitor once and for all. So we have to ask—why hasn't the government characterized this crash for what it is—a terrorist attack."

Scott turns his back to the TV and sips his tea out of a paper cup. He tries to tune out the voices.

"And just as important, who is this man? Scott Burroughs."

Hold on, what? Scott turns back. Onscreen is a photo of him taken sometime last decade—an artist portrait that accompanied a gallery show he did in Chicago.

"Yes, I know, they're saying he rescued a four-year-old boy, but who is he and what was he doing on that plane?"

Now a live image of Scott's house on the Vineyard. How is that possible? Scott sees his three-legged dog in the window, barking soundlessly.

"Wikipedia lists him as some kind of painter, but has no personal information. We contacted the Chicago gallery where Mr. Burroughs allegedly held his last show in 2010, but they claimed never to have met him. So ask yourself, how does a nobody painter who hasn't shown a painting in five years end up on a luxury plane with two of the richest men in New York?"

Scott watches his house on TV. A shingled, single-story home rented from a Greek fisherman for nine hundred dollars a month. It needs a paint job—and he waits for Cunningham's inevitable joke, the painter's house that needs a paint job—but it doesn't come.

"And so now, live on this network, this journalist is asking— if there's anyone out there who knows this mystery painter, please call the station. Convince me that Mr. Burroughs is real and not some sleeper agent posing as a has-been who just got activated by ISIS."

Scott sips his tea, aware of the stares of the two soldiers. He feels a presence behind him.

"Looks like going home is out of the question," Gus says, having wandered up behind Scott.

Scott turns.

"Apparently," he says, feeling a completely foreign disconnect— who he is inside versus this new idea of him, his new identity as a public persona, his name pronounced with vitriol by a famous face. And how if he goes home he will walk out of his life and onto that screen. He will become theirs.

Gus watches the TV for a moment, then goes over and turns it off.

"You got anywhere you can crash for a few days," he says, "under the radar?"

Scott thinks about it, comes up blank. He has called the one friend he has and ditched him in a convenience store parking lot. There are cousins somewhere, an old fiancé, but he has to believe that these people have already been discovered in the Google search of modern curiosity. What he needs is someone nonlinear, a name generated seemingly at random, that no private eye or computer algorithm could ever predict.

Then a name enters his head, some cosmic synapse firing. Two words spoken with an Irish lilt that paint a picture: a blond woman with a billion dollars.

"Yeah, I think I know who to call," he says.

ORPHANS

ELEANOR REMEMBERS WHEN they were girls. There was no *yours and mine*. Everything she and Maggie owned was communal, the hairbrush, the striped and polka-dot dresses, the hand-me-down Raggedy Ann and Andy. They used to sit in the farmhouse sink, facing the mirror, and brush each other's hair—a record on in the living room—Pete Seeger and Arlo Guthrie or the Chieftains—the sounds of their father cooking. Maggie and Eleanor Greenway, eight and six, or twelve and ten, sharing CDs, swooning over the same boys. Eleanor was the younger, towheaded and spritely. Maggie had a dance she did, twirling with a long ribbon until she got dizzy. Eleanor would watch and laugh and laugh.

For Eleanor there was never a time where she thought in terms of *I*. Every sentence in her head began with *we*. And then Maggie went to college and Eleanor had to learn how to be singular. She remembers that first three-day weekend, spinning in her empty room, listening for laughter that never came. And how that feeling, of being alone, felt like bugs in her skeleton. And so on Monday, when school started, she threw herself off the cliff of boys, opening her eyes for the first time to the idea of couplehood with someone else. She was going steady with Paul Aspen by Friday. And when that ended three weeks later, she switched to Damon Wright.

It was the lightbulb behind her eyes guiding her, this idea—never be alone again.

Over the next decade there was a series of men, crushes and infatuations, surrogates. Day in and day out Eleanor dodged her central defect, locking the door and rolling up the window, eyes doggedly forward, even as its knocks became louder and louder.

She met Doug three years ago in Williamsburg. She had just turned thirty-one, was working a temp job in Lower Manhattan and doing yoga in the evenings. She lived with two roommates in a three-story walk-up in Carroll Gardens. The most recent love of her life, Javier, had dropped her a week earlier—after she found lipstick stains on his boxers—and most days she felt like a rain-soaked paper bag. Her roommates told her she should try being alone for a while. Uptown, Maggie said the same, but every time she tried Eleanor felt that same old feeling, those bugs climbing back into her bones.

She spent the weekend with Maggie and David. Helping with the kids is how she remembers it, but really she just lay there on the sofa staring out the window and trying not to cry. Two nights later, she was out with some work friends at a blue-ribbon hipster joint near the L train when she spotted Doug. He had a heavy beard and wore overalls. She liked his eyes, the way they crinkled when he smiled. When he came up to the bar for another pitcher, she struck up a conversation. He told her he was a writer who avoided writing by hosting elaborate dinner parties. His apartment was full of obscure food prep machinery, vintage pasta rollers and a three-hundred-pound cappuccino machine he'd rebuilt screw by screw. Last year he started curing his own sausage, buying bung from a butcher in Gowanus. The trick was controlling the humidity so botulism didn't set in. He invited her over to try some. She said that sounded dicey to her.

He told her he was working on the great American novel or maybe just a paperweight made entirely out of paper. They drank Pabst together and ignored their friends. She went home with him an hour later and learned he slept on flannel sheets, even in the summer. His decor was lumberjack meets mad scientist. There was a vintage dentist chair he was rebuilding with a television mounted on the arm. Naked he looked like a bear and smelled of beer and sawdust. She felt like a ghost lying under him, watching him work, as if he were making love to her shadow.

He told her he had boundary issues and drank too much. She said, *Hey, me too.* And they laughed about it, but the truth was she didn't drink that much, but he did, and the great American paperweight called to him at odd hours, inspiring in him fits of self-pity and rage. She'd wake sweating under his flannel top sheet and find him tearing his desk (an old door laid across two sawhorses) apart.

But during daylight hours he was sweet, and he had a lot of friends who dropped by throughout the day and night, which meant Eleanor never had the chance to be alone. Doug welcomed the distraction, and he'd drop everything to go on a culinary adventure—tracking down a cherry pitter on Orchard Street, or riding the subway to Queens to buy goat meat from some Haitians. He was such a big presence that Eleanor never felt alone, even when he stayed out late. She moved into his apartment after a month, and if she ever felt lonely she put on one of his shirts and ate leftovers sitting on the kitchen floor.

She got her masseuse license and starting working at a high-end boutique in Tribeca. Her clients were movie stars and bankers. They were friendly and tipped well. Doug, meanwhile, did odd jobs— random carpentry and the like. He had a friend who remodeled restaurants and would pay Doug to track down and refurbish vintage stoves. In Eleanor's mind they were happy and doing what young couples should be doing in the modern age.

She introduced him to David, Maggie, and the kids, but she could tell that Doug didn't enjoy being around a man as accomplished and moneyed as David. They ate in the dining room at the town house (it was easier for the kids than going out) at a table for twelve, and she watched Doug drink a bottle of French wine and inspect the top-of-the-line kitchen appliances (an eight-burner Wolf range, a Sub-Zero fridge) with envy and disdain ("you can buy the tools, but you can't buy the talent to use them"). On the subway home, Doug railed against her sister's "Republican sugar daddy" and acted as if David had rubbed their faces in their inadequacy. Eleanor didn't understand. Her sister was happy. David was nice, and the kids were angels. And no, she didn't agree with her brother-in-law's politics, but he wasn't a bad person.

But Doug had the same clichéd overreaction to wealth that defined most bearded men his age. They defamed it, even as they coveted. He launched into a monologue that ran from the 6 train, through the change at Union Square, and all the way to their bedroom on Wyeth Avenue. How David was peddling hate to white people with guns. How the world was worse off now than it had ever been, because David trafficked in extremism and hate porn.

Eleanor told him she didn't want to talk about it anymore and went to sleep on the sofa.

They moved upstate in May. Doug had gone in on a restaurant in Croton-on-Hudson with some friends, more of an empty space really, and the idea was that they would move up there and he and his friends would build the place out from scratch. But money was tight, and one of the friends pulled out at the last minute. The other put in six months of half time, then knocked up a local high school girl and fled back to the city. And now the space sat half built—mostly just a kitchen and some boxes of white tile rotting in a spray of standing water.

Doug drives over there in an old pickup truck most days, but just to drink. He's set up a computer in the corner and will work on his paperweight if the mood strikes him, which it usually doesn't. The lease on the space expires at the end of the year, and if Doug hasn't managed to turn it into a functional restaurant (which feels impossible at this point), they will lose the space and all the money they've invested.

At one point, Eleanor suggested (just suggested) that David could maybe lend them ten grand to finish the space. Doug spit at her feet and went on a two-day rant about how she should have married a rich asshole like her fucking sister. That night he didn't come home, and she lay there feeling the old bugs crawling back inside her bones.

For a time it seemed their marriage would be just another house-plant that had failed to thrive, choked to death by the lack of money and the death of dreams.

And then David and Maggie and beautiful little Rachel died, and they found themselves with more money than they could ever spend.

. . .

Three days after the crash they sit in a conference room on the top floor of 432 Park Avenue. Doug, under protest, has put on a tie and brushed his hair, but his beard is still shaggy and Eleanor thinks he may have gone a day or two without a shower. She is wearing a black dress and low heels, and sits clutching her purse. Being here, in this office tower, facing a phalanx of lawyers makes her teeth itch—the import of it. To unseal their last will and testament, to be read the provisions of a document meant to be read in the event of death, sig-nifies with irrefutable evidence that someone you love is dead.

Eleanor's mother is watching the boy upstate. Eleanor felt a twist in her stomach as they were leaving. He looked so vacant and sad as she hugged him good-bye, but her mother assured her they'd be fine. He was her grandson, after all, and Eleanor forced herself to get in the car.

On the ride in, Doug kept asking how much money she thought they were going to get, and she explained to him that it wasn't their money. It was JJ's and there would be a trust and as the boy's guardian she would be able to spend the money to care for him, but not for their own personal gain. And Doug said, *Sure, sure*, and nodded and acted like *Of course I know that*, but she could tell from the way he drove and the fact that he smoked half a pack of cigarettes in ninety minutes that he felt like he'd won the lottery and was expecting to be handed an oversize novelty check.

Looking out the window she thinks about the moment she first saw JJ in the hospital, then flips to the moment three days earlier that the phone rang and she found out her sister's plane was missing. And how she sat there under the covers long after the call was over, holding the receiver while Doug slept beside her, on his back, snoring at the ceiling. She stared into the shadows until the phone rang again, sometime after dawn, and a man's voice told her that her nephew was alive.

Just him? she asked.

So far. But we're looking.

She woke Doug and told him they had to go to a hospital on Long Island.

Now? he said.

She drove, putting the car in gear before Doug had even gotten the door closed, his fly undone, sweatshirt half on. She told Doug there was a plane crash somewhere in the ocean. That one of the passengers had swum miles to shore, carrying the boy. She wanted him to tell her not to worry, that if they survived, then the others had survived as well, but he didn't. Her husband sat in the passenger seat and asked if they could stop for coffee.

The rest is a blur. She remembers jumping out of the car in a loading zone at the hospital, remembers the panicked search for JJ's room. Does she even remember hugging the boy, or meeting the hero in the bed beside him? He is a shape, a voice, flared out by the sun. Her adrenaline was so high, her surprise at the magnitude of events, at how big life could get—helicopters circling wave caps, naval ships deployed. So big that it filled the screens of three million televisions, so big that her life was now a historic mystery to be discussed, the details viewed and reviewed, by amateurs and professionals alike.

Now, in the conference room, she makes her hands into fists to fight off the pins and needles she's feeling, and tries to smile. Across from her, Larry Page smiles back. There are two lawyers on either side of him, split by gender.

"Look," he says, "there'll be time for all the minutiae later. This meeting is really just to give you an overview of what David and Maggie wanted for their children in case of—in the eventuality of their death."

"Of course," says Eleanor.

"How much?" asks Doug.

Eleanor kicks him under the table. Across from her, Mr. Page frowns. There is a decorum he expects in dealing with matters of extreme wealth, a studied nonchalance.

"Well," he says, "as I explained, the Batemans established a trust for both children, splitting their estate fifty–fifty. But since their daughter—"

"Rachel," says Eleanor.

"Right, Rachel. Since Rachel did not survive, the entirety of the trust goes to JJ. This includes all their real estate holdings—the town house in Manhattan, the house on Martha's Vineyard, and the pied-à-terre in London."

"Wait," says Doug. "The *what* now?"

Mr. Page presses on.

"At the same time, their wills both earmarked a large sum of cash and equities to a number of charitable organizations. About thirty percent of their total portfolio. The remainder lives in JJ's trust and will be available to him in stages over the next forty years."

"Forty years," says Doug, with a frown.

"We don't need much," says Eleanor. "That's his money."

Now it's Doug's turn to kick her under the table.

"It's not a question of what you need," the lawyer tells her. "It's about fulfilling the Batemans' last wishes. And yes, we're still waiting on the official pronouncement of death, but given the circumstance I'd like to free up some funds in the interim."

One of the women to his left hands him a crisp manila folder. Mr. Page opens it. Inside is a single piece of paper.

"At current market value," he tells them, "JJ's trust is worth one hundred and three million dollars."

Beside her, Doug makes a kind of choking noise. Eleanor's face burns. She's embarrassed by the clear greed he's showing, and she knows if she looked he'd have some stupid grin on his face.

"The bulk of the estate—sixty percent—will be available to him on his fortieth birthday. Fifteen percent matures on his thirtieth birthday, another fifteen percent on his twenty-first. And the remaining ten percent has been set aside to cover the costs of raising him to adulthood from this point forward."

She can feel Doug beside her, working out the math.

"That's ten million, three hundred thousand—again as of close of market yesterday."

Outside the window, Eleanor can see birds circling. She thinks about carrying JJ from the hospital that first day, the heft of him—so much heavier than she remembered, and how they didn't have a booster seat so Doug piled up some blankets in the back and they drove to a Target to buy one. Car idling in the parking lot, they sat there in silence for a moment. Eleanor looked at Doug.

What? he said, his face blank.

Tell them we need a booster seat, she said. *It should be front facing. Make sure they know he's four.*

He thought about arguing—*Me? In a Target? I fucking hate Target*—but to his credit he didn't, just shouldered the door open and went in. She turned in her seat and looked at JJ.

Are you okay? she asked.

He nodded, then threw up onto the back of her seat.

The man to Page's left speaks up.

"Mrs. Dunleavy," he says, "I'm Fred Cutter. My firm manages your late brother-in-law's finances."

So, thinks Eleanor, *not a lawyer.*

"I've worked out a basic financial structure to cover monthly expenses and education projections, which I'd be happy to review with you at your convenience."

Eleanor risks a look at Doug. He is, in fact, smiling. He nods at her.

"And I'm—" says Eleanor, "—I'm the executor of the trust. Me?"

"Yes," says Page, "unless you decide you do not wish to carry out the responsibilities afforded to you, in which case Mr. and Mrs. Bateman named a successor."

She feels Doug stiffen beside her at the idea of passing all that money on to some kind of runner-up.

"No," says Eleanor, "he's my nephew. I want him. I just need to be clear. I'm the one named in the trust, not—"

She flicks her eyes toward her husband. Page catches the look.

"Yes," he says. "You are the named guardian and executor."

"Okay," she says, after a beat.

"Over the next few weeks I'll need you to come in and sign some more papers—and by *come in*, I mean we can come to you. Some will need to be notarized. Did you want the keys to the various properties today?"

She blinks, thinking about her sister's apartment, now a museum filled with all the things she will never need again—clothes, furniture, the refrigerator filled with food, the children's rooms heavy with books and toys. She feels her eyes well with tears.

"No," she says. "I don't think—"

She stops to collect herself.

"I understand," says Page. "I'll have them sent to your house."

"Maybe somebody could collect JJ's things, from his room? Toys and books. Clothes. He probably, I don't know, maybe that would help him."

The woman to Page's right makes a note.

"Should you decide to sell any or all of the properties," says Cutter, "we can help you with that. Fair market value for the three combined is around thirty million, last time I checked."

"And does that money go into the trust," says Doug, "or—"

"That money would fold in with the current funds available to you."

"So ten million becomes forty million."

"Doug," says Eleanor, more sharply than she intended.

The lawyers pretend not to have heard.

"What?" her husband says. "I'm just—clarifying."

She nods, unclenching her fists and stretching her hands under the table.

"Okay," she says, "I feel like I should get back. I don't want to leave JJ alone too long. He's not really sleeping that well."

She stands. Across the table, the group stands as one. Only Doug is left in his chair, daydreaming.

"Doug," she says.

"Yeah, right," he says and stands, then stretches his arms and back like a cat waking from a long nap in the sun.

"Are you driving back?" Cutter asks.

She nods.

"I don't know what car you're in, but the Batemans owned several, including a family SUV. These are also available to you, or can be sold. It's whatever you want."

"I just—" says Eleanor, "I'm sorry. I can't really make any decisions right now. I just need to—think or take it all in or—"

"Of course. I'll stop asking questions."

Cutter puts his hand on her shoulder. He is a thin man with a kind face.

"Please know that David and Maggie were more than just clients. We had daughters the same age, and—"

He stops, his eyes filling, then nods. She squeezes his arm, grateful to find something human in this moment. Beside her, Doug clears his throat.

"What kind of cars did you say again?" asks Doug.

. . .

She is quiet on the ride home. Doug smokes the other half of the pack, window down, making calculations with his fingers on the steering wheel.

"I say keep the town house, right?" he says. "A place in the city. But, I don't know, are we really going to go back to the Vineyard? I mean, after what happened?"

She doesn't answer, just lays her head against the headrest and looks out at the treetops.

"And London," he says, "I mean, that could be cool. But how often are we really going to—I say we sell it and then if we want to go we can always stay in a hotel."

He rubs his beard, like a miser in a children's story, suddenly rich.

"It's JJ's money," she says.

"Right," says Doug, "but, I mean, he's four, so—"

"It's not about what we want."

"Babe—okay, I know—but the kid's used to a certain—and we're his guardians now."

"I'm his guardian."

"Sure, legally, but we're a family."

"Since when?"

His lips purse and she can feel him swallow an impulse to snap back.

He says:

"I mean, okay, I know I haven't been—but it's a shock, you know? This whole—and I know for you too. I mean, more than me, but— well, I want you to know I'm past all that shit."

He puts his hand on her arm.

"We're in this together."

She can feel him looking at her, hear the smile on his face, but she doesn't look over. It's possible that in this moment she feels more alone than she's ever felt in her life.

Except she isn't alone.

She is a mother now.

She will never be alone again.

PAINTING #2

IF ALL YOU looked at was the center frame, you could convince yourself that nothing was wrong. That the girl in question—eighteen perhaps, with a wisp of hair blown across her eyes—is just out for a walk in a cornfield on an overcast day. She is facing us, this woman, having only seconds before emerged from a tight labyrinth of towering green. And though the sky atop the cornfield is a somewhat ominous gray, the women and the front row of corn behind her is lit by a feverish sun, febrile and orange, so much so that she is squinting through her hair, one hand rising, as if to shield her eyes.

It is the quality of light that draws you in, makes you ask—*What combination of colors, applied in what order, with what technique, created this thunderstorm glow?*

To her left, in a canvas of equal size, separated by an inch of white wall, is a farmhouse, set at an angle to the field across a wide expanse of lawn, so that the woman in the foreground appears to dwarf the house, so powerful is the trick of perspective. The house is red clapboard, two stories with a slanted barn roof, shutters closed. If you squint, you can see the wooden flap of an earthen storm door flipped up from the ground on the side of the house, revealing a dark hole. And from that hole emerges a man's arm, clad in a long white sleeve, the tiny hand grasping a tethered rope handle, tense, frozen in motion. But is he opening the door or closing it?

You look back at the girl. She is not looking at the house. Her hair is across her face, but her eyes are visible, and though she faces forward her pupils have danced to her right, drawing the viewer's eye across the intricate splay of leafy green, across another inch of white gallery wall, to the third and final canvas.

It is then you see what this girl has just now noticed.

The tornado.

That swirling devil's clot, that black maelstrom of cylindrical majesty. It is a swirling gray spider egg unspooling, filled with rotten teeth. A biblical monster, God's vengeance. Whirring and churning, it shows you its food, like a petulant child, houses and trees cracked and spinning, a gritty hail of dirt. Viewed from anyplace in the room, it appears to be coming right at you, and when you see that you take a step back. The canvas itself is bent and fraying, its top right corner bent inward, cracked and twisted, as if by the sheer power of the wind. As if the painting is destroying itself.

Now you look back to the girl, eyes widening, hand rising, not to pull the hair from her face, you realize, but to shield her eyes from the horror. And then, hair rising, you look past her, to the house, but more specifically to that tiny storm door, that black pit of salvation, and within it a single man's arm, his hand grasping the frayed rope tether. And this time, as you take it in, you realize—

He is closing the storm door, shutting us out.

We are on our own.

117

LAYLA

THE THINGS MONEY *can't buy*, goes the famous quote, *you don't want anyway*. Which is bullshit, because in truth there is nothing money can't buy. Not really. Love, happiness, peace of mind. It's all available for a price. The fact is, there's enough money on earth to make everyone whole, if we could just learn to do what any toddler knows—share. But money, like gravity, is a force that clumps, drawing in more and more of itself, eventually creating the black hole that we know as *wealth*. This is not simply the fault of humans. Ask any dollar bill and it will tell you it prefers the company of hundreds to the company of ones. Better to be a sawbuck in a billionaire's account than a dirty single in the torn pocket of an addict.

At twenty-nine, Leslie Mueller is the sole heir to a technology empire. The daughter of a billionaire (male) and a runway model (female), she is a member of an ever-growing genetically engineered master race. They are everywhere these days, it seems, the moneyed children of brilliant capitalists, using a fraction of their inheritances to launch companies and fund the arts. At eighteen, nineteen, twenty, they buy impossible real estate in New York, Hollywood, London. They set themselves up as a new Medici class, drawn to the urgent throb of the future. They are something beyond hip, collectors of genius, winging from Davos to Coachella to Sundance, taking meetings, offering today's artists, musicians, and filmmakers the seductive ego stroke of cash and the prestige of their company.

Beautiful and rich, they don't take no for an answer.

Leslie—"Layla" to her friends—was one of the first, her mother a former Galliano model from Seville, Spain. Her father invented some ubiquitous high-tech trigger found in every computer and smartphone on the planet. He is the 9th richest person in the world, and even with only one-third of her inheritance vested, Layla Mueller is the 399th. She has so much money she makes the other rich people Scott has met—David Bateman, Ben Kipling—look like working stiffs. Wealth at Layla's level is beyond the fluctuations of the market. A sum so big she could never go broke. So great that the money makes its own money—growing by a factor of 15 percent every year, minting millions every month.

She makes so much money just being rich that the annual dividends her savings account earn make it the seven hundredth richest person on the planet. Think about that. Picture it if you can, which of course you can't. Not really. Because the only way to truly understand wealth at that level is to have it. Layla's is a path without resistance, without friction of any kind. There is nothing on earth she can't buy on a whim. Microsoft maybe, or Germany. But otherwise . . .

"Oh my God," she says, when she enters the study of her Greenwich Village home and sees Scott, "I'm obsessed with you. I've been watching all day. I can't take my eyes off."

They are in a four-story brownstone on Bank Street, two blocks from the river, Layla and Scott and Magnus, whom Scott called from the navy yard. As he dialed, Scott half pictured him still sitting in his car outside the convenience store, but Magnus said he was in a coffee shop putting the make on some girl and could be there in forty minutes, faster once Scott told him where he wanted to go. If Magnus was offended at being ditched before, he didn't say so.

"Look at me," he tells Scott after the housekeeper lets them in and they're sitting on a sofa in the living room. "I'm shaking."

Scott watches Magnus's right leg bouncing up and down. Both men know that the audience they're about to have could change their artistic fortunes irrevocably. For ten years Magnus, like Scott, has nibbled at the fringes of artistic arrival. He paints in a condemned paint warehouse in Queens, owns six stained shirts. Every night he prowls the streets of Chelsea and the Lower East Side, looking in windows. Each afternoon he works the phones, looking for invitations to openings and trying to get on the guest list for industry events. He's a charming Irishman with a crooked smile, but there is also an air of desperation in his eyes. Scott recognizes it easily, because until a few months ago he saw it every time he looked in the mirror. That same thirst for acceptance.

It's like living near a bakery but never eating any bread. Every day you walk the streets, the smell of it in your nose, your stomach growling, but no matter how many corners you turn, you can never enter the actual store.

The art market, like the stock market, is based on the perception of value. A painting is worth whatever someone is willing to pay, and that number is influenced by the perception of the artist's importance, their currency. To be a famous artist whose paintings sell for top dollar, either you have to already be a famous artist whose paintings sell for top dollar, or someone has to anoint you as such. And the person who anoints artists more and more these days is Layla Mueller.

She comes in wearing black jeans and a pre-wrinkled silk blouse, a brown-eyed blonde, barefoot, holding an electronic cigarette.

"There they are," she says brightly.

Magnus stands, holds out his hand.

"I'm Magnus. Kitty's friend."

She nods, but doesn't shake. After a moment, he lowers his hand. Layla sits on the sofa next to Scott.

"Can I tell you something weird?" she asks Scott. "I flew to Cannes in May with one of your pilots. The older one. I'm pretty sure."

"James Melody," he says, having memorized the names of the dead.

She makes a face—*holy shit, right?*—then nods, touches his shoulder.

"Does it hurt?"

"What?"

"Your arm?"

He moves it for her in its new sling.

"It's okay," he says.

"And that little boy. Oh my God. So brave. And then—can you believe?—I just saw a thing about the daughter's kidnapping, which— can you imagine?"

Scott blinks.

"Kidnapping?" he says.

"You don't know?" she says with what seems like real shock. "Yeah, the boy's sister back when she was little. Apparently, someone broke into their house and took her. She was gone for, like, a week. And now—I mean to survive something like that and then die so hor- ribly—you couldn't make this stuff up."

Scott nods, feeling bone-tired all of a sudden. Tragedy is drama you can't bear to relive.

"I want to throw a party in your honor," she tells him. "The hero of the art world."

"No," says Scott. "Thank you."

"Oh, don't be like that," she says. "Everybody's talking. And not just about the rescue. I saw slides of your new work—the disaster se- ries—and I love it."

Magnus claps his hands together suddenly at great volume. They turn and look at him.

"Sorry," he says, "but I told ya. Didn't I tell you? Fecking brilliant."

Layla draws on her electronic cigarette. *This is what the future looks like*, Scott thinks. *We smoke technology now.*

"Can you—" she says, "—if it's okay, what happened?"

"To the plane? It crashed."

She nods. Her eyes sober.

"Have you talked about it yet? To a therapist, or—"

Scott thinks about that. A therapist.

"Because," says Layla, "you'd love my guy. He's in Tribeca. Dr. Vanderslice. He's Dutch."

Scott pictures a bearded man in an office, Kleenex on every table.

"The cab didn't come," says Scott, "so I had to take the bus."

She looks puzzled for a moment, then realizes he's sharing a memory with her and leans forward.

Scott tells her he remembers his duffel bag by the door, faded black canvas, threadbare in places, remembers pacing, looking for headlights through the window (old milky glass), remembers his watch, the minute hands moving. His duffel held clothes, sure, but mostly it was full of slides, pictures of his work. The new work. Hope. His future. Tomorrow it would begin. He'd meet Michelle at her office and they'd review their submission list. His plan was to stay three days. There was a party Michelle said he had to go to, a breakfast.

But first the cab had to come. First he had to get to the airfield and get on a private plane—why had he agreed to that? The pressure of it, to travel with strangers—rich strangers—to have to make conversation, discuss his work or, conversely, be ignored, treated like he didn't matter. Which he didn't.

He was a forty-seven-year-old man who had failed at life. No career, never married, no close friends or girlfriends. Hell, he couldn't even handle a four-legged dog. Was that why he had worked so hard these last few weeks, photographing his work, building a portfolio? To try to erase the failure?

But the taxi never showed, and in the end he grabbed his bag and ran to the bus stop, heart beating fast, sweating from the thick August air. He got there just as the bus was pulling in, a long rectangle of windows lit blue-white against the dark. And how he climbed on, smiling at the driver, out of breath. He sat in the back, watching teenagers neck, oblivious to the domestic houseworkers riding beside them in tired silence. His heart rate slowed, but his blood still felt like it was racing. This was it. His second chance. The work was there.

It was good. He knew that. But was he? What if he couldn't handle a comeback? What if they gave him another chance and he choked? Could he really come back from the place he was? Napoleon in Elba, a beaten man, licking his wounds. Did he even want to—deep down? Life was good here. Simple. To wake in the morning and walk on the beach. To feed the dog scraps from the table and scratch her floppy ears. To paint. Simply to paint, with no greater goal.

But this way he could be somebody. Make his mark.

Except, wasn't he somebody already? The dog thought so. The dog looked at Scott like he was the best man who ever lived. They went to the farmers market together and watched the women in yoga pants. He liked his life. He did. So why was he trying so hard to change it?

"When I got off the bus," he tells Layla, "I had to run. They were gonna close the airplane doors, right? And, you know, there was part of me that wanted that, to get there and find the plane was already gone. Because then I'd have to get up early and take the ferry like anyone else."

He doesn't look up, but he can feel them both looking at him.

"But the door was open. I made it."

She nods, her eyes wide, and touches his arm.

"Amazing," she says, though what she means isn't clear. Is she speaking of the fact that Scott nearly missed the fateful flight, or the fact that he didn't?

Scott looks up at Layla, feeling self-conscious, like a small bird that has just sung for its supper and now waits for the seed.

"Look," says Scott, "it's very nice of you, to see me, to want to throw me a party, but I can't handle that right now. I just need a place to think and rest."

She smiles, nods. He has given her something no one else has, insight, details. She is part of the story now, his confidante.

"You'll stay here of course," she says. "There's a guest apartment on the third floor. You'd have your own entrance."

"Thank you," he says. "That's very—and I don't want to be blunt, but I feel like I should ask—what's in it for you?"

She takes a hit off her e-cigarette, exhales vapor.

"Sweetie, don't turn it into some kind of thing. I've got the room. I'm impressed with you and your work, and you need a place to be. Why can't it be simple?"

Scott nods. There is no tension in him, no desire for confrontation. He just wants to know.

"Oh, I'm not saying it's complicated. You want a secret maybe, or a story to tell at cocktail parties. I'm just asking so there's no confusion."

For a moment she looks surprised. People don't usually talk to her this way. Then she laughs.

"I like finding people," she says. "And the other thing is—fuck this twenty-four-hour news cycle. This people eater. Just wait, they're all on your side now, but then they turn. My mom went through it when my dad left her. It was all over the tabloids. And then when my sister had that problem with Vicodin. And last year I had that thing when Tony killed himself, and just because I showed his work they painted this whole picture of us, how I was, like, a gateway drug or something."

She holds his eye, Magnus forgotten on the other sofa, waiting for his chance to shine.

"Okay," says Scott after a moment. "Thank you. I just need— they're outside my house, all those camera, and—I don't know what to say other than *I went for a swim.*"

Her phone bloops. She takes it out, looks, then looks at Scott, and there's something on her face that makes him shrink inside.

"What?" he says.

She flips her phone around and shows him the Twitter app. He leans forward, squinting at a row of colorful rectangles (tiny faces, @ symbols, emojis, photo boxes) without a hint of comprehension.

"I'm not sure what I'm looking at," he says.

"They found bodies."

BEN KIPLING

FEBRUARY 10, 1963–AUGUST 26, 2015

SARAH KIPLING

MARCH 1, 1965–AUGUST 26, 2015

"PEOPLE USE THE word *money* like it's an object. A noun. Which is—that's just ignorance."

Ben Kipling stood at a tall porcelain urinal in the wood-paneled bathroom of Soprezzi. He was talking to Greg Hoover, who stood beside him, swaying, pissing against the concave sheen that shielded his dick from view, speckles of piss drizzling down on his six-hundred-dollar tasseled loafers.

"Money is the black vacuum of space," Ben continued.

"The what?"

"The black—it's an easement, yeah? A lubricant."

"Now you're talking my—"

"But that's not—

Kipling shook his dick, zipped. He went to the sink, put his hand under the soap dispenser, and waited for the laser to sense his warmth and spritz foam into his palm. And waited. And waited.

"It's friction, right?" he said without pausing. "This life of ours. The things we do and are done to us. Just getting through the day—"

He made increasingly insistent circular gestures under the sensor. Nothing.

"—the job, the wife, traffic, bills, whatever—"

He raised and lowered his hand, looking for the mechanical sweet spot. Nothing.

"—come on with this fucking thing already—"

Kipling gave up, moved to the next sink, as Hoover stumbled over to a third.

"I talked to Lance the other day," Hoover started.

"Hold on. I'm not—friction, I'm saying. Drag."

This time, when he put his hand under the sensor, foam fell gently into his hand. Kipling slumped with relief, rubbed them together.

"The pressure brought to bear on a man just getting out of bed in the morning," he said. "Money is the cure. It's a friction *reducer*."

He moved his hands under the water faucet, blindly expecting (once more) the sensor to do its job and send a signal to the switch that turns on the tap. Nothing.

"The more money you have—goddammit—the more—"

Enraged, he gave up entirely, shaking soap from his hands onto the floor—let someone else clean it up—and moved to the paper towel dispenser, saw it too was operated by a sensor, and didn't even make the attempt, choosing instead to wipe his hands on his eleven-hundred-dollar suit pants.

"—money you have, do you see what I'm—it alleviates the drag. Think of the slum rats in Mumbai crawling around in the muck versus, like, Bill Gates, literally on top of the world. Until, ultimately, you have so much dough your whole life is effortless. Like an astronaut floating free in the black vacuum of space."

Hands clean and dry finally, he turned and saw Hoover has had zero trouble with any of the sensors, soap, water, paper towels. He tore off more sheets than he needs, dried his hands vigorously.

"Sure. Okay," he said, "But what I'm saying is, I talked to Lance the other day, and he used a lot of words I really didn't like."

"Like what? *Alimony?*"

"Ha-ha. No, like *FBI*, for one."

A certain unpleasant clenching sensation hit Kipling right around the sphincter.

"Which is," he said, "—obviously—not a word."

"Huh?"

"It's a—never mind—why the fuck is Lance talking about the FBI?"

"He's hearing things," Hoover said. "*What kind of things? I* asked. But he won't go into it on the phone—we had to meet in a park. At two o'clock in the goddamn afternoon, like the great unemployed."

Kipling, nervous suddenly, went over and checked under the stall doors to make sure there were no other designer-suit types crapping in silence.

"Are they—did he say we should be—"

"No, but he may as well have. You know what I—because why else would he—especially when—especially because if you think of the trouble he could get in—"

"Okay. Okay. Not so—"

He couldn't remember suddenly if he'd checked under the last stall, checked it again, straightened.

"Let's table this," he said. "I wanna hear it, obviously, but—we need to finish with these guys. Not leave them hanging."

"Sure, but what if they're—"

"What if they're what?" said Kipling, the scotches working like a time delay on a 1940s long-distance phone call.

Hoover finished the sentence with his eyebrows.

"These guys?" said Kipling. "What are you—they came from Gillie."

"That doesn't mean—shit, Ben, anyone can be got to."

"*Got to?* Is that—are we in *The Parallax View* suddenly and no one bothered to—"

Hoover worked the wet wad of paper like it was a ball of dough, kneading and squeezing.

"It's a problem, Ben. That's all I'm—a major fucking—"

"I know."

"We need to—you can't just—"

"I won't. Don't be such a girl."

Kipling went to the door, pushed it open. Behind him, Hoover balled up his wet paper towel and fired it at the garbage can. It went in clean.

"Still got it," he said.

. . .

As he approached the table, Kipling saw that Tabitha was doing her job. She was lubricating the clients with booze and telling the men—two Swiss investment bankers vetted and referred by Bill Gilliam, a senior partner at the law firm that handles all their deals—inappropriate stories about men she blew in college. It was two thirty on a Wednesday. They'd been at this restaurant since noon, drinking top-shelf scotch and eating fifty-dollar steaks. It was the kind of restaurant men in suits go to to complain that their pools are too hot. Among the five of them, there was a net worth of almost a billion dollars. Kipling himself was worth three hundred million on paper, most of it tied up in the market, but there was also real estate and offshore accounts. Money for a rainy day. Cash the US government couldn't track.

Ben had become, at age fifty-two, the type of man who said *Let's take the boat out this weekend*. His kitchen could be used as backup if the power ever went out at Le Cirque. There was an eight-burner Viking range with grill and griddle. Every morning he rose to find half a dozen onion bagels laid out on a tray with coffee and fresh-squeezed orange juice, along with all four papers (*Financial Times*, *Wall Street Journal*, the *Post*, and the *Daily News*). When you opened the fridge at the Kiplings', it was like a farmers market (Sarah insisted they eat only organic produce). There was a separate wine fridge with fifteen bottle of champagne on ice at all times, in case a New Year's Eve party broke out unexpectedly. Ben's closet was like a Prada showroom. Wandering from room to room, one wouldn't be wrong to assume that Ben Kipling rubbed an urn one day and a genie popped out, and now all he has to do was say *I need new socks* out loud anywhere in his apartment and the next morning a dozen pairs would appear out of fucking nowhere. Except in this case the genie was a forty-seven-year-old house manager named Mikhail, who majored in hospitality at Cornell and had been with them since they moved into the ten-bedroom estate in Connecticut.

The TV over the bar was showing highlights from the Red Sox game last night, sportscasters running the odds of Dworkin breaking the single-season hit record. Right now the man was on a fifteen-game hitting streak. *Unstoppable* was a word they used, the hard consonants of it following Ben to his seat.

In forty minutes, he'd head back to the office and sleep off the meat and the booze on his sofa. Then at six the driver would take him up the parkway to Greenwich, where Sarah would have something on the table—takeout from Allesandro's probably—or no, wait, *shit*, they've got that dinner tonight with Jenny's fiancé's parents. A meet-and-greet kind of thing. Where were they doing that again? Someplace in the city? It's gotta be in his calendar, probably written in red like a twice-prolonged appointment for a barium enema.

Ben could picture them now, Mr. and Mrs. Comstock, he the portly dentist. His wife with too much lipstick, in from Long Island—*Did you take the Grand Central or the BQE?* And Jenny would sit there with Don or Ron or whatever her fiancé's name is, holding hands, and telling stories about how she and her parents "always summer on the Vineyard" without realizing how privileged and obnoxious that sounds. Not that Ben was one to talk. This morning he'd found himself debating the estate tax with his personal trainer and he'd said, *Well, look—Jerry—wait till you've got a hundred million plus in mixed assets that the government wants to tax twice and see if you still feel the same.*

Kipling sat, exhausted suddenly, and picked up his napkin reflexively, even though he was done eating. He dropped it into his lap, caught the waiter's eye, and pointed to his glass. *Another one*, he said with his eyes.

"I was just telling Jorgen," said Tabitha, "about that meeting we had in Berlin. Remember when the guy with the John Waters mustache got so mad he took off his tie and tried to strangle Greg?"

"For fifty million, I woulda let him," said Kipling, "except it turned out the fucking guy was broke."

The Swiss smiled patiently. They had zero interest in gossip. Nor did it seem that Tabitha's exaggerated cleavage was having its usual effect. *Could be they're queer*, thought Kipling with zero moral judgment, just a computer recording facts.

He chewed the inside of his cheek, thinking. What Hoover said to him in the men's room was ricocheting around in his brain like a bullet that had missed its target then took an unlucky hop off the pavement. What did he know about these guys, really? They'd come recommended from a reliable source, but how reliable was anyone when you get right down to it. Could they be FBI, these boys? SEC? Their Swiss accents were good, but maybe not great.

Kipling had a sudden impulse to drop cash on the table and walk away. He tamped it down, because if he was wrong, it was a hell of a lot of money to walk away from, and Ben Kipling wasn't a man to walk away from—*what did the Swiss say?* Potentially a billion dollars in hard-to-convert currency? Fuck it, Ben decided. If you're not going to retreat then you've got to charge. He opened his mouth and gave them the hard sell without getting too specific. No hot phrases that could be used against him in court.

"So, okay with the small talk," he said. "We all know what we're doing here. The same thing cavemen did in the age of the dinosaur, sizing each other up, seeing who you can trust. What's a handshake, after all, except a socially acceptable way to make sure the other guy doesn't have a knife behind his back."

He smiled at them. They looked back, unsmiling, but engaged. This was the moment they cared about—if they were who they said they were. The deal. The waiter brought Kipling his scotch, put it on the table. By habit, Ben moved it deeper toward the center of the table. He was a hand talker and had spilled his fair share of cocktails in the middle of a good monologue.

"You have a problem," he said. "You've got foreign currency you need to invest in the open market, but our government won't let you. Why? Because at some point that money found its way to a region they keep on a list in some federal building in DC. As if the money itself had a point of view. But you and me, we know that money is money. The dollar a black guy in Harlem uses to buy crack with today is the same dollar a suburban housewife uses to buy Hamburger Helper tomorrow. Or that Uncle Sam uses to buy weapons systems from McDonnell Douglas on Thursday."

On the television Ben watched plays of the day—a string of towering home runs, shoestring catches, and baseline rundowns. It was more than a passing interest. Ben was an encyclopedia of arcane baseball figures. It was a lifelong passion, one that taught him (coincidentally) the value of a dollar. Ten-year-old Bennie Kipling had the premier bubble-gum card collection in all of Sheepshead Bay. He dreamed one day of playing center field for the Mets and every year tried out for Little League, but he was small for his age and slow on the base path and couldn't hit the ball out of the infield, so he collected baseball cards instead, studying the market closely, exploiting the amateur mind-set of schoolmates—who focused only on players they liked—tracking rare cards and playing the rise and fall of each player. Every morning Bennie would read the obituaries, looking for signs that the recently deceased were baseball fans, and then he'd call the widows, saying he knew their husbands (or fathers) from the trading card circuit and how so-and-so had been a mentor to him. He never asked for the decedent's collection outright, just played up his saddest little-boy voice. It worked every time. On more than one occasion he took the subway into the city to collect a once prized box of baseball nostalgia.

"We come to you, Mr. Kipling," said Jorgen, the dark-haired Aryan in the cotton-weight suit, "because we hear good things. Obviously these are sensitive subjects, but my colleagues agree you are a straight man. That complications do not arrive. Additional expenses. The clients we represent, well, these are not people who appreciate complications or attempts to take advantage."

"And who is that again?" said Hoover, sweating at the brows. "Say without saying, if you can. Just so we're all clear."

The Swiss said nothing. They too feared a trap.

"The deal we make is the deal we keep," said Kipling. "Doesn't matter who's on the other side. I can't tell you exactly how we do what we do. That's our proprietary advantage, right? But what I will say is, accounts are opened. Accounts that cannot be connected back to you. After that, the money you invest with my firm gets a new pedigree and is treated like any other money. It goes in dirty and comes out clean. Simple."

"And how does it—"

"Work? Well, if we agree now, in principle, to move forward with this thing, then colleagues of mine will come to Geneva and help you set up the systems you'll need using a proprietary software package. My operative will then stay on site to monitor your investments and navigate the daily password and IP address changes. He doesn't need a fancy office. In fact, the less attention he draws the better. Put him in a men's room stall or in the basement next to the boiler."

The men thought about this. While they did, Kipling grabbed a passing waiter and handed him his black Amex card.

"Look," he said, "pirates used to bury treasure in the sand and then row away. And the minute they left, in my opinion, they were broke, because money in a box—"

Outside the window, he watched a group of men in dark suits approach the front door. In an instant Ben saw the whole thing unravel:

They would come in fast, guns out, wallets high, a sting operation, like a tiger trap in the jungle. Ben saw himself flipped on his belly, cuffed, his summer suit stained beyond repair, dirty footprints on his back. But the men kept walking. The moment passed. Kipling breathed again, finished his scotch in a single draft.

"—money you can't use has no value."

He sized them up, the men from Geneva—no bigger or smaller than a dozen other men he had sat across from, making this same pitch. They were fish to be caught on a hook, women to be flattered and seduced. FBI or no FBI, Ben Kipling was a money magnet. He had a quality that couldn't be put in writing. Rich people looked at him and saw a vault with two doors. They visualized their money going in one door, and coming out the other multiplied. A sure thing.

He slid his chair back, buttoning his jacket.

"I like you guys," he said. "I trust you, and I don't say that to just anyone. My feeling is, we should do this, but in the end it's up to you."

He stood.

"Tabitha and Jay are gonna stay behind, get your details. It was a pleasure."

The Swiss stood, shook his hand. Ben Kipling walked away from them, the front door opening before him as he exited. His car was at the curb, back door open, driver standing at attention, and he slid inside without slowing.

The black vacuum of space.

. . .

Across town, a yellow cab pulled up in front of the Whitney Museum. The driver was born in Katmandu, stole down into Michigan from Saskatchewan, paying a smuggler six hundred dollars for fake ID. He slept in an apartment now with fourteen other people, sent most of his pay overseas in the hope of one day bringing his wife and boys over on a plane.

The woman in back, on the other hand, who told him to keep the change from a twenty, lived in Greenwich, Connecticut and owned nineteen televisions she didn't watch. Once upon a time she was a doctor's daughter in Brookline, Massachusetts, a girl who grew up riding horses and got a nose job for her sixteenth birthday.

Everyone is from someplace. We all have stories, our lives unfolding along crooked lines, colliding in unexpected ways.

Sarah Kipling turned fifty in March—there was a surprise party in the Cayman Islands. Ben picked her up in a limo to go to Tavern on the Green (she thought), but took her out to Teterboro instead. Five hours later she was sipping rum punch with her toes in the sand. Now, outside the Whitney, she climbed out of a cab. She was meeting her daughter Jenny (twenty-six) to tour the biennial and get a quick download on her fiancé's parents before the dinner. This wasn't so much for Sarah's benefit, because she could talk to anyone, as it was for Ben's. Her husband had a hard time with conversations that weren't about money. Or maybe that wasn't it exactly. Maybe it was that he had a hard time talking to people who didn't *have* money. Not that he was aloof. It was just that he'd forgotten what it was like to have a mortgage or a car loan. What it was to be *getting by*, to go to a store and have to check the price of something before you buy it. And this could make him seem vulgar and aloof.

Sarah loathed the feeling she got in those moments—watching her husband embarrass himself (and her). There was no other words for it, in her mind. As his wife she was irrevocably tied to him—his opinions were her opinions. They reflected poorly on her, perhaps not because she held them exactly, but because by choosing Ben, by sticking with him, she showed herself (in the eyes of others) to be a poor judge of character. Though she grew up with money, Sarah knew that the last thing you did was *talk about it*. This was the difference between new money and old. Old-money kids were the ones in college with bed head and moth-hole sweaters. You found them in the cafeteria borrowing lunch money and eating off their friends' plates. They passed as poor, affecting a disposition that they were *beyond money*—as if one of the riches wealth had bought them was the right never think to about money again. In this way they floated through the real world the way that child prodigies stumbled through the daily travails of human existence, heads in the clouds, forgetting to wear socks, their shirts misbuttoned.

This made her husband's tone-deafness on the subject of money, his need to constantly remind others how much they had feel so gauche, so *rude*. As a result it had become her tired mission in life to soften his edges, to educate him on how to get rich without becoming tacky.

So Jenny would fill her in about her future in-laws, and Sarah would send Ben a text. *You can talk about politics with the husband (he votes Republican) or sports (Jets fan). The wife went to Italy last year with her book group (travel? reading?). They have a son with Down syndrome in an institution, so no retard jokes!*

Sarah had tried to get Ben to show more of an interest in people, to be more open to new experiences—they'd gone to counseling about it for two weeks, before Ben told her he'd rather cut off his ears than "listen to that woman for another day"—but eventually she'd done what most wives do and just gave up. So now it was she who had to make the extra effort to ensure that social engagements go well.

Jenny was waiting for her outside the main entrance. She had on flared slacks and a T-shirt, with her hair in the kind of beret the girls were wearing these days.

"Mom," she called when Sarah didn't see her right away.

"Sorry," her mother said, "my eyes are shot. Your father keeps telling me to go to the eye doctor, but who has time?"

They hugged briefly, efficiently, then moved inside.

"I got here early, so I got us tickets," said Jenny.

Sarah tried to shove a hundred-dollar bill in her hand.

"Mom, don't be silly. I'm happy to pay."

"For a cab later," her mother said jabbing the bill at her like a flyer to a mattress store they shoved at you on the street, but Jenny turned away and handed their tickets to the doyen, and Sarah was forced to put the bill back in her wallet.

"I heard the best stuff is upstairs," said Jenny. "So maybe we should we start at the top."

"Whatever you want, dear."

They waited for the elevator and rode up in silence. Behind them a Latin family talked in animated Spanish, the woman berating her husband. Sarah had studied Spanish in high school, though she hadn't kept up. She recognized the words for "motorcycle" and "babysitter," and it was clear from the exchange that something extramarital may have occurred. At their feet, two young children played games on handheld devices, their faces lit an eerie blue.

"Shane's nervous about tonight," Jenny said after they exit the elevator. "It's so cute."

"The first time I met your father's parents, I threw up," Sarah told her.

"Really?"

"Yes, but I think it might have been the clam chowder I had at lunch."

"Oh, Mom," said Jenny, smiling, "you're so funny." Jenny always told her friends that her mother was "slightly batty." Sarah knew it, or senses it on some level. And she was—what's the word?—a little absentminded, a little, well—sometimes she made unique connections in her head. And didn't Robin Williams have the same quality? Or other, you know, innovative thinkers.

So now you're Robin Williams? Ben would say.

"Well, he doesn't have to be nervous," said Sarah. "We don't bite."

"Class is a real thing," Jenny told her. "I mean again. The divide, you know. Rich people and—I mean, Shane's parents aren't poor, but—"

"It's dinner at Bali, not class warfare. And besides, we're not *that* rich."

"When was the last time you flew commercial?"

"Last winter to Aspen."

Her daughter made a sound as if to say, *Do you hear yourself?*

"We're not billionaires, dear. This is Manhattan, you know. Some of the parties we go to, *I* feel like the help."

"You own a yacht."

"It's not a—it's a sailboat, and I told your father not to buy it. *Is that who we are now,* I said, *boat people?* But you know *him* when he gets an idea."

"Whatever. The point is, he's nervous, so will you please—I don't know—keep it light."

"You're talking to the woman who charmed a Swedish prince, and boy was he a sourpuss."

With this they entered the main gallery space. Oversize canvases lined the walls, each a gesture of will. Thoughts and ideas reduced to lines and color. Sarah tried to let her daily brain go, to quiet the constant natter of thoughts, the chronic to-do list of modern life, but it was hard. The more you had, the more you worried. That was what she'd decided.

When Jenny was born, they'd lived in a two-bedroom apartment on the Upper West Side. Ben earned eighty thousand a year as a runner at the exchange. But he was handsome and good at making people laugh, and he knew how to seize an opportunity, so two years later he had graduated to trader and was pulling in four times that amount. They'd moved east to a condo in the 60s and started buying groceries at Citarella.

Before motherhood, Sarah had worked in advertising, and after Jenny was in preschool she'd flirted with the idea of going back to it, but she couldn't stomach the idea of a nanny raising her daughter while she was at work. So though she felt like she was giving up a piece of her soul, she'd stayed home and made lunch and changed diapers and waited for her husband to come home and do his share.

Her mother had encouraged her to do it, becoming—as her

mother described it—a *lady of leisure*. But Sarah didn't do well with unstructured time, possibly because her mind was so unstructured. And so she'd become a woman of lists, a woman with multiple calendars who left sticky notes on the inside of their front door. She was the kind of person who needed reminding, who would forget a phone number the second after someone recited it to her. She'd known it was bad when her three-year-old daughter started reminding her of things, even went to see a neurologist, who'd found nothing physically wrong with her brain and suggested Ritalin, suggesting she had ADHD, but Sarah hated pills and worried they would turn her into a different person, so she'd gone back to her lists, to her calendars and alarms.

On nights that Ben had worked late—which became increasingly frequent—she couldn't help but think of her mother in the kitchen when Sarah was young, washing up after dinner, supervising the end-of-day arts and crafts while packing lunches for the next day. Was this the cycle of motherhood? The constant return. Someone had told her once that mothers existed to blunt the existential loneliness of being a person. If that was true then her biggest maternal responsibility was simply companionship. You bring a child into this fractious, chaotic world out of the heat of your womb, and then spend the next ten years walking beside them while they figure out how to be a person.

Fathers, on the other hand, were there to toughen children up, to say *Walk it off* when mothers would hold them if they fall. Mothers were the carrot. Fathers were the stick.

And so Sarah had found herself in her own kitchen on East 63rd Street, packing preschool lunches and reading picture books during warm baths, her body and her daughter's body one and the same. On those nights when she'd fall asleep alone, Sarah would bring Jenny into bed with her, reading books and talking until they both nodded off, intertwined. This would be how Ben found them when he came home, smelling of booze, his tie askew, kicking his shoes off noisily.

"How are my girls?" he'd say. *His girls*, as if they were both his daughter. But he said the words with love, his face brightening, as if this was his reward for a long day, the faces of the women he loved looking up at him with sleepy eyes from the comfort of the family bed.

"I like this one," said Jenny, now a woman in her twenties, five years from children of her own. They'd managed to stay close through her divisive teen years, despite all odds. Jenny never was one for drama. The worst you could say now was that she didn't *respect* her mom the way she used to, the curse of the modern woman. You stay home and raise daughters, who grow up and get jobs and then feel pity for you, their stay-at-home mothers.

Beside her, Jenny was going on about Shane's parents—Dad fixed up old cars. Mom liked to do charity work for their church—and Sarah tried to focus, listening for red flags, things Ben would need to know, but her mind wandered. It struck her that she could buy any of the art in this room. What was the most these pieces by young artists could cost? A few hundred thousand? A million?

On the Upper West Side, they'd lived on the third floor. The condo on East 63rd was on the ninth. Now they owned a penthouse loft in Tribeca, fifty-three stories up. And though the house in Connecticut was only two floors, the zip code itself made it a space station of sorts. The "farmers" at the Saturday farmers market were the new breed of hipster artisans, championing the return of heirloom apples and the lost art of basket weaving. The things Sarah called problems now were wholly elective—*There are no first-class seats left on our flight, the sailboat is leaking*, et cetera. Actual struggle—they'd come to turn off the gas, your kid was knifed at school, the car's been repossessed—had become a thing of the past.

And all of this left Sarah to wonder, now that Jenny was grown, now that their wealth had exceeded their needs by a factor of six hundred, what was the point? Her parents had money, sure, but not this much. Enough to join the nicest country club, to buy a six-bedroom home and drive the latest cars, enough to retire with a few million in the bank. But this—hundreds of millions in clean currency stashed in the Caymans—it was beyond the boundaries of old money, beyond even the boundaries of what was once considered new. Modern wealth was something else entirely.

And these days—in the unstructured hours of her life—Sarah wondered, was she staying alive now just to move money around?

I shop therefore I am.

. . .

When Ben got back to the office, he found two men waiting for him. They sat in the outer office reading magazines, while Darlene typed nervously on her computer. Ben could tell from their suits—off the rack—that they were government. He almost spun on his heels and walked out, but he didn't. The truth was, he had—on the advice of his lawyer—a packed bag in a storage unit and a few untraceable million offshore.

"Mr. Kipling," said Darlene too loudly, standing. "These men are here to see you."

The men put down their magazines, stood. One was tall and square-jawed. The other had a dark mole under his left eye.

"Mr. Kipling," said Square Jaw, "I'm Jordan Bewes from the Treasury Department. This is my colleague, Agent Hex."

"Ben Kipling."

Kipling forced himself to shake their hands.

"What's this about," he asked as casually as he could.

"We'll do that, sir," said Hex, "but let's do it in private."

"Of course. Whatever I can do to help. Come on back."

He turned to lead them into his office, caught Denise's eye.

"Get Barney Culpepper up here."

He led the agents into his corner office. They were eighty-six stories up, but the tempered glass shielded them from the elements, creating a hermetic seal, a sense that one was in a dirigible, floating high above it all.

"Can I offer you anything," he said. "Pellegrino?"

"We're fine," said Bewes.

Kipling went to the sofa, dropped into the corner by the window. He had decided he would act like a man with nothing to fear. There was a bowl of pistachios on the sideboard. He took a nut, cracked it, ate the meat.

"Sit, please."

The men had to turn the guest chairs to face the sofa. They sat awkwardly.

"Mr. Kipling," said Bewes. "we're from the Office of Foreign Assets Control. Are you familiar with that?"

"I've heard of it, but honestly, they don't keep me around for my logistical know-how. I'm more the creative thinker type."

"We're an arm of the Treasury Department."

"I got that part."

"Well, we're here to make sure that American businesses and in-vestment firms don't do business with countries our government has deemed off limits. And, well, your firm has come to our attention."

"By *off limits* you mean—"

"Sanctioned," said Hex. "We're referring to countries like Iran and North Korea. Countries that fund terrorism."

"Their money's bad," said Hex, "and we don't want it here."

Ben smiled, showing them his perfectly capped teeth.

"The countries are bad. That's for sure. But the money? Well, money's a tool, gentlemen. It's neither good nor bad."

"Okay, sir, let me back up. You've heard of the law, yes?"

"Which law?"

"No, I'm saying—you know we have this thing called *laws* in this country."

"Mr. Bewes, don't patronize me."

"Just trying to find a language we both understand," said Bewes.

"The point is, we suspect your firm is laundering money for—well, shit, just about everyone—and we're here to let you know we're watching."

At this, the door opened and Barney Culpepper came in. Wearing blue-and-white seersucker, Barney was everything you'd want in a corporate attorney—aggressive, blue-blooded, the son of the former US ambassador to China. His father was pals with three presidents. Right now, Barney's had a red-and-white candy cane in his mouth, even though it was August. Seeing him, Kipling felt a wave of relief—like a kid called to the principal's office who rebounds when his dad arrives.

"Gentlemen," said Ben, "this is Mr. Culpepper, the firm's in-house counsel."

"This is a casual conversation," said Hex. "No need for lawyers."

Culpepper didn't bother shaking hands. He leaned his backside against the sideboard.

"Ask me about the candy," he said.

"Pardon," said Hex.

"The candy. Ask me about it."

Hex and Bewes exchanged a look, as if to say *I don't want to. You do it.*

Finally Bewes shrugged.

"What's with the—"

Culpepper took the candy cane out of his mouth, showed it to them.

"When my assistant said two agents from Treasury were here, all I could think was—it must be fucking Christmas."

"Very funny, Mr.—"

"Because I know my old racquetball buddy Leroy Able—you know him, right?"

"He's the secretary of the Treasury."

"Exactly. Well, I know my old racquetball buddy Leroy wouldn't send agents down here without calling me first. And since he didn't call—"

"This," said Hex, "is more of a courtesy call."

"Like where you bring over cookies and say welcome to the neighborhood?"

Culpepper looks at Kipling.

"Are there cookies? Did I miss the—"

"No cookies," says Ben.

Bewes smiles.

"You want cookies?"

"No," says Culpepper, "it's just, when your friend said '*a courtesy call*', I thought—"

Bewes and Hex exchange a look, stand.

"Nobody's above the law," says Bewes.

"Who said anything—" says Culpepper. "I thought we were talking about desert?"

Bewes buttons his jacket, smiling—a guy with a winning hand.

"A case is being built. Months, years. Sanctioned at the highest level. And you want to talk about evidence? How about you'd need two tractor trailers to haul it all to court."

"File a suit," said Culpepper. "Show a warrant. We'll respond."

"When the time comes," said Hex.

"Assuming you guys aren't parking cars in Queens after I make a phone call," said Culpepper, chewing on his candy cane.

"Hey," said Bewes, "I'm from the Bronx. You wanna call a guy out, call him out. But make sure you know what you're buying."

"It's so cute," said Culpepper, "that you think it matters the size of your dick. 'Cause, son, when I fuck someone, I use my whole arm."

He showed them the arm, and the hand attached to it, at the end of which a single finger was raised in salute.

Bewes laughed.

"You know how some days you come to work and it's a drag?" he said. "Well, this is gonna be fun."

"That's what they all say," said Culpepper, "until it goes in past the elbow."

. . .

That night at dinner, Ben was distracted. He reviewed his conversation with Culpepper in his head.

"It's nothing," Culpepper had said, dropping his candy cane in the trash after the agents left. "They're traffic cops writing bullshit tickets at the end of the month. Trying to get their quotas up."

"They said months," Ben responded. "Years."

"Look at what happened to HSBC. A fucking wrist slap. You know why? Because if they gave them the full extent of the law, they'd have had to take their banking license. And we all know that's not gonna happen. They're too big to jail."

"You're calling a billion-dollar fine a wrist slap?"

"It's walking-around money. A few months' profits. You know that better than anyone."

But Ben wasn't so sure. Something about the way the agents carried themselves. They were cocky, like they knew they had the high card.

"We need to close ranks," he'd said. "Anyone who knows anything."

"Already done. Do you know the level of nondisclosure paperwork you have to sign to even work the front desk here? It's Fort fucking Knox."

"I'm not going to jail."

"Jesus, don't be such a pussy. Don't you get it? There is no jail. Remember the LIBOR scandal? A conspiracy worth trillions with a *t*. A reporter says to the assistant attorney general, *This is a bank that has broken the law before, so why not be tougher?* The assistant attorney general says, *I don't know what tougher means.*"

"They came to my office," Ben had said.

"They took an elevator ride. Two guys. If they really had something it'd be hundreds of guys, and they'd walk out with a lot more than their dicks in their hands."

And yet sitting in a corner booth with Sarah and Jenny and her fiancé's family, Ben couldn't help but wonder if that was really all they'd walked out with. Ben wished he had videotape of the meeting so he could watch his own face, see how much he'd given away. His poker face was usually top-notch, but in that room he'd felt off his game. Did it come through in the tension around his mouth? A crinkle in his eyes.

"Ben?" said Sarah, shaking his arm. From the look on her face, it was clear a question has been thrown his way.

"Huh?" he said. "Oh, sorry. I didn't catch that. It's pretty loud in here."

He said this, even though the place was dead quiet, just a few blue-hairs whispering into their soup.

"I said, we still think real estate is the way to go, money-wise," said Burt or Carl or whatever Shane's father's name was. "And then I asked your opinion."

"Depends on the real estate," said Ben, sliding out of the banquette. "But my advice after Hurricane Sandy is, if you're buying in Manhattan, pick a high floor."

He excused himself, dodging Sarah's disapproving look, and went outside. He needed some air.

On the curb he bummed a smoke from a late commuter and stood under the restaurant's awning smoking. A light rain fell, and he watched the taillights sheen on the black macadam.

"Got another?" asked a man in a turtleneck, stepping out behind Ben.

Kipling turned, eyed him. A moneyed man in his forties, but with a nose that had been broken at least once.

"Sorry. I bummed this one."

The man in the turtleneck shrugged, stood looking out at the rain.

"There's a young lady in the restaurant trying to get your attention," he said.

Ben looked. Jenny was waving at him. *Come back to the table.* He looked away.

"My daughter," he said. "It's meet-the-new-in-laws night."

"Congrats," said the man.

Kipling puffed, nodded.

"With boys you worry, will they ever leave the house?" said the man. "Find their way. In my day they kicked you to the curb the minute you hit voting age. Sometimes before. Adversity. It's the only way to make a man."

"That what happened to your nose?" said Kipling.

The man smiled.

"You know how on your first day in prison they say find the biggest guy and kick his ass? Well, like anything else, there are consequences."

"That's—you've been to prison?" said Kipling, feeling a tourist's thrill.

"Not here. Kiev."

"Jesus."

"And later in Shanghai, but that was a piece of pie, compared."

"Are we talking bad luck or—"

The man smiled.

"Like an accident? No, man. The world's a dangerous place. But you know that, right?"

"What?" said Kipling, feeling a slight premonitory chill.

"I said you know the world's a dangerous place. Cause and effect. Wrong place, wrong time. You could fill a thimble with the times in human history a good man did a bad thing without thinking."

"I didn't, uh, I didn't catch your name."

"How about my Twitter handle? You want to Instagram me?"

Kipling dropped his cigarette on the sidewalk. As he did, a black car pulled up to the curb in front of the restaurant and sat, idling.

"Nice talking to you," said Ben.

"Hold on. We're almost through, but not quite."

Kipling tried to get through the door, but the man was in the way. Not blocking him exactly, just there.

"My wife——" said Ben.

"She's fine," said the man. "Probably right now thinking about dessert. Maybe have the meringue. So take a breath—or take a ride in the car. Your choice."

Kipling's heart was going a mile a minute. He'd forgotten this feeling existed. What was it? Mortality?

"Look," said Ben, "I don't know what you think——"

"You had a visit today. The party police. Señor Buzz Kill. I'm being obtuse deliberately. Except to say—maybe they spooked you."

"Is this, like, a threat scenario or——"

"Don't get excited. You're not in trouble. With them maybe. But not with us. Not yet."

Kipling could only imagine who *us* meant. The realities of the situation were clear. Though he had always dealt with factotums and middlemen (white-collar criminals at best), Kipling had made his bones at the firm by exploiting previously *underutilized* revenue streams. Revenue streams that—as his visit from the Treasury agents only reinforced—were of an extra-legal nature. Which is to say, in plain English, that he laundered money for countries that sponsor terrorism, like Iran and Yemen, and countries that murder their own citizens, like Sudan and Serbia. And he did it from a corner office in a downtown high-rise. Because when you deal with *billions* of dollars, you did it in plain sight, creating shell companies and disguising wire-transfer origin points six ways from Sunday, until the money was so clean it might as well be new.

"There's no problem," Ben told the man in the turtleneck. "Just a couple of young agents getting overeager. But upstairs from them we've got things locked down. At the level where it matters."

"No," said the man, "you've got a few problems there too. Changes in executive policy. Some new marching orders. I'm not saying *panic*, but——"

"Look," said Ben. "We're good at this. The best. That's why your employers——"

A hard glare.

"We don't talk about them."

Ben felt something electric run down his back and pucker his ass-hole.

"You can trust us, I'm saying," he managed. *"Me.* That was always my pledge. No one's going to jail over—because of this. That's what Barney Culpepper says."

The guy looked at Ben as if to say, *Maybe I believe you, maybe I don't.* Or maybe he was trying to say, *It's not up to you.*

"Protect the money," he said. "That's what matters. And don't forget who owns it. Because, okay, maybe you cleaned it so good it doesn't connect to us, but that doesn't make it yours."

It took a second for Ben to translate the implication. They thought he was a thief.

"No. Of course."

"You look worried. Don't look like that. It's okay. You need a hug? All I'm saying is, don't forget the most important things. And that's the following—your ass is of secondary importance. Only the money matters. If you have to go to jail, go to jail. And if you feel the urge to hang yourself, well, maybe that's not a bad idea either."

He took out a pack of cigarettes, shook one between his lips.

"Meanwhile," he said. "Get the flan. You won't regret it."

Then the man in the turtleneck walked to the waiting black sedan and got in. Kipling watched as it pulled away.

THEY WENT TO the Vineyard on Friday. Sarah had a charity auction. Something about Save the Tern. On the ferry out she brooded about their failed dinner with the maybe in-laws. Kipling apologized. *A work thing*, he told her. But she'd heard that too many times before.

"Just retire then," she said. "I mean, if it's stressing you out this much. We have more money than we could ever use. We could sell the apartment even, or the boat. Honestly, I could care less."

He bristled at the words, the implication that this money that he'd made, that he continued to make, was somehow worthless to her. As if the art of it, the expertise he'd accumulated, his love of the deal, of every new challenge, was valueless. A burden.

"It's not about the money," he told her. "I have responsibilities."

She didn't bother arguing further, doesn't bother saying, *How about your responsibilities to me? To Jenny?* As far as Sarah was concerned she'd married a perpetual motion machine, an engine that must keep spinning or never spin again. Ben was work. Work was Ben. It was like a mathematical equation. It had taken her fifteen years and three therapists to accept that—acceptance being the key to happiness, she believed. But sometimes it still stung.

"I don't ask for much," she said, "but the dinner with the Comstocks was important."

"I know," he said, "and I'm sorry. I'll invite the guy to the club, play nine or eighteen. By the time I'm finished buttering, he'll be president of our fan club."

"It's not the husband that matters. It's the wife. And I can tell she's skeptical. She thinks we're the kind of people who try to buy their way into heaven."

"She said this?"

"No, but I can tell."

"Fuck her."

She gritted her teeth. This was always his way, to dismiss people. It only made things worse, she believed, even as she was jealous of him for being so carefree.

"No," she said. "It matters. We have to be better."

"Better what?"

"People."

An acerbic reply died on his tongue when he saw her face. She was serious. In her mind they were bad people somehow, just by being rich. It went counter to everything he believed. Look at Bill Gates. The man had committed half his wealth to charitable causes in his lifetime. Billions of dollars. Didn't that make him a better person than what—a local priest? If impact was the measure, wasn't Bill Gates a better man than Gandhi? And weren't Ben and Sarah Kipling, by donating millions to good causes each year, better people than the Comstocks, who gave—at most—fifty grand?

. . .

Sarah was up early Sunday morning. She puttered in the kitchen, straightening, figuring out what they needed, then put on her walking shoes, grabbed her wicker basket, and walked across the island to the farmers market. It was muggy out, the marine layer in the process of burning off, and the sun magnified through airborne water molecules made the world feel liquid somehow. She passed the leaning mailboxes at the end of their turnoff and turned to walk along the shoulder of the main road. She liked the sound of her shoes on the sand that lined the macadam. Her rhythmic soft shoe. New York was so loud with its traffic and subterranean subway clatter that you couldn't hear yourself moving in time and space, couldn't hear your breath sounds coming and going. Sometimes with the jackhammering and the explosive hiss of kneeling buses you had to pinch yourself just to know you were still alive.

But here, the steel chill of night giving way to the mug of a summer day, bubbling rainbows in the air, Sarah could feel herself breathing, her muscles moving. She could hear her own hair as it brushed against the collar of her light summer jacket.

The farmers market was busy already. You could smell the seconds fermenting in hidden baskets out of sight, bruised tomatoes and stone fruit boxed for cosmetic reasons, even though the mottled fruit was the sweetest. Every week the vendors set up in a slightly different order, sometimes the kettle corn at one end, sometimes another. The flower vendor favored the middle, the baker the end closest to the water. Ben and Sarah had been coming here for fifteen years, first as renters and then, when rich became wealthy, as owners of a modern concrete sleeve with an ocean view.

Sarah knew all the farmers by name. She had watched their children grow from toddler to teen. She walked beside weekenders and locals, not shopping as much as feeling part of the place. They were going to catch an afternoon ferry. It would be pointless to buy more than a single peach, but she couldn't *not* come to the farmers market on a Sunday morning. Those weeks when it rained and the market was canceled, she felt rootless. Back in the city, she would wander the streets like a rat in a maze, looking for something, yet never knowing exactly what.

She stopped and studied some watercress. The fight she and Ben had had after the dinner—his cold shoulder, the mid-meal walkout— had been short but fierce. She let him know in no uncertain terms that she wasn't going to put up with his selfishness anymore. The world did not exist to satisfy the needs of Ben Kipling. And if that's what he wanted—to surround himself with people that he could walk on as he pleased—well, then, he should find another wife.

Ben had been uncharacteristically apologetic, taking her hand and telling her she was right, that he was sorry and would make every effort to make sure it never happened again. It took her off guard. She was so used to fighting with the back of his head. But this time he looked her in the eye. He told her he knew he had taken her for granted, that he'd taken everything for granted. He'd been arrogant. *Hubris* was the word he used. But from here on out it was a new day. He actually looked a little scared. She took the fear to be a sign that her threat had actually landed, that he believed she would leave him and didn't know what she would do without him. Later she would realize that he was already afraid—afraid that everything he had, everything he was, was on the verge of eclipse.

And so today, having witnessed her husband's contrition, having lain with him in their marital bed, his head between her breasts, his hands upon her thighs, she felt a new chapter in her life begin. A renaissance. They had talked into the late-night hours of taking a month off and going to Europe. They would walk the streets of Umbria, hand in hand, newlyweds again. Sometime after midnight he had opened his mahogany box and they had smoked some pot, the first she'd smoked since Jenny was born. It made them giggle like kids, sitting on the kitchen floor in front of the open refrigerator, eating strawberries straight out of the crisper.

She wandered past English cucumbers and baskets of loose-leaf lettuces. The berry man had arranged his wares into a trinity—green baskets of blueberries grouped with blackberries and gum-red raspberries. She peeled back the rough husks of summer corn, her fingers hungry to feel the yellow silk below, lost in an illusion. Here on the Vineyard, at the farmers market, at this precise spot, in this moment in time, the modern world vanished, the unspoken division of our silent class wars. There was no rich or poor, no privilege, there was only food tugged from loamy earth, fruit plucked from sturdy branches, and honey stolen from the beehive bush. *We are all equal in the face of nature*, she thought—which was, in and of itself, an idea born of luxury.

Looking up, she saw Maggie Bateman in the middle distance. The moment was this: A young couple with a baby stroller passed through her center of vision and in their passing, Maggie was revealed in profile, caught in mid-sentence, and then—as the couple with the stroller cleared completely—the man she was speaking to was, himself, revealed. He was a handsome man in his forties, dressed in jeans and a T-shirt, both paint-stained, the T-shirt covered by an old blue cardigan. The man had longish hair, swept back carelessly but creeping forward, and as Sarah watched he reached up and swept it back again, the way a horse swats flies with its tail, distracted.

The first thought that hit Sarah was simply recognition. She *knew* that person (Maggie). The second thought was context (that's Maggie Bateman, married to David, mother of two). The third thought was that the man she was talking to was standing a little too close, that he was leaning in and smiling. And that the look on Maggie's face was similar. That there was an *intimacy* between them that felt more than casual. And then Maggie turned and saw Sarah. She raised a hand and shielded her eyes from the sun, like a sailor searching the horizon.

"Hey there," she said, and there was something about the openness of the greeting, the fact that Maggie didn't act like a woman who'd just been caught flirting with a man who was not her husband, that made Sarah rethink her first assumption.

"I thought you might be here," Maggie said. Then, "Oh, this is Scott."

The man showed Sarah his palm.

"Hi," said Sarah, then to Maggie, "Yeah, you know me. If the market's up I'll be here squeezing avocados, rain or shine."

"Are you going back today?"

"The three o'clock ferry, I think."

"Oh no. Don't—we've got the plane. Come with us."

"Really?"

"Of course. That's what it's—I was just telling Scott. He's got to go into the city tonight too."

"I was thinking of walking," said Scott.

Sarah frowned.

"We're on an island."

Maggie smiled.

"Sarah. He's kidding."

Sarah felt herself flush.

"Of course."

She forced a laugh.

"I'm such a ditz sometimes."

"So that's it," said Maggie. "You have to come. Both of you. And Ben. It'll be fun. We can have a drink and, I don't know, talk about art."

To Sarah she said, "Scott's a painter."

"Failed," he clarified.

"No. Now that's—didn't you just tell me you have gallery meetings next week?"

"Which are bound to go badly."

"What do you paint?" Sarah asked.

"Catastrophe," he said.

Sarah must have looked puzzled, because Maggie said, "Scott paints disaster scenes from the news—train wrecks, building collapses, and things like monsoons—they really are genius."

"Well," said Scott, "they're morbid."

"I'd like to see them sometime," said Sarah politely, though morbid is exactly how it sounded to her.

"See?" said Maggie.

"She's being polite," said Scott perceptively. "But I appreciate it. I live pretty simply out here."

It's clear he would say more if asked, but Sarah changed subjects. "What time are you guys going back?" she asked.

"I'll text you," said Maggie, "but I think around eight. We fly to Teterboro and then into the city from there. We're usually home and in bed by ten thirty."

"Wow," said Sarah, "that would be amazing. Just the thought of Sunday-afternoon gridlock—*eek*—I mean it's worth it, but that would be—Ben is going to be thrilled."

"Good," said Maggie. "I'm glad. That's what it's there for, right? If you've got a plane—"

"I wouldn't know," said Scott.

"Don't be snarky," said Maggie, turning to him. "You're coming too."

She was grinning, teasing him, and Sarah decided that this was just how Maggie was, a good sport, a people person. Scott certainly wasn't giving off a vibe that the two of them were anything other than farmers market friends.

"I'll think about it," he said. "Thanks."

He gave them both a smile and walked off. For a moment it felt that all three of them would go their separate ways, but Maggie lingered a bit and Sarah felt the obligation to keep talking if she wanted to, so the two of them leaned away and then back.

"How do you know him?" Sarah asked.

"Scott? Just—from around. Or—he's always at Gabe's, you know, having coffee, and I used to bring the kids down all the time, just a place to go to get out of the house. Rachel liked their muffins. And we just got chatty."

"Is he married?"

"No," said Maggie. "I think he was engaged once. Anyway, the kids and I went out to his place once, saw his work. It really is terrific.

155

I keep trying to get David to buy something, but he said he's in the disaster business, so he doesn't really want to come home and look at that. And to be fair, they are pretty graphic."

"I bet."

"Yeah."

They stood there for a moment, out of words, like two rocks in a stream, the movement of the crowd a constant around them.

"Things are good?" said Sarah.

"Good, yes. You?"

Sarah thought about the way Ben kissed her this morning. She smiled.

"They are."

"Great. Well, let's catch up on the plane, huh?"

"Amazing. Thanks again."

"Okay. See you tonight."

Maggie gave her a quick air kiss and then she was gone. Sarah watched her go, then went to find some more strawberries.

. . .

At the same time, Ben sat on the deck—reclaimed wood, ivied trellis—and watched the waves. Laid out on the kitchen counter were a dozen bagels with lox, heirloom tomatoes, capers, and a local artisanal cream cheese. Ben sat on a wicker chair with the Sunday *Times* and a cappuccino, a light wind in his face off the ocean. He had traded texts with Culpepper all weekend, using an app called Redact that blacked out messages as you read them, then erased them for good.

Out on the ocean, sailboats inch across the wave caps. Culpepper wrote cryptically that he had been digging into the government's case through back channels. He used emoticons instead of key words, assuming it would make the texts harder to use as evidence, were the government to somehow crack the app.

Looks like they have a key :-(feeding them dirt.

Ben wiped tomato runoff from his chin, finished his first bagel half. A whistleblower? Is that what Culpepper was saying? Ben remembered the man with the turtleneck outside Bali, his nose broken in a Russian prison. Did that really happen?

Sarah came out onto the porch with half a grapefruit. Where he'd just gotten up, she'd already been to a Spin class in town.

"Ferry leaves at three thirty," Ben told her. "So we should be there at two forty-five."

Sarah handed him a napkin, sat.

"I ran into Maggie at the farmers market."

"Bateman?"

"Yes. She was with some painter. I mean, not *with*, but they were talking."

"Uh-huh," he said, preparing to tune out the rest of the conversation.

"She said there's room on their plane tonight."

This got his attention.

"She offered?"

"Unless you want to take the ferry. But, you know, the traffic Sunday night."

"No, that sounds—did you say yes?"

"I said I'd talk to you, but assume we're in."

Ben sat back. He'd text his assistant to have a car sent to Teterboro. He was taking out his phone to do it when he had another thought.

David. He could talk to David. Not in detail, of course, but to the extent that he was having some troubles—one mogul to another. Was there a strategy David recommended? Should they hire a crisis manager preemptively? Start looking for a scapegoat? David also had close ties to the executive branch. If there really were new marching orders to the Justice Department, maybe David could get them some advance word.

He put his half-eaten bagel down, wiped his hands on his pants, stood.

"I'm gonna take a walk on the beach, sort some things out."

"If you wait a minute, I'll go with you."

He started to tell her he needed the time to think, but paused. After the fiasco with Jenny's boyfriend, he needed to go the extra mile. So he nodded and went inside to get his shoes.

. . .

The ride to the airport was short, the car picking them up just after nine p.m. They rode in the air-conditioned rear, moving through dimming twilight, the sun low on the horizon, an orange yolk dipped slowly into a cool meringue. Ben reviewed what he wanted to say to David, how to sidle up on the thing—not *There's a crisis*, but *Have you heard anything coming out of the White House that might affect the market in general?* Or no, that's too inside baseball. Maybe it was as simple as *We're hearing rumblings about some new regulations. Can you confirm or deny?*

He was sweating, despite the sixty-eight-degree interior. Next to Ben, Sarah was watching the sunset with a whispered smile. Ben squeezed her hand encouragingly, and she looked over and gave him a big grin—*her man*. Ben smiled back. He could just about slay a gin and tonic right now.

Ben was getting out of the car on the tarmac when Culpepper called. It was nine fifteen, and balmy, a heavy fog hanging on the edges of the runway.

"It's happening," said Culpepper as Ben took his overnight bag from the driver.

"What?"

"Indictments. A birdie just told me."

"What? When?"

"In the morning. The feds'll come in force, waving warrants. I had a shitstorm call with Leroy, but he's gotta side with the president on this one. *We need to send a message to Wall Street,* or some such shit. I've got a hundred temps in there right now taking care of things."

"Things?"

"What does the cookie monster do to cookies?"

Ben was shaking. His creative reasoning center was closed.

"Jesus, Barney. Just say it."

"Not on the phone. Just know that what Stalin did to the USSR is happening to our data. But you don't know anything. As far as you're concerned it's just another Sunday night."

"What should I—"

"Nothing. Go home, take a Xanax, sleep. In the morning put on a comfortable suit and moisturize your wrists. They're going to arrest you at the office. You and Hoover and Tabitha, et cetera. We have lawyers on retainer standing by to bail you out, but they'll be dicks and hold you the maximum time allowed."

"In jail?"

"No. At Best Buy. Yes, in jail. But don't worry. I've got a good lice guy."

He hung up. Ben stood on the tarmac, oblivious to the warm wind and Sarah's concerned stare. Everything looked different now. The creeping fog, the shadows below the plane. Ben half expected fast lines to drop from a helicopter sky, shock troops descending.

It's happening, he thought. The absolute worst-case scenario. *I will be arrested, indicted.*

"Jesus, Ben, you're like a ghost."

Behind them the two-man ground crew finished gassing up the plane.

"No," he said, trying to pull himself together. "No, it's—I'm fine. Just—some bad news from the markets. Asia."

The two men pulled the hose back, away from the fuselage. They were wearing khaki coveralls and matching caps, their faces darkened by shadow. One of them took a few steps away from the gas line, pulled out a pack of cigarettes. He lit one, the flame illuminating his face with an orange flicker. Ben squinted at him. *Is that——?* he thought, but the face went dark again. His fight-or-flight instinct was so strong right now it was as if every fear he had ever had was surrounding him in the fog. His heartbeat was thunderous, and he shivered despite the heat.

After a moment he realized that Sarah was talking to him.

"What?" he said.

"I said, should I worry?"

"No," he told her. "No. It's just——you know, I'm really looking forward to the trip we talked about. Italy, Croatia. I think it'll be——I don't know——maybe we should go tonight."

She took his arm.

"You're so crazy," she told him, squeezing. He nodded. The second man finished securing the fuel hose, climbed into the cab of the truck. The second man dropped his cigarette, grinded it out, walked to the passenger door.

"I wouldn't wanna be flying in this," he said.

And there's something about the way he said it. An *implication*. Ben turned.

"What?" he said. But the man was already closing his door. Then the truck pulled away. Was that a threat of some kind? A warning? Or was he being paranoid? Ben watched the truck roll back to the hangar until its taillights were just two red spots in the fog.

"Babe?" said Sarah.

Ben exhaled loudly, trying to shake it off.

"Yeah," he said.

Too Big to Jail. That's what Barney had said. It was just a ploy. The government was trying to make an example, but when it came down to it——the secrets he had, the implications to the financial markets—— he had to believe that Barney was right. That this thing would settle quietly for a few million dollars. The truth was, he'd prepared for this day, planned for it. He'd have been an idiot not to, and if there was one thing Ben Kipling wasn't it was an idiot. He had insulated himself financially, hiding funds—not everything, of course, but a couple of million. There was a litigator on retainer. Yes, this was the worst-case scenario, but it was a scenario they had built a fortress to handle.

Let them come, he thought, surrendering himself to fate, then he squeezed Sarah's hand, breathing again, and walked her to the plane.

2.

CUNNINGHAM

IT'S NEVER BEEN a secret that Bill Cunningham has problems with authority. In some ways that's his brand, the fire-breathing malcontent, and he's translated it into a ten-million-dollar-a-year contract with ALC. But in the same way a man's nose and ears become exaggerated as he ages, so do the psychological issues that define him. We all become caricatures of ourselves, if we live long enough. And so over the last few years, as his power grew, so too did Bill's *fuck you and the horse you rode in on* attitude. Until now, he's been like some blood-drinking Roman caesar who believes deep down he may be a god.

Ultimately, this is why he's still on the air, after all the bullshit corporate crybabying over his alleged "phone hacking." Though, if he's being honest (which he isn't), he'd have to admit that David's death had a lot to do with it. A grief response and power vacuum in a moment of crisis that Bill was able to exploit by delivering what he calls "leadership," but was really a kind of moral bullying.

"You're gonna—" he said, "let me get this straight, you're gonna can me in a moment of all-out war."

"Bill," said Don Liebling, "don't you do that."

"No, I want—you need to say it on the record—so when I sue your asses for a billion dollars I can be specific on the stand while I'm jerking off into some caviar."

Don stares at him.

"Jesus. David's dead. His wife is dead. His—"

He gets quiet for a moment, overcome by the immensity of it.

"His goddamn daughter. And you're—I can't even say it out loud."

"Exactly," said Bill, "you can't. But I can. That's what I do. I say things out loud. I ask the questions no one else is willing to—and millions of people watch this channel because of that. People who are gonna run to CNN if they turn on our coverage of the death of our own fucking boss and see some second-string automaton with Fisher-Price snap-on hair reading his opinions off a teleprompter. David and his wife and daughter—who, I held her at her fucking baptism—are lying somewhere at the bottom of the Atlantic with Ben Kipling—who I'm hearing was about to be indicted—and everybody's using the word *accident* like nobody on earth had reason to want these people dead, except then why did the man travel in a bulletproof limousine and his office windows could take a hit from a goddamn bazooka?"

Don looks over at Franken, Bill's lawyer, already knowing that in the war between common sense and marketing genius, marketing is going to win out. Franken smiles.

Gotcha.

And that's how it came to pass that Bill Cunningham was back on the air Monday morning, three hours after news of the crash broke.

He sat before the cameras, his hair unbrushed, in shirtsleeves, his tie askew, looking for all intents and purposes like a man felled by grief. And yet, when he spoke, his voice was strong.

"Let me be clear," he said. "This organization—this planet—has lost a great man. A friend and leader. I wouldn't be sitting in front of you right now—"

He paused, collected himself.

"—I'd still be throwing weather in Oklahoma, if David Bateman hadn't seen potential where no one else could. We built this network together. I was his best man when he married Maggie. I am—I *was*—godfather to his daughter, Rachel. And that is why I feel it is my *re-*

sponsibility to see that his *murder* is solved, and that the killer or killers are brought to justice."

He leaned forward and stared into the lens.

"And yes, I said *murder*. Because whatever else could it be? Two of the most powerful men in a city of powerful men, whose plane disappears over the dark Atlantic, a plane serviced just the day before, flown by top-notch pilots who reported no mechanical issues to flight control, but somehow dropped off radar eighteen minutes after takeoff—look at my face—no one on earth can convince me there wasn't some kind of foul play involved."

The ratings that morning were the highest in the history of the network, and they continued to climb from there. As the first wreckage was found, the first bodies washed up on shore—Emma Lightner found by a dog walker on Fisher Island on Tuesday, Sarah Kipling hauled in by lobstermen on Wednesday morning—Bill seemed to rise above himself, like a relief pitcher in the bottom innings of a too-close-to-call game seven.

That day Bill spun the grim discovery of human remains toward further intrigue. Where was Ben Kipling? Where was David Bateman? Didn't it seem convenient that of the eleven people on the plane, passengers and crew, only seven bodies remained missing, including those of the two men most likely to have been targeted by as-yet-unknown forces? If Ben Kipling was sitting with his wife, as had been reported, why was her body recovered and not his?

And where was this Scott Burroughs character? Why did he still insist on hiding his face from the world? Is it possible he was involved somehow?

"Clearly he knows more than he's saying," Bill told the viewers at home.

Sources inside the investigation had been funneling ALC information since the first boots hit the ground. From this, they were able to break the seating chart before anyone else. They were also the first to break news of Kipling's imminent indictment.

It was Bill who broke that the boy, JJ, had been asleep when he arrived at the airfield and was carried onto the plane by his father. His personal connection to the story, the marathon hours he spent behind the anchor desk, frequently having to pause to collect himself, made it hard for viewers to change the channel. Would he break down entirely? What would he say next? Hour after hour, Bill cast himself as a kind of martyr, Jimmy Stewart on his feet in the Senate chambers, refusing to succumb or surrender.

But as the days went on, even the back-channel leaks began to seem false. Could there really be no new leads on the location of the wreckage? And now that all the other outfits had the Kipling story—the *Times* ran a six-thousand-word piece on Sunday that showed in minute detail how his firm had laundered billions from North Korea, Iran, and Libya—Bill became less interested in digging for dirt there. He was reduced to opinion pieces, to going over old ground—pointing at time lines, yelling at maps.

And then he had an idea.

. . .

Bill meets Namor at a dive bar on Orchard Street—black box, no sign. He chooses it because he figures none of the grungy liberal elite of the Williamsburg Lower East Side knows his face. All the bearded Sarah Lawrence graduates with their artisanal ales who think every conservative pundit is just another friend of their dad's.

In preparation, Bill trades his trademark suspenders for a T-shirt and leather bomber jacket. He looks like a former president, trying to be cool—Bill Clinton at a U2 concert.

The bar—Swim!—is defined by low lighting and glowing fish tanks, giving it the look of mid-1990s sci-fi action movie. He orders a Budweiser (un-ironically) and finds a table behind a big saltwater tank, then watches the door for his man. Sitting behind the tank gives the illusion that he is underwater, and through the glass the room takes on a funhouse-mirror quality—like what a hipster bar would look like after the oceans rise and consume the earth. It's just after nine p.m. and the place is half filled with bro-clusters and hipster first dates. Bill sips the king of beers and checks out the local talent—blond girl, decent tits, a little chubby. Some kind of East Asian number with a nose ring—*Filipino?* He thinks about the last girl he fucked, a twenty-two-year-old intern from GW he bent over his desk, coughing his orgasm into her brown hair after six glorious minutes of *watch the door!* jackhammering.

His man enters in a raincoat, an unsmoked cigarette tucked behind his ear. He looks around casually, sees Bill's comically oversize head magnified through the fish tank, and approaches.

"I'm assuming you thought you were being stealth," he says, sliding into the booth, "choosing this dump."

"My core audience are fifty-five-year-old white men who need two heaping tablespoons of fiber to take a halfway-decent shit every morning. I think we're in the clear here."

"Except you came by town car, which is loitering at the curb this very minute, drawing attention."

"Shit," says Bill, pulling out his phone and telling his driver to *circle.*

Bill met Namor on a junket to Germany during the second Bush's first regime. Namor was introduced to him by a local NGO as *a man to know.* And right off the bat the kid was feeding him gold. So Bill cultivated him, buying him meals, theater tickets, whatever, and making himself available whenever Namor felt like talking, which was usually north of one thirty in the morning.

"What did you find out?" he asks Namor after his phone is back in his pocket.

Namor looks around, gauging volume and distance.

"The civilians are easy," he says. "We're already up on the flight attendant's father, the pilot's mother, and the Bateman aunt and uncle."

"Eleanor and—what's it?—Doug."

"Right."

"They must be giddy," says Bill, "winning the goddamn orphan lottery. It's gotta be something like three hundred million the kid inherits."

"But also," says Namor, "he's an orphan."

"Boo hoo. I *wish* I was an orphan. My mother raised me in a boardinghouse and used bleach for birth control."

"Well, taps are up there on all three phones, hers, his, and home. And we're seeing all their electronic messages before they do."

"And this feed goes where?"

"I set up a dummy account. You'll get the info by coded text when we walk out tonight. I also hacked her voice mail so you can listen late at night while you're humping your pillow."

"Trust me, I get so much pussy—when I go home at night the only thing I put my cock in is ice."

"Remind me not to order a margarita at your house."

Bill finishes his beer, waves at the bartender for a second.

"And what about King Neptune," he says, "the long-distance swimmer?"

Namor sips his beer.

"Nothing."

"Whaddya mean, *nothing*? It's two thousand fifteen."

"What can I say? He's a throwback. No cell phone, doesn't text, pays all his bills by mail."

"Next thing you're gonna tell me is he's a Trotskyite."

"Nobody's a Trotskyite anymore. Not even Trotsky."

"Probably 'cause he's been dead for fifty years."

A waitress brings Bill a new beer. Namor signals he wants one too.

"At least," says Bill, "tell me where this fucking Boy Scout is—on what planet."

Namor thinks about that.

"What's got you so bent about this guy?" he asks.

"What are you talking about?"

"I'm just saying—this swimmer—everybody else thinks he's a hero."

Bill makes a face like the word has made him physically sick.

"That's like saying everything that's wrong with the country is what makes it great."

"Yeah, but—"

"Some failed drunk hobnobbing with men of actual accomplishment, a hitchhiker on the bootstrap express."

"I don't know what that—"

"He's a fraud, I'm saying. A nobody. Muscling his way into the spotlight, playing the humble knight, when the actual heroes, the great men, are dead at the bottom of the deep blue bullshit. And if that's what we call a hero in two thousand fifteen, then, buddy, we're fucked."

Namor picks his teeth. It's no skin off his nose either way, but there's a big ask here, a lot of laws about to be broken, so it's probably worth being sure.

"He saved the kid," he says.

"So what? They train dogs to wear whiskey barrels and find warm bodies in an avalanche, but you don't see my teaching my kids to grow up to be malamutes."

Namor thinks about that.

"Well, he didn't go home."

Bill stares at him. Namor smiles without teeth.

"I'm sifting through some chatter. Maybe he'll turn up."

"But you don't know—is what you're saying."

"Yes. For once. I don't know."

Bill pumps his leg, suddenly uninterested in his second beer.

"I mean, what are we talking about here? A drunken degenerate? A black ops sleeper agent? Some kind of Romeo?"

"Or maybe he's just a guy who got on the wrong plane and saved a kid."

Bill makes a face.

"That's the hero story. Everybody's got the fucking hero story. It's human interest bullshit. You can't tell me that this dried-up has-been gets a seat on that plane just because he's a good guy. I couldn't even get a ride on the plane three weeks ago. Had to take the goddamn ferry."

"And you're definitely not a good guy."

"Fuck you. I'm a great American. How is that not more important than what? Being nice?"

The waitress brings Namor's second beer. He sips it.

"Here's the thing," he says. "Nobody stays buried forever. Sooner or later, this guy goes to the deli to buy a bagel and somebody gets a cell phone photo. Or he calls someone we've already tapped."

"Like Franklin at NTSB."

"I told you. That one's tricky."

"Fuck you. You said anybody. You said pick a name from the phone book."

"Look, I can get his personal line, but not the satphone."

"What about email?"

"In time, maybe. But we gotta be careful. They monitor everything anymore, since the Patriot Act."

"Which you called amateur hour. Get some sack already."

Namor sighs. He has his eye on the blonde, who's texting someone while her date is in the can. Once he has her name he can fish up naked selfies in less than fifteen minutes.

"My memory is you said we had to cool it for a while," he says. "Wasn't that the phone call? Burn everything. Wait for my signal."

Bill waves him off.

"That was before ISIS killed my friend."

"Or whoever."

Bill stands, zips his bomber.

"Look," he says, "it's a simple equation. Secrets plus technology equals no more secrets. What this thing needs is a brain trust, someone at twenty thousand feet who's got access to all the intel—governmental, personal, fucking forensic weather data—and he—this elevated godhead—uses that information to paint the real picture, uncover who's lying and who's telling the truth."

"And that someone is you."

"Fucking A right," says Bill, and walks out to his town car.

FUNHOUSE

SCOTT SITS ALONE that night and watches himself on television. It is less an act of narcissism and more a symptom of vertigo. To see his face onscreen, features reversed, to have childhood photos—*how did they get them?*—unearthed and displayed in a public forum (between commercials for adult diapers and minivans), to be told the story of his own life, as if in a game of telephone. A story that resembles his own, but isn't. Born in the wrong hospital, attended a different elementary school, studied painting in Cleveland instead of Chicago—like looking down and seeing someone else's shadow following you on the street. He has a hard enough time these days knowing who he is without this sentient doppelgänger out there. This third-person him now a subject of rumor and speculation. *What was he doing on that plane?* Last week he was an ordinary man, anonymous. Today he is a character in a detective story. *The Last Man to See the Victims Alive* or *Savior of the Child.* Each day he plays his role, scene by scene, sitting on sofas and hard-backed chairs, answering questions from the FBI and NTSB, going over and over the details—what he remembers, what he doesn't. And then seeing the headlines in the paper, hearing disembodied voices from the radio.

A hero. They are calling him a hero. It is not a word he can handle right now, being so far outside his own sense of himself, the narrative he has created that allows him to function—a broken man with modest ambitions, a former blackout drunk who lives moment-to-moment now, hand-to-mouth. And so he keeps his head down, dodging the cameras.

Occasionally he is recognized on the subway or walking down the street. To these people he is something more than a celebrity. *Yo, you saved that kid. I heard you fought a shark, bro. Did you fight a shark?* He is treated not like royalty—as if his fame is based on something rare—but more like a guy from the neighborhood who got lucky. Because what did he do really, except swim? He is one of them, a nobody who did good. And so when he is recognized, people approach smiling. They want to shake his hand, take a picture. He survived a plane crash and saved a kid. There is juju to touching him, the same boost you get from a lucky penny or a rabbit's foot. By doing the impossible he—like Jack—proved that impossible is possible. Who wouldn't want to rub up on that?

Scott smiles and tries to be friendly. These conversations are different from what he assumes it will feel like to talk to the press. They're contact on a human level. And though he feels self-conscious he makes sure he is never rude. He understands that they want him to be special. It's important to people that he be special, because we need special things in our lives. We want to believe that magic is still possible. So Scott shakes hands and accepts the hugs of random women. He asks that they not take his picture, and most respect that.

"Let's keep this private," he says. "It means more when it's just you and me."

People like this idea, that in a time of true mass media, they could have a unique experience. But not everyone. Some take his picture brazenly, as if it is their right. And others get upset when he refuses to pose for a photo with them. An older woman calls him an asshole outside Washington Square Park, and he nods and tells her she's right. He is an asshole and he hopes she has a great day.

"Fuck you," she tells him.

Once anointed a hero by your fellow man, you lose the right to privacy. You become an object, stripped of some unquantifiable humanity, as if you have won a cosmic lottery and woke one day to find yourself a minor deity. *The Patron Saint of Good Luck.* It stops mattering what you wanted for yourself. All that matters is the role you played in the lives of others. You are a rare butterfly held roughly at a right angle to the sun.

On the third day he stops going outside.

He is living in Layla's third-floor guest apartment. It is a space of pure white—white walls, white floor, white ceiling, white furniture—as if he has died and moved on to some kind of heavenly limbo. Time, once mired in hard-fought routine, becomes fungible. To wake in a strange bed. To make coffee with unfamiliar beans. To lift rich bath towels from self-closing cupboards and feel their hotel texture against your skin. In the living room there is a bar filled with Scottish malts and clear Russian courage. A cherrywood, mid-century case with an elaborate folding lid. Scott stared at it for a long time that first night, the way a man in a certain mental state regards a gun cabinet. So many ways to die. Then he covered the bar with a blanket, moved a chair in front of it, never to look at it again.

Somewhere, the Kipling wife and that beautiful flight attendant are lying faceup on a steel slab. *Sarah*, that was her name, and the model in the short skirt was *Emma Lightner*. Several times a day he reviews the names like a Zen koan. *David Bateman, Maggie Bateman, Rachel Bateman* . . .

He thought he had come to terms with this thing, its full import, but there was something about the news that bodies had been found that threw him off balance. They're dead. All of them. He knows they're dead. He was there, in the ocean. He dove beneath the wave. There could be no survivors, but hearing the news, seeing the footage—*first bodies recovered from Bateman crash*—made the whole thing real, the way your legs go out from under you only after a crisis is over.

The mother is still out there, the father and sister. So are the pilots, Charlie Busch and James Melody. So is Kipling, the traitor, and the Batemans' security man, buried somewhere deep beneath the waves, swaying in permanent black.

He should go home, he knows, back to the island, but he can't. For some reason he finds himself unable to face the life he once lived (*once*, in this case, being nine days ago, as if linear time means anything to a man who's survived what he's survived. There is before and there is after), unable to approach the little white gate on a quiet sandy road, to step over the old slip-on shoes left absently by the door, one behind the other—the toe of the back shoe still resting on the heel of the front, where he stepped out of it. He feels unable to return to the milk in the fridge gone sour, and his dog's sad eyes. That is *his* home, the man on TV who wears Scott's shirts and squints into the lens of old photographs—*are my own teeth that crooked?* Unable to face the gauntlet of cameras, the endless barrage of questions. Talking to people on the subway is one thing, but addressing the masses—that's something he can't handle. A statement becomes a pronouncement when delivered to the crowd. Random observations become part of the public record to be replayed for all eternity, Auto-Tuned and memified. Whatever the reason, he feels unable to retrace his steps, to withdraw to the place he lived "before." And so he sits on his borrowed sofa of the now and stares out at the treetops and brownstones of Bank Street.

Where is the boy at this moment? On a farm somewhere in upstate New York? At a breakfast table surrounded by spiky green strawberry tops and calcifying oatmeal splotches? Every night before bed, Scott has the same thought. In sleep he will dream of the boy lost in an endless black ocean, dream of his Dopplered cries—nowhere and everywhere at once—as Scott splashes around, half drowning, searching but never finding. But the dream does not come. Instead there is only the deep vacuum of sleep. It occurs to him now, sipping cold coffee, that maybe these are the boy's dreams.

A projection of his anxiety, floating on the jet stream like a dog whistle only Scott can hear.

Is the bond between them real or implied, a product of guilt, an idea he has contracted like a virus? To save this child, to have him cling to you for eight exhausting hours, to carry him in your arms to the hospital—did that create new pathways in the brain? Isn't the life saved enough? He is home now, this child the world knows as JJ, but whom Scott will always think of simply as *the boy*. Safe and cared for by a new family, by the aunt and her—well, let's be honest—*shifty* husband. An instant millionaire hundreds of times over who will never want for anything, and him not even five. Scott saved his life, gave him a future, the chance of happiness. Isn't that enough?

He dials information and asks for the aunt's number in upstate New York. It is nine p.m. He has sat alone in the apartment for two days straight. The operator connects him and as he listens to the phone ring he wonders what he is doing.

On the sixth ring she answers, Eleanor. He pictures her face, the rosy cheeks and sad eyes.

"Hello?"

She sounds wary, as if only bad news comes after dark.

"Hey, it's Scott."

But she's already talking.

"We already made a statement. Can you please respect our privacy?"

"No, it's Scott. The painter. From the hospital."

Her voice softens.

"Oh, sorry. They just—they won't leave us alone. And he's just a boy, you know? And his mom and dad are—"

"I know. Why do you think I'm hiding out?"

A silence as she switches from the call she thought it was to the reality—a human moment with her nephew's savior.

"I wish we could," she says. "I mean, it's hard enough going through this all in private, without—"

"I'm sure. Is he—"

A pause. Scott feels he can hear her thinking—how much should she trust him? How much can she say?

"JJ? He's, you know, he's not really talking. We took him to a psychiatrist—I mean, I did—and he said, just—*give him time.* So I'm not pressing."

"That sounds—I can't imagine what it's like—"

"He doesn't cry. Not that he—I mean, he's four, so how much can he really understand? But still, I thought he'd cry."

Scott thinks about this. What's there to say? "He's just processing, I guess. Something that—traumatic. I mean, for kids whatever they go through is normal, right? I mean, in their heads. They are learning what the world is, so that's what he thinks now. That planes crash and people die and you end up in the drink. Which, maybe he's having second thoughts about the whole thing if that's what life on this earth is all—"

"I know," she says. And they sit for a minute in a silence that is neither awkward nor uncomfortable. Just the sound of two people thinking.

"Doug doesn't talk much either. Except about the money. I caught him the other day downloading spreadsheet software. But—emotionally? I think he's freaked out by the whole thing."

"Still?"

"Yeah, he's—you know, he's not good with people. He had a hard childhood too."

"You mean, twenty-five years ago?"

He can hear her smile over the phone.

"Be nice."

Scott likes the sound of her voice, the pace of it. There is an implication of intimacy to it, as if they have known each other a long, long time.

"Not that I'm one to talk," he tells her. "Given my track record with women."

"That is bait I will not take," she says.

They talk for a while about the daily routine. She gets up with the boy while Doug sleeps—he goes to bed late, it seems. JJ likes toast for breakfast and can eat a whole container of blueberries in one sitting. They do art projects until nap time and in the afternoons he likes to look for bugs in the yard. On trash days they sit on the porch and wave at the haulers.

"A normal kid, basically," she says.

"Do you think he really understands what happened?"

A long pause, then she says:

"Do you?"

ON WEDNESDAY THE funerals begin. Sarah Kipling is first, her remains buried at Mount Zion Cemetery in Queens, a graveyard in the shadow of looming pre-war smokestacks, as if there is a factory next door manufacturing bodies. Police hold the news trucks to a cordoned area on the south side of the wall. It's a cloudy day, the air stilted, tropical. Thunderstorms are forecast for the afternoon and already you can feel the unsettled electricity in the atmosphere. The line of black cars stretches all the way to the BQE, family, friends, political figures. There will be eight more before this is through—assuming all the bodies are recovered.

Overhead, helicopters circle. Scott arrives in a yellow cab. He's wearing a black suit found in Layla's guest closet. It's a size too big, long in the sleeves. In a dresser drawer he found, conversely, a small white shirt, too tight in the neck, that leaves a noticeable gap under his necktie. He's shaved badly, cutting himself in two places. The sight of his blood in the bathroom mirror and the sharp slice of pain startled him back to a kind of reality.

He can still taste salt water in the back of his throat, if he's being honest, even in sleep.

Why is he alive and they dead?

Scott tells the driver to leave it running and steps out into the mug.

181

For a moment he wonders if the boy will be here—he forgot to ask—but then he thinks, *Who would bring a toddler to a stranger's funeral?*

The truth is, he doesn't know why he came here. He is neither family nor friend.

Scott can feel the eyes on him as he walks up. There are two dozen guests in black ringing the grave. He sees them see him. He is like lightning that has struck twice in the same place. An anomaly. He lowers his eyes out of respect.

Standing at a respectful distance he sees half a dozen men in suits. One is Gus Franklin. He recognizes two of the others, Agent O'Brien from the FBI and the other is—Agent something or other from, what is it, the SEC? They nod to him.

As the rabbi talks, Scott watches dark clouds move over the skyline. They are on a planet called earth at the heart of the Milky Way galaxy. Spinning, always spinning. Everything in the universe appears to move in a circular pattern, celestial objects rotating in orbit. Forces of push and pull that dwarf the industry of man or beast. Even in planetary terms we are small—one man afloat in an entire ocean, a speck in the waves. We believe our capacity for reason makes us bigger than we are, our ability to understand the infinite vastness of celestial bodies. But the truth is, this sense of scale only shrinks us down.

The wind kicks up. Scott tries not to think about the other bodies still buried with the plane—Captain Melody, Ben Kipling, Maggie Bateman and her daughter, Rachel. He pictures them there, like a lost letter in the lightless deep, swaying silently to unheard music as the crabs consume their noses and toes.

When the funeral ends, a man approaches Scott. He has a military carriage and a handsome, leathery face, as if he spent years of his life in the hot Arizona sun.

"Scott? I'm Michael Lightner. My daughter was—"

"I know," says Scott softly. "I remember her."

They stand among the tombstones, surrounded by white statues of the Madonna. In the distance there is a domed mausoleum, topped by a sculpted friar holding a staff and cross. He is dwarfed by the city skyline, gleaming in the late-afternoon sun, so that if you unfocused your eyes you could convince yourself that all the buildings are just tombstones of a different kind, towering edifices of remembrance and regret.

"I read somewhere that you're a painter," Michael says. He takes a pack of cigarettes from his shirt pocket, taps out a smoke.

"Well, I paint," says Scott. "If that makes me a painter, I guess I'm a painter."

"I fly airplanes," says Michael, "which I always thought made me a pilot."

He smokes for a moment.

"I want to thank you for what you did," he says.

"Living?" says Scott.

"No. The boy. I ditched once in the Bering Strait on a life raft, and that was—I had supplies."

"Do you remember Jack LaLanne?" asks Scott. "Well, I went to San Francisco when I was a kid and he was swimming across the bay pulling a boat behind him. I thought he was Superman. So I joined the swim team."

Michael thinks about that. He is the kind of man you wish you could be, poised and confident, but salty somehow, as if he takes things seriously, but not too seriously.

"They used to broadcast every rocket launch on TV," he says. "Neil Armstrong, John Glenn. I'd sit on the living room rug and you could almost feel the flames."

"Did you ever make it up?"

"No. Flew fighter planes for a long time, then trained pilots. Couldn't bring myself to go commercial."

"Have they told you anything?" asks Scott. "About the plane?"

Michael unbuttons his jacket.

"Mechanically it seemed sound. The pilot didn't report any issues on an earlier run across the Atlantic that morning, and maintenance did a full service the week before. Plus, I looked over Melody's record, your pilot, and he's spotless—though human error—can't rule it out. We don't have the flight recorder yet, but they let me see the air traffic control reports and there were no maydays or alarms."

"It was foggy."

Michael frowns.

"That's a visual problem. Maybe you get some turbulence from temperature variation, but in a jet like that, flying by instruments, it wouldn't have been a factor."

Scott watches a helicopter come in from the north, gliding along the river, too far away to hear the blades.

"Tell me about her," he says.

"Emma? She's—was—You have kids and you think *I made you, so we're the same,* but it's not true. You just get to live with them for a while and maybe help them figure things out."

He drops his cigarette on the wet ground, puts a foot on it.

"Can you—" he says, "anything about the flight, about her, you can tell me?"

Her last moments, he is saying.

Scott thinks about what he can say—that she served him a drink? That the game was on and the two millionaires were jawing and one of the millionaire's wives was talking about shopping?

"She did her job," he says. "I mean, the flight was, what, eighteen minutes long? And I got there right before the doors closed."

"No, I understand," says the father, bowing his head to hide his disappointment. To have one more piece of her, an image, to feel one more time that he can learn something new, it's a way to keep her alive in his mind.

"She was kind," Scott tells him.

They stand there for a moment, nothing left to say, then Michael nods, offers his hand. Scott shakes it, tries to think of something to say that could address the grief the other man must be feeling.

But Michael, sensing Scott's turmoil, turns and walks away, his back straight.

The agents approach Scott on his way back to the cab. O'Brien is in the lead, with Gus Franklin on his heels—one hand on the agent's shoulder as if to say, *Leave the fucking guy alone.*

"Mr. Burroughs."

Scott stops, his hand on the taxi door.

"We really don't want to bother you today," says Gus.

"It's not called *bothering*," says O'Brien. "It's called *our job.*"

Scott shrugs, no way around it.

"Get in," says Scott. "I don't want to do this on camera."

The cab is a minivan. Scott rolls the door back, climbs inside, and sits on the back bench seat. The agents look at each other, then climb in also. Gus in front, O'Brien and Hex in the middle jump seats.

"Thank you," says Scott. "I've lived this long without being captured by helicopter camera—"

"Yeah, we noticed," say O'Brien. "You're not a big fan of social media."

"Any media," says Hex.

"How's the search going?" Scott asks Gus.

Gus turns to the driver, a Senegalese man.

"Can you give us a minute?"

"It's my cab."

Gus takes out his wallet, gives the man twenty dollars, then another twenty when that doesn't work. The driver takes it, climbs out.

"Hurricane Margaret is moving north from the Caymans," Gus tells Scott. "We've had to call off the search for now."

Scott closes his eyes. Maggie, Margaret.

"Yeah," says Gus. "It's a bad joke, but they name these things at the beginning of the season."

"You seem pretty upset," says O'Brien.

Scott squints at the agent.

"A woman died in a plane crash and now there's a hurricane named after her," he says. "I'm not sure how I'm supposed to seem."

"What was your relationship with Mrs. Bateman?" asks Hex.

"You guys have a way of saying words that's very judgmental."

"Do we?" says O'Brien. "It's probably comes from a deep-seated philosophical belief that everybody lies."

"I might give up on conversation entirely, if I thought that," says Scott.

"Oh no. Makes it fun," says O'Brien.

"People are dead," Gus snaps. "This isn't a game."

"With respect," says O'Brien, "*you* focus on what made the plane go down. We'll zero in on the human factor."

"Unless," says Hex, "the two things are actually the same."

Scott sits back and closes his eyes. They appear to be having this conversation without him now and he feels weary. The ache in his shoulder has subsided, but there is a headache creeping up the rim of his brain, a deep-tissue echo of the swelling barometric pressure outside.

"I think he fell asleep," says Hex, studying him.

"You know who sleeps in a police station?" says O'Brien.

"The guy who did it," says Hex.

"You boys should get your own radio station," says Gus. "Morning sports. Traffic and weather together on the eights."

O'Brien taps Scott's chest.

"We're thinking of getting a warrant to look at your paintings."

Scott opens his eyes.

"What would that look like?" he asks. "A warrant to look at art?" He pictures a drawing of a document, an artist's rendering.

"It's a piece of paper signed by a judge that lets us seize your shit," says O'Brien.

"Or maybe come over Thursday night," says Scott. "I'll serve white wine in paper cups and put out a tray of Stella D'oro breadsticks. Have you been to a gallery opening before?"

"I've been to the fucking Louvre," snaps O'Brien.

"Is that near the regular Louvre?"

"This is my investigation," says Gus. "Nobody's seizing anything without talking to me."

Scott looks out the window. All the mourners are gone now. The grave is just a hole in the ground, filling with rainwater as two men in coveralls stand under a canopy of elm and smoke Camel Lights.

"What practical value could my paintings have, in your mind," he asks.

He truly wants to know, as a man who has spent (wasted?) twenty-five years smudging color on canvas, ignored by the world, chasing windmills. A man who has resigned himself to impracticality and irrelevance.

"It's not what they are," says O'Brien. "It's what they're about."

"Disaster paintings," says Hex. "That's from your agent. Pictures of car wrecks and train crashes."

"Which," says O'Brien, "putting aside the intrinsic fucked-upness of that as an art form, is interesting to us on a procedural level. As in, maybe you got tired of looking for disaster to paint, decided to cause your own."

Scott looks at them with interest. What fascinating brains these men have, creating plots and deception from whole cloth. His eyes move to Gus, who is punching the bridge of his nose as if in great pain.

"How would that work?" Scott asks. "On a practical level. A penniless painter with a three-legged dog. A man who spends his days chasing something he can't define. A story with no verbs. How does this man—I don't even know how to put it—turn?"

"It happens all the time," says O'Brien. "Small men in small rooms thinking big thoughts. They start thinking things, going to gun shows, looking up fertilizer bombs online."

"I don't go online."

"The physical fucking library then. *Notice me*, is the point. Revenge."

"On who, for what?"

"Anyone. Everyone. Their mothers, God. The kid who buggered them in gym class."

"In the actual class?" says Scott. "In front of everybody?"

"See now you're joking, but I'm being serious."

"No. It's interesting to me is all," says Scott. "How your mind works. Like I said, I walk on the beach. I sit in coffee shops and stare into my cup. I think about image, about color and mixing media. This is new to me, this kind of television projection."

"Why do you paint what you paint?" asks Gus quietly.

"Well," says Scott, "I mean, I'm not sure really. I used to do landscapes and then I just started putting things in them. I guess I'm trying to understand the world. I mean, when you're young you expect your life to go well, or at least you accept that that's possible. That life can be navigated. If you choose a path, or even if you don't, because how many people do you know who end up on top by accident. They fall into something. But what I fell into was bourbon and my own asshole."

"I'm falling asleep over here," says O'Brien.

Scott continues because Gus asked, and, because he asked, Scott assumes he actually wants to know.

"People get up in the morning and they think it's another day. They make plans. They move in a chosen direction. But it's not another day. It's the day their train derails or a tornado touches down or the ferry sinks."

"Or a plane crashes."

"Yes. It's both real, and—to me—a metaphor. Or it was—ten days ago. Back when I thought painting a plane crash was just a clever way to hide the fact that I'd ruined my life."

"So you did paint a plane crash," says Hex.

"We're gonna wanna see that," says O'Brien.

Through the window, Scott watches the men drop their cigarette butts in the mud and grab their shovels. He thinks about Sarah

Kipling, who humored him on a sunny day in August, a weak hand-shake, a perfunctory smile. Why is she in the ground and not him? He thinks of Maggie, of her daughter, nine years old. They're both at the bottom of the ocean somewhere and he is here, breathing, having a conversation about art that is really a conversation about death.

"Come by anytime," he tells them. "The paintings are there. All you have to do is turn on the lights."

. . .

He has the cab drop him at Penn Station, figuring that with all the press at the funeral someone will have followed the cab, and as he pushes through the doors he sees a green SUV pull up to the curb and a man in a denim jacket jump out. Scott moves quickly to the subway, descending to the downtown number 3 train platform. Then he doubles back and makes his way to the uptown platform. As he does he sees his pursuer in the denim jacket appear on the downtown side. He has a camera out and as the uptown train sharks in, the man sees Scott and raises his camera to get a shot. Scott turns on his heels as the train screeches past him, obscuring his face. He hears the sluice of air and the subway ding and backs through the doors. He sits, holding his hand in front of his face. As the doors close he peers through his open fingers, and as the train pulls out he catches a glimpse of denim on the far track, camera still raised, praying for a shot.

Scott rides uptown three stops, then gets out and takes the bus go-ing downtown. He is in a new world now, collision city, filled with suspicion and distrust. There is no room for abstract thought here, no room to ruminate on the nature of things. This is the other thing that died in the turbulent Atlantic. To be an artist is to live at once in the world and apart from it. Where an engineer sees form and function, an artist sees meaning. A toaster, to the engineer, is an array of me-chanical and electrical components that work together to apply heat to bread, creating toast. To the artist, a toaster is everything else. It is a comfort creation machine, one of many mechanical boxes in a dwelling that create the illusion of home. Anthropomorphized, it is a hang-jawed man who never tires of eating. Open his mouth and put in the bread. But poor Mr. Toaster Oven. He's a man who, no matter how much he eats, is never truly fed.

· · ·

Scott eats cereal for dinner, still dressed in his borrowed suit, tie askew. It feels disrespectful to take it off somehow. Death, so permanent for the dead, should be more than just an afternoon activity for the mourners. So he sits and shovels and chews in all black, like a breakfast undertaker.

He is standing at the sink, washing his single dish and spoon, when he hears the front door open. He know it's Layla without looking, the sound of her heels and the smell of perfume.

"Are you decent?" she says, coming into the kitchen.

He lays his bowl on the dish rack to drain.

"I'm trying to figure out why you need place settings for thirty," he says. "Cowboys used to travel the country with a single plate and fork and spoon."

"Is that what you are," she asks. "A cowboy?"

He goes to the living room and sits on the sofa. She pulls the blanket off the roll-top bar and pours herself a drink.

"Are you keeping the booze warm or—?"

"I'm an alcoholic," he tells her. "I think."

She sips her drink.

"You think."

"Well, probably a safe bet, given that when I start drinking I can't stop."

"My father is the richest alcoholic on the planet. *Forbes* did an article, how he probably drinks three hundred thousand a year in top-shelf booze."

"Maybe put that on his tombstone."

She smiles, sits, her shoes dropping from her feet. She curls her right leg under her left.

"That's Serge's suit."

He reaches for the tie.

"I'm sorry."

"No," she says. "It's fine. He's in Romania now, I think. On to his next epic fuck."

Scott watches her drink her scotch. Outside the rain smacks and streaks the windows.

"I ate a peach once," he says, "in the Arizona desert, that was better than any sex I've ever had."

"Careful," she tells him. "I may take that as a challenge."

After she's gone he carries her glass to the sink. There is still a finger of scotch inside and before he pours it into the sink he holds it to his chin and smells, transported by that familiar earthy peat. *The lives we live*, he thinks, *are filled with holes*. He rinses the glass and lays it upside down to drain.

Scott goes into the bedroom and lies down on the bed, suit still on. He tries to imagine what it's like to be dead, but can't, and so he reaches over and turns off the light. The rain drums against the window glass. He stares at the ceiling, watching shadow streaks moving in reverse, raindrops slithering from down to up. Tree branches splayed in a Rorschach weave. The whiteness of the apartment is an empty canvas, a place waiting for its occupant to decide how to live.

What will he paint now? he wonders.

THREADS

THERE WAS AN answer. They just didn't have it yet. This was what Gus told his bosses when they pressed. It had been ten days since the crash. There was a hangar on a naval base out on Long Island where they collected the debris they'd recovered. A six-foot section of wing, a tray table, part of a leather headrest. It's where the remaining bodies would be brought when they were recovered—assuming they were found with the wreckage and didn't wash up on a beach like Emma Lightner or get pulled from a fisherman's net, like Sarah Kipling. Those bodies had been sent to local morgues and had to be recovered by federal mandate over a period of days. Jurisdiction was one of the many headaches you dealt with when investigating a crash into coastal waters.

Every day the divers put on wet suits, the pilots gassed their choppers, and captains divvied up the grid. Deep water is dark. Currents shift. What doesn't float, sinks. Either way, the more time that went by, the less likely it was that they would find what they were looking for. Sometimes, when the waiting was too great, Gus would call in a chopper and fly out to the lead ship. He'd stand on the deck and help coordinate the search, watching the gulls circle. But even in the middle of the action Gus was still just standing around. He was an engineer, a specialist in airplane design who could find the flaw in any system. The caveat was he needed a system to analyze—propulsion, hydraulics, aerodynamics. All he had was a torn pieces of wing, and the top-down pressure of a man being buried alive.

And yet even a small piece of wreckage tells a story. From the wing fragment they'd determined that the plane hit the water at a ninety-degree angle—diving straight down like a seabird. This is not a natural angle of descent for an airplane, which wants to glide on contoured wings. That suggested pilot error, even possibly a deliberate crash—although Gus reminded everyone of the possibility that the plane had actually descended at a more natural angle, only to impact a large wave head-on, simulating a nose-down crash. In other words, *We don't know anything for sure.*

A few days later, a chunk of the tail section was spotted off Block Island. From this they got their first look at the hydraulic system—which appeared uncompromised. The next day two more pieces of luggage were found on a Montauk beach—one intact, the other split open, just a shell. And so it went, piece by piece, like searching a haystack for hay. The good news was that the wreckage seemed to be breaking up underwater, revealing itself a little at a time, but then, four days ago, the finds stopped coming. Now Gus is worried they might never find the bulk of the fuselage, that the remaining passengers and crew are gone for good.

Every day he faces pressure from his superiors in Washington, who, in turn, face mounting demands from the attorney general and from a certain angry billionaire to find answers, recover those missing, and put the story to rest.

There is an answer. We just don't know it yet.

On Thursday he sits at a conference table reviewing the obvious with twenty-five bureaucrats, going over the things they already know they know. This is in the federal building on Broadway, home turf for Agent O'Brien of the FBI and Hex of the SEC, plus the half dozen subordinates they control. To O'Brien this crash is part of a larger story—terrorist threats and splinter cell attacks targeting American interests. To Hex the crash is only the latest piece in a war story about the US economy and the millionaires and billionaires who devote massive capital to the breaking of rules and laws. Gus is the only one in the room thinking about the crash as a singularity.

These people on *that* aircraft.

Beside him, the CEO of the private security firm responsible for the Bateman family is describing the process they use to assess threat levels. He's brought a six-man team with him, and they hand him documents as he speaks.

"—in constant contact with dedicated agents of Homeland Security," he is saying. "So if there was a threat, we knew about it within minutes."

Gus sits at the conference table, looking at his reflection in the window. In his mind he is on a Coast Guard cutter, scanning the waves. He is standing on the bridge of a naval frigate reviewing sonar imagery.

"I supervised a comprehensive review of all intel and activity myself," the CEO continues, "for a full six months before the crash, and I can say with complete confidence—nothing was missed. If somebody was targeting the Batemans, they kept it to themselves."

Gus thanks him, hands off to Agent Hex, who begins a review of the government's case against Ben Kipling and his investment firm. Indictments, he says, were handed down as planned the day after the crash, but Kipling's death gave the other partners the perfect scapegoat. So to a man, all have said that any trades with rogue nations (if they existed) were the brainchild of a dead man, laundered through their books as something else. They were duped, in other words. *I'm as much of a victim here as you*, they said.

Eighteen of the firm's accounts have been frozen. Total value, $6.1 billion. Investigators have tied the money to five countries, Libya, Iran, North Korea, Sudan, and Syria. They know from Kipling's phone records that Barney Culpepper called him thirty-nine minutes before the flight departed. Culpepper has declined to comment on what they discussed, but it's clear the call was to warn Kipling about the indictment.

As far as Agent Hex and his superiors at the SEC are concerned, the crash was a move by a hostile nation to silence Kipling and hamper their investigation. The question of exactly when the Kiplings were invited to fly back with the Batemans arises. The CEO of the security firm checks the logs. There's a communiqué from the Batemans' body man at eleven eighteen the morning of the flight, reporting a conversation with the principal (David Bateman, aka Condor) in which Condor stated Ben and Sarah would be flying back with them.

"Scott," says Gus absently.

"What?" says Hex.

"The painter," Gus clarifies. "He told us Maggie invited Sarah and her husband—it was earlier that morning at the farmers market, I think. And he'd already been invited—check the notes, but I think it was sometime Sunday morning. He ran into Maggie and the kids at the local coffee shop."

Gus thinks about his last conversation with Scott, sitting in a taxi at the cemetery. He'd hoped to have a more detailed discussion, going minute by minute through Scott's memories of the flight, boarding, the subsequent takeoff, and what he remembered from the air, but the conversation was hijacked by men looking for faces in the clouds.

In the absence of facts, he thinks, *we tell ourselves stories*.

This is clearly what the news media is doing—CNN, Twitter, *Huffington Post*—the twenty-four-hour cycle of speculation. Most of the reputable outfits are sticking to facts and well-researched op-eds, but the others—Bill Cunningham at ALC being the worst offender—are building legends, turning the whole mess into some giant soap opera about a lothario painter and his millionaire patrons.

Gus thinks of the boy, settled in now with his aunt and uncle in the Hudson River Valley. He drove out to meet them two days ago, sitting in their kitchen and drinking herbal tea. There is never a good time to question a young child, no perfect technique. Memories, which are untrustworthy even in adults, are unreliable at best in children, especially after a trauma.

He's not talking much, Eleanor said, bringing him his tea. *Ever since we got him home. The doctor says that's normal. Or, not normal, but not abnormal.*

The boy sat on the floor playing with a plastic front loader. After letting him get used to Gus's presence in the room, Gus settled on the floor beside him.

JJ, he said, *my name is Gus. We met before. At the hospital.*

The boy looked up, squinting, then went back to playing.

I thought we could talk about the airplane, when you went on the plane with your mommy and daddy.

And sissie, the boy said.

That's right. And your sister.

Gus paused, hoping the child would fill the silence, but he didn't.

Well, said Gus, *do you remember the plane? I know you were—Scott tells me you were asleep when it took off.*

The boy looked up at Scott's name, but didn't speak. Gus nodded to him encouragingly.

But, he said, *did you—do you remember waking up at all, before—*

The boy looked over at Eleanor, who had taken a place behind him on the floor.

You can tell him, sweetie. Just—anything you remember.

The boy thought about this, then took his digger and crashed it into a chair.

Raar, he yelled.

JJ, said Eleanor. But the boy ignored her, getting up and running around the room with the digger, smashing it into walls and cabinets.

On the floor, Gus nodded, climbed wearily to his feet, his knees popping.

It's okay, he said. *If he remembers anything, it'll come out. Better not to push.*

Now, in the conference room, a logistical conversation is in progress about the techniques a hit squad (from Libya, North Korea, et cetera) might have used to bring down the plane. The most likely scenario is a bomb planted at some point during the flight's time either at Teterboro or on the Vineyard itself. Schematics of the plane are brought out and they stand around the table pointing at possible hiding spots. The exterior of the plane is unviable, given the pilot's thorough visual examination before takeoff.

Gus has spoken to the ground-crew techs who refueled the jet on the runway, working-class men with Massachusetts accents who drink green beer on Saint Patrick's Day and eat hot dogs on July Fourth. No gaps can be found where a third party could have come aboard and planted an explosive device.

O'Brien floats (again) the idea that they should look at Charlie Busch, a last-minute addition to the crew. There are rumors, unconfirmed, that he may have dated the flight attendant, Lightner, but no hard proof. Gus reminds him that a thorough background check of Busch has been done. He was a jock from Texas, nephew of a US senator and something of a playboy, if his personnel file was to be believed. Nothing in the man's past suggests he might have crashed the plane deliberately, no matter what his dating profile said. He certainly didn't fit any known terrorist profile.

The day before Gus had been summoned to Washington to meet with Busch's uncle, Senator Birch. Birch was a lifer in the Senate, four terms in. He had a full head of white hair and the broad shoulders of a former college running back. Off to the side, his chief of staff sat typing on his cell phone, ready to step in if the conversation floated too far afield.

"So—what's the answer?" Birch asked him.

"Too early to tell, sir," Gus said. "We need the plane, need to analyze the systems, recover the bodies."

Birch rubbed his face.

"What a mess. Bateman *and* Kipling. And meanwhile, my poor sister."

"Yes, sir."

"Look," said Birch, "he was a good kid. Charlie. A little bit of a fuckup early on, but he pulled his shit together, as far as I can tell. Made something of himself. What are Jim Cooper's people saying at GullWing?"

"His record was good. Not great, but good. We know he was in London the night before the crash, that he socialized with a number of GullWing employees, and that Emma Lightner was there as well. But as far as anyone can tell, it was just another night. They went to a bar. Emma left early. We know that sometime that night your nephew switched flights with Peter Gaston. He wasn't meant to be on Flight Six Thirteen."

Birch shook his head.

"Bad luck."

Gus bobbled his head to say, *Maybe it was bad luck. Maybe it wasn't.*

"Your nephew caught a jump seat on a charter to New York the next day. We don't yet know why. Gaston says the switch was Charlie's idea. Said he just felt like going to New York. Apparently he was like that, though—impulsive."

"He was young."

Gus thought about that.

"He may also have had some boundary issues with women."

Birch made a face as if to say, *That's not a real thing.*

"What are you gonna do? He was a handsome guy. His whole life he basically skated by on a smile. If he was my kid I'da taken him out to the woodshed and beat some discipline into him, but his mama thought the sun rose and set up his ass. But I did what I could, made some calls, got him into pilot training at the guard, helped him find his footing."

Gus nodded. He was less interested in knowing what kind of person the copilot was, and more interested in understanding his physical and mental state on the day of the event. Planes don't crash because pilots grew up without fathers. Backstory gives you context, but it doesn't tell you what you really need to know. Which is, what happened in the eighteen minutes between the wheels leaving the tarmac and the plane touching down in the ocean? Were there any mechanical faults with the aircraft?

As far as he was concerned, the rest was just something to do while they waited for a real lead.

Across from him, Birch nodded to his aide. Time to wrap it up. He stood, extended his hand.

"If this things looks like it's going to reflect badly on Charlie, I want you to tell me. I'm not asking you to do anything illegal, just a heads-up. I'd like to protect the boy's mother as much as possible."

Gus stood, shook the senator's hand.

"Of course, sir," he said. "Thank you for seeing me."

Now, in a high-rise conference room, Gus watches himself in the glass, tuning out the suited men around him. They too are filling time. Right now the investigation is a game of Clue where the cards are missing. He needs a plane. Until then, all they can do is guess.

Hex bumps Gus's arm. He realizes O'Brien is talking to him.

"What?"

"I said I got a warrant," says O'Brien.

"For what?" Gus asks.

"The paintings. We seized them from Burroughs's studio about an hour ago."

Gus rubs his eyes. He knows from O'Brien's file that he is the son of a boarding school principal, Andover or Blair Academy, he can't remember which. This seems like as good way as any to design a judgment machine, one whose function is to police and punish—which is clearly how O'Brien sees his role in life.

"The man saved a child," he says.

"He was in the right place at the right time, and I'm wondering why."

Gus tries to keep his temper under control.

"I've done this job for twenty years," he says, "and no one has ever described being in a plane crash as being in the right place at the right time."

O'Brien shrugs.

"I gave you the chance to make this your idea. Now I'm moving on it myself."

"Just—bring them to the hangar," Gus tells him, then, before O'Brien can protest. "And you're right. We should look. I would have done it differently, but it's done now. So bring them to the hangar. And then pack your bags, because you're off the task force."

"What?"

"I brought you on because Colby said you were his best man, but we're not going to do *this*. It's my investigation, and how we treat the survivors *and* the suspects is a tone that I set. So it's done now. You seized artwork created by a man who may one day get a medal of honor from the president. You've decided he's hiding something, or maybe you just can't accept that life is full of random coincidence, that not everything that *seems* meaningful *is* meaningful, but the truth is, it's not your decision to make. So pack your shit. I'm giving you back to the FBI."

O'Brien stares at him, jaw tight, then stands slowly.

"We'll see," he says, and walks out.

PAINTING #3

YOU ARE UNDERWATER. Below you there is only darkness. High above, you see light, a gradual gray hinting toward white. There is texture to the murk, what appear to be black crosses peppering your field of vision. They are not obvious at first, these slashes of black, like something has been drawn and crossed out, but as your eyes adjust to the painting you realize they are everywhere, not simply brush technique, but content.

In the bottom right corner of the frame you can make out something shiny, a black object catching some glint of light from the surface. The letters *USS* are visible, the final *S* sinking below the edge of frame. Seeing it draws your eye to something else, cresting the very bottom of the canvas, the tip of something triangular, something primordial rising.

It is in this moment you realize that the crosses are bodies.

Leaked Document shows tension inside the Bateman crash Investigation, raises questions about the role of a mysterious passenger.

(Sept. 10, 2015, 8:16 p.m.)

BILL CUNNINGHAM (Anchor): Good evening, America. I'm Bill Cunningham. We're interrupting our regular programming to bring you this special report. ALC has acquired an internal memo written by Special Agent Walter O'Brien of the FBI to NTSB lead investigator, Gus Franklin, penned just hours ago. The memo discusses the team's current theories of the crash, and raises questions about the presence on the plane of purported crash hero, Scott Burroughs.

(BEGIN VIDEOTAPE)

CUNNINGHAM: As seen here, the document—which starts off cordial—shows disagreement between the investigators in how to handle the case going forward. As listed in the memo, investigators are currently working on four main theories. The first is mechanical error. The second is pilot error. The third is listed as *sabotage, possibly to impede a government investigation into Ben Kipling and his investment firm.* The final reads as quote *a terrorist attack, aimed at David Bateman, chairman of ALC News.*

But there is a fifth theory, raised here for the first time, one that questions the role played by Scott Burroughs in the crash. It is a theory Agent O'Brien clearly raised in person with the lead investigator earlier that day, only to be rebuffed, and so now, as he writes, quote: *and though I know you've said in person that you have no interest in this line of questioning, given recent revelations, I feel I must put in writing a possible fifth theory, and that is the idea that passenger Scott Burroughs either knows more than he's saying, or bears some culpability in events leading to the downing of the aircraft.*

And wait till you hear why, my friends. Quote, *Interviews with local vendors and residents of Martha's Vineyard suggest that Burroughs and Mrs. Bateman, wife of David, were very close and appeared to have a comfortable physical relationship—hugging in public. It is known that Mrs. Bateman had visited Mr. Burroughs at his studio and seen his work.*

And friends, as a personal friend of the family, I can tell you I don't read those words lightly, nor am I suggesting that an affair took place. But the question of why Mr. Burroughs was on that plane continues to nag at me. But fine, say they were friends, even good friends. There's no harm or shame in that. It's the next thing Agent O'Brien writes that is, to me, the bombshell.

And I quote, *Interviews with Mr. Burroughs's manager in New York confirm that he had several meetings with gal-*

lerists set for the week. Upon further questioning, however, a startling (to me) detail emerged, and that concerns the content of Mr. Burroughs most recent work. As described by Mrs. Crenshaw, there are fifteen paintings in total and all present a different photorealistic disaster scenario, with many of the images focused on large-scale transportation accidents. These include (1) a train derailment, (2) a fog-bound highway pileup, and (3) a large passenger plane crash.

Continuing on, O'Brien writes: *Given this, I can't stress enough the need for further questioning of the man who, at very least, is our only witness to events that resulted in the crash of this flight, and claims that he was knocked unconscious when the plane first pitched should be tested.*

Ladies and gentlemen, I have a hard time understanding why Gus Franklin, the team's lead investigator, would hesitate for a second to listen to the advice of what is clearly a very smart and very experienced agent of our nation's greatest law enforcement agency. Is it possible that Franklin has his own agenda? That the government agency he works for has an agenda or is being pressured by this liberal administration to bury this case quickly, lest it become a rallying cry for men and women who, like our heroic former leader, David Bateman, can't stomach any more business as usual?

For more on the story we turn now to ALC's Monica Fort.

ALLIES

WHEN SHE PULLS into the driveway, a car Eleanor doesn't recognize is parked under the elm tree. A Porsche SUV with a press sticker in the front window. Seeing it, Eleanor panics—the boy is inside with her mother—and she ditches Doug and runs to the house, banging through the front door, already calling—

"Mom?"

She scans the living room, moving deeper into the house.

"Mom?"

"In the kitchen, hon," her mother calls back.

Eleanor throws her bag onto a chair, hurries down the hall. She is already chewing two people out in her mind, her mother and whoever owns the Porsche.

"You're sweet," she hears her mother say, and then Eleanor is through the door and into the kitchen. There's a man in a suit and red suspenders sitting at the table.

"Mom," Eleanor barks, as the man hears the door and turns.

"Eleanor," he says.

Eleanor stops in her tracks, recognizing Bill Cunningham, news anchor. She has met him before, of course, at David and Maggie's parties, but he exists in her mind mainly as an oversize head on television, brow furrowed, taking about the moral bankruptcy of liberal minds.

When he sees her, he opens his arm, a patrician gesture, as if expecting her to run to him.

"The things we must endure," he says. "Savagery and setbacks. If you knew how many funerals I've been to in the last ten years—"

"Where's JJ?" says Eleanor, looking around.

Her mother pours herself some tea.

"Upstairs," she says. "In his room."

"Alone?"

"He's four," her mother tells her. "If he needs something he'll ask."

Eleanor turns and goes into the hall. Doug is coming toward her, looking puzzled.

"Who is it?" he asks.

She ignores him, takes the stairs two at a time. The boy is in his room, playing with a pair of plastic dinosaurs. Crossing the threshold, Eleanor takes a cleansing breath and forces a smile.

"We're back, we're back," she says breezily.

He looks up, smiles. She kneels on the floor in front of him.

"Sorry it took so long," she says. "There was traffic and Doug was hungry."

The boy points to his own mouth.

"Are you hungry?" Eleanor asks.

He nods. She thinks about what that means, bringing him downstairs into the kitchen. She is about to tell him to wait here, but then she thinks, *He's hungry*, followed by an intuition about the power of the boy in her arms. The strength he will give her, she who was always such a people pleaser.

"Okay, come on."

She holds out her arms. He climbs in and she lifts him from the floor and carries him downstairs. He plays with her hair as they go.

"There's a man in the kitchen," she tells him. "You don't have to talk to him if you don't want to."

Bill is sitting where she left him. Doug is at the fridge, digging around.

"I've got a Belgian ale," he says, "and this Brooklyn microbrew some friends of mine make."

"Surprise me," says Bill, then sees Eleanor and JJ.

"There he is," says Bill. "The little prince."

Doug grabs two bottles of the microbrew, comes over.

"It's a pilsner," he says, handing one to Bill, "not too hoppy."

"Fine," says Bill dismissively, putting the bottle down without looking at it. He smiles at the boy.

"You remember your uncle Bill."

Eleanor switches JJ to her right hip, away from him.

"Is that what this is," Eleanor asks, "a family visit?"

"What else?" he says. "I'm sorry I couldn't get here sooner. It's a terrible thing when your life becomes the news and the news becomes your life. But somebody had to be up there telling the truth."

Is that what you do? she thinks. *I thought you reported the news.*

"What is the latest on this thing?" asks Doug, sipping his beer. "We're, you know, we try to stay focused on the kid and not—" Then, worried he's alienated his celebrity guest, "I mean, you understand—watching the news isn't really—"

"Of course," says Bill. "Well, they're still looking for the rest of the plane."

Eleanor shakes her head. *Are they insane?*

"No. Not in front of JJ."

Doug's mouth gets tight. He has never liked being scolded by women, especially in front of other men. Eleanor sees it, adds it to the list of today's offenses. She puts the boy in a chair and goes to the fridge.

"She's right, of course," says Bill. "Women are better at these things than men. Feelings. We tend to focus on the facts. What we can do to help."

Eleanor tries to tune him out, focuses on feeding her nephew. He's a picky eater, not fussy but selective. He'll eat cottage cheese, but not cream cheese. He likes hot dogs, but not salami. It's just a question of dialing it in.

Bill, meanwhile, has decided it's his mission to get the boy to smile.

"You remember Uncle Bill, right?" he says. "I was at your baptism."

Eleanor brings the boy a cup of water. He drinks.

"And your sister," Bill continues, "at hers too. She was—such a beautiful girl."

Eleanor gives Bill a look. *Watch it.* He nods, shifts focus without hesitating, trying to show her he's a good listener, a good partner. That they're in this together.

"And I know I haven't been around much lately, unfortunately. Work and, well, your dad and me didn't always see eye-to-eye. *Too* close maybe. But, you know, there was love there. Especially on my end. But in the end it's what we do, grown-ups. You'll see. Or I hope you won't, but probably you will. We work too much at the expense of love."

"Mr. Cunningham," says Eleanor. "It's nice of you to visit, but this is—after we eat it's nap time."

"No. He napped this morning," her mother offers. Eleanor glares at her. She too is a people pleaser, Bridget Greenway, especially men. The original welcome mat. Their father, Eleanor and Maggie's, left their mother when Eleanor went off to college, divorcing her and moving to Florida. It was the smiling he couldn't take, their mother's constant Stepford grin. Today he lives in Miami and dates brooding divorcées with fake tits. He's meant to come next week, after Bridget leaves.

Bill picks up on the tension between mother and daughter. He looks at Doug, who raises his half-drunk beer as if in a toast.

"Good, right?" he says, oblivious.

"What?" says Bill, who has clearly decided Doug is some kind of hipster douchebag.

"The beer."

Bill ignores him, reaches over and ruffles the boy's hair. Four hours ago he stood in Don Liebling's office and faced down Gus Franklin from the NTSB and representatives of the Justice Department. They said they wanted to know where he got O'Brien's memo.

I bet you do, he told them, thumbing his suspenders.

Don Liebling straightened his tie and told the government shock troops that of course their sources were confidential.

Not good enough, said the attorney from Justice.

The black guy, Franklin, seemed to have his own theory.

Did O'Brien give it to you? Because of what happened?

Bill shrugged.

It didn't just fall out of the sky, he said. *That much we know. But I've been to court before, defending a source, and I'm happy to go again. I hear they validate your parking now.*

After the agents stormed out, Liebling closed the door and put himself in front of it.

Tell me, he said.

On the sofa, Bill spread his legs wide. He'd been raised without a dad by a weak woman who clung to shitbird men like she was drowning. She used to lock Bill in his room at night and go paint the town red with menstrual blood. And look at him now, a multimillionaire who tells half the planet what to think and when. The fuck if some silver spoon, Ivy League lawyer was going to shake him in his shoes. No way was he going to out Namor. This was about David. About his mentor. His friend. And okay, maybe they didn't get along that well at the end, but that man was his brother, and he will get to the truth here, no matter what the cost.

Like the spook said, he told Don, *it was the FBI man. They kicked him off the team and he was pissed.*

Liebling stared at him, wheels turning in his head.

If I find out, he started.

Gimme a break, said Bill, standing, then walked to the door, step by step, putting himself in the lawyer's face. *Forget you're in an office,* he said with his body. *Forget hierarchy and the laws of social behavior. This is a warrior you're facing, king stud on the open savanna, poised and ready to rip off your face, so either lower your horns or get the fuck out of my way.*

He could smell the salami on Liebling's breath, saw him blink, off balance, unprepared for the old bear versus bear, the dirt-pit cock-fight. For thirty seconds, Bill hate-fucked him with his eyes. Then Don stepped aside and Bill sauntered out.

Now, in the kitchen, he stands, deciding to take the high ground.

"Just a friendly visit," he says. "These are difficult times and you—well, to me you're family—you were family to David and that makes us—so I want you to know I'm looking out for you. Uncle Bill is looking out—watching over."

"Thank you," says Eleanor, bringing JJ a plate. "But I think we're going to be fine."

He smiles generously.

"I'm sure. The money will help."

There's something in his tone, a bite that belies the sympathy on his face.

"We're thinking of moving into the town house in the city," says Doug.

"Doug," Eleanor snaps.

"What? We are."

"It's a beautiful place," says Bill, thumbs hooking into his suspenders. "A lot of memories."

"I don't mean to be rude," says Eleanor coldly, "but I need to feed JJ."

"Of course," says Bill, "You're the—I mean, a boy this age still needs mothering, especially after—so don't feel you have to—"

Eleanor turns away from him, seals the ziplock with the turkey in it, puts it in the fridge. Behind her, she hears Bill stand. He's not used to being dismissed.

"Well," he says, "I should go."

Doug stands.

"I'll walk you out."

"Thanks, but there's—I can find it."

Eleanor brings JJ his plate.

"Here you go," she says. "There's more pickles if you want them."

Behind her, Bill walks to the kitchen door, stops.

"Have you spoken to Scott?" he asks.

At the name, the boy looks up from his meal. Eleanor follows his eyes to Bill.

"Why?"

"No reason," says Bill, "just, if you're not watching the news then maybe you haven't heard the questions."

"What questions?" asks Doug.

Bill sighs, as if this is hard for him.

"There's just—people are wondering, you know. He was the last one on the plane, and—what was his connection to your sister, really? And then, have you heard about his paintings?"

"We don't need to talk about this now," says Eleanor.

"No," says Doug, "I wanna know. He calls, you know. In the middle of the night."

Doug looks at his wife.

"You think I don't know, but I do."

"Doug," says Eleanor. "That's not his business."

Bill thumbs his suspenders, bites his lower lip.

"So you are talking to him," Bill says. "That's—I mean, just—be careful, you know? He's—look, it's just questions right now, and this is America. I'll fight to the death before I let this administration take away our right to due process. But it's early days, and these are real questions. And I just—I worry about—you've been hurt so much—already. And who knows how bad this'll get? So, my question is, do you need him?"

"That's what I said," says Doug. "I mean, we're grateful. What he did for JJ."

Bill makes a face.

"Of course, if you—I mean, a who-knows-how-long swim in the middle of the night. And with a busted arm, dragging a little boy."

"Stop," says Eleanor.

"You're saying," says Doug, picking up the idea like a germ—that the hero maybe isn't that much of a hero after all—"hold on. Are you saying—?"

Bill shrugs, looks at Eleanor, his face softening.

"Doug," says Bill, "come on. Eleanor's right. This isn't—"

He leans right, trying to see JJ around Eleanor's blocking body, then keeps bending "comically" until the boy looks at him. Bill smiles.

"You be a good boy," he tells him. "We'll talk soon. If you need anything, tell your—tell Eleanor to call me. Maybe we'll go see the Mets sometime. You like baseball?"

The boy shrugs.

"Or the Yankees. I've got a box."

"We'll call you," says Eleanor.

Bill nods.

"Anytime," he says.

. . .

Later, Doug wants to talk, but Eleanor tells him she's going to take JJ to the playground. She feels as if she's being squeezed inside a huge fist. At the playground she forces herself to be fun. She slides with the boy and bounces on the seesaw. Trucks in the sand, digging it, piling it, watching it fall. It's a hot day and she tries to keep them in the shade, but the boy just wants to run, so she feeds him water to keep him hydrated. A thousand thoughts are going in her head, colliding, each new idea interrupting the last.

Part of her is trying to put together why Bill came. Another part is parsing through what he said, specifically about Scott. What is she supposed to think, that the man who saved her nephew actually crashed the plane somehow and then faked his heroic swim? Every idea in that sentence is absurd in its own right. How does a painter crash a plane? And why? And what did he mean about Scott's relationship with Maggie? Was he saying there was an affair? And why drive out to the house to tell her this?

The boy taps her arm and points to his pants.

"You have to go potty?" she asks.

He nods, and she picks him up and carries him to the public bathroom. As she helps him with his pants, it hits her with a sway of vertigo that given his youth there is little chance he will remember his real parents when he's an adult. She will be the mother he thinks of the first Sunday of every May. Not her sister. But, she thinks, does that mean that Doug will be his father? The thought of it sickens her a little. Not for the first time she curses herself for the weakness of her youth, this need for constant companionship like an elderly widow who leaves the TV on and gets a dog.

But then she thinks maybe all Doug needs is a chance. Maybe inheriting a four-year-old boy will motivate him, turn him into a family man. Then again, isn't thinking a child can save your marriage the classic delusion? They've had JJ with them for two weeks now, and Doug isn't drinking any less, hasn't changed his comings and goings, hasn't treated her any better. Her sister is dead and the boy is now an orphan, but *What about Doug's needs?* he says with every thoughtless comment. What about how this affects him?

She helps JJ get his pants up and wash his hands. Uncertainty is making her light-headed. Maybe she's not being fair. Maybe she's still upset about meeting the estate attorneys and business managers, the finality of the thing. And maybe Doug's right. Maybe they should move into the house in the city, give JJ a sense of continuity—use the money to re-create the luxury he knows? But her instinct is that that would only confuse him. Everything has changed. To pretend otherwise feels like fraud.

"Ice cream?" she asks him as they walk back outside and the full heat of the day hits him. He nods. She smiles and takes his hand, leading him to the car. Tonight she will talk to Doug, lay it all out, how she's feeling, what she thinks the boy needs. They will sell the real estate and put the money into the trust. They will give themselves a monthly stipend that's big enough to cover any additional expenses the boy brings, but not enough to allow them to quit their jobs or become people of luxury. Doug won't like it, she knows, but what can he say?

The decision is hers.

RACHEL BATEMAN

JULY 9, 2006–
AUGUST 26, 2015

SHE REMEMBERED NONE of it. What details she knew had been told to her, except for the image of a rocking chair in a bald, bare attic, rocking back and forth on its own. She saw that chair from time to time in her mind, mostly in the ether on the verge of sleep, an old wicker rocker creaking toward and away, toward and away, as if to soothe a ghost, dog-tired and cross.

Her parents named her Rachel after Maggie's grandmother. When she was really little (she was nine now) Rachel decided she was a cat. She studied their cat Peaches, trying to move like it. She would sit at the breakfast table and lick the back of her hand, wiping her face with it after. Her parents put up with it until she told them she was going to sleep during the day and roam the house at night. Maggie, her mother, said, "Babe, I just don't have the energy to stay up."

Rachel was the reason they had bodyguards, the reason men with Israeli accents and shoulder holsters followed them everywhere. There were three normally. In the lingo of the business, Gil, the first, was a body man—paid to stay in direct physical proximity to the principal. In addition, there was an advance team, usually rotating, of four to six men who watched them from farther away. Rachel knew they were here because of her, because of what had happened, though her father denied it. *Threats*, he said vaguely, implying that running a TV news network was somehow more relevant to their daily threat level than the fact that his daughter had been kidnapped in her youth, and that quite possibly one or more of the kidnappers were still out there.

At least those were the facts in her head. Her parents had assured her, as had men from the FBI (as a favor to her father last year) and a high-paid child psychiatrist, that the kidnapping had been the work of a single, deranged man (Wayne R. Macy, thirty-six), and that Macy had been killed (shot through the right eye) during the ransom exchange by a lawman in a flak jacket, but not before Macy had shot and killed a second lawman in the opening salvo of a fleeting firefight. The dead lawman was Mick Daniels, forty-four, a former FBI agent and veteran of the First Gulf War.

All she remembered was a chair.

. . .

She was supposed to feel things. She knew that. A nine-year-old girl in summer, on the verge of her teen years. She had been out on the Vineyard with her mother and brother for the last two weeks, lying about. As a child of great wealth there were countless options available to her—tennis lessons, sailing lessons, golf lessons, horseback riding, whatever—but she didn't feel like being trained. She had studied piano for two years, but ultimately wondered *to what end* and moved on. She liked being home with her mom and her brother. That was basically it. She felt useful there—*a four-year-old boy is more than a handful*, her mother would say—and so Rachel played with JJ. She fixed him lunch and changed his pants when he had an accident.

Her mother told her she didn't have to do it, that she should go out, enjoy the day, but it was hard to do with a large Israeli man (three sometimes) following your every move. Not that she could argue the need for it. Wasn't she herself proof that you can't be too careful?

So she stayed home, lying on the porch or the back lawn,

staring at the ocean—blinded by it sometimes, that diamond sparkle. She liked to read books about wayward girls, girls who fit in nowhere, then discovered they had magic powers. Hermione, Katniss Everdeen. She'd read *Harriet the Spy* when she was seven and Pippi Longstocking, and they were competent, but in the end simply human. As she grew, Rachel felt she needed more from her heroines, more teeth, more fight, more power. She liked the thrill of danger they faced, but didn't want to have to actually worry about them. It made her too anxious.

Whenever she reached a particularly distressing section (Hermione versus the troll in *Harry Potter and the Sorcerer's Stone*, for example), she would walk the book inside and hand it to her mother.

"What's this?"

"Just tell me—does she make it?"

"Does who make what?"

"Hermione. A troll escaped, a giant—and she's—can you—just read it and tell me she's okay."

And her mother, who knew her well enough not to push, would stop whatever she was doing and sit, reading as many pages as it took to get the answer. Then she would hand the book back, her thumb marking a new spot.

"Start here," she'd say. "She didn't have to fight it. She just yelled at it that it was in the girls' bathroom and should go away."

They had a giggle about that, yelling at a troll, and then Rachel went back outside to read.

. . .

It started with the housekeeper. They didn't realize it, though, at the time. Her name was Francesca Butler, but everyone called her Frankie. This was when the family summered on Long Island, at Montauk Point, before private planes and helicopters, when they would just pile in the car and drive out on a Friday night, battling the shifting bulge, like the LIE was just a giant anaconda that had swallowed a traffic jam, the clot of snarled cars shifting downward in surges.

Her brother wasn't even an idea yet. It was just David and Maggie and toddler Rachel, sleeping in her car seat. The news channel was six years old and already a profit- and controversy-generating machine, but her father liked to say, *I'm just a figurehead. A general in a back room. Nobody knows me from Adam.*

The kidnapping would change that.

That was the summer of the Montauk Monster, which washed up on shore on July 12, 2008. A local woman, Jenna Hewitt, and three of her friends were walking on Ditch Plains Beach and found the creature.

"We were looking for a place to sit," she was later quoted saying, "when we saw some people looking at something... We didn't know what it was... We joked that maybe it was something from Plum Island."

Described by some as a "rodent-like creature with a dinosaur beak," the monster was about the size of a small dog and mostly hairless. The body was stocky and the limbs slender. It had two front paws with elongated, pale claws. Its tail was slim and approximately equal in length to the head and neck combined. It was short-faced, wearing an expression of agony or dismay; the postorbital part of the skull appeared long and stout. It had no teeth visible in the upper jaw, instead showing what could be described as a hooked beak of bone. The lower jaw contained a large pointed canine and four post-canines with tall, conical cusps.

Was it a raccoon, as some suggested, that had decomposed in the ocean? A sea turtle whose shell had been removed? A dog?

For weeks, photos of the bloated, distended corpse appeared in tabloids and online. Speculation increased that it was something cooked up in a lab at the Plum Island Animal Disease Center, a mile or so offshore. The Real Island of Dr. Moreau, they started calling it.

But eventually, as with all things, a lack of answers led to a lack of interest, and the world moved on.

But when David and Maggie arrived in Montauk that weekend, monster fever was full-blown. Roadside T-shirt kiosks had sprung up. For five dollars you could see the spot where the monster was found, now just an anonymous patch of sand.

The Batemans were renting a house on Tuthill Road. It was a two-story white clapboard across the road from a small lagoon. Mostly secluded, the house was directly parallel to a stalled modern remodel, sheet plastic flapping over a gaping wound to the living room. In years prior, Rachel's family had rented a house farther north, on Pinetree Drive, but that one had sold to a hedge-fund billionaire in January.

Their new clapboard home (Maggie would stay out there with Rachel through Labor Day weekend, and David would drive out on Fridays and take off the last week of August) was cozy and quaint. It had a large farmhouse kitchen and a sloped and creaky porch. The bedrooms were on the second floor, Mom and Dad facing the ocean. Rachel's room (complete with a Victorian-era crib) faced the lagoon. They brought Frankie (the nanny) with them, a third pair of hands, as Maggie liked to say. Frankie sat in the back of the Audi with Rachel, engaged in a road-trip-long game of pick up Rachel's pacifier, wipe it off, and hand it back. Frankie was a night-school nursing student at Fordham who helped take care of Rachel three days a week. She was twenty-two, an émigré from the wilds of Michigan who moved to New York with a boyfriend after college, only to have him leave her for the bass player in a Japanese surf punk band.

Maggie liked her, because spending time with Frankie made her feel young, something that being with David in his world—populated entirely by people like David, in their forties, and some even in their fifties and sixties—did not. Maggie had just turned twenty-nine. She and Frankie were seven years apart. The only difference between them, really, was that Maggie had married a millionaire.

"You got lucky," Frankie used to tell her.

"He's nice," Maggie would say.

"So even luckier," Frankie would say and smile. Among her friends there was a lot of talk about landing a rich man. They used to put on short skirts and tall boots and go to bottle-service clubs, hoping to land a Wall Street up-and-comer with a full head of hair and a dick of steel. But Frankie wasn't really like that. She had a softer edge, having been raised with goats and chickens. Maggie never worried that Frankie was out to steal her husband away. It would be absurd, after all, to trade in your twenty-nine-year old trophy wife for a twenty-two-year-old, like a cliché on steroids. And yet, she supposed, stranger things had happened.

Just a few years earlier she had been the one paid to teach other people's children. A twenty-two-year-old preschool teacher, living in Brooklyn. She rode her bike over the Brooklyn Bridge every morning, using hand signals like she was supposed to. The foot traffic on the bridge was minimal at that hour. Joggers mostly. A few health-conscious commuters brown-bagging their way across the river. She wore a lemon-yellow helmet, her long brown hair fluttering behind her like a cape. She didn't wear headphones or sunglasses. She braked for squirrels, stopping mid-span to take in the view and have some water. In the city she took Chambers to Hudson and rode north, checking behind her every minute or so for taxi drivers on cell phones or slicksters in German automobiles who'd stopped looking at the road.

She got to work every morning by six thirty. She liked to straighten up before the kids arrived, to restock supplies. The schoolhouse was small, just a few rooms in an old brick building next to a parking lot that had been turned into a playground. It was on a tree-lined street in a part of the West Village that had an almost old London feel. Sidewalks curved like crooked fingers. On Facebook she once posted that she liked this part of the city best, its timeless, genteel nature. Like most right-brained people in New York, she tried never to go above 14th Street.

The first student usually arrived at eight, strolling or shuffling or scootering, hand in hand with Daddy or Momma, sometimes still half asleep, lying in a futuristic Maclaren or Stokke supercarriage. Little Penelope or Daniel or Eloise, shoes so small they could fit on a doll, tiny short-sleeved shirts with checks or stripes like one day they would grow up to be wealthy nerds, just like Daddy. Four-year-old girls in eighty-dollar dresses with one pigtail or flowers in their hair picked from a pot outside a brownstone by a harried parent on the way to school.

Maggie was always there to greet them, standing in the asphalt playground, smiling with sunny exuberance as soon as they appeared, like a dog who jumps to its feet at the sound of a key in the front door.

Good morning, Miss Maggie, they cried.

Good morning, Dieter, good morning Justin, good morning Sadie.

She gave them a hug or mussed their hair, then said good morning to Mommy or Daddy, who often grunted their replies, having started texting the moment their kid's feet touched school property. They were lawyers and advertising executives, magazine editors and architects. The men were forty or older (the oldest father in her class was sixty-three). The women ranged from late-twenties supermodels with children named Raisin or Mudge to harried working moms in their thirties who had given up on finding a living, breathing husband and convinced a gay friend to cum in a cup in exchange for six weekends a year at the summer house in the Catskills and the honorary title of "uncle."

She was a patient teacher, sometimes inhumanly so, warm and thoughtful, but firm when necessary. In their evaluations, some parents wrote that they wished they could be more like her, a twenty-two-year-old girl who always had a smile and a kind word, even to a screaming child who had just screwed their nap.

Maggie usually left the school around four, walking her mahogany-colored bike to the curb before snapping her chin strap and lurching into traffic. In the afternoons she liked to ride over to the river and take the bike path south. She stopped sometimes to sit on a bench by the water and watch boat traffic, the helmet forgotten atop her head. She would close her eyes every time the wind blew. On days when the temperature was over ninety she might buy a shaved ice from a Mexican man with a cart—usually cherry—and sit in the grass eating it with the flat thumbnail of a tiny spoon. On those days she would take off her helmet and lay it on the grass like a lemon drop. She'd relax on her back in the cool green and stare at the clouds for a long time, flexing her toes on the lawn, before reaffixing her helmet and starting the long ride home, her lips stained the color of childhood.

How distant it seemed to her now, just seven years later, the unemployed mother of a toddler or, more precisely, the pampered wife of a millionaire.

As soon as they arrived at the house, she and David would go to the market and stock up on supplies, while Frankie stayed home with Rachel. Montauk at this point wasn't the brand-name scene of the Hamptons, but you could feel it creeping in. The local general store now sold specialty butters and artisanal jams. The old hardware store stocked heirloom linens and had been remodeled in distressed white bead board.

From a roadside stand they bought tomatoes, fat and cracked, and went home and sliced them thick and ate them with sea salt and olive oil. There was no such thing as hardship anymore, certainly nothing more than a fleeting inconvenience, and yet when she reflected on it late at night Maggie was amazed by how her sense of life's difficulties ebbed and adapted to fit her new circumstances. Whereas, before David, she would have to bike home in the rain some days through gridlock traffic and scour her apartment for pennies to do laundry (and even that couldn't truly be considered hardship in a world where children went to bed hungry), now she found herself exasperated by foolish things—misplacing the keys to her Lexus, or being told by the clerk at D'Agostino that he didn't have change for a hundred. When she realized this, how soft she was becoming, how *privileged*, Maggie felt a wave of self-loathing. They should give all their money away, she told David, raise their kids hand-to-mouth with the proper values.

"I want to go back to work," she'd say.

"Okay."

"No. I mean it. I can't just sit around all day. I'm a worker. I'm used to working."

"You're taking care of Rachel. You tell me all the time how much work that is."

She would twist the phone cord between her fingers, keeping her voice down so as not to wake the baby.

"It is. I know. And I just can't—I'm not going to have my daughter raised by nannies."

"I know. We both feel that way, which is why it's so magical that you can—"

"I just—I don't feel like myself anymore."

"That's a normal postpartum—"

"Don't do that. Don't make it about my body, like I can't control myself."

Silence from the other end. She couldn't tell if he was being taciturn or writing an email.

"I still don't understand why you can't take more time," she said. "We're only up here a month."

"I hear you. It's frustrating for me too, but we're in the middle of a big expansion on a corporate level—"

"Never mind," she said, not wanting to hear the details of his job. It's not like he enjoyed her war stories—the woman who cut ahead of them at the supermarket, the playground soap operas.

"Okay. I'm just saying—I'm going to try to make it out Thursday night at least twice."

Now it was she who was silent. Upstairs Rachel was asleep in her crib. Maggie could hear sounds from the other side of the kitchen that made her think Frankie was changing over the laundry. On the edge of things was the sound of the ocean, that tectonic drum, the heart-beat of the earth. At night she slept like the dead because of it, some core genetic pulse once again in phase with the rhythm of the sea.

It was late the following week that Frankie disappeared. She had gone into town to see a movie at the little old art house theater. She was meant to be home by eleven and Maggie didn't wait up. It was her night with Rachel—rising at her earliest cries and soothing her back to sleep—and her instinct on those nights was always to front-load her sleep, so as soon as the sun went down (sometimes before) her head would be down on the pillow, her tired eyes perpetually reading and rereading the same short pages of her book, without ever making it past the second chapter.

In the morning when she rose with Rachel (who had come to bed with her just after midnight) and Frankie wasn't up, Maggie thought it was a little strange, but the girl was young and maybe she met some-one at the movie or went for a drink after at the old sailor pub on the way home. It wasn't until eleven when she knocked on Frankie's door—they'd agreed that Maggie would have the day to herself—and then opened it and found the bed empty and unused, that Maggie be-gan to worry.

She called David at the office.

"What do you mean *she's gone?*" he said.

"Just, I don't know where she is. She didn't come home and she's not answering her phone."

"Did she leave a note?"

"Where would she leave a note? I checked her room and the kitchen. She went to a movie. I called her cell, but she's not—"

"Okay, let me—I'll make a few calls, check to see if she came back to the city—remember she was having troubles with that boy—Troy something—and if I don't turn up anything or she's still not back, I'll call the local police."

"Is that—I don't want to overreact."

"Well, we're either worried or we're not. You tell me."

There was a long pause, while Maggie thought it through—during which time she also made a snack for Rachel who was biting at her ankles.

"Babe?"

"Yeah," she said, "it's weird. You should call."

Three hours later, she was sitting across from the local sheriff, Jim Peabody, whose face looked like the last piece of jerky in the jar.

"Maybe I'm just being silly," she said, "but she's usually so responsible."

"Don't do that to yourself, Mrs. Bateman. Take your power away. You know this girl and you had an instinct. You gotta trust that."

"Thank you. I—thank you."

Jim turned to his deputy—female, heavyset, about thirty.

"We'll visit the theater, talk to Sam, see if he remembers her. Grace'll go by the pub. Maybe she stopped in there. You said your husband was calling her people?"

"Yes. He phoned some friends and some of her family—nobody's heard from her."

Rachel was coloring—mostly on the paper—at a small round kid's table Maggie had picked up at a flea market, the kind that came with two adorable little folding chairs. Maggie was amazed the girl hadn't bothered them once during the entire visit, as if she understood the importance of what was happening. But then she had always been a sensitive and serious child, so much so that Maggie sometimes worried she was depressed. She'd read an article about it in the *Times*—children with depression—and now it hung in the back of her mind, a Big Idea that could tie all the little ideas together—the poor sleeping, the shyness—or maybe she was just allergic to wheat.

This is what motherhood was, one fear eclipsed by another.

"She's not depressed," David would say. "She's just focused."

But he was a boy, and a Republican to boot. What did he knows about the intricacies of female psychology?

When there was still no word by sundown, David put the rest of the week's activities on hold and drove out. In the minutes after he arrived, Maggie felt like a balloon deflating: The strong business-as-usual facade she had put on disappeared. She poured herself (and him) a stiff drink.

"Rachel asleep?" he asked.

"Yes. I put her in her room. Do you think that's a mistake? Should I have put her in ours?"

He shrugged. It made no real-world difference, he thought. It was just an issue in his wife's head.

"I called the sheriff on the way in," he told her when they were sitting in the living room. The ocean roared in through the screens, invisible in the black night air. "He said she definitely went to the movie. People remembered her—a pretty girl dressed like the city—but nothing from the bar. So whatever happened, it happened on her way home."

"I mean, what could have happened?"

He shrugged, sipped his drink.

"They checked the local hospitals."

Halfway through her drink, Maggie grimaced.

"Shit. I should have done that. Why didn't I—"

"It's not your job. You were busy with Rachel. But they checked the hospitals and no one fitting her description came in last night. No Jane Does or anything."

"David, is she dead? Like lying in a ditch or something?"

"No. I don't think so. I mean, the longer this goes the less positive I'm gonna spin it, but right now it could just be—I don't know—a bender."

But they both knew Frankie wasn't the bender type.

That night Maggie slept fitfully. She had a dream that the Montauk Monster had come to life and was slithering out of the lagoon and across the road, moving inevitably toward their house, leaving a slug trail of gore behind. She stirred and rolled, imagining it surging up the siding to the second-floor window—Rachel's window. Had she left the window open? It was a warm night, stuffy. She usually closed it, but this time—given her absent brain, her distraction over Frankie—had she left it open?

Maggie woke with her feet already on the floor, a mother's panic moving her down the short hall to her daughter's room. The first thing that struck her was that the door was closed. Maggie knew she hadn't closed it. In fact, she always put a doorstop in front of it to keep it from closing in the wind. She hit the door almost at a run, and the knob wouldn't turn. Her shoulder hit the door hard, making a loud bang.

Behind her she heard David stir, but from inside the room she heard nothing. She tried the knob again. It was locked.

"David!" she yelled, then again, her voice taking on a tinge of hysteria.

Then he was behind her, moving fast but still sluggish, some part of his sleeping brain left behind.

"It's locked," she said.

"Move," he told her.

She did, flattening herself against the wall to let him get in there. He grabbed the knob in his big hand and tried to turn it.

"Why isn't she crying?" Maggie heard herself say. "She must be awake. I must have woken her up. Banging."

He tried the knob again, then gave up, put his shoulder into it. Once, twice, three times. The door stretched the jamb but didn't open.

"Motherfucker," he said, now fully awake, taken by fear. Why wasn't his daughter crying? Instead, all that came under the door was the surge of the ocean.

He stepped back and kicked the door hard, reaching down for some primal Neanderthal strength. The jamb shattered this time, one of the hinges popping, the door flying open and bending backward, like a boxer who's been gut-punched.

Maggie pushed past him into the room and screamed.

The window was wide open.

The crib was empty.

. . .

Maggie stood staring at it for a long time, as if the sight of an empty crib was a surreal impossibility. David ran to the window and looked out, first one way, then another. Then he was out of the room past her. She heard his feet thundering down the stairs, then heard the front door slam and heard his feet running through first grass, then sand, then gravel, as he made his way to the road.

He was on the phone downstairs when she found him.

"Yes," he said. "This is life or death. I don't care what it costs."

A pause as he listened.

"Okay. We'll be up."

He hung up, eyes locked on some point in the middle distance.

"David?" she said.

"They're sending someone."

"Who?"

"The company."

"What do you mean someone? Did you call the cops?"

He shook his head.

"This is my daughter. They *took* my daughter. We're not using public servants."

"What are you talking about? Who took her? She's missing. They need to—we need to have someone, a lot of someones, out there looking for her right now."

He stood and started turning on lights, going room to room, making the house look awake. She followed.

"David?"

But he was lost in thought, some kind of masculine scheme playing out in his head. She turned and grabbed the car keys off the hook.

"Well, I can't just sit here."

He caught up to her at the door, grabbed her wrist.

"It's not—" he said, "she didn't wander off. She's two. Someone climbed up to her window and took her. *Why?* For money."

"No."

"But first," he said, "first they took Frankie."

She leaned against the wall, her head spinning.

"What are you—"

He put his hands on her, not in a rough way, but firmly, to let her know she was still connected to the earth, to him.

"Frankie knows us. She knows our routines, our finances—or at least a general sense of our finances—she knows which room Rachel sleeps in. Everything. They took Frankie so she could give them Rachel."

Maggie went over and sat down on the sofa, purse still on her arm.

"Unless she's working with them," said David.

Maggie shook her head, shock calming her, making her limbs feel like seaweed floating on the waves.

"She's not. She's twenty-two. She goes to night school."

"Maybe she needs money."

"David," said Maggie, looking at him. "She's not helping them. Not on purpose."

They thought about this, what it might take to compel a conscientious young woman to give up a sleeping toddler placed in her charge.

Forty-five minutes later, they heard car tires on the driveway. David went outside to meet them. He came back in with six men. They were clearly armed and had what could only be described as a military demeanor. One of the men wore a suit. He was olive-skinned, graying at the temples.

"Mrs. Bateman," he said. "I'm Mick Daniels. These men are here for your protection and to help me ascertain the facts."

"I had a dream," she found herself telling him.

"Honey," said David.

"About the Montauk Monster. That it was sliding up the side of our house."

Mick nodded. If he found this odd at all, he didn't say so.

"You were sleeping," he told her, "but some part of you heard something. It's genetic training. An animal memory of spending a few hundred thousand years as prey."

He had them show him their bedroom and then Rachel's room, had them retrace their steps. Meanwhile, two of his men examined the perimeter. The other two set up a command center in the living room, bringing in laptops, telephones, and printers.

They met up again with the full group ten minutes later.

"A single set of footprints," they were told by a black man working a piece of bubble gum, "and two deeper marks directly under the window. We think that's from the ladder. Tracks lead to a smaller structure on the property, then disappear. We found a ladder inside. Extendable. Tall enough to reach the second floor, I think."

"So he didn't bring his own ladder," said Mick, "he used one that was already here. Which means he knew it was here."

"We had a rain gutter fall last weekend," said David. "The landlord came and put it up, used a ladder. Not sure where he got it, but he drove up in a sedan, so he didn't bring it with him."

"We'll look at the landlord," said Mick.

"No visible tire marks on the road," said a second man, holding a rifle. "Nothing fresh, at least. No sense of which direction he or they may have taken."

"I'm sorry," said Maggie, "but who are you people? Somebody took my baby. We need to call the police."

"Mrs. Bateman," said Mick.

"Stop calling me that," she said back.

"I'm sorry, what would you like me to call you?"

"No. Just—will somebody please tell me what's happening?"

"Ma'am," Mick said, "I am a paid security consultant for the biggest private security firm in the world. Your husband's employer retained my services at no cost to you. I served eight years with the Navy SEALs, and eight more with the Federal Bureau of Investigation. I've worked three hundred kidnapping cases with a very high rate of success. There is a formula at work here. As soon as we figure it out, I promise you we will call the FBI, but not as helpless bystanders. My job is to control the situation from now until we get your daughter back."

"And can you do that?" Maggie said, as if from another dimension. "Get her back?"

"Yes, ma'am," said Mick. "I can."

BLANCO

IT'S THE WHITE walls that wake him. Not just in the bedroom; the whole apartment is embossed in pure ivory—walls, floors, furniture. Scott lies there, eyes open, heart beating fast. To sleep in white limbo, like a new soul suspended in ether waiting for a door to open, for the bureaucratic check box of body assignment, praying breathlessly for the invention of color, can drive a man mad apparently. Scott tosses and turns under white sheets on white pillows, his bed frame painted the color of eggs. At two fifteen a.m. he throws off the covers and puts his feet on the floor. Traffic sounds creep through the double-pane windows. He is sweating from the exertion of forcing himself to stay in bed, and he can feel his heart beating through the walls of his rib cage.

He goes to the kitchen, and considers making coffee, but it feels wrong somehow. Night is night and morning is morning and to confuse the two can lead to lingering displacement. A man out of time, phase-shifted, drinking bourbon for breakfast. There is an itch behind Scott's eyes. He goes into the living room, finds a credenza, opens all the drawers. In the bathroom he finds six tubes of lipstick. In the kitchen he finds a black Sharpie and two Hi-Liters (pink and yellow). There are beets in the fridge, frazzled and fat, and he takes them out and puts a pot of water on the stove to boil.

They are talking about him on the television. He doesn't need to turn it on to know that. He is part of the cycle now, the endless worrying. Whitewashed floorboards creak underfoot as he pads into the living room (white). The fireplace is still charred from recent use, and Scott crouches on the cool brick lip and searches the ashes. He finds a lump of charcoal by feel, pulling it forth like a diamond from a mine. There is a floor-length mirror on the far wall, and as he straightens he catches sight of himself. By coincidence his boxers are white and he wears a white T-shirt—as if he too is slowly being consumed by some endless nothing. Seeing himself in the mirror in this all-white world— a pale, white man draped in white cloth—he considers the possibility that he is a ghost. *What is more likely*, he wonders, *that I swam for miles with a dislocated shoulder and a toddler on my back, or that I drowned in the churning salt, like my sister all those years back, her panicked eyes and mouth drawn under the greedy black water of Lake Michigan?*

Charcoal in hand, he goes around the apartment turning on lights. There is an instinct to it, a feeling not exactly rational. Outside he can hear the grinding brakes of the day's first trash truck, its geared jaws pulverizing the things we no longer need. The apartment now fully illuminated, he turns a slow circle to take it all in, white walls, white furniture, white floors, and this single turn becomes a kind of spin, as if once started it cannot be stopped. A white cocoon punctuated by black mirrors, window covers raised.

Everything capable of producing color has been piled on the low white coffee table. Scott stands with ashen charcoal in hand. He switches the lump from left to right, his eyes drawn to the feral black stain there on his left palm. Then, with gusto, he claps his dirty palm to his chest and draws it down across his belly, smearing black ash onto the cotton.

Alive, he thinks.

Then he starts on the walls.

. . .

An hour later he hears a knock on the door, and then the sound of the key in the lock. Layla enters, still dressed for evening in a short gown and high heels. She finds Scott in the living room, throwing beets at the wall. His T-shirt and shorts are *ruined* in the common parlance, or *much improved* in the eyes of this particular painter—stained black and red. The air smells vaguely of charcoal and root vegetables. Without acknowledging her arrival, Scott pads over to the wall and crouches, lifting the smashed tuber. Behind him, he hears footsteps in the hall, hears the sound of a breath drawn in. A startled rush.

He hears it and doesn't hear it, because, at the same time, there is nothing but the sound of his own thoughts. Visions and memory, and something more abstract. Urgent—not in the sense of earth shattering, but as it feels to urinate finally after a long drive home, stuck in stop-and-go traffic, the long run to the front door, fumbling for keys, fly unbuttoned shakily on the hurried move. And then the artless stream. A biological necessity fulfilled. A light, once off, now turned on.

The painting is revealing itself to him with every stroke.

Behind him, Layla watches, lips parted, taken by a feeling she doesn't really understand. She is an intruder on an act of creation, an unexpected voyeur. This apartment, which she owns and decorated herself, has become something else. Something unexpected and wild. She reaches down and unstraps her high heels, carrying them to the speckled white sofa.

"I was at a thing uptown," she says. "One of those endless *who cares*—and I saw your light on from the street. All the lights."

She sits, one leg folded under the other. Scott runs his hand through his hair, his scalp now the color of cooked lobster. Then he goes to the coffee table, chooses a lipstick.

"A fifty-year-old man said he wanted to smell my panties," she says. "Or wait, that's not it—he wanted me to take off my panties and slip them into his pocket and then later, when his wife was sleeping, he said he would hold them to his nose and jerk off into the sink."

She unfolds and walks to the liquor cabinet to pour herself a drink.

Seemingly oblivious, Scott tests the lipstick color on the wall, then re-caps it, chooses a different shade.

"Imagine his wide eyes when I told him I wasn't wearing any," Layla says, watching him select a color called Summer Blush. She sips her drink. "Do you ever wonder what things were like before?"

"Before what?" says Scott, not turning.

She lies back on the sofa.

"I worry sometimes," she says, "that people only talk to me because I'm rich or they want to fuck me."

Scott is a laser beam, focused on a spot.

"Sometimes," he says, "they're probably just wondering—do you want to order an appetizer or potentially a cocktail."

"I'm not talking about if it's their job. I'm saying in a room full of people. I'm saying socially or at a business meeting. I'm talking about somebody looking at me and thinking, *There's a human being with something meaningful to add to the great debate.*"

Scott caps the lipstick and steps back to inspect his work.

"When I was seven," he says, "I ran away from home. I mean, not from home, but from the house. I climbed a tree in the backyard. *This'll show them*, I thought, for who remembers what reason. My mom—from the kitchen window—saw me up there, a boy in the bough of a tree with his knapsack and a pillow, glaring, but she just went about making dinner. Later, I watched them eating at the kitchen table—Mom, Dad, my sister. *Pass the biscuits.* After the dishes were done, they sat on the sofa watching TV. *Real People*, possibly *Full House*. I started getting cold."

He smudges charcoal, perfecting an effect.

"Have you ever tried sleeping in a tree?" he asks. "You have to be a panther. One by one the house lights go out. I'd forgotten to bring food, is the thing, or a sweater. So after a while I climb down and go inside. The back door is open. My mother has left a plate of food on the table for me with a note. *Ice cream in the freezer!* I sit and eat in the dark, then go upstairs to bed."

"What are you saying?"

"Nothing. It's just something I did."

He smudges charcoal lines on the drywall, adding shadows.

"Or maybe," he says, "what I mean is, people can say all kinds of things without ever opening their mouths."

She stretches her arms and legs away from her body, turning her hip to the ceiling.

"They're saying on the news that the boy stopped talking," she says. "That he hasn't spoken a word since the accident. I don't know how they know, but that's what they're saying."

Scott scratches his face, leaving an inky smudge on his temple.

"When I was drinking," he says, "I was what they call a motormouth. Just one thing after another, mostly the things I thought people wanted to hear, or—that's not true—things I thought were provocative. The *truth*."

"What was your drink?"

"Whiskey."

"So male."

He uncaps the yellow Hi-Liter, rubs the wet felt absently across his left thumb.

"The day I sobered up, I stopped talking," he says. "What was there to say? You need hope to form a thought. It takes—I don't know—*optimism* to speak, to engage in conversation. Because, really, what's the point of all this communicating? What difference does it really make what we say to each other? Or what we do, for that matter?"

"There's a name of that," she says. "It's called depression."

He puts the Hi-Liter down, turns slowly, taking in the work. Shape and color, open to interpretation. He feels exhausted all of a sudden, now that the room has depth, dimension. As his eyes reach Layla, he sees she has removed her dress and is lying naked on the sofa.

"You weren't kidding about the underwear," he says.

She smiles.

"All night I was so happy," she says, "knowing I had a secret. Everybody talking about what happened, the mystery—a plane crashed. Was it terrorism? Some kind of *kill the rich* beginning-of-the-end scenario. Or some North Korean mosquito swat to keep Kipling from narcing. You should have been there. But then things turn, become more—personal. All these moneyed elitists talking about the boy, will he ever talk again."

She studies him.

"Talking about you."

Scott goes to the kitchen sink, washes his hands, watching ash and lipstick run down the drain. When he comes back the sofa is empty.

"In here," she calls from the bedroom.

Scott thinks about that—what a naked woman in his bed will lead to—then he turns and goes into the study. The walls here are still white. It offends his sense of accomplishment, so he presses his stained torso to the drywall, leaving a body shape like Wile E. Coyote. He goes over to the desk and picks up the phone.

"Did I wake you?" he asks when she answers.

"No," says Eleanor. "We're up. He had a nightmare."

Scott pictures the boy tossing and turning, the inside of his head a raging sea.

"What's he doing right now?"

"Eating cereal. I tried to get him back to sleep, but he wouldn't have it. So I found *WordWorld* on PBS."

"Can I talk to him?"

He hears her put down the phone, hears the muffled sound of her voice—*JJ!*—across the room. Surrendering to gravity, Scott lies on the floor, the phone cord stretching along with him. After a second he hears the plastic of the receiver dragged across a hard surface, then breathing.

"Hey, pal," says Scott. He waits. "It's Scott. I was—looks like we both woke up, huh? You had a bad dream?"

From the other room, Scott hears Layla turn on the TV, mainlining the twenty-four-hour news cycle. Through the phone he hears the little boy breathing.

"I was thinking about maybe coming up there—to see you," says Scott. "You could show me your room or—I don't know. It's been hot here. In the city. Your aunt says you're near the river. I could maybe teach you how to skip stones, or—"

He thinks about what he has just said, *Let's you and I visit another large body of water.* Part of him wonders if the boy screams every time the toilet flushes, if he shies from the sound of the filling tub.

"What helps me with fear," he says, "being afraid, is preparation, you know? Knowing how to do things. Like if a bear attacks they say you're supposed to play dead. Did you know that?"

He feels the weight of exhaustion pulling on him from deep below the floor.

"What about lions?" the boy says.

"Well," says Scott, "I'm not sure there. But I tell you what. I'll get the answer and tell you when I see you, okay?"

A long silence.

"Okay," says the boy.

Scott hears the boy drop the phone, then the sound of its retrieval.

"Wow," says Eleanor. "I don't know what to—"

It hangs between them, this miracle worker exchange. Scott doesn't want to talk about it. The fact that the boy will speak to him and no one else is simply a fact, as far as he's concerned, without what psychologists call *meaning*.

"I told him I'd visit," says Scott. "Is that okay?"

"Of course. He'd—we'd like that."

Scott thinks about the inflection of her voice.

"What about your husband?" he asks.

"There are very few things he likes."

"You?"

A pause.

"Sometimes."

They think about that for a while. From the bedroom, Scott hears a sigh, but he can't tell if it's a human noise or a sound effect off the screen.

"Okay," says Scott. "Sun'll be up soon. Try to get a nap today."

"Thanks," she says. "Have a nice day."

A nice day. The simplicity of it makes him smile.

"You too," he says.

After they hang up, Scott lies there for a beat, flirting with sleep, then climbs to his feet. He follows the sound of the television, peeling off his T-shirt and dropping it on the floor, then takes off his boxers and walks to the bedroom, turning off lights as he goes. Layla is half under the covers, posing hip-up—she knows what she looks like, the power of it—her eyes arranged coyly on the screen. Chilly now, Scott climbs into bed. Layla turns off the TV. Outside, the sun is just starting to rise. He lays his head on the pillow, feeling first her hands and then her body move toward him. Waves climbing a white sand beach. She arranges herself across his hips and torso. Her lips find his neck. Scott feels the warmth of the comforter pulling him down. The white box has been vanquished. Limbo is now a place. Her hand touches his chest. Her leg floats up along his shin and settles across his thighs. Her body is hot, the arc of her breasts flush against his arm. She nuzzles and whispers into the groove of his neck, taking her time.

"You like talking to me," she says, "right?"

But he is already asleep.

PAINTING #4

AT FIRST IT looks like a blank canvas. A long white rectangle covered in gesso. But stepping closer you can see there's a topography to the white, shadows and valleys. White paint has been built up in layers, and there are hints of colors underneath, the blush of something hidden. And you think, maybe the canvas isn't blank after all. Maybe the image has been covered, erased by white. The truth is, the naked eye alone will never be able to uncover the story. But if you take your hand and run it over the valleys and ridges of gesso, if you close your eyes and allow the topographic truth to seep through, then maybe the contours of a scene begin to leak through.

Flames. The outline of a building.

Your imagination does the rest.

PUBLIC / PRIVATE

A CAR HORN wakes him, long and insistent. Layla is gone. The horn comes again. Scott gets to his feet, walks naked to the window. There is a news crew outside, satellite van parked on the curb, dish deployed.

They have found him.

He steps back from the curtain, finds the remote, turns on the television. The image of a house appears, a white three-story with blue windows and black stars on a tree-lined street in New York City. It is the house he's standing in. A news scroll slides along under the house, displaying words and numbers—the NASDAQ down 13 points, Dow Jones up 116. On the left-hand side of the screen, Bill Cunningham occupies his own box, leaning into the lens.

"—he's shacking up, apparently, with the famous radical heiress, whose father gave over four hundred million dollars to lefty causes last year. You remember, dear viewers, the man who tried to buy the 2012 election. Well, this is his little girl. Although—not so little anymore—look at these pictures of her from a film festival in France earlier this year."

Onscreen, the house slides to a smaller box, replaced in the main window by still images of Layla in a series of revealing ball gowns, clipped from style sheets and scandal rags. There is a bikini shot long-lensed from an actor's yacht.

Scott wonders if Layla is in the house, watching this.

As if hearing his thoughts, the apartment door opens. Layla comes in. She is dressed for a day of meetings, it appears.

"I didn't tell anyone," she says. "I swear."

Scott shrugs. He never assumed she did. In his mind they are both an endangered species, discovered mid-molt by a curious child with poor impulse control.

Onscreen, he watches fifteen curtained windows, a narrow front door painted blue, two garage doors, also blue. The only thing shading his safe house from view is a narrow sapling, just a stick really with a halfhearted spray of green leaves. Scott studies the house he's in on TV, concerned but also strangely fascinated, like a man watching himself being eaten alive. It seems he cannot avoid becoming a public figure now. That he must participate in this commercial dance.

How strange, he thinks.

Layla stands beside him. She is thinking about saying more, but doesn't. After a moment she turns and wanders out of the apartment again. Scott hears the apartment door close, then the sound of her heels on the staircase. He stands staring at the house on television.

Bill Cunningham, looking energized, says:

"—movement in an upstairs window just moments ago. Sources tell us that Ms. Mueller lives in the house alone, which—how many bedrooms are there, dear viewers? Looks like at least six to me. And I can't help but make some connections here—the head of a conservative news network dies in mysterious circumstances, and then the lone survivor of the plane crash shacks up with the daughter of a left-wing activist. Well, some people might call it a coincidence, but I do not."

Onscreen one of the garage doors starts to open. Scott leans forward, watching more than just television now. He half expects to see himself pull out, but instead a black Mercedes emerges, Layla behind the wheel wearing oversize sunglasses. The news cameras move in, looking to block her way, but she pulls out quickly—more than willing to run them over—and makes a left turn, roaring off up Bank Street toward Greenwich before they can pen her in.

In her wake, the garage door closes.

"—the homeowner, definitely," says Cunningham. "But I'm wondering, potentially, was this Burroughs fellow crouched down in the rear seat well, like some jailbreaker from a Peckinpah film."

Scott turns off the TV. He is alone in the house now, standing naked in a white room, sun casting shadows on the floor. If he rations what he has, eats one meal a day, he can stay in this apartment for six days. Instead, he takes a shower, dresses for the day. *Magnus*, he thinks. If anyone talked, it was him. But when he calls Magnus, the Irishman claims ignorance.

"Slow up," says Magnus. "What house is on television?"

"I need you to rent me a car," Scott tells him after talking in circles around it. Magnus is uptown in what used to be Spanish Harlem, half in the bag, though it's only ten in the morning.

"You put in a good word, yeah?" says Magnus. "With Layla? Whispered a little something in that beautiful ear. Magnus is the best painter. Something along those—"

"Last night. I went on at length about your use of color and light."

"Right on, boyo. Right fecking on."

"She was hoping to come by this weekend, maybe see the new work."

"I've gone full chubby," says Magnus, "just in the last few seconds. The head is purple and engorged, like a snakebite."

Scott crosses to the window. The curtains are sheer, but not see-through. Scott tries to look down, aware that people are out there looking back at him. He catches a glimpse of a second news van pulling into the curb.

"Doesn't have to be a big car," he says. "I just need it for a couple of days to drive upstate."

"Want me to come?" says Magnus.

"No. I need you here," Scott replies. "Holding down the fort. Layla likes to stay up all night, if you get my meaning."

"Consider it held, my friend. I've got enough Viagra to last until Halloween."

After they hang up, Scott grabs his jacket, walks into the living room, then stops short. In all the chaos he has forgotten the hours he spent last night eradicating the white. He stands now in a cube of charcoal and lipstick, beet stains dried in ruby streaks. The Martha's Vineyard farmers market surrounds him—a study for a painting in three dimensions—so that the room's furniture appears to be set in the middle of the open square. There is the fishmonger on the far wall, open coolers of ice below a long white card table; rows of vegetables, triple trays of berries. And faces, reconstructed from memory, sketched quickly with crumbling coal.

And there, seated on a white canvas chair, is Maggie, her head and shoulders sketched on the wall, her body outlined on the fabric of the chair. She is smiling, eyes shadowed by a big summer hat. Her two children flank her on either side of the chair, the girl, standing to her shoulder, on the right. The boy, half obscured behind a side table, on the left—just his tiny arm visible, attached to a slice of shoulder, a striped shirt, stripes the color of beets, stopping in the middle of his biceps, the rest of him hidden by wood.

Scott stands frozen in the middle of this scene, out of time, surrounded by ghosts. Then he goes downstairs to face the crowd.

JACK

I NEVER LIKED to exercise," said Jack LaLanne. "But I like results."

This was clear from his triceps definition alone, not to mention the Clydesdale heft of his beer-barrel thighs. A man of average height, bursting at the seams of his short-sleeved jumpsuit. In his house he kept an exercise museum, packed with obscure tech, most of it self-made. Jack invented the leg extension machine in 1936, you see. His approach was to work a muscle until it failed, believing, as he did, in the power of transformation through deep-tissue annihilation.

In the beginning, he wore a T-shirt and your standard pair of pants to train. He liked the feeling he got from stressing the weave. Then he had the idea to display himself in fitted jumpsuits—a uniform of self-improvement—so he went to the Oakland Pants Factory. He gave them sketches, an array of color choices. Blues and grays mostly. An Afro-American woman took his measurements with a cloth tape, rolling around him on a squeaky metal chair. In those days wool was the only fabric that would stretch, and so they made the jumpsuits out of that, milled as thin as the material would allow. Jack liked them shiny, he told her, peacocking, and sleeveless to show his rolling arms and taper at the waist.

Jack wore them so tight you could see what he ate for breakfast.

A local health store paid Jack to create a local access show for

KGO-TV. He taught people about the power of diet, designing workouts for every muscle, from toe to tongue. Six years later, the show went national. People ate breakfast to images of Jack bouncing on his tiptoes. They ran in front of their television, aping what they saw, bending at the waist and rotating their arms in bird-like windmills. As things picked up steam, certain words and phrases entered the American lexicon. *Jumping jack, squat thrust, leg lift.*

His jumpsuits had a tone-on-tone belt that cinched at the waist.

In his prime, Jack was a square-jawed hourglass of a man, his ink-black shag cut into a classic Italian wave on his head. Frankie Valli, for example. To most people in the early years he existed only in black and white, an ethnic fireplug pointing at anatomy charts, explaining what went on inside the human body. *See*, he seemed to say, *we're not just animals. We're architecture. Bones and sinew and ligament as a foundation for a rolling musculature.* Jack showed us that everything about the human anatomy was connected and could be used in glorious tandem.

To smile was to use an entire system of muscles, powered by joy.

One day he showed Americans how to get their faces "ath-u-letic looking," opening and closing his mouth comically wide, to the take-me-out-to-the-ball-game lilt of a sports organ.

Then, in the 1970s, Jack went full color, bounding onto a wood-paneled set in shiny blues and purples. He became a kind of talk-show host, interviewing bodybuilders about diet and lifestyle. It was the era of *Mutual of Omaha's Wild Kingdom*. Vietnam had been lost, American men had walked on the moon, and Nixon seemed poised to resign in disgrace. You tuned in because you liked his boundless energy. You tuned in because you were tired of looking down and seeing your own stomach. You tuned in to get your heart rate moving and turn your life around.

"Now, direct from Hollywood," boomed the announcer, "here's your personal health and fitness instructor, Jack LaLanne."

For thirty minutes what you got was *can do* gumption. You got a corporate-sponsored attitude adjustment. You got mountains to climb, inspiration. You got skills.

"Isn't it better to be happy with a problem," he said, "than to be miserable with it?"

Don't wallow, Jack told a nation stumbling under recession. *When life gets hard, you need to get harder.*

This was during Jack's inspirational phase, when he realized that what people needed was not just a muscular regimen, but a better way of looking at the world. The network would throw back from commercials and there he'd be, the jumping jack man, sitting backward on a metal chair, laying down the science.

"You know," he'd say, "there are so many slaves in this country. Are you a slave? You're probably saying, Jack, how can you be a slave in this wonderful free country of America? I don't mean a slave in the idea that you're thinking of it. I'm talking about you're a slave when you can't do the things you want when you want to do them. Because you are a slave, just like the slaves of old who were captured and put in chains. They were shackled, you know, and not allowed to go anyplace."

Jack looked directly into the lens.

"You're a slave just about as much as that."

And at this point he leaned forward and pointed right at the camera, enunciating each syllable.

"You're a slave to your own body."

The mind, said Jack, *remains active until the day you die, but it is a slave to the body—bodies that have become so lazy all they want to do is sit. The dawn of the couch potato. And you've allowed it to be that way.*

"Instead of you ruling your body," he said, "your body is ruling you."

It was the dawn of the television age, and already the lethargy had set in, that flicker-glow hypnotism. The idiot box. And here was Jack speaking truth to power, trying to break you from the smothering shackles of the modern world.

This is not complicated shit, he told you with his eyes, the movement of his body seeming to answer every question he asked. No French philosopher living or dead could convince Jack LaLanne that the problems of man were existential. It was a matter of will, of perseverance, of mind over matter. Where Sartre saw ennui, Jack saw energy. Where Camus saw pointlessness and death, Jack saw the board-breaking power of repetition.

Jack rose to power in the era of Buzz Aldrin and Neil Armstrong, the age of John Wayne. America was the go-getter nation, as far as he was concerned. There was no challenge too great, no obstacle too big.

Jack told us that America was the nation of the future, that we were all on the verge of traveling to a science-fiction nirvana in gleaming rocket ships.

Except, as far as Jack was concerned, we should be running there.

HE IS ASSAULTED by artificial light, framed by cameras with halogen spots. Scott squints reflexively, ensuring that the first image the world sees of him is of a man wincing slightly, left eye bowed in squint. Bodies surge forward as he steps from the front door, men with shoulder-mounted cameras and women with balled microphones, trailing chords across the gum-stained sidewalk.

"Scott," they say. "Scott, Scott."

He settles in on the threshold, door half open, in case he needs an easy escape.

"Hello," he says.

He is a man starting a conversation with a crowd. Questions are hurled toward him, everybody speaking at once. Scott thinks of what this street once was, a forested stream winding toward a muddy river. He holds up his hand.

"What's the goal here?" he asks.

"Just a few questions," says one of the journalists.

"I was here first," says another, a blond woman holding a microphone with the letters *ALC* embossed on a rectangular box. Her name, she says, is Vanessa Lane, and she has Bill Cunningham speaking into her ear from mission control.

"Scott," she says, pushing to the front, "what are you doing here?"

249

"Here on this street?" he asks.

"With Ms. Mueller. Is she a friend of yours, or more maybe?"

Scott thinks about this. *Is she a friend or more maybe.* He's not sure what the question means really.

"I'd have to think about that," he says. "Whether we're friends. We just met really. And then there's her point of view—how she sees things—because maybe I get it wrong, the meaning, which—who hasn't done that before, thinking something is black when it's really white."

Vanessa frowns.

"Tell us about the crash," she says, "what was it like?"

"In what sense?"

"Out there alone, the raging ocean, and then you hear the boy crying."

Scott thinks about this, his silence peppered by other questions, shouted in 5/6 time.

"You're looking for a comparison. This is like that. An analogy to help you understand."

"Scott," yells a brunette with a microphone, "why did the plane crash? What happened?"

A young couple approaches from the east. Scott watches as they cross the street to avoid the spotlight. He is the accident now, rubbernecked by pedestrians.

"I suppose I'd have to say it was like nothing," Scott tells Vanessa, not ignoring this new question, but simply focused on the last. "Certainly there's no comparison for me. The size of the ocean. Its depth and power. A moonless sky. Which way is north? Survival, at its basest form, isn't a story. Or, I don't know, maybe it's the only story."

"Have you spoken to the boy?" someone shouts. "Was he scared?"

Scott thinks about that.

"Wow," he says, "That's—I don't know that that's a question for me to—the four-year-old brain—I mean, that's an entirely different conversation. I know what the experience was for me—a speck in a vast and hostile darkness—but for him, at this moment in development, biologically, I mean. And with the nature of fear—at a certain level— the animal power of it. But again, at his age—"

He breaks off, thinking, aware that he is not giving them what they want, but concerned that their questions are too important to answer in the moment, to define in passing, simply to meet some kind of arbitrary deadline. *What was the experience like? Why did it happen? What does it mean going forward?* These are subjects for books. They are questions you meditate over for years—to find the right words, to identify all the critical factors, both subjective and objective.

"It's an important question," he says, "and one we may never really know the answer to."

He turns to Vanessa.

"I mean, do you have kids?"

She is twenty-six at most.

"No."

Scott turns to her cameraman, in his forties.

"You?"

"Uh, yeah. A little girl."

Scott nods.

"And see, then there's gender, and the time of night, how he was asleep when the plane went down, and did he think it was a dream maybe? At first. Like maybe he was still sleeping. So many factors."

"People say you're a hero," shouts a third reporter.

"Is that a question?"

"Do you think you're a hero?"

"You'd have to define the word for me," says Scott. "Plus, what I think doesn't really matter. Or—that's not true—what I think about myself hasn't always proven to be accurate, according to the world at large. Like, how in my twenties I thought I was an artist, but really I was just a kid in his twenties who thought he was an artist. Does that make sense?"

"Scott," they shout.

"I'm sorry," says Scott, "I can tell I'm not giving you what you want."

"Scott," says Vanessa. "This is from Bill Cunningham directly. Why were you on that plane?"

"You mean, in a cosmic sense, or—"

"How did you end up on the plane?" she says, correcting herself.

"Maggie invited me."

"Maggie is Margaret Bateman, wife of David."

"Yes."

"And were you having an affair with her, with Mrs. Bateman?"

Scott frowns.

"Like a sexual affair?"

"Yes. Just as you are now having an affair with Ms. Mueller, whose father donates millions to liberal causes."

"Is that a real question?"

"People have a right to the truth."

"Just because I've been inside her house, you're saying I've had—that she and I have had sex. This is your Einstein conclusion."

"Isn't it true that you wooed your way onto that plane?"

"In order to what—crash into the sea and have to swim ten miles to shore with a busted shoulder?"

He feels no anger, just bafflement at the line of questioning.

"Isn't it true the FBI has questioned you multiple times?"

"Does two count as multiple?"

"Why are you in hiding?"

"You say *in hiding* like I'm John Dillinger. I'm a private citizen, living his life in private."

"You didn't go home after the crash. Why not?"

"I'm not sure."

"Maybe you feel you've got something to hide."

"Staying out of sight is not the same thing as hiding," says Scott. "I miss my dog. That's for sure."

"Tell us about the paintings? Is it true the FBI has seized them?"

"No. Not that I—they're just pictures. A man stands in a shed on an island. Who knows why he paints what he paints? He feels like his life is a disaster. Maybe that's where it starts. With irony. But then—he sees something greater there, a key maybe to understanding. Is this—? Am I answering your—"

"Is it true you painted a plane crash?"

"Yes. That's one of the—it feels like, to me, I mean, we're all gonna die. That's—biology. All animals—but we're the only ones that—know. And yet we—somehow we manage to put this profound knowledge into some kind of a box. We know, but at the same time we don't. And yet in these moments of mass death—a ferry sinks, a plane crashes—we are brought face-to-face with the truth. We too will die one day, and for reasons that have nothing to do with us, our hopes and dreams. One day you get on a bus to go to work and there's a bomb. Or you go Walmart looking for savings on Black Friday and get crushed by a mob. So—what started as irony—my life, the disaster—opened a door."

He chews his lip.

"But the man in the shed is still just a man in a shed, you know?"

Vanessa touches the plastic in her ear.

"Bill would like to invite you to come to the studio for a one-on-one interview."

"That's nice of him," says Scott. "I think. Except the look on your face doesn't seem like you're being nice. More like the police."

"People are dead, Mr. Burroughs," she says. "Do you really think now is the time for nice."

"Now more than ever," he tells her, then turns and walks away.

It takes a few blocks, but eventually they stop following him. He tries to walk normally, aware of himself both as a body in space and time, and as an image viewed by thousands (millions?). He takes Bleecker to Seventh Avenue and jumps in a cab. He is thinking about how they found him—a man in a locked apartment with no cell phone. Layla says she didn't talk, and he has no reason to doubt her. A woman with a billion dollars doesn't lie unless she wants to, and from the way she acted it seemed like Layla liked having Scott as her own little secret. And Magnus, well, Magnus lies about a lot of things, but this doesn't feel like one of them. Unless they gave him money, but then why did Magnus end their phone call by hitting Scott up for a hundred bucks?

The universe is the universe, he thinks. *I suppose it is enough to know there is a reason without having to know what it is. Some new kind of satellite maybe? Software that burrows into our bones while we sleep? Yesterday's science fiction becomes today's IPO.*

He was an invisible man and now he's not. What matters is that he runs toward something and not away. Sitting in the back of a cab, Scott pictures the boy eating cereal in front of the television late at night—unable to sleep—watching a dog drawn from the letters *d-o-g* talk to a cat drawn from the letters *c-a-t*. If only real life were that simple, where everyone we met and every place we went was fashioned from the pure essence of its identity. Where you looked at a man and saw the letters *f-r-i-e-n-d*, and looked at a woman and saw the word *w-i-f-e*.

The screen is on in the cab, playing clips from late-night television. Scott reaches forward and turns it off.

GIL BARUCH

JUNE 5, 1967–
AUGUST 26, 2015

THERE WERE LEGENDS about him, stories, but more than stories. *Theories* might be a better word. Gil Baruch, forty-eight, Israeli expat. (Though one of the theories was that he owned a home on the razor's edge of the West Bank, an edge he himself had forged single-handedly from Palestinian land, driving up one day in an old jeep and setting up his tent, enduring the stares and taunts of the Palestinians. Rumors he had chopped the wood himself, poured the foundation, a rifle strap over his chest. That the first house had been torched by an angry mob, and Gil—rather than using his prodigious sniper skills or hand-to-hand prowess—had simply watched and waited, and when the crowd dispersed he urinated his disdain into the ashes and started again.)

That he was the son of Israeli royalty, no one disputed, his father, Lev Baruch, being the trusted right hand of Moshe Dayan, renowned military leader, mastermind of the Six Day War. They say Gil's father was there in 1941 when a Vichy sniper put a bullet through the left lens of Dayan's binoculars, that it was Gil's father who cleaned out the glass and shrapnel and stayed with Dayan for hours until they could be evacuated.

They said Gil was born on the first day of the Six Day War, that his birth coincided with the opening shot down to the second. Here was a child forged in war from the loins of a military hero, born of cannon recoil. Not to mention, people said, that his mother was the favorite granddaughter of Golda Meir, the only woman tough enough to forge an entire nation inside the belly of an Arab state.

But then there were others who said Gil's mother was just a milliner's daughter from Kiev, a pretty girl with a wandering eye who never left Jerusalem. This is the nature of legend. There's always someone lurking in the shadows, trying to poke holes. What's undisputed is that his oldest brother, Eli, was killed in Lebanon in 1982, and that both his younger brothers, Jay and Ben, were killed in the Gaza Strip during the Second Intifada—Jay annihilated by a land mine and Ben in an ambush. And that Gil lost his only sister in childbirth. This was part of the legend, that Gil was a man surrounded by death, that everyone close to him died sooner than later, and yet Gil prevailed. He was rumored to have been shot six times before turning thirty, to have survived a knife attack in Belgium, and to have shielded himself from an explosion in Florence by hiding in the belly of a cast-iron tub. Snipers had targeted him and missed. Bounties on his head, too numerous to list, went perpetually uncollected.

Gil Baruch was an iron nail in a burning building, left gleaming in the ashes after everything else had been destroyed.

And yet all that death and sorrow hadn't gone unnoticed. There was a biblical quality to the travails of Gil Baruch. Even in Jewish terms his suffering was exceptional. Men would clap him on the back in bars and buy him drinks, and then remove themselves to a safe distance. Women laid themselves at his feet, as they would on the tracks of a train, hoping that in the collision of bodies they would be annihilated. Crazy women with fiery tempers and bountiful G-spots. Depressive women, fighters, biters, poets. Gil ignored them all. At his core he knew that what he needed in his life was *less* drama, not more.

And yet the legends prevailed. During his tour in private security, he had bedded some of the most beautiful women in the world, models, princesses, movie stars. There was a theory, prominent in the 1990s, that he had taken Angelina Jolie's virginity. He had the olive skin, hawk nose, and heavy brow of a great romantic. He was a man with scars, both physical and emotional, scars he carried without complaint or remark, a taciturn man with a glint of the ironic in his eyes (as if deep down he knew he was the butt of a comic joke), a man who carried weapons and slept with a gun under his pillow, his finger on the trigger.

They said a man had not yet been born that Gil Baruch could not best. He was an immortal who could only be killed by an act of God.

And yet what else can one call a plane crash, except the fist of God sent to punish the bold?

. . .

He had been with the family for four years, joining their detail when Rachel was five. It had been three years since the kidnapping, three years since David and Maggie felt the cold chill of discovery—an empty crib, an open window—in the middle black of night. Gil slept in what old-world architects would have called the maid's quarters—a monk's cell behind the laundry room in the city, and a larger room facing the driveway on the Vineyard estate. Depending on the current threat level—ascertained from email analysis, as well as conversations with foreign and domestic analysts, both private and in the government, based on the current melange of extremist threats and the controversial nature of current ALC network programs—Gil's support team grew and shrank, numbering at one point after the 2006 Iraq surge a dozen men with Tasers and automatic weapons. But, baseline, there were always three. A trinity of eyes watching, calculating, coiled, and ready to act.

Their travel was planned in the home office, always in consultation with the on-site team. Commercial flights were no longer optimal, nor was public transportation, although Gil indulged David's desire to ride the subway to the office a few times a month, but never in any kind of pattern, a day chosen at random, and on those days they first sent a decoy in the town car, exiting the building dressed in David's clothes, head down, hurried out by his team and stuffed into the backseat.

On the subway, Gil stood far enough from David to let him feel like a man of the people, but close enough to intervene if outside agents chose to strike. He stood with his thumb resting on the hilt of a curved folding blade, hidden on his belt. A blade so sharp it could cut paper and was rumored to be poisoned with the venom of the molten brown recluse. There was a small semi-automatic pistol tucked somewhere undetectable, one David had seen his body man pull once without seeming to move. A homeless man charged them screaming outside the Time Warner building, holding some kind of pipe, and David took a fast step back, looking to his aide. One minute Gil's hand was empty. The next he held a snub-nosed Glock, produced from the ether like a magician revealing a dull and scarred coin.

Gil liked the rocking of the subway, the corner shriek of metal on metal. He had a deep-marrow certainty that his life would not end underground. It was an instinct he had learned to trust. Not that he feared death. There were so many people he had lost, so many familiar faces now waiting for him on the other side—if there was another side, and not just tar-black silence. But even that didn't sound bad, an end to the Sisyphean immensity of life. At least the eternal question would be answered, once and for all.

The Torah, it should be noted, makes no clear reference to the afterlife whatsoever.

As he did every morning, Gil rose before dawn. It was the fourth Sunday in August, the family's last on the Vineyard. They had been invited to Camp David for the Labor Day weekend, and Gil had spent much of yesterday coordinating security with the Secret Service. He spoke four languages, Hebrew, English, Arabic, and German, joking that it was important for a Jew to know the language of his enemies, so he could tell when they were plotting against him.

This joke, of course, was lost on most listeners. It was the look on his face when he told it, like a mourner at a funeral.

The first thing Gil did after he rose was change his status to *active*. He did it instantly, the moment his eyes opened. At most, he slept four hours a night, waiting an hour or two after the family went to sleep, and rising an hour or two before they woke. He liked that quiet time when the lights were out, sitting in the kitchen, listening to the mechanical hum of the appliances, the trigger click of the HVAC as it engaged to cool or heat the house. He was a master of immobility, having sat still—the legend went—for five days straight on a Gaza roof, deep inside enemy territory, his Barrett M82 balanced on metal legs, waiting for a high-value target to emerge from an apartment complex, the threat of discovery by Palestinian forces a constant.

Compared with that, sitting in the air-conditioned, luxury kitchen of a multimillionaire's estate was like an ocean cruise. He sat with a thermos of green tea (no one ever saw him make it), eyes closed, listening. As opposed to the domestic craziness of the waking day, the night sounds of a house—even a big one like this—were consistent and predictable. The house was wired, of course, sensors on all the windows and doors, motion detectors, cameras. But that was technology, and technology could be tricked, disabled. Gil Baruch was old school, a sensualist. Some said he wore a garrote for a belt, but no one had ever seen the proof.

The truth was, when Gil was a child, he and his father fought all the time, about everything. Gil was the middle child, and by the time he was born the paterfamilias was already well on his way to drinking himself to death. Which he did, in 1991, when cirrhosis became heart failure and heart failure became silence.

And then, according to the Torah, Gil's father ceased to be. Which was just fine with Gil, who sat now in the air-conditioned kitchen and listened to barely audible hush of the surf as it pounded the beach outside.

The security logs from that Sunday are unremarkable. The husband

(Condor) stayed home (*read newspaper 8:10 am–9:45, napped in upstairs guest room 12:45–1:55, made and received several phone calls 2:15–3:45, prepared and cooked supper 4:30–5:40 pm*). The wife (Falcon) went to the farmers market, accompanied by Rachel and a body man, Avraham. The boy played in his room and had a soccer lesson. He napped from eleven thirty to one. Anyone looking back at the log later, trying to piece together a mystery, would find nothing but times and dry entries. It was a lazy Sunday. What made it meaningful were not the facts or details, but the imperceptibles. Inner life. The smell of the beach grass and the feel of sand on a bathroom floor when changing out of a swimsuit.

The heat of American summer.

Line ten of the log read simply: *10:22 Condor ate second breakfast.* It couldn't capture the perfect toasting of the onion bagel or the saltiness of the fish in contrast with the thickness of cream cheese. It was time lost in a book—a journey of imagination, transportation—which to others simply looks like sitting or lying stomach-down on the rug in front of a summertime fire, legs bent at the knees, up ninety degrees, kicking absently, feet languid in the air.

To be a body man did not mean being in a state of constant alarm. In fact it was the opposite. One had to be open to changes in the way things were—receptive to subtle shifts, understanding that the frog was killed not by being dropped into boiling water, but by being boiled slowly, one degree at a time. The best body men understood this. They knew that the job required a kind of tense passivity, mind and body in tune with all five senses. If you thought about it, private security was just another form of Buddhism, tai chi. To live in the moment, fluidly, thinking of nothing more than where you are and what exists around you. Bodies in space and time moving along a prescribed arc. Shadow and light. Positive and negative space.

In living this way, a sense of *anticipation* can evolve, the voodoo preknowledge that the wards you are watching are going to do or say something expectable. By being one with the universe you become the universe, and in this way you know how the rain will fall, the way cut grass will blow in fixed starts in a summer wind. You know when Condor and Falcon are about to fight, when the girl, Rachel (Robin), is getting bored, and when the boy, JJ (Sparrow), has missed his nap and is going to melt down.

You know when the man in the crowd is going to take one step too close, when the autograph fan is, instead, looking to serve legal papers. You know when to slow down on a yellow light and when to take the next elevator.

These are not things you have *feelings* about. They are simply things that are.

Falcon was up first, in her robe, carrying Sparrow. The machine had already made coffee. It ran on a timer. Rachel came down next. She went straight to the living room and put on cartoons. Condor was up last, an hour later, shuffling in with the newspaper, thumbs digging into the blue Sunday plastic bag. Gil lurked, staying out of the way, eyes on the periphery, hugging the shadows.

After breakfast he approached Condor.

"Mr. Bateman," he said. "Okay if I brief you now?"

Condor looked up over his reading glasses.

"Should I be worried?"

"No, sir, just an overview for the week."

Condor nodded, stood. He knew Gil didn't like to talk shop in casual settings. They went into the parlor. It was lined with books that Condor had actually read. Old maps lined the walls, photos of Condor with notable global figures—Nelson Mandela, Vladimir Putin, John McCain, the actor Clint Eastwood. There was an autographed baseball in a glass case on the desk. Chris Chambliss's tenth-inning blast from *that* game, because who in the tristate area didn't remember the way the stands emptied onto the field, the way Chambliss had to push and twist through civilian lunatics to round the bases—did he even touch home plate?

"Sir," said Gil, "would you liked me to get command central on the line to do a more formal briefing?"

"God no. Just run it down for me."

Condor sat behind his desk, picked up an old football. He juggled it mindlessly, hand to hand, as Gil spoke.

"Sixteen email threats intercepted," he began, "sent to mostly public addresses. Your private lines seem uncompromised since our last reshuffle. At the same time, corporate is tracking some specific threats against American media companies. They're working with Homeland Security to stay up to the moment."

Condor studied him as he spoke, spiraling the nerf from left to right and back.

"You were in the Israeli army."

"Yessir."

"Infantry, or—?"

"That's not something I can talk about. Let's say I did my duty and let that be that."

Condor flipped the ball, missed the catch. It bounce-rolled in a sloppy parabola, settling under a curtain.

"Any direct threats?" he asked. "*David Bateman, we're going to kill you.* That type of thing."

"No, sir. Nothing like that."

Condor thought about it.

"But okay, so this guy? The one we don't talk about who took my girl. When did he ever make a threat against a media conglomerate or send a bullshit email? This was a scumbag who thought he could get rich and didn't mind murdering the maid."

"Yessir."

"And what are you doing to protect us from those guys? The ones who don't make threats."

If Gil felt dressed down he didn't show it. To him it was a fair question.

"Both homes are secure. Cars are armored. Your protection detail is visible, high-profile. If they're looking for you, they see us. We're sending a message. There are easier targets."

"But you can't guarantee?"

"No, sir."

Condor nodded. The conversation was over. Gil headed for the door.

"Oh, hey," said Condor. "Mrs. Bateman invited the Kiplings to fly back with us later."

"Is that Ben and Sarah?"

Condor nodded.

"I'll let command know," said Gil.

The key to being a good body man, he had decided over the years, was to be a mirror: not invisible—the client wanted to know you were there—but reflective. Mirrors weren't intimate objects. They reflected change. Movement. A mirror was never static. It was the part of your environment that shifted with you, absorbing angle and light.

And then, when you stood flush in front of it, it showed you yourself.

. . .

He had read the file, of course. What kind of bodyguard would he be if he hadn't? The truth was, he could quote certain sections from memory. He had also spoken to the surviving agents at length, looking for sensory details, for information on how the principals comported themselves—was Condor calm under pressure or explosive? Did Falcon succumb to panic and grief, or did she show a mother's steel? The kidnapping of a child was the nightmare scenario in his line of work, worse than a death (though—to be realistic—a kidnapped child was, nine times out of ten, a dead child). But a kidnapped child removed the normal human safety mechanisms from a parent's mind. Survival of the self was no longer a concern. Protection of wealth, of home, became secondary. Reason, in other words, went out the window. So mostly what you fought with in the kidnap-and-ransom scenario (other than the clock) was the principals themselves.

The facts at the time of Robin's kidnapping were these: Twenty-four hours earlier the nanny, Francesca Butler ("Frankie"), had been taken, most likely while traveling on foot on her way home from the movies. She had been coerced at a second location to share information about the Batemans' rental home and routines—most important, which room was the baby girl in? On the night of the abduction (between twelve thirty and one fifteen a.m.), a ladder had been removed from a shed on the property and propped against the south wall, extending to the lip of the guest room window. There were signs that the window lock had been jimmied from the outside (it was an old house with original windows and over the years they had swollen and shrunk until there was a healthy gap between the upper and lower frames).

Later, investigators would conclude that the kidnapping was the work of a single perpetrator (though there was some dispute). And so the official story was that one man set the ladder, climbed up, retrieved the girl, and took her back down. The ladder was then re-stowed in the shed (what had he done with the child, placed her in a car?). And the child removed from the property. In the words of the principals, *She disappeared.* But of course, Gil knew that no one really disappeared. They were always someplace, bodies at rest or in motion in three-dimensional space.

And in this case, where this single kidnapper had taken Rachel Bateman (aka Robin) was across the street, to the stalled modern remodel, hidden away behind plastic. To a sweltering attic space, soundproofed with newspaper, where food came out of a plastic red cooler and water from a hose connected to a second-floor bathroom sink. The nanny, Frankie Butler, lay dead in the open foundation, covered with cardboard.

It was from this spot that the kidnapper—a thirty-six-year-old ex-con named Wayne R. Macy—watched the comings and going across the street. From his vantage point in the future, Gil knew that Macy was not the criminal mastermind they first thought they were dealing with. When you have a principal like David Bateman—worth millions, as well a high-profile political target—you must assume that the child's kidnapper has targeted the principal for specific reasons, with full knowledge of his profile and resources. But the fact is, all Macy knew was that David and Maggie Bateman were rich and unprotected. He had done a stretch in Folsom Prison in the 1990s for armed robbery and had come home to Long Island with the idea that he might turn his life around. But straight life was punishing and unrewarding, and Wayne liked his booze, and so he burned through job after job, until finally one day—hauling trash bags out of the back of the Dairy Queen—he had decided, *Who am I kidding? It's time to take my fortune into my own hands.*

So he set out to grab a rich man's kid and make a few dollars. Details came out later that he had cased two other families first, but certain factors—the husbands were on the premises full-time, both houses had alarm systems—deterred him from acting, and ultimately steered him to settle on a new target—the Bateman family—the last house on a quiet street, unguarded, populated by two young women and a child.

The consensus was that he had killed Frankie that first night, after getting all the information out of her he could—there were signs of physical cruelty and also evidence of sexual assault, possibly posthumous.

The child was taken at twelve forty-five a.m. on July 18. She would be missing for three days.

. . .

The word came back as they were already in transit. Command relayed it to the lead car and the lead car transmitted it to Gil, who listened to the voice in his ear, speaking to him through fiber and void, without betraying anything.

"Sir," he said in a certain tone of voice, as the car left their road. Condor looked over, saw Gil's expression, nodded. Behind them, the kids were animated, like push-button toys. They always got this way before getting on the plane, excited, nervous.

"Kids," he said with a *look* on his face. Maggie saw it.

"Rachel," she said, "that's enough."

Rachel sulked, but stopped the game of poke and tickle. JJ was too young to get the message the first time. He poked Rachel and laughed, thinking they were still playing.

"Stop," she whined.

Condor leaned over to Gil, who closed the gap, speaking quietly into Condor's ear.

"There's a problem with your guest," he said.

"Who, Kipling?" said Condor.

"Yessir. Command did the routine check and a flag came back."

Condor didn't respond, but the question was implicit: *What flag?*

"Our friends in State are saying Mr. Kipling may be indicted to-morrow."

The blood drained from Condor's face.

"Jesus," he said.

"The actual charges are sealed, but research think he may be laundering money for non-friendlies."

Condor thought about that. *Non-friendlies.* Then it hit him. He was about to host an enemy of the state on his plane. A traitor. How would that look in the press, if the press found out? Condor pictured the bored paparazzi at Teterboro, waiting for all the celebrity returns. They would stand when the plane taxied in, then—when it was clear Brad and Angelina weren't on board—they'd snap a few photos just in case and go back to their iPhones. Photos of David Bateman arm in arm with a traitor.

"What do we do?" he asked Gil.

"Up to you."

Falcon was looking at them, clearly worried.

"Is there something—?" she said.

"No," Condor told her quickly. "Just—it looks like Ben's in some legal trouble."

"Oh no."

"Yeah, bad investments. So I was just—the question comes up for me—do we want to—if we're seen together—after the news comes out—are we going—it could be a headache is all I mean."

"What's Daddy saying?" Rachel asked.

Falcon was frowning.

"Nothing. Just a friend of ours is having some trouble. So we're going to—"

—this directed at Condor—

"—we're going to stand by him, because that's what friends do. Sarah especially is just such a lovely person."

Condor nodded, wishing now that he'd dodged the question and handled things privately.

"Of course," he said. "You're right."

He looked forward, met Gil's eye. The Israeli had a look on his face, which implied he needed direct confirmation that they were going with the status quo. Against his better judgment, Condor nodded.

Gil turned and looked out the window as they talked. It wasn't his job to be part of things. To have opinions. On the road, he could see the marine layer hanging low, lampposts vanishing into the mist. Only a hoary glow at height indicated they were whole.

Twenty minutes later, parked on the tarmac, Gil waited for the lead car to disgorge the advance team before he gave the okay to exit. The two lead men were scanning the airfield for irregularities. Gil did the same, trusting them and not trusting them at the same time. As he reviewed the area (entrance points, blind spots), the family climbed from the car. Sparrow was asleep by this point, draped across Condor's shoulder. Gil made no offer to help carry bags or children. His job was to protect them, not to valet.

From the corner of his eye, Gil saw Avraham sweep the plane, climbing the deployable stairs. He was inside for six minutes, walking fore to aft, checking the washroom and the cockpit. When he emerged, he gave the high sign and descended.

Gil nodded.

"Okay," he said.

The family approached the gangway, boarding in random order. Knowing the plane was swept clear, Gil was the last to board, protecting against attack from the rear. He could feel the chill of the cabin before he was halfway up, a ghostly kiss on his exposed neck, cutting through the August musk. Did he feel something stir in his lizard brain in that moment, a low foreboding, a wizard's sense of doom? Or is that wishful thinking?

Inside, Gil remained standing, placing himself by the open door. He was a big man—six foot two—but thin, and somehow found a place in the narrow entryway that kept him out of the aisle as passengers and crew settled in for the flight.

"The second party has arrived," said a voice in his earpiece, and through the door Gil could see Ben and Sarah Kipling on the tarmac, showing ID to the advance men. Then Gil felt a presence off his right shoulder and turned. It was the flight attendant holding a tray.

"I'm sorry," she said, "did you want some champagne before we take off, or—can I get you something."

"No," he said. "Tell me your name?"

"I'm Emma—Lightner."

"Thank you, Emma. I'm providing security for the Batemans. May I speak to your captain?"

"Of course. He's—I think he's doing his walk-around. Should I ask him to speak to you when he comes back?"

"Please."

"Okay," she said. Clearly, Gil felt, something was making her nervous. But sometimes the presence of an armed man on a plane did that to people. "I mean, can I get you anything, or—"

He shook his head, turned away, because now the Kiplings were climbing the front stairs of the plane. They had been fixtures at Bateman events over the years, and Gil knew them on sight. He nodded as they entered, but moved his gaze quickly to deter conversation. He heard them greet the others on the plane.

"Darling," said Sarah. "I love your dress."

At that moment the captain, James Melody, appeared at the foot of the stairs.

"Did you see the fucking game?" Kipling said in a blustery voice. "How does he not catch that ball?"

"Don't get me started," said Condor.

"I mean, I could have caught that fucking ball and I've got French toast hands."

Gil moved to the top of the stairs. The fog was thicker now, blowing in trails.

"Captain," said Gil. "I'm Gil Baruch with Enslor Security."

"Yes," said Melody, "they told me there'd be a detail."

He had a slight, unplaceable accent, Gil realized. British maybe or South African, but recycled through America.

"You haven't worked with us before," he said.

"No, but I've worked with a lot of security outfits. I know the routine."

"Good. So you know if there's a problem with the plane or any change in the flight plan I'll need the copilot to tell me right away."

"Absolutely," said Melody. "And you heard we had a change in first officer?"

"Charles Busch is the new man, yes?"

"That's right."

"And you've flown with him before?"

"Once. He's not Michelangelo, but he's solid."

Melody paused for a moment. Gil could sense he wanted to say more.

"There's no such thing as an insignificant detail," he told the pilot.

"No, just—I think there may be some history between Busch and our flight attendant."

"Romantic?"

"Not sure. Just the way she acts around him."

Gil thought about that.

"Okay," he said. "Thank you."

He turned and went back inside, glancing into the cockpit as he did. Inside, Busch was in the copilot's seat, eating a plastic-wrapped sandwich. He looked up and met Gil's eye and smiled. He was a young man, clean-cut but with a slight glaze to him—he'd shaved yesterday, not today, his hair was short, but unbrushed—handsome. Gil only had to watch him for a moment to know that he'd been an athlete at some point in his life, that he'd been popular with girls since childhood, and that he liked the way it made him feel. Then Gil was turning back to the main cabin. He saw the flight attendant, Emma, approaching with an empty tray.

He gestured to her with one finger. *Come here.*

"Hi," she said.

"Is there an issue I should know about?"

She frowned.

"I'm not—"

"Between you and Busch, the copilot."

She flushed.

"No. He's not—that's—"

She smiled.

"Sometimes they like you," she said. "And you have to say no."

"That's all?"

She fixed her hair self-consciously, aware that she had drink orders to fill.

"We flew together before. He likes to flirt—with all the girls, not just—but it's fine. I'm fine."

A moment.

"And you're here," she said, "so—"

Gil thought about that. It was his job to assess—a darkened doorway, the sound of footsteps—he was, by necessity, a connoisseur of people. He had developed his own system for knowing the types—the brooder, the nervous talker, the irascible victim, the bully, the sprite—and within those types had developed subtypes and patterns that signaled possible shifts in anticipated behavior—the circumstances under which the nervous talker might become the brooder, and then the bully.

Emma smiled at him again. Gil thought about the copilot, the half-eaten sandwich, the captain's words. Travel time was just under an hour, gate-to-gate. He thought about Kipling's indictment, about the case-closed kidnapping of Robin. He thought about everything that could go wrong, no matter how far-fetched, running it all through the gray matter abacus that had made him a legend. He thought about Mosha Dayan's eye and his father's drinking, about his brothers' deaths, each in turn, and the death of his sister. He thought about what it meant to live your life as an echo, a shadow, always standing behind a man and his light. He had scars he wouldn't discuss. He slept with his finger on the trigger of a Glock. He knew that the world was an impossibility, that the state of Israel was an impossibility, that every day men woke and put on their boots and went off to do the impossible no matter what it might be. This was the hubris of mankind, to rally in the face of overwhelming odds, to thread the needle and climb the mountain and survive the storm.

He thought of all this in the time it took the flight attendant to pass, and then he got on the radio and told command that they were good to go.

COUNTRYSIDE

SCOTT DRIVES NORTH, paralleling the Hudson past Washington Heights and Riverdale. Urban walls give way to trees and low-slung towns. Traffic stalls, then abates, and he takes the Henry Hudson Parkway past the low mall clot of central Yonkers, shifting to Route 9 heading up through Dobbs Ferry, where American revolutionaries once camped in force, probing the Manhattan border for British weakness. He rides with the radio off, listening to the slush of his tires on the rain-slick road. A late-summer thunderstorm has moved through in the last few hours, and he navigates the tail end of it, windshield wipers moving in time.

He is thinking about the wave. Its silent rumble. The loom of it. A towering hump of ocean brine exposed by moonlight, sneaking up on them from the rear, like a giant from a children's story. Eerie and soundless it came, an enemy without soul or agency. Nature at its most punishing and austere. And how he grabbed the boy and dove.

His mind shifts to the image of cameras—leering mechanically, thrust forward on anonymous shoulders, judging with their unblinking convex eyes. Scott thinks of the lights in his face, the questions overlapping, becoming a wall. Were the cameras a tool for the advancement of man, he wonders, or was man a tool for the advancement of the cameras? We carry *them*, after all, valeting them from place to place, night and day, photographing everything we see. We believe we have invented our machine world to benefit ourselves, but how do we know we aren't here to serve it? A camera must be aimed to be a camera. To service a microphone, a question must be asked. Twenty-four hours a day, frame after frame, we feed the hungry beast, locked in perpetual motion as we race to film it all.

Does television exist for us to watch, in other words, or do we exist to watch television?

Overhead, the wave crested, teetering, a five-story building on the verge of smooth collapse, and he dove, squeezing the boy to him, no time to take a breath, his body taking over, survival no longer trusted to the abstract functions of the mind. Legs kicking, he entered the blacks, feeling the spin-cycle tug of the wave pulling all things to it, and then the tilt and inevitable gravity of descent, grabbed by a monster's hand and thrust deeper, and now it was all he could do to hold the boy to his body and survive.

Was Scott having an affair with Maggie? That's what they asked. A married mother of two, a former preschool teacher. And to them she was what—a character on a reality show? A sad and lusty housewife from post-modern Chekhov?

He thinks of Layla's living room, the late-night OCD of an insomniac transforming it into some kind of memory palace. And how this charcoal rendering will most likely be the last picture of Maggie ever created.

Would he have slept with her if she'd asked? Was he attracted to her, and perhaps her to him? Did he stand too close when she came to view his work, or did he bounce nervously on his toes, keeping his distance? She was the first person he'd shown the work to, the first civilian, and his fingertips were itchy. As she walked the barn he felt the urge for a drink, but it was a scar, not a scab, and he didn't pick it.

This is his truth, the story he tells himself. Publicly, Scott is just a player in a drama not his own. He is "Scott Burroughs," heroic scoundrel. It's just the hint of an idea now, a theory. But he can see how it could blossom, becoming—what? A kind of painting. Fact turned to fiction step by step.

He thinks of Andy Warhol, who used to make up different stories for different journalists—*I was born in Akron. I was born in Pittsburgh*—so when he spoke to people he would know which interviews they'd read. Warhol, who understood the idea that the self was just a story we told. Reinvention used to be a tool of the artist. He thinks of Dalí's urinal, of Claes Oldenburg's giant ashtray. To take reality and repurpose it, bend it to an idea, this was the kingdom of make-believe.

But journalism was something else, wasn't it? It was meant to be objective reporting of facts, no matter how contradictory. You didn't make the news fit the story. You simply reported the facts as they were. When had that stopped being true? Scott remembers the reporters of his youth, Cronkite, Mike Wallace, Woodward and Bernstein, men with rules, men of iron will. And how would they have covered these events?

A private plane crashes. A man and a boy survive.

Information versus entertainment.

It's not that Scott doesn't understand the value of "human interest." What was his fascination with the King of Exercise, if not a fascination in the power of the human spirit? But he could count on one hand the things he knows about Jack's love life, his romantic history. There was a wife, a decades-long marriage. What more did he need to know?

It's fascinating to him, as a man who concerns himself with image, to think of how his own is being fabricated—not in the sense of being faked, but how it's being manufactured, piece by piece. *The Story of Scott. The Story of the Crash.*

All he wants is to be left alone. Why should he be forced to clarify, to wade into the swamp of lies and try to correct these poisoned thoughts? Isn't that what they want? For him to engage? To escalate the story? When Bill Cunningham invites him on the air, it is not to set the story straight so the story ends. It is to add a new chapter, a new twist that propels the narrative forward into another week of ratings cycles.

A trap, in other words. They are setting a trap. And if he is smart he will continue to ignore them, move forward, live his life.

As long as he doesn't mind the fact that nobody on earth will ever see him as he sees himself again.

THE HOUSE IS small and hidden by trees. There's a port lean to it, as if the wide-plank slats on the left end of the building have given up over the years, slumping from exhaustion or boredom or both. Driving in, Scott thinks it has a kind of shadowy charm, with its blue trim and scalloped white window shutters, a postcard childhood you remember in your dreams. As he pulls in over rough paving stones and parks under an oak tree, Doug comes out of the house carrying a canvas tool bag. He throws it in the open back of an old Jeep Wrangler with some force and moves to the driver's door without looking up.

Scott waves as he climbs out of the rental, but Doug doesn't make eye contact, slapping the truck in gear and pulling out in a spray of wood chips. Then Eleanor comes to the front door, holding the boy. Scott finds he has butterflies in his stomach seeing them (her red-checked dress framed against the blue trim and scalloped white shutters, the boy matched in a plaid shirt and short pants). But unlike Eleanor, whose eyes are on Scott, the boy seems distracted, looking back into the house. Then Eleanor says something to him and he turns. Seeing Scott, his face breaks into a smile. Scott offers him a little wave (*When did I become such a waver?* he wonders). The boy offers a shy wave back. Then Eleanor puts him down and he half runs, half walks over to Scott, who bends a knee and thinks about scooping him up, but ends up just putting his hands on the boy's shoulders and looking him in the eye, like a soccer coach.

"Hey, you," he says.

The boy smiles.

"I brought you something," says Scott.

He stands and goes to the trunk of the rental car. Inside is a plastic dump truck he found at the gas station. It's bound to a cardboard box by unbreakable nylon ties, and they spend a few minutes trying to wrestle it free before Eleanor goes inside and fetches some scissors.

"What do we say?" she asks the boy, once the truck is free and the subject of vigorous digging.

"Thank you," she offers after a moment, when it's clear the boy isn't going to speak.

"I didn't want to show up empty-handed," says Scott.

She nods.

"Sorry about Doug. We had—things are hard right now."

Scott musses the boy's hair.

"Let's talk inside," he says. "I passed a news van on the way in. My feeling is I've been on TV enough this week."

She nods. Neither of them wants to be on display.

They catch up at the kitchen table while the boy watches *Thomas and Friends* and plays with his truck. It will be bedtime soon and the boy is fidgety, his body flopping around on the sofa, his eyes glued to the screen. Scott sits at the kitchen table and watches him through the doorway. The boy's hair has been cut recently, but not completely— so the bangs are blunt, but the back is bushy. It seems like a junior version of Eleanor's hair, as if he has adapted in order to fit into the family.

"I thought I could do it myself," Eleanor explains, putting the kettle on the stove, "but he was so agitated after a few minutes I had to give up. So now every day I try to cut a little bit more, sneaking up on him when he's playing with his trucks, or—"

As she says it she grabs the scissors from the drawer by the stove and pads in toward the boy, trying to stay out of his field of vision. But he sees her and waves her off, making a kind of primal growl.

"Just—" she says, trying to reason with an unreasonable animal. "It's longer on the—"

The boy makes the sound again, eyes on the TV. Eleanor nods, comes back into the kitchen.

"I don't know," says Scott. "There's something perfect about a cute kid with a bad haircut."

"You're just saying that to make me feel better," she says, dumping the scissors back into the drawer.

She pours them both a cup of tea. Since they sat, the sun has dropped into view at the top edge of the window frame, and when Eleanor leans in to pour his tea, her head slips into the creamy light, creating an eclipse. He squints up at her.

"You look good," he tells her.

"Really?" she says.

"You're still standing. You made tea."

She thinks about that.

"He needs me," she says.

Scott watches the boy flip around, absently chewing on the fingers of his left hand.

Eleanor stares into the setting sun for a moment, stirs her tea.

"When my grandfather was born," he says, "he weighed three pounds. This was in West Texas in the 'twenties. Before ICUs. So for three months he slept in a sock drawer."

"That's not true."

"As far as I know," he says. "People can survive much more than you think is my point. Even kids."

"I mean, we talk about it—his parents. He knows they're—passed—as much as he understands what that means. But I can tell from the way he looks to the door whenever Doug comes home that he's still waiting."

Scott thinks about that. To know a thing and not know it at the same time. In some ways, the boy is the lucky one. By the time he is old enough to truly understand what happened, the wound will be old, the pain of it faded with time.

"So you said Doug—" says Scott. "—some problems?"

Eleanor sighs, dips her tea bag absently in the cup.

"Look," she says, "he's weak. Doug. He's just—and I didn't—I thought it was something else at first—how insecurity, you know, defensiveness, can seem like confidence? But now I think his opinions are louder because he's not really sure what he believes. Does that make sense?"

"He's a young man. It's not a new story. I had some of that myself. Dogma."

She nods, a ray of hope returning to her eyes.

"But you grew out of it."

"Grew? No. I burned it all down, drank myself into a stupor, pissed off everyone I knew."

They think about that for a moment, how sometimes the only way to learn not to play with fire is to go up in flames.

"I'm not saying that's what he'll do," says Scott, "but it's not realistic to think he'll just wake up one morning and say, *You know what? I'm an asshole.*"

She nods.

"And then there's the money," she says quietly.

He waits.

"I don't know," she says. "It's—I get nauseous just thinking about it."

"You're talking about the will?"

She nods.

"It's—a lot," she says.

"What they left you?"

"Him. It's—it's his money. It's not—"

"He's four."

"I know, but I just want to—couldn't I just keep it all in an account until he's old enough to—"

"That's a version," says Scott. "But what about food or housing. Who's going to pay for school?"

She doesn't know.

"I could—" she says, "I mean, maybe I make two meals. A fancy one for him or—I mean, he gets nice clothes."

"And you get rags?"

She nods. Scott thinks about walking her through all the ways that her idea makes no sense, but he can tell she knows it. That she is working her way toward accepting the trade-off she's been given for the death of her family.

"Doug sees it differently, I'm guessing."

"He wants—can you believe?—he thinks—*we should definitely keep the town house in the city, but I don't know, we could probably sell London and just stay in a hotel whenever we visit.* Like when did we turn into people who go to London? The man owns half a restaurant he'll never open because the kitchen's not done."

"He could finish it now."

She grits her teeth.

"No. It's not for that. We didn't earn it. It's not—the money is for JJ."

Scott watches the boy yawn and rub his eyes.

"I'm guessing Doug doesn't agree."

She worries her hands together until the knuckles are white.

"He said we both want the same thing, but then I said, *If we both want the same thing, why are you yelling?*"

"Are you—scared—at all?"

She looks at him.

"Did you know that people are saying you had an affair with my sister?"

"Yes," he says. She narrows her eyes. "I know that. But I didn't."

He reads her eyes, her doubt, not knowing who she can trust anymore.

"Someday I'll tell you what it means to be a recovered alcoholic.

Or *recovering*. But mostly it's about avoiding—pleasure—about staying focused on the work."

"And this heiress in the city?"

He shakes his head.

"She gave me a place to hide, because she liked having a secret. I was the thing that money couldn't buy. Except—I guess that's not true."

Scott is about to say something when JJ pads in. Eleanor straightens, wipes her eyes.

"Hey there, boo. Is it over?"

He nods.

"Should we go read some books and get ready for bed?"

The boy nods, then points at Scott.

"You want him to read?" asks Eleanor.

Another nod.

"Sounds good," says Scott.

. . .

While the boy goes upstairs with Eleanor to get ready for bed, Scott calls the old fisherman he rents his house from. He wants to check in, see how the three-legged dog is doing.

"It's not too bad, is it?" he asks. "The press?"

"No, sir," says Eli. "They don't bother me, plus—turns out they're scared of the dog. But Mr. Burroughs, I gotta tell you. The men came. They had a warrant."

"What men?"

"Police. They broke the lock on the barn and took it all."

Scott has a chill in the base of his spine.

"The paintings?"

"Yes, sir, all of them."

There's a long pause as Scott thinks about that. The escalation. What it means. The work is out there now. His life's accomplishment.

What damage will come to it? What will they make him do to get it back. But there's another feeling deep down, a giddy nerve jangling at the idea that finally the paintings are doing what they're meant to do. They're being seen.

"Okay," he tells the old man. "Don't worry. We'll get them back."

After teeth are brushed and pajamas acquired, and after the boy is in bed, under the covers, Scott sits in a rocking chair and reads from a stack of books. Eleanor hovers in the doorway, not knowing whether to stay or go, unclear of the boundaries of her role—is she allowed to leave them alone? Should she, even if she is?

After three books the boy's lids are droopy, but he doesn't want Scott to stop. Eleanor comes over and lies on the bed, nestling in beside the boy. So Scott reads three more, reading on even after the boy is asleep, after Eleanor too has surrendered to it and the late-summer sun is finally down. There is a simplicity to the act, to the moment, a purity that Scott has never experienced. Around him, the house is quiet. He closes the last book, lays it quietly on the floor.

Downstairs, the phone rings. Eleanor stirs, gets out of bed carefully, so as not to wake the boy. Scott hears her pad downstairs, hears the murmur of her voice, the sound of the hang-up, then she wanders back up and stands in the doorway, a strange look on her face, like a woman riding a roller coaster that's plummeting to earth.

"What?" says Scott.

Eleanor swallows, exhales shakily. It's as if the door frame is holding her up.

"They found the rest of the bodies."

3.

SCREEN TIME

WHERE IS THE intersection between life and art? For Gus Franklin, the coordinates can be mapped with GPS precision. Art and life collide in an aircraft hangar on Long Island. This is where twelve oversize paintings now hang, shadowed in the light that spills in through milky windows, the large hangar doors kept closed to keep out the prying eyes of cameras. Twelve photorealistic images of human disaster, suspended by wire. At Gus's urging great care has been taken to ensure no harm comes to the work. Despite O'Brien's witch-hunt dogma, Gus still isn't convinced they've done anything except harass the victim, and he won't be responsible for damaging an artist's legacy or impeding a well-earned second chance.

He stands now with a multi-jurisdictional team of agents and representatives from the airline and aircraft manufacturer, studying the paintings—not for their artistic pedigree, but as evidence. Is it possible, they ask themselves, that within these paintings are clues to the erasure of nine people and a million-dollar aircraft? It is a surreal exercise, made haunting by the location in which they stand. In the middle of the space, folding tables have been erected, upon which technicians have laid out the debris from the crash. With the addition of the paintings, there is now a tension in the space—a push/pull between wreckage and art that causes each man and woman to struggle with an unexpected feeling—that somehow the evidence has become art, not the other way around.

Gus stands in front of the largest work, a three-canvas spread. On the far right is a farmhouse. On the far left, a tornado has formed. In the center a woman stands at the lip of a cornfield. He studies the towering stalks, squints at the woman's face. As an engineer, he finds the act of art beyond him—the idea that the object itself (canvas, wood, and oil) is not the point, and that instead some intangible experience created from suggestion, from the intersection of materials, colors, and content has been created. Art exists not inside the piece itself, but inside the mind of the viewer.

And yet even Gus has to admit, there is an unsettling power in the room now, a haunting specter of mass death that comes from the volume and character of images.

It is in the acknowledgment of this thought that something else strikes him.

In each painting there is a woman.

And all the women have the same face.

"What do you think?" Agent Hex of the SEC asks him.

Gus shakes his head. *It's the nature of the human mind to look for connections*, he thinks. Then Marcy approaches and tells them that divers have found what they believe to be the missing wreck.

The room erupts with voices, but Gus stares at the painting of drowning men in a hangar full of drying debris. One thing is real. The other is fiction. How he wishes it was the painting that were death and the truth fiction. But then he nods and crosses to a secure phone line. There is a moment in every search, he thinks, when it feels like the hunt will never end. And then it does.

Agent Mayberry coordinates with the Coast Guard ship that found the wreck. Divers with helmet cameras, he tells Gus, are being deployed. The feed will be sent to them via a secure channel, already in place. An hour later, Gus sits before a plastic card table inside the hangar. This is where he has taken most of his meals for the last two weeks. The other members of his team stand behind him, drinking Dunkin' Donuts coffee from Styrofoam cups. Mayberry is on a satphone, talking directly to the Coast Guard cutter.

"The feed should be coming up now," he says.

Gus adjusts the angle of monitor, though rationally he knows this will do nothing to help speed the connection. It is a nervous busyness. For a moment there is just a video window with no connection—FEED MISSING—then a sudden snap of blue signal. Not ocean blue, but an electronic blue, pixilated. Then that hue gives way to the soundless green of an underwater lens. The divers (Gus has been told there are three) are each projecting light from a head rig, and the video has an eerie handheld quality. It takes Gus a moment to orient himself, as the divers are already very close to what appears to be the fuselage—a scratched white shell bisected by what appears to be thick red lines.

"There's the airline logo," says Royce and he shows them a photo of the plane. GULLWING is scripted on the side of the plane in slanting red letters.

"Can we communicate?" Gus asks the room. "See if they can find the ID number."

There is a scramble to try to reach someone on the Coast Guard cutter. But by the time word gets to the divers they are already moving, floating on, working their way—Gus intuits—toward the rear of the aircraft. As they pass over the port wing, Gus can see that it has snapped off with great force. The metal around the tear is twisted and curved. He looks over to the partial wing lying on the hangar floor next to a tape measure grid.

"The tail's gone," says Royce. Gus looks back at the screen. White lights are passing over the fuselage, moving in a slow nod as the divers kick their fins. The rear of the jet is gone, the aircraft reclining in the silt, so that the jagged tear is half buried—a machine consumed by nature.

"No," says the woman from the airline. "It's there, isn't it? In the distance?"

Gus squints at the screen, and believes he can make out a glimmer on the edge of the light, man-made shapes tilted and swaying gently in the current. But then the diver's camera turns and they are looking at the hole in the back of the plane, and as the camera tilts up, the full length of the fuselage is revealed for the first time. And suddenly they have perspective.

"I've got a crumple zone," says one of the engineers.

"I see it," says Gus, wanting to cut off speculation. The craft will have to be raised and transported back here for a full examination. Lucky for them it's not too deep. But another hurricane is anticipated next week, and the seas are already becoming unpredictable. They will have to move fast.

A diver appears before the camera, his legs moving. He points to the blackness at the back of the plane, then to himself. The camera nods. The diver turns.

Gus sits forward in his chair, aware of the power of the moment.

They are entering the cemetery.

How to describe the things we see onscreen, experiences we have that are not ours? After so many hours (days, weeks, years) of watching TV—the morning talk shows, the daily soaps, the nightly news and then into prime time (*The Bachelor, Game of Thrones, The Voice?*)— after a decade of studying the viral videos of late-night hosts and *Funny or Die* clips emailed by friends, how are we to tell the difference between them, if the experience of watching them is the same? To watch the Twin Towers fall and on the same device in the same room then watch a marathon of *Everybody Loves Raymond*.

To Netflix an episode of *The Care Bears* with your children, and then later that night (after the kids are in bed) search for amateur couples who've filmed themselves breaking the laws of several states. To videoconference from your work computer with Jan and Michael from the Akron office (about the new time-sheet protocols), then click (against your better instincts) on an embedded link to a jihadi beheading video. How do we separate these things in our brains when the experience of watching them—sitting or standing before the screen, perhaps eating a bowl of cereal, either alone or with others, but, in any case, always with part of us still rooted in our own daily slog (distracted by deadlines, trying to decide what to wear on a date later)—is the same?

Watching, by definition, is different from doing.

To be a diver 150 feet below the surface of the ocean, your oxygen and nitrogen levels regulated, encased in the slim cocoon of a wet suit, face mask on, feet kicking in a steady pulse, seeing only what your headlamp reveals. To feel the pressure of the deep, focused on the effort of your own breathing—something previously mechanical and automatic that now requires foresight and effort. To wear weights— literal weights—to keep your otherwise buoyant body from floating to the surface, and the way this makes your muscles strain and your breath feel bigger than your chest. In this moment there is no living room, no deadlines at work, no dates that must be dressed for. In this moment you are connected only to the reality you are experiencing. It is, in fact, *reality*.

Whereas Gus is simply another man seated before a desktop monitor. But even so, as the divers slip into the dark mechanical chasm that holds the dead, he experiences something visceral, outside his own room-bound reality, something that can only be described as dread.

It is darker here inside the confines of the plane. What has been lost in the crash, along with the tail, is the rear lavatory and galley, and there is a pinch to the fuselage where it has torqued from the impact. Directly ahead of the camera, flickering in the headlamp, the flippers of the forward diver move in a rhythmic paddle. That diver also wears a headlamp, and it is in the vaguer light of that diver that the first headrest becomes visible, and floating around it like a halo, a seaweed spray of hair.

The hair is visible for only a second before the forward diver blocks it with his body, and in that moment everyone watching leans to the right trying to see past him. It is an instinctual move, one the rational brain knows is impossible, but so great is the desire to see what has been revealed that each person leans as one.

"Move," says Mayberry under his breath.

"Quiet," Gus snaps.

Onscreen, the camera pans as the operator's head turns. Gus sees that the cabin's wood paneling has splintered and warped in places. A shoe floats past. A child's sneaker. Behind Gus, one of the women draws a quick breath. And then there they are, four of the remaining five passengers, David Bateman, Maggie Bateman, daughter Rachel, and Ben Kipling, floating futilely against the reinforced nylon bonds of their lap belts, their bodies bloated.

The body man, Gil Baruch, is nowhere to be found.

Gus closes his eyes.

When he opens them, the camera has moved past the bodies of the passengers and is facing the darkened galley. The forward diver turns and points at something. The camera operator has to swim forward to find it.

"Are those—what are those holes?" Mayberry asks as Gus leans forward. The camera moves closer, zooming in on a grouping of small holes around the door's lock.

"They look like—" one of the engineers says, then stops.

Bullet holes.

The camera goes tighter. Through the watery light, Gus can make out six holes. One of them has shorn the door lock away.

Someone shot up the cockpit door, trying to get in.

Did the shots hit the pilots? Is that why the plane crashed?

The camera moves off the door, floating to the right and up.

But Gus remains focused. Someone shot up the cockpit door? Who? Did they make it inside?

And then the camera finds something that makes everyone in the room suck in their breath. Gus looks up, sees Captain James Melody, his dead body trapped in a pocket of high air in the rounded ceiling of the forward galley.

On the wrong side of the locked cockpit door.

JAMES MELODY

MARCH 06, 1965–
AUGUST 26, 2015

HE MET CHARLES Manson once. That's the story James Melody's mother tells. *You were two. Charlie held you on his lap.* This was Venice, California, 1967. James's mother, Darla, was over from Cornwall, England, on an expired travel visa. She'd been in country since 1964. *I came with the Beatles*, she used to say, though they were from Liverpool and took a different flight. Now she lived in an apartment in Westwood. James tried to visit whenever he was on a layover at any of the Greater Los Angeles airports—Burbank, Ontario, Long Beach, Santa Monica, and on and on.

Late at night, after a few sherries, Darla sometimes intimated that Charles Manson was James's real father. But then there were lots of stories like this. *Robert Kennedy came to Los Angeles in October 'sixty-four. We met in the lobby of the Ambassador Hotel.*

James had learned to ignore them mostly. At fifty, he had resigned himself to never knowing the true identity of his biological dad. It was just another of life's great mysteries. And James was a believer in mystery. Not like his mum, who never met a phantasmagorical ideology she didn't embrace instantly and completely, but in the manner of Albert Einstein, who once said, "Science without religion is lame. Religion without science is blind."

As a pilot, James had seen the vastness of the air. He had flown through tumultuous weather with no one between him and catastrophe but God.

Here's something else Einstein said: "The further the spiritual evolution of mankind advances, the more certain it seems to me that the path to genuine religiosity does not lie through the fear of life, and the fear of death, and blind faith, but through striving after rational knowledge."

James was a great fan of Albert Einstein, the former patent clerk who divined the Theory of Relativity. Where James's mother looked for answers to life's mysteries in the great spiritual miasma, James preferred to think that every question is ultimately answerable by science. Take, for example, the question *Why is there something and not nothing?* For spiritualists, of course, the answer is God. But James was more interested in a rational blueprint of the universe, down to the subatomic level. To be a pilot required advanced math and scientific understanding. To become an astronaut (which James once fancied he'd do) required these even more so.

On layovers, you could always find James Melody reading. He'd sit by the pool at a hotel in Arizona paging through Spinoza, or eat at the bar of a nightclub in Berlin reading social science texts like *Freakanomics*. He was a collector of facts and details. In fact, this was what he was doing now at the restaurant in Westwood, reading the *Economist* and waiting for his mother. It was a sunny day in August, eighty-three degrees out, prevailing winds from the southeast at ten miles per hour. James sat drinking a Lillet on the rocks and reading an article on the birth of a red heifer on a farm on Israel's West Bank. The cow's birth had both Jews and fundamentalist Christians in an uproar, as both Old and New Testaments tell us that the new Messiah cannot come until the Third Temple is constructed on the Temple Mount in Jerusalem. And as everyone knows, the Third Temple cannot be built until the ground is purified by the ashes of a red heifer.

As the article explained (but which James already knew), Numbers 19:2 instructs us, "Speak unto the children of Israel, that they bring thee a red heifer without spot, wherein is no blemish, and upon which never came yoke." The animal must not have been used to perform work. In the Jewish tradition, the need for a red heifer was cited as the prime example of a *hok*, or biblical law for which there was no apparent logic. The requirement was therefore deemed of absolute divine origin.

As the reporter wrote, the *Economist* published the story, not because of its religious significance, but because it had reignited the hot-button issue of ownership of the Temple Mount. They cited the region's geopolitical significance without commenting on the religious validity of fundamentalist claims.

After he was done reading the article, James tore it out of the magazine and carefully folded it into thirds. He flagged down a passing waiter and asked him to throw it in the trash. The danger in leaving the article inside the magazine was that his mother would pick it up in passing, see the article, and go off on one of her "tangents." The last tangent took her down the rabbit hole of Scientology for nine years, during which time she accused James of being a suppressive person, and cut all contact, which he didn't mind so much, except he worried. Darla surfaced again years later, chatty and warm, as if nothing had happened. When James asked her what had happened, she said simply, "Oh, those sillies. They act like they know everything. But as the Tao Te Ching tells us, *Knowing others is wisdom. Knowing the self is enlightenment.*"

James watched the waiter disappear into the kitchen. He had the impulse to follow him and make sure the article was thrown away—in fact he wished he'd told the waiter to bury it under other refuse, or that he himself had torn it into small, unreadable pieces—but he resisted. These obsessive impulses were best ignored, a lesson he had learned the hard way. The article was gone. Out of sight. Unreachable. That was what mattered.

And just in time, for in rode his mother on her Ventura 4 Mobility Scooter with adjustable angle, delta tiller (bright red, of course). She rolled down the handicapped ramp, saw him, and waved. James stood as she approached, navigating past diners (who had to move their chairs so she could pass). It's not that his mother was obese (in fact, just the opposite: She weighed no more than ninety pounds) or that she had a disability (she walked just fine). It's that she liked the statement the fire-engine-red scooter made, the import it brought. This was clear from the entrance she'd just made, wherein everyone in the restaurant had to stand, and adjust their seats, as if for the entrance of a queen.

"Hi there," said Darla as James held out a chair for her. She stood without effort and took it. Then, seeing his Lillet, "What are we drinking?"

"It's Lillet. Would you like one?"

"Yes, please," she said.

He signaled to the waiter to bring another. His mother put her napkin in her lap.

"So? Tell me I look wonderful."

James smiled.

"You do. You look great."

There was a voice he used only with her. A slow and patient elucidation, as if speaking to a child with special needs. She liked it, as long as he didn't go too big with it, pushing to the point of patronization.

"You seem fit," she said. "I like the mustache."

He touched it, realizing she hadn't seen him with it.

"A little Errol Flynn, ay?" he said.

"It's so gray, though," she suggested with a wince. "Maybe a little boot black."

"I think it makes me look distinguished," he said lightly as the waiter brought her drink.

"You're a darling," she told him. "Have another ready, will you. I'm dreadfully thirsty."

"Yes, ma'am," he said, withdrawing.

Over the decades, his mother's British accent had morphed into something James had taken to calling pure affectation. Like Julia Child, she had a grandness about her that made the accent seem simply aristocratic. As in, *This is just the way we speak, darling.*

"I researched the specials," he said. "I'm told the veal is divine."

"Ooh good," she said. There was nothing she loved more than a good meal. *I'm a sensualist,* she told people, which was something that sounded sexy and fun when she was twenty-five, but now—at seventy—just sounded wrong.

"Did you hear about the red heifer?" she asked after they ordered. He had a brief, panicked flash that somehow she had seen the article, but then he remembered that she watched CNN twenty-four hours a day. They must have done a story.

"I saw it," he told her, "and I'm excited to hear your thoughts, but let's talk about something else first."

This seemed to placate her, which told him that she hadn't connected to the story completely yet, the way a plug connects to a socket, drawing power.

"I've taken up the harmonica," he said. "Trying to get in touch with my musical roots. Although I'm not sure *roots* is the right—"

She handed her empty Lillet glass to the waiter, who arrived with another just in time.

"Your stepfather played the harmonica," she told him.

"Which one?"

She either didn't hear his quip or ignored it.

"He was very musical. Maybe you got it from him."

"I don't think it works that way."

"Well," she said, and sipped her drink. "I always thought it was a little silly."

"The harmonica?"

"No. Music. And God knows I had my share of musicians. I mean, the things I did to Mick Jagger would make a hooker blush."

"Mother," he said, looking around, but they were far enough from the other diners that no heads had turned.

"Oh please. Don't be such a prude."

"Well, I like it. The harmonica."

He took it out of his jacket pocket, showed it to her.

"It's portable, right? So I can take it anywhere. Sometimes I play quietly in the cockpit with the autopilot on."

"Is that safe?"

"Of course it's safe. Why wouldn't it be—"

"All I know is I can't keep my phone on for takeoff and landing."

"That's—they changed that. And also, are you suggesting the sound waves from the harmonica could impact the guidance system, or—"

"Well, now—that's your area—technical understanding—I'm just calling it like I see it."

He nodded. In three hours he was scheduled to take an Ospry to Teterboro and pick up a new crew. Then a short jaunt to Martha's Vineyard and back. He'd gotten a room reserved at the Soho House downtown, with a one-night layover, then tomorrow he flew to Taiwan.

His mother finished her second drink—*they pour them so small, dear*—and ordered a third. James noticed a red string on her right wrist—*so she's back on Kabbalah*. He didn't need to check his watch to know that it had only been fifteen minutes since she arrived.

When he told people he grew up in a doomsday cult he was only partially kidding. They were there—he and Darla—for five years, from '70 to '75, *there* being a six-acre compound in Northern California. The cult being The Restoration of God's Commandments (later shortened to simply The Restoration), run by the right reverend Jay L. Baker. Jay L. used to say that he was the baker and they were his bread. God, of course, was the baker who'd made them all.

Jay L. was convinced the world would end on August 9, 1974. He had had a vision on a river rafting trip—family pets floating up to heaven. When he came home, he consulted the scriptures—the Old Testament, the Book of Revelation, the Gnostic Gospels. He became convinced there was a code in the Bible, a hidden message. And the more he dug, the more notes he took in the margins of religious texts, the more he banged out sums on his old desktop calculator, the more convinced he became that it was a date. *The* date.

The end of the world.

Darla met Jay L. on Haight Street. He had an old guitar and a school bus. His followers numbered exactly eleven (soon to grow to just under a hundred), mostly women. Jay L. was a handsome man (under all that hair), and he'd been blessed with an orator's voice, deep and melodious. He liked to gather his followers in intertwining circles, like the symbol for the Olympics, so that some sat face-to-face, and he'd wander among them espousing his belief that when the rapture came only the purest souls would ascend. *Purity* in his eyes meant many things. It meant that one prayed at least eight hours a day, that one committed oneself to hard work and to caring for others. It meant that one ate no chicken or chicken-related products (such as eggs), that one bathed only with soaps made by hand (sometimes cleaning one's face with the ash of a birch tree). Followers had to surround themselves with only pure sounds—sounds straight from the source, no recorded materials, television, radio, film.

Darla liked it, these rules, for a while. She was a searcher at heart. What she claimed to be looking for was enlightenment, but really what she wanted was order. She was a lost girl from a working-class home with a drunken father who wanted to be told what to do and when to do it. She wanted to go to bed at night knowing that things made sense, that the world was the way it was for a reason. Though he was young, James remembers the fervor his mother brought to this new communal way of life, the headlong way she threw herself in. And when Jay L. decided that children should be raised collectively and had them build a nursery, her mother didn't hesitate to add James to the group.

"So are you here now or what?" his mother said.

"Am I here?"

"I can't keep track of it. All your comings and goings. Do you even have an address?"

"Of course I do. It's in Delaware. You know that."

"Delaware?"

"For tax purposes."

She made a face as if thinking about things like that were subhuman.

"What's Shanghai like?" she asked. "I always thought it would be magical to see Shanghai."

"It's crowded. Everybody smokes."

She looked at him with a certain bored pity.

"You never did have a sense of wonder."

"What's that supposed to mean?"

"Nothing. Just—we're put on this earth to revel in the majesty of creation, not—you know—live in Delaware for tax purposes."

"It's just on paper. I live in the clouds."

He said this for her benefit, but it was also true. Most of his best memories were of the cockpit. Colors seen in nature, the way light bends around the horizon, the cathartic adrenaline rush of a storm ceiling bested. And yet what did it mean? That had always been his mother's question. *What does it all mean?* But James didn't worry about that. He knew deep down in the core of his being that it didn't *mean* anything.

A sunrise, a winter squall, birds flying in a perfect V. These were things that *were*. The truth, visceral and sublime, of the universe, was that it existed whether we witnessed it or not. Majesty and beauty, these were qualities we projected upon it. A storm was just weather. A sunrise was simply a celestial pattern. It's not that he didn't enjoy them. It's that he didn't require anything more from the universe than that it exist, that it behave consistently—that gravity worked the way it always worked, that lift and drag were constants.

As Albert Einstein once said, "What I see in Nature is a magnificent structure that we can comprehend only very imperfectly, and that must fill a thinking person with a feeling of humility. This is a genuinely religious feeling that has nothing to do with mysticism."

He walked his mother back to the apartment after lunch. She rode beside him waving to people she knew, like a mermaid on her very own holiday parade float. At the door, she asked James when he'd be back again, and he told her he had a layover in LA next month. She told him to watch for the signs. The red heifer had been born in the Holy Land. In and of itself this was not proof of God's plan, but if the signs multiplied, then they should be ready.

He left her in the lobby. She would drive onto the elevator and then straight into her apartment. She had her book group later, she said, and then dinner with some friends from her prayer group. Before he left she kissed his cheek (he bent down to receive it, as one does to the pope or a cardinal) and told him she would be praying for him. She said she was glad that he was such a good son, one who bought his mother such a nice lunch and never forgot to call. She said she'd been thinking about the commune a lot lately and did he remember that? The Reverend Jay L. Baker. What was it he used to say? *I am the baker and you are all my bread. Well*, she told him, *I was your baker. I made you in my oven, and don't you forget it.*

He kissed her cheek, feeling the peach fuzz of old age against his lips. At the revolving door he turned and waved one last time, but she was already gone, just a flash of red in the closing elevator doors. He put on his sunglasses and spun out into the afternoon light.

In ten hours he would be dead.

. . .

There was chop—medium to heavy—dropping through the cloud ceiling into Teterboro. He was flying a Cessna 282 carrying four executives from the Sony Corporation. They landed without incident and taxied to meet the limousine. As always, James stood in the cockpit door wishing his disembarking passengers safe travels. In the past he sometimes said *God bless you* (a habit picked up in childhood), but he noticed it made the men in ties uncomfortable, so he switched to something more neutral. James took his responsibility as captain very seriously.

It was three in the afternoon. He had a few hours to kill before his next flight, a quick jog over to Martha's Vineyard to pick up a payload of six. For this flight he'd pilot an OSPRY 45XR. He hadn't flown the particular model before, but he wasn't worried. OSPRY made a very capable airplane. Still, as he sat in the crew lounge waiting, he read up on the specs. The plane was just under seventy feet in overall length, with a wingspan of sixty-three feet, ten inches. It'd do Mach .083, though he'd never push it that hard with paying passengers aboard. It'd fly coast-to-coast on a full tank at a top speed of 554 mph. The specs said it topped out at forty-five thousand feet, but he knew from experience that that was a cautious number. He could take it up to fifty thousand feet without incident, though he couldn't imagine needing to on this flight.

August 9, 1974, that was the day the world was supposed to end. At The Restoration they spent months preparing. God told Noah it would be the fire next time, so that's what they prepared for. They learned to drop and roll, in case the rapture missed them. Jay L. spent more and more time in the woodshed channeling the Angel Gabriel. As if by unspoken agreement, everyone in the group gorged themselves for ten days and then ate only matzoh. Outside the temperature rose and dropped in significant measure.

In the crew lounge, James checked the prevailing weather conditions. Weather-wise they were looking at poor visibility around the Vineyard, with a low cloud base (two hundred to four hundred feet) and heavy coastal fog. Winds were out of the northeast at fifteen to twenty miles per hour. As James knew from basic meteorology, fog is just a cloud near or in contact with the earth's surface—either land or sea. In simple terms, minute water droplets hang suspended in the air. The water droplets are so tiny that gravity has almost no effect, leaving them suspended. At its lightest, fog may only consist of wisps a few feet thick. At its worst, it might have a vertical depth of several hundred feet.

Marine fog tends to be thick and long lasting. It can rise and fall over time, without fully dissipating. At altitude it becomes a low stratus cloud deck. In middle and higher latitudes (like New England), marine fog is primarily a summer occurrence. Low visibility isn't the worst problem a pilot faces—the inboard HGS system can land the plane with zero visibility if it knows the runway GPS. The HGS converts signals from an airport's Instrument Landing System into a virtual image of the runway displayed on the monitor. But if the wind shifts abruptly on manual approach, a pilot can be caught off guard.

"Come ye out from among them and be ye separate." This was what the Bible said, the words that convinced Jay L. Baker to gather his flock and flee to the woods outside Eureka, California. There was an old abandoned summer camp there, without heat or electricity. They bathed themselves in the lake and ate berries from the trees. Jay L. began to filibuster, sermonizing for hours, sometimes days at a time. The signs were everywhere, he told them. Revelations. In order to be saved they had to renounce all sin, to cast venal wickedness from their hearts. Sometimes this involved inflicting pain on their genital areas and the genital areas of others. Sometimes it required visiting "the confessional," an old wooden outhouse that could reach interior temperatures of 105 degrees in the summer sun. His mother once stayed in there for three days, ranting that the devil had come to claim her soul. She was a fornicator and (possibly) a witch, having been caught in bald flagrante with Gale Hickey, a former dentist from Ojai. At night James would try to sneak her water, moving furtively from bush to bush, pushing his canteen through a hole in the pitch, but his mother always refused. She had brought this on herself and would endure the full purge.

James made a note to check the HGS system before takeoff. If he could he would talk to flight crews coming off inbound flights to get an anecdotal sense of conditions in the air, though things can change quickly at altitude, and pockets of turbulence move around.

He sipped a cup of Irish breakfast tea as he waited—he carried foil packets in his carry-on. Lifting the cup to his lip, he saw a drop of blood break the surface, creating ripples. Then another. His lip felt wet.

"Shit."

James hurried to the men's room, napkin to his face, head tilted back. He'd been getting nosebleeds recently, maybe twice a week. The doctor he saw told him it was the altitude. Dry capillaries plus pressure. He'd ruined more than one uniform in the last few months. At first, he'd been worried, but when no other symptoms arrived Melody chocked it up to age. He'd be fifty-one next March. Halfway there, he thought.

In the bathroom, he put pressure on his nose until the bleeding stopped, then cleaned himself up. He was lucky this time. There was no blood on his shirt or jacket, and James was back in the lounge drinking a fresh cup of tea before his seat was cold.

At five thirty p.m. he gathered his things and walked out to meet the plane.

The fact was, nothing ended on August 9, 1974, except the presidency of Richard M. Nixon.

• • •

He started his pre-flight check in the cockpit, running through the systems one by one. He checked the paperwork first—he'd always been a stickler for precision of detail. He checked the movement of the yoke, listening for any unusual sounds, eyes closed, feeling for any catches or chinks. The starboard motion felt a little sticky, so he contacted maintenance to take a look. Then he switched on the master and checked fuel levels, setting full flaps.

His copilot today was Peter Gaston, an idiosyncratic Belgian who liked to talk philosophy on long flights. James always enjoyed their conversations, especially when they delved into areas between science and ideology. Except when the copilot boarded, it wasn't Gaston but a glassy-eyed man perhaps in his twenties, his tie askew.

"Afternoon, Captain," he said.

Melody recognized him—Charlie something. He'd flown with him once before and though technically the kid performed well, James frowned.

"What happened to Gaston?" he said.

"You got me," said Charlie. "Stomach thing, I think. All I know is I got a call."

James was annoyed, but he wasn't about to show it, so he shrugged. It was the front office's problem.

"Well, you're late. I called maintenance about some stickiness in the yoke. I was just about to do a walk-around. Stow your bag and let's go."

The kid's eyes went to the flight hangar.

"Just, uh, give me a minute," he said and went out again.

After he left, James climbed down the gangway steps and walked the perimeter of the plane, doing a visual inspection. Though it was a warm summer night, he checked for any ice that might have accumulated on the exterior. He looked for missing antennas, for dents, loose bolts, missing rivets, making sure the plane's lights were all fully functional. He found some bird droppings on the wing, removed them by hand, then assessed the way the plane sat on its wheels—a leftward lean would mean the air in the rear port tire was low—inspecting the trailing edges of the wings and eyeballing the engines. He used both his rational left brain, running down a mental checklist, and his instinctual right brain, open to the sense that something felt *off* about the plane. But nothing did.

Back in the cabin, he conferred with the mechanic who told him the altitude system checked out. He chatted with the flight attendant, Emma Lightner, with whom he hadn't worked before. As seemed to be the case on these private flights, she was prettier than was reasonable for such a basic and menial job, but he knew it paid well and the girls got to see the world. He helped her stow some heavier bags. She smiled at him in a way he recognized as friendly, but not flirtatious. And yet her beauty in and of itself felt like gravity—as if nature had designed this woman to pull men to her, and so that's what she did, whether she wanted to or not.

"Just a quick one tonight," he told her. "Should have you back in the city by eleven. Where are you based?"

"New York," she said. "I've got a place in the Village with two other girls. I think they're gone now, though—South Africa, maybe."

"Well, straight to bed for me," said James. "I was in LA this morning. Asia yesterday."

"They sure move us around, don't they?"

He smiled. She couldn't be more than twenty-five. For a moment he thought of the kind of men she must date. Quarterbacks and rock musicians—was that still a thing? Rock music? He himself was mostly celibate. It wasn't that he didn't like the company of women. It was more that he couldn't stand the complications of it, the immediate sense of obligation, the expectation of complete intermingling. He was a man who lived out of a suitcase at fifty. He liked things the way he liked them. His tea, his books. He liked going to the movies in foreign lands, watching modern American films with subtitles in baroque old-world theaters. He liked walking cobblestone streets, listening to people argue in tongues. He loved the hot rush of desert air when one walked the gangway down onto Muslim soil. Yemen, the UAE. He had flown over the Alps at sunset, had battled thunderstorms over the Balkans. In James's mind he was a satellite, graceful and self-sufficient, orbiting the earth, fulfilling its designated purpose without question.

"We were supposed to have Gaston on the other stick," said James. "You know Peter?"

"No," she said. "I've heard of him."

"You'd like him. A Belgian who quotes Proust. What's not to like?"

She smiled, showing teeth, and it was enough. To make a beautiful woman smile, to feel the warmth of her attention. He went into the cockpit and ran through the systems again, checking maintenance's work.

"Ten minutes," he called out.

As he rechecked the systems he felt the plane shift. *That will be the kid coming back*, he thought. He waited for him to reenter the cockpit, thinking he would give him another chance. The kid flew well last time. Maybe he'd just had a late night before, a bachelor party. But the kid didn't come in, not right away. Instead, James heard whispering from the main cabin, and then something that sounded like a slap. He stood at the sound, frowning, and was almost to the cockpit door when the kid came in holding his left cheek.

"Sorry," he said, "I got held up in the office."

James could see Emma behind him. She'd retreated into the main cabin and was smoothing the linens on the headrests.

"Everything okay out here?" James asked, more to her than the kid.

She smiled at him in a far-off way, keeping her eyes down. He looked at Charlie.

"All good, Captain," said Charlie. "Just singing a song I shouldn't have been singing."

"Well, I don't know what that means, but I don't tolerate funny business on my bird. Do I need to call the front office, get another man?"

"No, sir. No funny business. Just here to get the job done. Nothing else."

James studied him. The kid held his eyes. A rogue of sorts, he decided. Not dangerous, just used to getting his way. He was handsome in a crooked sort of fashion, with a Texas twang. *Loose.* That's how James would describe him. Not a planner. More of a *go with the flow* sort. And James was okay with that, in principle. He could be flexible when it came to staff. As long as they did what they were told. The kid needed discipline was all, and James would give it to him.

305

"Okay then, take your seat and get on with control. I want to be wheels-up in five. We've got a schedule to keep."

"Yessir," said Charlie with an unreadable grin, and got to work.

And then the first passengers came aboard, the client and his family—plane shifting as they climbed the gangway—and James made himself available for conversation. He always liked to meet the souls he flew, to shake hands and put faces to names. It made the work more meaningful, especially when there were children. He was captain of this ship, after all, responsible for all lives. It didn't feel like servitude. It felt like a privilege. Only in the modern world did people believe that they should be the ones receiving. But James was a giver. He didn't know what to do when people tried to pamper him. If he caught a seat on a commercial flight, he always found himself getting up to help the flight attendants stow baggage or grabbing blankets for pregnant passengers. Someone had once said to him, *It's hard to be sad when you're being useful.* And he liked that idea. That service to others brought happiness. It was self-involvement that led to depression, to spiraling questions about the meaning of things. This had always been his mother's problem. She thought too much of herself, and not enough of others.

James had built himself to be the opposite. Often he considered what his mother would do in any situation—what the *wrong* decision was—and it clarified for him what he should do instead. In this way he used her as the North Star on a journey where you always want to go south. It was helpful, aligning himself in this way. It gave him something to tune to, like a violin to a piano.

They were in the air five minutes later, taking off to the west and banking back toward the coast. The yoke still felt a little sticky when he moved it starboard, but he put it down to an idiosyncrasy of the plane.

THE BLACKS

THE FIRST NIGHT, Scott sleeps on a pullout sofa in the sewing room. He hadn't planned on staying, but in the aftermath of the day's news he felt Eleanor might need the support, especially since her husband seemed to have disappeared.

He turns off his phone when he's working, said Eleanor, though the way she said it seemed to indicate that the word *working* really mean *drinking.*

Now, on the verge of a dream, Scott hears Doug come home around one, the sound of tires on the driveway waking him with a jolt of adrenaline. There is that animal surge of primitive nerves, eyes opening in an unfamiliar room, unsure for a long moment of where he is. A sewing table sits under the window, the machine a strange looming predator in the shadows. Downstairs, the front door closes. Scott hears the sound of feet on the stairs. He listens as they approach, then stop outside his door. Silence again, like a breath held. Scott lies coiled, tense, an unwanted guest in another man's house. Outside he becomes aware of Doug breathing, a bearded man in overalls, drunk on artisanal bourbon and microbrews. Outside the window the cicadas are cutting a bloody racket in the yard. Scott thinks of the ocean, filled with invisible predators. You hold your breath and dive into the closing darkness, like sliding down a giant's throat, no longer even human in your mind. Prey.

A floorboard pops in the hall as Doug shifts his weight. Scott sits up and stares at the doorknob, a dim copper ball in the darkness. What will he do if it turns? If Doug enters drunk, ready for a fight?

Breathe. Again.

Somewhere the air conditioner's compressor kicks on, and the low duct thrust of forced air breaks the spell. The house is just a house again. Scott listens as Doug walks down the hall to the bedroom.

He exhales slowly, realizing he's been holding his breath.

In the morning, he takes the boy out looking for rocks to skip. They scour the grounds of the riverbank, looking for flat smooth stones—Scott in his city shoes and the boy in little pants and a little shirt, each shoe smaller than Scott's hand. He shows the boy how to stand, cockeyed to the water, and sidearm projectiles across the surface. For a long time the boy can't do it. He furrows his brow and tries over and over, clearly frustrated, but refusing to give up. He chews his tongue inside his closed mouth and makes a working sound, half song, half drone, selecting his stones carefully. The first time he gets a two-hopper, he jumps in the air and claps his hands.

"Nice, buddy," Scott tells him.

Energized, the boy runs off to collect more stones. They are on a thin strip of brambly bank on the edge of the woods at a wide bend in the Hudson. The morning sun is behind them, blockaded by trees, on the rise, its first rays cresting the far shore. Scott sits on his heels and puts his hand in the moving water. It is cool and clear, and for a moment he wonders if he will ever go swimming again, ever fly on another plane. He can smell silt in the air and somewhere a tinge of cut grass. He is aware of his body as a body, muscles engaged, blood flowing. Around him, unseen birds call to each other without urgency, just a steady interchange of heckle and woop.

The boy throws another stone, laughing.

Is this how healing starts?

Last night Eleanor came into the living room to tell him he had a call. Scott was on his knees, playing trucks with the boy.

Who would be calling me here?

"She said her name was Layla," Eleanor said.

Scott got to his feet, went into the kitchen.

"How did you know I was here?" he asked.

"Sweetie," she said, "what else is money for?"

Her voice dropped, moving to a more intimate octave.

"Tell me you're coming back soon," she said. "I'm spending, like, all my time on the third floor sitting inside your painting. It's so good. Did I tell you I've been to that farmers market? When I was a kid. My dad had a place on the Vineyard. I grew up eating ice cream in that courtyard. It's eerie. The first time I ever handled cash was to go buy peaches from Mr. Coselli. I was six."

"I'm with the boy now," Scott told her. "He needs me—I think. I don't know. Kids. Psychology. Maybe I'm just in the way."

Through the phone, Scott heard Layla take a sip of something.

"Well," she said, "I've got buyers lined up for every painting you make in the next ten years. I'm talking to the Tate later about mounting a solo show this winter. Your rep sent me the slides. They're breathtaking."

These words, once so coveted, were Chinese to him now.

"I have to go," he told her.

"Hold on," she said, purring, "don't just run. I miss you."

"What's going on?" he asked. "In your mind. With us."

"Let's go to Greece," she told him. "There's a little house on a cliff I own through, like, six shell companies. Nobody knows a thing. Complete mystery. We could lie in the sun and eat oysters. Dance after dark. Wait till the dust clears. I know I should be coy with you, but I've never met anyone whose attention is harder to get. Even when we're together it's like we're in the same place, but different years."

After he hung up, Scott found JJ had moved to the desk in the living room. He was using Eleanor's computer, playing an educational game, moving letter tiles.

"Hey, buddy."

The boy didn't look up. Scott pulled up a chair and sat down next to him. He watched the boy drag the letter *B* onto a matching square. Above it a cartoon bug sat on a leaf. The boy dragged the *U*, then the *G*.

"Do you mind if I—" said Scott. "Could I—"

He reached for the mouse, moved the cursor. He didn't own a computer himself, but he had spent enough time watching people on laptops in coffee shops to understand what to do, he thought.

"How do I—" he asked, after a moment, more to himself than the boy, "—search for something?"

The boy took the mouse. Concentrating, chewing his tongue, he opened a browser window, went to Google, then gave the mouse back to Scott.

"Great," said Scott. "Thanks."

He typed *Dwo*—then stopped, not knowing the spelling. He erased the word, then typed, *Red Sox, video, longest at bat*, hit ENTER. The page loaded. Scott clicked on a video link. The boy showed him how to maximize the window. He felt like a caveman staring into the sun.

"You can—it's okay to watch I think," he told the boy, then hit PLAY. Onscreen the video began. The quality was pixilated, the colors saturated, as if—rather than record the game the normal way—the poster had filmed their own television screen. Scott imagined that, a man sitting in his living room filming a baseball game on TV, creating a game within a game, the image of an image.

"Dworkin—struck out and singled to center field," the announcer said. Behind him the roar of the crowd was loud, filtered through TV speakers and compressed further by the viewer's camera. The batter stepped into the box. He was a tall Hoosier with a Mennonite beard, no mustache. He took a few practice swings. In the control room they cut to the pitcher, Wakefield, bobbling the rosin. Behind him, towers of floodlights flared the corners of the screen. A night game in summer, eighty-six degrees with winds out of the southwest.

From Gus, Scott knew that Dworkin's at-bat started as the wheels of their plane left the tarmac. He thought about that now, the speed of the plane, the flight attendant in her jump seat, and how much quicker the private jet left the ground than a commercial flight. He watched Dworkin take a pitch low and outside. Ball one.

The camera moved to the crowd, men in sweatshirts, kids with hats and gloves, waving at the lens. The pitcher wound up. Dworkin readied himself, bat hovering above his right shoulder. The ball was released. Scott clicked the mouse, pausing the image. The pitcher froze, back leg raised, left arm extended. Sixty feet away, Dworkin readied himself. From the news Scott knew that twenty-two more pitches were coming. Twenty-two pitches thrown over a span of eighteen minutes, pitch after pitch fouled into the stands, or back into the net. The slow drawl of baseball time, a game of lazy Sundays and dugout chatter. Wind up and pitch.

But right now the game was paused, frozen, the ball floating in midair. Twenty-two pitches, the game already nearly three weeks old, but for a first-time viewer it was as if the events onscreen were happening for the first time. As if the whole earth had rewound. Who knew what would happen next? Dworkin could strike out or homer into deep left field, high above the green monster. Sitting there with the boy, Scott couldn't help but think, *What if everything else reset with the game?* If the whole world cycled back to ten p.m. on the night of August 26, 2015, then stopped. He imagined the cities of the planet frozen, red-light traffic pressed in perfect unison. He pictured smoke hovering motionless above suburban chimneys. Cheetahs caught in mid-stride on the open plains. Onscreen the ball was just a white dot trapped between a point of departure and its destination.

If it was true. If somehow the world had wound itself back, then somewhere he was on an airplane. They were all on an airplane. A family of four, the banker and his wife. A beautiful flight attendant. Children. They were alive. Paused. The girl listening to music. The men jawing, watching the game. Maggie in her seat, smiling into the face of her sleeping son.

As long as he didn't restart the game they would live. As long as he never clicked the mouse. The ball in midair was the plane in midair, its destiny unmet. He stared at it and was surprised to find his eyes watering, the pixels onscreen blurring, the man at the plate just a smudge, the ball a random snowflake, out of season.

At the river, Scott lowers his hand into the water, lets the current pull at his wrist. He remembers looking out the window this morning and watching Doug pack his pickup truck with bags. He was yelling words that Scott couldn't make out, and then he slammed the cab door and pulled out of the driveway, spraying gravel.

What happened? Is he gone for good?

A noise rises on the periphery. It starts as an industrial hum—a distant chain saw maybe, trucks on the interstate (except there is no interstate nearby)—and Scott pays it no attention as he watches the boy dig into the muddy shore and pull out coins of shale and quartz. He begins at a far point and works his way back, searching the mud first with his eyes, then his fingers.

The chain saw gets louder, taking on a low bass rumble. Something is coming. Scott stands, becoming aware of wind, the westward lean of trees, leaves shimmering, mimicking the sound of applause. In the distance the boy stops what he's doing and looks up. In that moment a Jurassic roar overtakes them as the helicopter comes in low over the trees behind them. Scott ducks his head reflexively. The boy starts to run.

The helicopter swoops through bright sun, like a bird of prey, then slows as it reaches the far bank and begins to circle back. It is black and shiny, like a pincered beetle. JJ approaches at a full run, a look of fear on his face. Scott picks him up without thinking and moves into the trees. He runs in his city shoes through low brush, snaking between poplars and elms, poison ivy brushing his cuffs. Once again he is a muscle of survival, an engine of rescue. The boy's arms are wrapped around his neck, legs around his waist. He faces backward, his eyes wide, chin on Scott's shoulder. His knees dig into Scott's sides.

When they get back to the house, Scott sees the helicopter settle in the backyard. Eleanor has come out onto the front porch and has a hand on her head, trying keep her hair from blowing out of her face.

The pilot shuts off the engine, rotors slowing.

Scott hands the boy to Eleanor.

"What's going on?" she says.

"You should take him inside," Scott tells her, then turns to see Gus Franklin and Agent O'Brien climb out of the whirlybird. They approach, O'Brien ducked low, hand on his head, Gus walking up-right—confident that he is shorter than the blades.

The engine whirl slows and quiets. Gus sticks out his hand.

"Sorry for the drama," he says. "But given all the leaks I thought we should reach you before the news got out."

Scott shakes his hand.

"You remember Agent O'Brien," says Gus.

O'Brien spits into the grass.

"Yeah," he says. "He remembers."

"Wasn't he off the case?" says Scott.

Gus squints into the sun.

"Let's just say some new facts are moving the FBI to the front of the investigation."

Scott looks puzzled. O'Brien pats his arm.

"Let's go inside."

They sit in the kitchen. Eleanor puts on an episode of *Cat in the Hat* to distract the boy (*too much TV,* she thinks. *I'm giving him too much TV*), then sits on the edge of her seat, jumping up every time he stirs.

"Okay," says O'Brien. "This is me taking off the gloves."

Scott looks at Gus, who shrugs. There's nothing he can do. The divers recovered the cockpit door this morning, lasering the hinges and floating it to the surface. Tests showed the holes were indeed bullet holes. This triggered a shift in procedural authority. Phone calls were made from government offices and Gus was told in no uncertain terms that he should give the FBI as much operational leeway as they required. Oh, and by the way, he was getting O'Brien back. Apparently, the brass was convinced that O'Brien wasn't their leak. Plus, it turned out, he was being *groomed for big things*—Gus's liaison explained—so they were putting him back on the case.

Ten minutes later, O'Brien walked into the hangar with a team of twelve men and asked for a "sit rep." Gus saw no point in fighting— he was a pragmatist by nature, as much as he disliked the man personally. He told O'Brien that they'd recovered all remaining bodies except for Gil Baruch, the Batemans' body man. It looked as if he had either been thrown clear of the others or had floated out of the fuselage in the days after the crash. If they were lucky his body would wash up somewhere, as Emma's and Sarah's had. Or, quite possibly, it was simply gone.

The obvious questions as Gus saw them were as follows.

1. Who fired the shots? The obvious suspect was the security man, Gil Baruch, the only passenger known to be armed, but since none of the passengers or crew had gone through a security screening before boarding the plane, they were all potential shooters.
2. Why had the shots been fired? Was the shooter attempting to force his way into the cockpit in order to hijack the plane? Or simply to crash it? Or was the shooter attempting to get inside the cockpit to avert the crash? Villain, or a hero? That was the question.
3. Why was the captain in the main cabin and not the cockpit? If it was a possible hijack scenario, was he a hostage? Had he come out to defuse the situation? But if that was the case...
4. Why was there no mayday from the copilot?

Speaking of the copilot, divers had found Charles Busch strapped into his seat in the cockpit, hands still gripping the yoke. One of the bullets had buried itself in the floor behind him, but there was no evidence that anyone had made it inside the cockpit before the plane hit the water. Gus told the agent that autopsy results on Busch would be back that afternoon. None of them knew what they were hoping for. The *best-case scenario*, in Gus's mind, was that the young man had suffered a stroke or heart attack. The worst case, well, the worst case was this was a calculated act of mass murder.

All loose debris had been tagged and bagged and was here now, being cataloged. The good news was that the black box and data recorders had been recovered. The bad news was that it appeared one or both may have been damaged in the crash. Techs would work around the clock to recover every last trace of data. By the end of the day, Gus told him—barring an unexpected turn of weather—the fuselage should be up and on its way to the hangar.

O'Brien listened to everything Gus said, then called in the helicopter.

Now, in the kitchen, Agent O'Brien makes a show of taking a small notebook out of his pocket. He removes a pen, unscrews the cap, lays it next to the pad. Gus can feel Scott's eyes on him, questioning, but he keeps his focus on O'Brien, as if to signal to Scott—*this is where you should be looking now*.

They have agreed not to discuss the case on the phone, not to put anything in writing until they find out how O'Brien's memo was leaked. From now on, all conversations will take place in person. It is the paradox of modern technology. The tools we use can be used against us.

"As you know," says O'Brien. "We found the plane. And Mrs. Dunleavy, I'm afraid I have to tell you that, yes, we have officially recovered the bodies of your sister, her husband, and your niece."

Eleanor nods. She feels like a bone that has been left to bleach in the sun. She thinks about the boy, in the living room watching TV. *Her* boy. And what she will say to him, or should say to him. She thinks about Doug's last words this morning.

This isn't over.

"Mr. Burroughs," says O'Brien, turning to Scott. "You need to tell me everything you remember about the flight."

"Why?"

"Because I told you to."

"Scott," says Gus.

"No," O'Brien snaps. "We're done holding this guy's hand."

He turns to Scott.

"Why was the pilot outside the cockpit during the flight?"

Scott shakes his head.

"I don't remember that."

"You said you heard banging before the plane crashed. We asked if you thought it was mechanical. You said you didn't think so. What do you think it was?"

Scott looks at him, thinking.

"I don't know. The plane pitched. I hit my head. It's—they're not memories really."

O'Brien studies him.

"There are six bullet holes in the cockpit door."

"What?" says Eleanor, her face draining of blood.

The words push Scott back in his chair. *Bullet holes?* What are they saying?

"Did you ever see a gun?" O'Brien asks Scott.

"No."

"Do you remember the Batemans' body man? Gil Baruch?"

"The big guy by the door. He didn't—I don't—"

Scott loses his words, mind racing.

"You never saw him pull a gun?" O'Brien asks.

Scott racks his brain. *Somebody shot up the cockpit door.* He tries to make sense of that. The plane pitched. People screamed and somebody shot up the door. The plane was going down. The captain was outside the cockpit. Somebody shot up the door trying to get in.

Or was the gun pulled first and the pilot—no, the *copilot*—put the plane into a dive to—what? Throw him off balance? Either way, they're saying this wasn't mechanical error, or human error. It was something worse.

There is a visceral twist of nausea in Scott's guts, as if it's only hitting him now how close he came to death. And then a wave of light-headedness as the next thought strikes him. If this wasn't an accident, then it means *someone tried to kill him.* That instead of an act of fate, he and the boy were victims of an attack.

"I got on the plane," he says, "and took a seat. She brought me some wine. Emma. I don't—I said, *No, thank you,* asked for some water. Sarah—the banker's wife—was talking in my ear about taking her daughter to the Whitney Biennial. The game was on TV. Baseball. And the men—David and the banker—they were watching, cheering. My bag was in my lap. She wanted to take it—the flight attendant— but I held on to it, and as we taxied I started—I started going through it. I don't know why. Something to do. Nerves."

"What made you nervous?" asks O'Brien.

Scott thinks about it.

"It was a big trip for me. And the plane—having to run for the plane—I was discombobulated—a little. It all seems meaningless now, how much it mattered. Meetings with art reps, gallery visits. I had all the slides in my bag, and—after the run—I wanted to make sure I still had them. For no reason."

He looks at his hands.

"I was in the window seat, looking out at the wing. Everything was foggy, and then suddenly the fog cleared. Or we rose above it, I guess is what happened. And it was just night. And I looked over at Maggie, and she smiled. Rachel was in the seat behind her, listening to music, and the boy was asleep with a blanket over him. And I don't know why, but I thought she might like a drawing, Maggie, so I took out my pad and started sketching the girl. Nine years old, headphones on, looking out the window."

He remembers the look on the girl's face, a child lost in thought, but something in her eyes—a sadness—hinting at the woman she would one day become, and how she had come to the barn that day with her mother to look at Scott's work, a growing girl all legs and hair.

"We hit a couple of bumps going up," he says. "Enough to shake the glasses, but it was pretty smooth, otherwise, and nobody seemed worried. The security man sat in the front with the flight attendant for takeoff on the—what do you—jump seat, but he was up as soon as the seat belt sign was off."

"Doing?"

"Nothing, standing."

"No drama?"

"No drama."

"And you were drawing."

"Yes."

"And then?"

Scott shakes his head. He remembers chasing his pencil across the floor, but not what happened before. The lie of an airplane is that the floor is always level, the straight angles of the plane tricking your mind into thinking you're sitting or standing at a ninety-degree angle to world, even when the plane is on its side. But then you look out the window, and find yourself staring at the ground.

The plane banked. The pencil fell. He unbuckled his seat belt to chase it, and it rolled across the floor, like a ball going downhill. And then he was sliding, and his head hit something.

Scott looks at Gus.

"I don't know."

Gus looks at O'Brien.

"I have a question," Gus says. "Not about the crash. About your work."

"Okay."

"Who's the woman?"

Scott looks at him.

"The woman?"

"In all the paintings—I noticed—there's always a woman, and it's always—from what I can see—the same woman. Who is she?"

Scott exhales. He looks at Eleanor. She is watching him. What must she think? Days ago her life was a straight line. Now all she has are burdens.

"I had a sister," says Scott. "She drowned when I was—she was sixteen. Night swimming in Lake Michigan with some—kids. Just—dumb kids."

"I'm sorry."

"Yeah."

Scott wishes there was something profound he could say about it, but there isn't.

. . .

Later, after the boy is asleep, Scott calls Gus from the kitchen.

"Was that okay today?" he asks.

"It was helpful, thank you."

"Helpful how?" Scott wants to know.

"Details. Who sat where. What people were doing."

Scott sits at the table. There was a moment, after the helicopter departed and Eleanor and Scott were left alone, when both of them seemed to realize that they were strangers, that the illusion of the last twenty-four hours—the idea that the house was a bubble they could hide in—had dissolved. She was a married woman, and he was—what? The man who rescued her nephew. What did they really know about each other? How long was he staying? Did she even want him to? Did he?

An awkwardness arose between them then, and when Eleanor started cooking, Scott told her he wasn't hungry. He needed a walk to clear his head.

He stayed out until after dark, wandering back to the river and watching the water turn from blue to black as the sun set, and the moon came out.

He was farther than he'd ever been from the man he thought he was.

"Well," Gus tells him over the phone. "Nobody knows this yet, but the flight recorder's damaged. Not destroyed, but it's gonna take work to get to the data. I've got a team of six guys in there working now, and the governors of two states are calling every five minutes for up-dates."

"I can't help you with that. I can barely open a tube of paint."

"No. I'm just—I'm telling you because you deserve to know. Everybody else can go to hell."

"I'll tell Eleanor."

"How's the boy? I couldn't really get a sense of it earlier."

"He's not—talking, really, but he seems to like that I'm here. So maybe that's therapeutic. Eleanor's really—strong."

"And the husband? I didn't see him there today."

"He left this morning with luggage."

A long pause.

"I don't have to tell you how that's going to look," says Gus.

Scott nods.

"Since when does how a thing looks matter more than what it is?" he asks.

"Two thousand twelve, I think," says Gus. "Especially after—your hideout in the city. How that made the news. The heiress, which—I said *find someplace to hide*, not shack up in a tabloid story."

Scott rubs his eyes.

"Nothing happened. I mean, yeah, she took off her clothes and climbed into bed with me, but I didn't—"

"We're not talking about what did or didn't happen," says Gus. "We're talking about what it looks like."

In the morning, Scott hears Eleanor down in the kitchen. He finds her at the stove making breakfast. The boy's on the floor, playing between rooms. Wordlessly, Scott sits on the floor next to him and picks up a cement truck. They play for a moment, rolling rubber wheels on the wooden floors. Then, the boy offers Scott a gummy bear from the bag and he takes it.

Outside, the world continues to spin. Inside, they go through the motions of daily life, pretending that everything is normal.

EMMA LIGHTNER

JULY 11, 1990–
AUGUST 26, 2015

IT WAS ABOUT setting boundaries and sticking to them. You smiled at the client, served them drinks. You laughed at their jokes and made small talk. You flirted. You were a fantasy to them, just like the plane. The beautiful girl with the million-dollar smile making men feel like kings as they sat on a luxury jet, talking on three cell phones at once. Under no circumstances did you give out your phone number. You certainly did not kiss an Internet millionaire in the galley or have sex with a basketball star in a private bedroom. And you never went with a billionaire to a second location, even if that second location was a castle in Monaco. You were a flight attendant, a service professional, not a prostitute. You had to have rules, boundaries, because in the land of the rich it was easy to lose your way.

At twenty-five, Emma Lightner had traveled to all seven continents. Working for GullWing, she had met movie stars and sheiks. She had flown with Mick Jagger and Kobe Bryant. One night after a cross-country flight—LAX to JFK—Kanye West chased her onto the tarmac and tried to give her a diamond bracelet. She didn't take it, of course. Emma had long since stopped being flattered by the attention. Men old enough to be her grandfather routinely suggested she could have anything she wanted if she joined them for dinner in Nice or Gstaad or Rome. It was the altitude, she sometimes thought, the possibility of death by falling. But what it really was was the arrogance of money, and the need of the wealthy to possess everything they saw. The truth was, Emma was nothing more to her clients than a Bentley or a condo or a pack of gum.

To female passengers, wives of clients or clients themselves, Emma was both a threat and a cautionary tale. She represented the old paradigm, where beautiful women in conical bras catered to the secret needs of powerful men in smoky clubs. A geisha, a Playboy Bunny. She was a stealer of husbands, or, worse, a reflection in the mirror, a reconstruction of their own paths to moneyed wifery. A reminder. Emma felt their eyes on her as she moved through the cabin. She endured the steely-tongued jabs of women in oversize sunglasses who sent back their drinks and told her to be more careful next time. She could fold a napkin into the shape of a swan and mix a perfect gimlet. She knew which wines to pair with oxtail stew or venison paella, could perform CPR, and had been trained to do an emergency tracheotomy. She had skills, not just looks, but that never mattered to these women.

On the bigger jets there would be three to five girls working. On the smaller plane it was just Emma, in a short blue skirt suit, handing out drinks and demonstrating the safety features of the Cessna Citation Bravo or Hawker 900XP.

The exits are here. The seat belts work just so. Oxygen masks. Your seat may be used as a flotation device.

She lived her life in turnaround time, the hours and days spent between flights. The travel company kept apartments in most major international cities. It was cheaper than buying hotel rooms for the crew. Anonymously modern with parquet floors and Swedish cabinetry, each apartment was designed to resemble the other—the same furniture, the same fixtures—in the words of the company handbook, "in order to lessen the effects of jet lag." But to Emma, the uniformity of the space had the opposite effect, increasing her feeling of displacement. It was easy to wake in the middle of the night and not know which city you were in, which country. Occupancy of any company safe house usually hovered around ten people. This meant that at any one time there might be a German pilot and six South Africans sleeping two to a room. They were like modeling agency apartments, filled with beautiful girls, except in one room there'd be a couple of forty-six-year-old pilots farting in their sleep.

Emma had been twenty-one when she started, the daughter of an air force pilot and a stay-at-home mom. She had studied finance in college, but after six months working for a big New York investment bank had decided she wanted to travel instead. The luxury economy was exploding, and jet companies and yacht companies and private resorts were desperate for attractive, competent, bilingually discreet people who could start right away.

The truth was, she loved planes. One of her first (and best) memories was of riding in the cockpit of a Cessna with her dad. Emma couldn't have been more than five or six. She remembers the clouds through the tiny oval windows, towering white shapes her mind transformed into puppies and bears. So much so that when they got home Emma told her mother that her dad had taken her to see the zoo in the sky.

She remembers her father from that day, seen from a low angle, strong-jawed and immortal, his close cropped hair and aviator sunglasses. Michael Aaron Lightner, twenty-six years old, a fighter jet pilot, with arms like knotted ropes. No one in her life would ever be a man the way her father was a man, sharp-toothed and steely-eyed, with a dry Midwestern wit. A man of few words who could cut a cord of firewood in ten minutes and never wore a seat belt. She had seen him once knock a man out with a single punch, a lightning strike that was over before it began, the knockout a foregone conclusions, her father already walking away as the other man crumpled to the ground.

This was at a gas station outside San Diego. Later, Emma would learn that the man had said something lewd to her mother as she went to the restroom. Her father, pumping gas, saw the exchange and approached the man. Words were had. Emma doesn't remember her father raising his voice. There was no heated argument, no macho chest bump or warning shove. Her father said something. The man said something back. And then the punch, a whip crack to the jaw that started at the hip, and then her father was walking back to the car, the man tipping backward and toppling, like a tree. Her dad lifted the nozzle from the gas tank and set it back on its arm, screwing the gas cap in place.

Emma, her face pressed to the window, watched her mother return from the restroom, saw her glance at the unconscious stranger and slow, her face confused. Her father called to her and then held the door for his wife before climbing into the driver's seat.

Emma knelt in the backseat and stared out the back window, waiting for the police. Her father was something else now, not just a dad. He was her knight, her protector, and when they taxied down private runways, Emma would close her eyes and picture that moment, the words exchanged, the man falling. She would fly high into the troposphere, into the dark recesses of space, slipping weightless inside a single perfect memory.

Then the captain would turn off the FASTEN SEAT BELT sign and Emma would snap back to reality. She was a twenty-five-year-old woman with a job to do. So she'd stand and smooth the wrinkles of her skirt, already smiling her collusive yet professional smile, ready to play her part in the ongoing seduction of wealth. It wasn't hard. There was a checklist you went through as you prepared for takeoff and another one as you started your final descent. Jackets were distributed, cocktails refreshed. Sometimes, if the flight was short and the meal comprised more than four courses, the plane would sit on the runway for an hour while dessert and coffee were served. When it came to high-end private travel, the journey *was* the destination. And then, after your guests had disembarked, there were dishes to be cleared and stowed. But the real dirty work was left for the locals, Emma and the others descending the gangway and sliding into their own sleek transport.

Emma Lightner lived her life in turnaround time, but it was the turnaround she found the most depressing. It wasn't just the luxury of her work surroundings that made it difficult to return to a normal life, wasn't just the town car that took you to and from work, or the Swiss-watch precision and opulence of the plane. It wasn't simply that you spent your days and nights surrounded by millionaires and billionaires, men and women who, even as they reminded you that you were their servant, also (if you were beautiful like Emma) made you feel like part of the club—because in today's economy beauty is the great equalizer, a backstage pass.

For Emma, what made it so hard to return to the tiny apartment in the West Village she shared with two other girls was the sudden realization that for all those weeks of traveling she had been a stow-away in someone else's life, an actor on a stage playing a part. She was the royal escort, the chaste concubine, immersed in servitude for weeks at a time, until the rules and boundaries she set to navigate her professional life became the backbone of her personal life as well. She found herself growing increasingly lonely, an object to be looked at, but never touched.

On Friday, August 24, she flew from Frankfurt to London on a Learjet 60XR. It was her and Chelsea Norquist, a gap-toothed blonde from Finland, in the main cabin. The clients were German oil company executives, meticulously dressed and unfailingly polite. They landed at six p.m. GMT at Farnborough Airport, bypassing all the drag and bureaucracy of Heathrow or Gatwick. The executives, over-coated with mobile phones glued to their ears, descended the external stairway to a limousine waiting on the tarmac. Parked behind the limo was a black SUV waiting to take the flight crew into the city. Here in London, the company apartment was in South Kensington, a short walk from Hyde Park. Emma had stayed there at least a dozen times. She knew which bed she wanted, which nearby bars and restaurants she could escape to, the ones where she could order a glass of wine or a cup of coffee, open a book, and recharge.

The pilot on the Frankfurt flight, Stanford Smith, was a former British air force lieutenant in his early fifties. The first officer, Peter Gaston, was a thirty-six-year-old chain smoker from Belgium who hit on all the girls with a tenacity and good humor that ironically made him seem toothless. He had a reputation among GullWing crews as the guy to see if you needed ecstasy or coke, the man to call in a pinch if you last-minute had to find clean piss for a company drug screen.

Traffic on the A4 was bumper-to-bumper. Sitting next to Emma in the middle row of the Cadillac, Chelsea worked her iPhone, setting and revising the social agenda for the night. She was twenty-seven, a party girl with a weakness for musicians.

"No, you stop it," she said, giggling.

"I'm telling you," Stanford announced from the back row, "you roll a pair of pants. You don't fold them."

"*Merde*," said Peter. "You want flat surfaces for stacking."

Like all people who travel for a living, Stanford and Peter believed they were experts at the art of packing. The subject was a constant source of disagreement among crews all over the world. Sometimes the differences were cultural—Germans believed that shoes had to be stored in sleeves; the Dutch were strangely fond of garment bags. Veterans tested rookies randomly, usually after a few drinks, grilling them on the proper strategy in packing for an SAT of possible trips—a midwinter overnighter from Bermuda to Moscow. A two-day layover in Hong Kong in August. What size and brand of suitcase? A single heavy coat or layers? The order in which items went into a suitcase was critical. Emma had little interest in the subject. She felt what she put inside her suitcase was a private matter. To derail the subject, she would smile demurely and announce that she slept naked and never wore panties—which was a lie. The girl wore flannel pajamas to bed, which she rolled separately and vacuum-sealed in reusable plastic bags when traveling—but the ploy usually worked in changing the subject from packing to nudity, at which point Emma would make an excuse and walk away, letting the others carry the thread to its natural conclusion—which was a discussion of sex.

But tonight Emma was tired. She had just finished back-to-back flights—Los Angeles to Berlin with a big-name director and famous female movie star for a film premiere, after which the crew immediately refueled and flew to Frankfurt to pick up the oil company executives. She had slept a few hours on the first leg, but now, with the change in time zones, and the knowledge that she needed to stay awake for at least four more hours, Emma found herself stifling a yawn.

"Oh no," Chelsea said, catching her. "We're going out tonight. Farhad has it all lined up."

Farhad was Chelsea's London boy, a fashion designer who wore unlaced high-tops with slim-fit suits. Emma liked him well enough, except the last time she was in London he had tried to set her up with a Manchester ragamuffin artist who couldn't keep his hands to himself.

Emma nodded and drank from her water bottle. At this time tomorrow, she would be on a charter to New York, then a quick trip to Martha's Vineyard and home to Jane Street for a weeklong vacation. In the city, she planned to sleep for forty-eight hours, then sit down and figure out what the hell she was doing with her life. Her mother was planning to come to the city for three nights, and Emma was excited to see her. It had been too long, and Emma felt the need for a giant mom hug and a hot pot of mac and cheese in her bones. She had planned to spend her last birthday in San Diego, but a charter had come up at double her normal rate and she had taken it, spending her twenty-fifth birthday freezing her ass off in St. Petersburg.

From now on, she thought, she would put her own needs first, family, love. She couldn't afford to end up one of these lifer-widows with too much makeup and a boob job. She was old enough already. Time was running out.

They pulled up in front of the corporate town house just after seven, the dusky London sky a rich midnight blue. Rain was forecast for tomorrow, but right now it was perfect summer weather.

"Looks like there's only one other crew tonight," Stanford said, pocketing their itinerary as they climbed from the car. "Chicago-based."

Emma felt a twinge of something—worry? dread?—but it vanished almost as quickly when Chelsea gave her arm a squeeze.

"A quick bath and a vodka and we're off," she said.

Inside, they found Carver Ellis, the copilot for the Chicago flight, and two flight attendants dancing to French pop songs from the 1960s. Carver was a muscular black man in his thirties. He wore chinos and a white tank top, and smiled when he saw her. Emma had flown with Carver a couple of times and liked him. He was lighthearted and always treated her professionally. Seeing him, Chelsea made a purring sound. She had a thing for black guys. The flight attendants were new to Emma. A blond American and a pretty Spaniard. The Spaniard was in a towel.

"Now it's a party," Carver said as the Frankfurt crew rolled in.

Hugs and handshakes were exchanged. There was a bottle of Chopin vodka on the kitchen counter and a crate of fresh-squeezed orange juice. From the living room windows you could see the treetops of Hyde Park. The song on the stereo was a drum and bass loop, sultry and infectious.

Carver took Emma's hand and she let herself be twirled. Chelsea kicked off her heels and jutted a hip, her hands lifted toward the ceiling. For a moment they danced, letting the energy of the music and the thrum of their libidos rule them. The groove had a pocket you felt in your loins. How amazing to be young and alive in a modern European city.

Emma took the first shower, standing under scalding water with her eyes closed. As always there was that feeling in her bones that she was still moving, still hurtling through space at four hundred miles per hour. Without realizing, she began to hum in the steamy glass stall.

People of the Earth can you hear me?
Came a voice from the sky on that magical night.

She towel-dried, her toiletry kit hanging from a hook by the sink. It was a testament to MAC's efficiency, organized by region—hair, teeth, skin, nails. Standing naked, she brushed her hair with long even strokes, then put on deodorant. She moisturized, first her feet, then her legs and arms. It was a way to ground herself, to remind herself she was real, not just an object hovering in midair.

There was a quick knock at the door, and Chelsea slipped into the bathroom with glass tumbler in hand.

"Bitch," she said to Emma, "I hate that you're so thin."

She handed the glass to Emma and used both hands to squeeze the imaginary fat around her own middle. The glass was half full of vodka over ice with a floating lime. Emma took one sip, then another. She felt the vodka moving through her, warming her from the inside.

Chelsea pulled a glassine envelope from her skirt pocket and cut a line of coke on the marble countertop, working with professional efficiency.

"Ladies first," she said, handing Emma a rolled dollar bill.

Emma wasn't a huge fan of cocaine—she preferred pills—but if she was going to make it out the door tonight she needed the pick-me-up. She bent and put the roll to her nose.

"Not all of it, you saucy cunt," said Chelsea, slapping Emma's naked ass.

Emma straightened, wiping at her nose. As always, there was a physical click in her head as the drug hit her bloodstream, the sensation of something in her brain being turned on.

Chelsea racked the line and rubbed the remaining powder into her gums. She took Emma's brush and started in on her hair.

"It's gonna get wild tonight," she said. "Trust me."

Emma wrapped herself in a towel, feeling every thread on her skin.

"I can't promise I'll stay out too late," she said.

"Go home early and I'll smother you in your sleep," said Chelsea. "Or worse."

Emma zipped her toiletry kit. She knocked back what was left of the vodka. She pictured her father in a dirty white tee, frozen forever at twenty-six. He walked toward her in slow motion. Behind him a bigger man fell to the ground.

"Just try it, bitch," she told Chelsea. "I sleep with a blade."

Chelsea smiled.

"That's my girl," she said. "Now let's go out there and get proper fucked."

Coming out of the bathroom Emma heard a man's voice. Later she would remember the way her stomach lurched and time seemed to slow down.

"I took the knife away from him," said the man. "What did you think I'd do. Broke his arm in three places, too. Fucking Jamaica."

Panicking, Emma turned to duck back into the bathroom, but Chelsea was behind her. They knocked heads.

"Ow, shit," said Chelsea, loudly.

In the living room everyone looked up. They saw Chelsea and Emma (in a white towel) doing a strange dance, as Emma made one last attempt to disappear. And then Charlie Busch was on his feet, coming toward her, his arms wide.

"Hey, beautiful," he said. "Surprise."

Cornered, Emma turned. The coke had turned on her, making the world jittery and uneven.

"Charlie, Charlie," she said, trying to sound upbeat.

He gave her a kiss on both cheeks, his hands holding her by the shoulders.

"Put on a few, huh?" he said. "Too many desserts."

Her stomach lurched. He grinned.

"Just kidding," he said. "You look fantastic. Doesn't she look great?"

"She's in a towel," said Carver, sensing Emma's discomfort. "Of course she looks great."

"What do you say, babe?" said Charlie. "Wanna run on in and put on something sexy. I hear we got big plans tonight. Big plans."

Emma forced a smile and stumbled to her room. The vodka made her legs feel like they were made out of paper. She closed the door and put her back to it, standing for a long moment with her heart pounding in her chest.

Fuck, she thought. *Fuck, fuck, fuck.*

It had been six months since she last saw Charlie. Six months of phone calls and texts. He was like a bloodhound after a scent. Emma had changed her phone number, had blocked his emails and un-friended him on Facebook. She ignored the texts, ignored the gossip from co-workers, how he was talking trash about her behind her back, how he called other girls by her name in bed. Her friends had told her to file a complaint with the company, but Emma was afraid. Charlie was somebody's nephew, she seemed to remember. Besides, she knew it was the squeaky wheel that got let go.

She had done so well, she thought. She had made rules and stuck by them. She was the girl with her head on straight. Charlie was her one mistake. It wasn't his fault really. He couldn't help who found him attractive. He was tall and handsome with a rogue's scruff. A charmer with green eyes that had reminded Emma of her father. Which, of course, was what it was. Charlie was a man who occupied the same space as her father, embodied the same archetype, the strong, silent loner, the Good Man, but it was a mirage. The truth was, Charlie was nothing like her father. With him, the good-guy thing was just an act. Where her father was confident, Charlie was arrogant. Where her father was chivalrous, Charlie was patronizing and smug. He had wooed her, seduced her with empathy and warmth, and then, out of nowhere, he turned into Mr. Hyde, berating her in public, telling her she was stupid, she was fat, she was a slut.

At first she treated this change as if it were her fault. Clearly, he was reacting to something. Maybe she had put on a few pounds. Maybe she had been flirting with that Saudi prince. But then, as his behavior intensified—culminating in a terrifying bedroom choking—she realized that Charlie was crazy. All of his jealousy and viciousness was the bad side of his bipolar heart. He wasn't a good man. He was a natural disaster, and so Emma did what any sane person does in the face of a natural disaster. She ran.

Now she dresses quickly, pulling on her least flattering outfit. She wipes the makeup from her cheeks with a towel, takes out her contact lenses, putting on the cat's-eye glasses she bought in Brooklyn. Her first instinct is to say she feels sick and stay home, but she knows what Charlie will do. He'll offer to stay and take care of her, and the last thing Emma can handle is being alone with him.

Someone bangs on the bedroom door, making Emma jump.

"Come on, whore," yells Chelsea. "Farhad's waiting."

Emma grabs her coat. She will stay close to the others, sticking to Chelsea and Carver, latching on to the pretty Spaniard. She will stick to them like glue, and then, when the time is right, she will slip away. She will come back to the apartment, grab her things, and check into a hotel under an assumed name, and if he tries anything, she will call the company tomorrow and file a formal complaint.

"Coming," she yells, hurriedly packing. She will put her suitcase by the door and be gone before anyone's the wiser. Ten seconds, in and out. She can do this. She wanted to change her life anyway. This is her chance. And as she opens the door, she finds that her pulse has almost returned to normal. And then she sees Charlie standing by the front door, smiling with his X-ray eyes.

"Okay," says Emma. "I'm ready."

HURT

MORNING TRAFFIC—human and vehicular—moves up Sixth Avenue in ever-shifting patterns. Each body, car, and bicycle is a water molecule that would travel in a straight line at maximum speed if not for all the other molecules competing for space in an ever-shrinking channel, like an ocean strained through a fire hose. It is a sea of earbuds, bodies moving to their own beat. Working women in sneakers text on the go, their minds a thousand miles away, cabdrivers half watching the road and half scrolling through messages from faraway lands.

Doug stands outside the entrance to the ALC Building smoking a final cigarette. He has slept three hours in the last two days. A smell test of his beard would yield hints of bourbon, drive-through cheeseburgers, and the peaty curl of Brooklyn lager. His lips are chapped, synapses firing too fast and in too many directions. He is a revenge machine, one that has convinced itself that truth is subjective, and that a man wronged has the right, no the moral duty, to Set The Record Straight.

Krista Brewer, Bill Cunningham's producer, meets him in the lobby, moving at a near run. She actually pushes a black guy with a messenger bag out of the way, her eyes locked on Doug's shuffling form.

"Doug, hi," she says, smiling like a hostage negotiator who's been taught not to break eye contact. "Krista Brewer. We spoke on the phone."

"Where's Bill?" Doug asks nervously, having second thoughts. He had a vision of how this would go in his head, and this isn't it.

She smiles.

"Upstairs. He can't wait to see you."

Doug frowns, but she takes his arm, leads him past security and onto a waiting elevator. It is the morning rush, and they are packed in with a dozen other molecules, all destined for different floors, different lives.

Ten minutes later, Doug finds himself in a chair in front of a triple mirror framed in bright lights. A woman with a lot of bracelets brushes his hair and puts foundation on his forehead, dabbing him with powder.

"You got plans for the weekend?" she asks him.

Doug shakes his head. His wife has just thrown him out of the house. He spent the first twelve hours drunk and the last six sleeping in his pickup truck. He feels like Humphrey Bogart in *The Treasure of Sierra Madre*, that same sense of crazed loss (so close!), not that it's about the money. It's the principle. Eleanor is his wife and the kid is their kid, and, yes, $103 million (plus 40 more for the real estate) is a lot of money, and, yes, he had already shifted his worldview, luxuriating in the idea that he is now a man of means. And, no, he doesn't think that money solves every problem, but certainly it will make their lives easier. He can finish the restaurant, no problem, and finally finish that novel. They can afford child care for the kid and maybe fix up the Croton house for weekends while they move into the town house on the Upper East Side. The Batemans' cappuccino machine alone is worth relocating. And, yes, he knows that's shallow—but isn't that what the whole artisanal return-to-simplicity movement is all about— making sure that every single thing we do is thoughtful and perfect? That every bite of every meal, every step of every day, everything from our hemp throw pillows to our handcrafted bicycles is like a koan from the Dalai Lama.

We are the enemies of industrialization, killers of the mass market. No more "10 billion served." Now it's one meal at a time, eggs cooked from your own chickens. Seltzer infused by your own CO_2 tank. This is the revolution. Back to the soil, the loom, the still. And yet the struggle is hard, the way each man has to claw his way into some kind of future. To overcome the obstacles of youth and *establish himself* without getting lost along the way. And the money would help with that. It would remove the worry, the risk. Especially now, with the kid, and how hard that can be—like, say, if you weren't really ready yet to have that much responsibility, to put your own needs aside for the needs of something small and irrational that can't even wipe its own butt.

In the chair he's starting to sweat. The makeup lady blots his forehead.

"Maybe take off your coat," she suggests.

But Doug is thinking about Scott, about the snake in his home, and how this fucking guy just drives up like he owns the place, like just because he's got this bond with the kid he's invited somehow to move in. And what did Doug ever do to deserve being thrown out of his own home? Yeah, okay, he came home drunk after midnight and maybe he was a little pissed off and yelling, but it's his house, after all. And she's *his* woman. And what kind of bizarro world are we living in if some has-been painter has more of a right to be in a man's home than he does? So he says all this to Eleanor, orders her to send the guy packing as soon as the sun comes up. Tells her that she's his wife and he loves her, and they have a beautiful thing, a thing worth protecting, cherishing, especially now that they're *parents*, right? That he's a father.

And Eleanor listens. Just listens. Sits very still. Doesn't get upset. Doesn't seem scared or pissed or—anything. She just listens to him rant and stomp around the bedroom, and then—when he runs out of gas—she tells him she wants a divorce and that he should go sleep on the couch.

Krista comes back smiling. They're ready for him, she says. Bill is ready, and Doug is *so brave* for coming in, and the country, the world, is so grateful that there are men like Doug out there who are willing to tell the truth about things, even if it's hard. And Doug nods. This is him in a nutshell. He is the common man, noble, hardworking. A man who doesn't complain or demand, but one who expects the world to be square with him. Who expects a day's work to earn a day's pay. Expects that the life you build, the family you make, is your life, your family. You earned it and nobody should be able to take that away from you.

A lottery won should stay won.

So he takes off the paper bib and goes to meet his destiny.

. . .

"Doug," says Bill, "thank you for being here today."

Doug nods, trying not to look into the camera. *Just focus on me*, Bill has told him. And this is what he does, focuses on the other man's eyebrows, the tip of his nose. He's not handsome, Bill Cunningham, not in the traditional sense, but he has that alpha bravado—the indefinable nexus of power, charisma, and confidence, the unblinking gaze and crotch-forward carriage of a man at the height of his visceral global impact. Is it physical? Pheromonal? An aura? For some reason, Doug thinks of the way a school of reef sharks will scatter when a great white appears. The way some woodland deer will simply surrender to the jaws of the wolf, ceasing their struggles and lying still, subdued by inevitable and irresistible forces.

And then he thinks, *Am I the deer?*

"These are troubling times," says Bill. "Don't you agree?"

Doug blinks.

"Do I agree that the times are troubling?"

337

"For you. For me. For America. I'm talking about loss and injustice."

Doug nods. This is the story he wants to tell.

"It's a tragedy," he says. "We all know it. The crash and now—"

Bill leans forward. Their feed is being beamed by satellite to nine hundred million possible screens worldwide.

"For people who don't know the story as well as me," he says, "give a little background."

Doug fidgets nervously, then becomes conscious that he's fidgeting and gives an odd shrug.

"Well, uh, you know about the crash. The plane crash. And how only two people survived. JJ, my nephew. My, uh, wife's nephew. And this painter, Scott, uh, something, who supposedly swam to shore."

"Supposedly?"

"No," says Doug, backpedaling. "I'm just going off something you—I mean, it was heroic—definitely, but that doesn't—"

Bill shakes his head imperceptibly.

"And so you took him in," he says, "your nephew."

"Yes. Of course. I mean, he's only four. His parents are—dead."

"Yes," says Bill. "You took him in 'cause you're a good man. A man who cares about Doing The Right Thing."

Doug nods.

"We don't have much, you know," says Doug. "We're—I'm a writer, and Eleanor, my wife, she's a, like a physical therapist."

"A caregiver."

"Right, but, you know, whatever we have is his—he's family, right? JJ? And look—"

Doug takes a breath, trying to focus on the story he wants to tell.

"—look, I'm not perfect."

"Who is?" asks Bill. "Plus, you're—how old are you even?"

"I'm thirty-four."

"A baby."

"Not—I mean—I work hard, okay? I'm trying to start a restaurant, to rebuild—while also—and, okay, sometimes I have a few beers."

"Who doesn't?" says Bill. "At the end of a long day. In my book that makes a man a patriot."

"Right, and—look, the guy's a—hero—Scott—clearly, but—well, he kind of moved in—"

"Scott Burroughs? He moved into your house."

"Well, he—he showed up a couple of days ago to see the kid, which—again—he saved him, right? So that's—nobody's saying he can't *see* JJ. But—a man's home is supposed to be his—and my wife— you know, it's a lot to handle, with the boy—a lot to process—so maybe she's just—confused, but—"

Bill bites his lip. Though he doesn't show the audience at home, he's losing his patience with Doug, who is clearly a basket case and who—left to his own devices—will implode without communicating the story Bill has brought him here to tell.

"Let me see," he interrupts, "not to interrupt, but let me see if I can clarify a few things here, because, well, you're clearly upset."

Doug stops, nods. Bill turns slightly so he's speaking into the camera.

"Your wife's sister and her husband were killed, along with their daughter, under very suspicious circumstances in a private plane crash, leaving their son, JJ, an orphan at four. So you and your wife took him in, out of the goodness of your hearts, and have been trying to give him some kind of family, help him through this terrible time. And then another man—Scott Burroughs—a man rumored to have been romantically involved with your sister-in-law, who was last seen leaving the home of a loose and notoriously single heiress—has moved into your house, while you—meanwhile—have been asked to leave by your wife."

He turns to Doug.

"You were thrown out," he says, "to call it what it is. Where did you sleep last night?"

"In my truck," Doug mumbles.

"What?"

"In my truck. I slept in my truck."

Bill shakes his head.

"You slept in a truck, while Scott Burroughs slept in your house. With your wife."

"No. I mean, I don't know if there's—that it's something romantic—I'm not—"

"Son, please. What else would it be? The man saves the boy—allegedly—and your wife takes him in, both of them, as if to make, what? A new family? Who cares that her actual husband is now homeless. Heartbroken."

Doug nods, the urge to cry suddenly unstoppable. But he pulls himself together.

"Don't forget about the money," he says.

Bill nods. *Bingo.*

"What money?" he says innocently.

Doug wipes his eyes, aware that he is slumped over. He straightens, trying to regain control.

"So—David and Maggie, JJ's parents—they were—well, you know—he ran this network. That's not to say anything shady, but—I mean, they were very wealthy people."

"Worth what? Approximately."

"Uh, I don't know that I should—"

"Ten million, fifty?"

Doug hesitates.

"More?" asks Bill.

"Maybe double," says Doug reluctantly.

"Wow. Okay. A hundred million dollars. And this money—"

Doug rubs his beard a few quick times with his hand, like a man trying to sober up.

"A lot of it goes to charity," he says, "but then, of course, the rest is JJ's. In a trust. Which—you know—he's four, so—"

"You're saying," says Doug, "I think you're saying, that whoever gets the boy, gets the money."

"That's, I mean, a coarse way of—"

Bill stares at him with disdain.

"I prefer the word *blunt*. My point is—and maybe I'm being dumb here—but there are tens of millions of dollars at stake for whoever parents this kid—my godchild, I should add. So—yeah—I'm not—in the spirit of full transparency—I'm not objective here by a long shot. After what he's been through, the death of his—everybody he loves— that this kid would become a pawn—"

"Well, I mean, Eleanor's not—she a good person. Means well. I just—my thought is, she must be—it's manipulation somehow."

"By the painter."

"Or—I don't know—maybe the money made her—the idea of it—changed her somehow."

"Because you thought you had a happy marriage."

"Well, I mean, there's some struggle, right? We don't always—but that's—in your twenties, thirties—it's hard work—life. Making your mark? And you're supposed to—stick by each other, not—"

Bill nods, sits back. In his right pant pocket, his phone vibrates. He slips it out and looks at the text message, his eyes narrowing. As he does, a second message comes in, then a third. Namor has been bugging the wife's home phone, and is writing to say he heard something.

Calls btwn swimmer and heiress last night. Sexy stuff.

And then . . .

Also swimmer and NTSB. Flight recorder damaged.

Followed by . . .

Swimmer admits bedding heiress.

Bill pockets his phone, pulls himself up to his full sitting height.

"Doug," he says, "what if I told you we had confirmation that Scott Burroughs bedded Layla Mueller, the heiress, just hours before driving out to your home?"

"Well, I mean—"

341

"And that he is talking to her still, calling her from your home?"

Doug feels his mouth go dry.

"Okay. But—does that mean—do you think—is he *with* my wife, or—"

"What do you think?"

Doug closes his eyes. He's not equipped for this, for the feelings he's having, the sense that somehow in the last two weeks he has gone from winner to loser, as if his life is a practical joke the world is playing on him.

In the studio, Bill reaches out and pats Doug's hand.

"We'll be right back," he says.

BULLETS

WHO AMONG US really understands how recording works? How an Edison machine, in the old days, laid grooves in a cylinder of vinyl and from those grooves, when played back with a needle, came the exact replica of the sounds recorded. Words or music. But how is that possible, for a needle and a groove to re-create sound? For a scratch in a plastic wheel to capture the exact timbre of life? And then the change to digital, and how the human voice now passes through a microphone into a hard drive and somehow is codified into ones and zeros, translated to data, and then reassembled through wires and speakers to reconstruct the precise pitch and tone of human speech, the sounds of reggae or birds calling to each other on a summer day.

It is just one of a million magic acts we have mastered over the centuries, technologies invented—from anatomical stents to war machines—their origins traced back to the dirty days of the Neanderthal and the creation of fire. Tools for survival and conquest.

And how ten thousand years later, men in skinny jeans and Oliver Peoples eyeglasses can disassemble a black box inside a sterile case and probe it with wiry pentalobes and penlights. How they can replace damaged ports and run diagnostic software, itself created from binary code. Each line simply a version of *on* or *off.*

Gus Franklin sits on the back of his chair, feet on the seat. He has been awake for thirty-six hours, wearing yesterday's clothes, his face unshaved. They're close. That's what they tell him. Almost all of the data has been recovered. He'll have a printout any second, the flight recorder data detailing every move the plane made, every command entered. The voice recorder may take longer, their ability to go back in time—the translation of ones and zeros into voices—hampering their ability to float inside that ghost cockpit and bear witness to the flight's final moments.

Ballistics show that the bullet holes are consistent with Gil Baruch's service weapon. Agent O'Brien—tired of looming over NTSB techs and asking *How much longer?*—is in the city, trying to find out more about the Batemans' body man. Because his body is missing, Agent O'Brien has floated a new theory. Maybe Gil turned on his employer, sold his services to another buyer (al-Qaeda? the North Koreans?), then—after the flight was under way—pulled his weapon and somehow crashed the plane, then escaped.

Like a villain in a James Bond movie? Gus asked to no response. He offered O'Brien the more likely theory that Baruch, whom they know wasn't buckled in, was killed in the crash, his body thrown clear, swallowed by the deep or eaten by sharks. But O'Brien shook his head and said they needed to be thorough.

On a parallel track, the autopsy results on Charles Busch came back about an hour ago. Toxicology was positive for alcohol and cocaine. Now there's an FBI team digging deeper into the copilot's history, interviewing friends and family, reviewing work history and school records. There's no evidence of any mental health issues in his files. Did he have a psychotic episode, like the Germanwings copilot? Had Busch always been a time bomb, and somehow managed to keep it secret?

Gus stares at the art gallery on the far side of the hangar. A train derailed. A tornado approaching. He was a married man once, two toothbrushes in the medicine cabinet. Now he lives alone in a sterile apartment by the Hudson, hermetically sealed inside a glass cube. He owns one toothbrush, drinks from the same glass at every meal, rinsing it afterward and placing it on the rack to dry.

A tech comes over carrying a clutch of paper. The printout. He hands it to Gus, who scans it. His team assembles around him, waiting. Somewhere the same information is being brought up onscreen, a second group gathered around that. Everyone is looking for narrative, a story told in latitude and altitude, the literal rise and fall of Flight 613.

"Cody," says Gus.

"I see it," says Cody.

The data is pure numbers. Vectors of thrust and lift. They're clean. They graph. To trace a journey mathematically, all you need are coordinates. Reading the data, Gus relives the final minutes of the airplane's journey—data divorced from the lives and personalities of the passengers and crew. This is the story of an airplane, not the people on board. Engine performance records, flap specifics.

Forgotten is the disaster scene around him, the art gallery and its patrons.

The data shows that the flight takes off without incident, banking left, then straightening out, the plane rising to twenty-six thousand feet over a period of six minutes and thirteen seconds, as ordered by ATC. At minute six, the autopilot is switched on and the flight heads southwest along a planned route. Nine minutes later, control of the plane is switched from pilot to copilot, Melody to Busch, for reasons the data can't project. Course and altitude remain constant. Then, sixteen minutes into the flight, the autopilot is turned off. The plane banks sharply and dives, what started as a slow port turn becoming a steep spiral, like a mad dog chasing its tail.

All systems were normal. There was no mechanical error. The copilot turned off the autopilot and took manual control. He put the plane into a dive, ultimately crashing into the sea. Those are the facts. Now they know the root cause. What they don't know is, (a) why? and (b) what happened next? They know Busch was drunk, high. Was

his perception or judgment altered by drugs? Did he think he was flying the plane normally, or did he know he had begun a death spiral?

More important, did the copilot wait for the pilot to go and then
deliberately crash the plane? But why would he do that? What possible root cause would lie behind such an action?

Gus sits for a moment. Around him there is a sudden rush of activity, numbers fed into algorithms, double-checked. But Gus is still.
He knows for certain now. The crash was no accident. Its origins
lie not in the science of tensile strength or joint wear, caused not by
computer failure or faulty hydraulics, but in the murky whys of psychology, in the torment and tragedy of the human soul. Why would a
handsome, healthy young man put a passenger plane into a steep and
irrevocable dive, ignoring the panicked pounding of the captain outside the cockpit and his own shrieking survival instinct? What possible
root cause lay in the gray matter of his brain—what previously un-
diagnosed mental illness or recent deafening gripe at the injustices of
the world—could inspire a senator's nephew to kill nine people, including himself, by turning a luxury jet into a missile?

And can they conclude then that the shots fired were an attempt to
reenter the cockpit and take control of the plane?

The solution to this mystery, in other words, lies outside the
purview of engineers, and in the realm of voodoo speculation.

All Gus Franklin can do is grit his teeth and wade into the storm.

He reaches for the phone, then thinks better of it. News like this,
in the aftermath of multiple leaks, is best delivered in person. So he
grabs his jacket and heads for the car.

"I'm heading in," he tells his team. "Call me when the techs crack
the recorder."

GAMES

THEY ARE PLAYING Chutes and Ladders in the living room when the call comes. *Doug is on TV.* Eleanor comes back from the kitchen phone shaking. She meets Scott's eye, pantomimes that they need a way to keep the boy busy so they can talk.

"Hey, buddy," Scott tells him, "go grab my bag from upstairs, huh? I got a present for you."

The boy runs upstairs, hair flying behind him, footsteps a sloppy cascade on the stairs. Eleanor watches him go, then turns, her face pale.

"What's wrong?" Scott asks.

"My mother," she says, looking for the TV remote.

"What—"

She is pawing through the junk drawer below the TV. "Where's the remote?"

He spies it on the coffee table, grabs it. She takes it, turns on the TV, pushes buttons. The black screen blinks on, a center star coming to life, becoming sound, birthing an elephant on a savanna, looking for water. Eleanor flips channels, searching.

"I don't understand," Scott says.

He throws a glance at the stairs. Overhead, he can hear the boy's feet on the ceiling, the closet door opening in the guest room.

Then there's a sharp intake of breath from Eleanor, and Scott turns back. Onscreen is a flanneled and bearded Doug, sitting across from the a red-suspendered Bill Cunningham. They are on a newsroom set, behind an anchor desk. It is a surreal sight, as if two different programs have been spliced together, side by side. A show about money and a show about trees. Doug's voice fills the room, mid-sentence. He is talking about Scott and how Eleanor threw her own husband out of the house, and maybe Scott is in it for the money, and Bill Cunningham is nodding and interrupting, and restating Doug's points—at one point even stepping in to tell the story himself.

—a washed-up painter who beds married women and glorifies disaster scenes.

Scott looks at Eleanor, who is clutching the remote to her chest, her knuckles white. For some reason he thinks of his sister lying in her coffin, a sixteen-year-old girl who drowned on a late-September day, swallowed by the murky deep, air bubbles rising. A virginal body that had to be dried and cleaned, muscled into its best dress by a forty-six-year-old mortician, a stranger who coated her skin with blush and brushed her waterlogged hair until it shone. And how her hands were raised to her chest, a spray of yellow daisies laced between her unfeeling fingers.

And how his sister was allergic to daisies, which upset Scott to no end, until he realized that it didn't matter anymore.

"I don't understand," Eleanor says, then repeats it—more quietly this time, to herself, a mantra.

Scott hears footsteps on the stairs, and turns. He intercepts the boy as he spills down the stairs carrying Scott's bag, a confused (potentially hurt) look on his face, as if to say *I can't find the present.* Scott approaches him at a raking angle, mussing his hair and detouring him smoothly into the kitchen.

"Couldn't find it?" he says, and the boy shakes his head.

"Okay," says Scott, "let me look."

He sits the boy at the kitchen table. Outside a mail truck pulls up to the driveway. The mail carrier wears an old-school pith helmet. Past him, Scott can see the raised dishes of the news trucks, parked at the end of the cul-de-sac, waiting, watching. The mailman opens the mailbox, puts in a supermarket circular and some bills, oblivious to the drama inside.

From the living room, Scott hears Doug say, "We were fine before he showed up. Happy."

Scott digs through his bag, looking for something he can claim is a present. He finds the fountain pen his father gave him when he left for college. A black Montblanc. It is the one thing Scott has kept through the years, his fortunes rising and falling, the one constant as he fumbled his way through spells of drinking, through his *great painter* phases, kamikaze-ing into periods of abject terror, numbing himself with booze, zeroing in on failure. And then through his rise from whatever ashes were left to a new body of work. A fresh start.

And how at his lowest point he threw all his furniture out the window, every plate and dish, everything he owned.

Except the pen.

He signs his paintings with this pen.

"Here," he tells the boy, pulling it out of his bag. The boy smiles. Scott unscrews the cap, shows the boy how it works, uses it to draw a dog on a paper napkin.

"My father gave it to me when I was young," he says, then realizes the implication, that he is now passing the pen on to his own son. That he has adopted the boy somehow.

He has the thought and pushes through it. Life can paralyze us, freeze us into statues if we think about things too long.

He hands the pen to the boy, arguably the last piece of the man he once was, his spine, the only thing about him that has stayed straight and true, unfailing, reliable. He was a boy once himself, an explorer setting out for undiscovered lands. Not a single cell of that boy remains now, Scott's body changed at the genetic level, every electron and neutron replaced over the decades by new cells, new ideas.

A new man.

The boy takes the pen, tries it on the napkin, but can't get a line.

"It's—" says Scott, "—it's a fountain pen, so you have to hold it—"

He takes the boy's hand, shows him how to hold it. From the kitchen he hears Bill Cunningham say, "—so first he befriends the sister—a wealthy woman—and now that she's dead and the money has passed to her son—suddenly he's in your house, and you're sleeping in an old truck."

The boy gets a black line out of the pen, draws another. He makes a happy sound. Watching him, something inside Scott snaps into place. A sense of purpose, a decision he didn't even know he was making. He walks to the phone, like a man on hot coals, determined not to look down. He dials information, gets the number for ALC, then asks for Bill Cunningham's office. After a few misdirects, he finds his way to Krista Brewer, Bill's producer.

"Mr. Burroughs?" she says, sounding breathless, as if she has run a great distance to reach the phone.

Because of the nature of time, the next moment is both endless and instantaneous.

"Tell him I accept," says Scott.

"Pardon?"

"The interview. I'll do it."

"Wow. Great. Should we—I can have a remote truck to you in an hour."

"No. Stay away from the house, from the boy. This is between me and the gargoyle. A conversation about how maybe bullying and belittling people from a distance is a bullshit coward's way to be a man."

The quality of her voice, in the next moment, can only be described as *elated*.

350

"Can I quote you on that?"

Scott thinks of his sister, her hands crossed, eyes closed. He thinks of the waves, towering, and the struggle to stay afloat, one arm dislocated.

"No," he says. "I'll see you this afternoon."

PAINTING #5

WE ARE SORRY FOR YOUR LOSS.[1]

---

1   (White letters on black canvas.)

THE HISTORY OF
VIOLENCE

GUS IS ON Second Avenue headed back to the hangar when the call comes.

"Are you following this?" Mayberry asks.

"Following what?" he says. He has been lost in thought, ruminating about his meeting with the state attorney general and heads of the FBI and the SEC. The copilot was high. He crashed the plane deliberately.

"It's turned into a real soap opera," Mayberry says. "Doug, the uncle, went on TV to say he'd been thrown out of the house and that Burroughs had moved in. And now they're saying Burroughs is headed into the studio for an interview."

"Jesus," says Gus. He thinks about calling Scott to warn him off, but then remembers that the painter has no cell phone. Gus slows for a red light, a taxi merging signal-less in front of him, forcing him to slam on the brakes.

"Where are we on the flight recorder?" he asks.

"Close," says Mayberry. "Ten minutes maybe."

Gus joins a line of traffic headed for the 59th Street Bridge.

"Call me the second you have it," he says. "I'm on my way back."

. . .

Sixty miles north, a white rental car threads its way through Westchester, toward the city. It's greener here, the parkway surrounded by trees. Unlike Gus's route, the road here is mostly empty. Scott changes lanes without signaling.

He tries to exist solely in the moment he's living, a man driving a car on an Indian summer day. Three weeks ago, he was a speck of dust in a raging sea. A year before that he was a hopeless drunk waking on a famous painter's living room rug, staggering out into the harsh sunlight and discovering an aquamarine swimming pool. Life is made of these moments—of one's physical being moving through time and space—and we string them together into a story, and that story becomes our life.

So as he is sitting in his rented Camry on the Henry Hudson Parkway, he is also sliding into a chair in studio 3 of the ALC Building an hour later, watching a young man with glasses hide a wire microphone under Bill Cunningham's lapel. And simultaneously he is a teenager home from college, sitting on a ten-speed Schwinn beside a country road at night, waiting for his younger sister to finish her swim in Lake Michigan. Because what if instead of a story told in consecutive order, life is a cacophony of moments we never leave? What if the most traumatic or the most beautiful experiences we have trap us in a kind of feedback loop, where at least some part of our minds remains obsessed, even as our bodies move on?

A man in a car, and on a bike, and in a television studio. But also in the front yard of Eleanor's house thirty minutes earlier, walking to the car, and Eleanor is asking him not to go, telling him that he's making a mistake.

"If you want to tell your story," she says, "fine, call CNN, call the *New York Times*. Not him."

Not *Cunningham*.

In the ocean, Scott grabs the boy and dives beneath a wave too big to comprehend.

And at the same time, he slows behind a dented station wagon, then puts on his turn signal and changes lanes.

In the dressing room, Scott watches Bill Cunningham grimace, hearing him roll his *r*'s and execute a succession of quick voice exercises, trying to decide if the feeling in his stomach is fear or dread or the thrill of the boxer before a fight he thinks he can win.

"Will you come back?" Eleanor asked him in the driveway.

And Scott looked at her, the boy on the porch behind her, eyes confused, and he said, "Is there a pool around here? I think I should teach the boy to swim."

And how Eleanor smiled and said, "Yes." There was.

In the hair and makeup room, Scott waited for Bill. It would be wrong to say he was nervous.

What was the threat of one man after he had faced down the entire ocean? So Scott simply closed his eyes and waited to be called.

"First of all," says Bill, when they're across from each other and the cameras are rolling. "I want to thank you for sitting down with me today."

The words are kind, but Bill's eyes are hostile, so Scott doesn't respond.

"It's been a long three weeks," says Bill. "I don't—I'm not sure how much any of us has slept. On the air—me personally—more than a hundred hours, on the hunt for answers. For the truth."

"Am I supposed to look at you or the camera?" Scott interrupts.

"At me. It's like any other conversation."

"Well—" says Scott. "I've had a lot of conversations in my life. None of them was like this."

"I'm not saying the content," says Bill. "I'm talking about two men talking."

"Except this is an interview. A damn interview isn't a conversation."

Bill leans forward in his chair.

"You seem nervous."

"Do I? I don't feel nervous. I just want to be clear on the rules."

"What do you feel then, if not nervous? I want viewers at home to be able to read your face."

Scott thinks about this.

"It's strange," he says, "you hear the word *sleepwalking* sometimes. How some people sleepwalk through life and then something wakes them up. I don't—that's not how I feel. Maybe the opposite."

He watches Bill's eyes. It's clear Bill doesn't know yet what to make of Scott, how to trap him.

"The whole thing feels like some kind of—*dream*," says Scott. He too is striving for truth. Or maybe he alone.

"Like maybe I fell asleep on the plane and I'm still waiting to wake up."

"Unreal, you're saying." says Bill.

Scott thinks about that.

"No. It's very real. Too real maybe. The way people treat each other these days. Not that I thought we lived on Planet Hugs, but—"

Bill sits forward, not interested in a conversation about manners.

"I'd like to talk about how you came to be on that plane."

"I was invited."

"By who?"

"Maggie."

"Mrs. Bateman."

"Yes. She said call her Maggie, so I call her Maggie. We met on the Vineyard last summer. June maybe. We went to the same coffee shop, and I'd see her at the farmers market with JJ and her daughter."

"She came to your studio."

"Once. I work out back of my house in an old barn. There were workmen in her kitchen, she said, and she needed something to do for the afternoon. The kids were with her."

"You're saying the only time you saw her outside of the market or a coffee shop, the kids were with her."

"Yes."

Bill makes a face to indicate maybe he thinks that's bullshit.

"Some of your work could be considered pretty disturbing, don't you think?" he says.

"For children you mean?" says Scott. "I suppose. But the boy was napping, and Rachel wanted to see."

"So you let her."

"No. Her mother. It wasn't my—and it's not like—for the record—the pictures aren't—*graphic*. It's just—an attempt."

"What does that mean?"

Scott thinks about that, what he's trying to say.

"What is this world?" he says. "Why do things happen? Does it *mean* something? That's all I'm doing. Trying to understand. So I showed them around—Maggie and Rachel—and we talked."

Bill sneers. Scott can tell that the last thing he wants to do is talk about art. In the cacophony of time he is sitting in a television studio, but part of him is still in his car, driving into the city—the wet road smeared with the red trails of taillights, and he is also somehow sitting on the plane, trying to get oriented—a man who minutes earlier had been running from the bus stop.

"You had feelings for her, though," says Bill. "Mrs. Bateman."

"What does that mean, feelings? She was a nice person. She loved her children."

"But not her husband."

"I don't know. It seemed that way. I've never been married, so what do I know. It's not something we ever—she was very comfortable, it seemed, as a person. They had fun, her and the kids. They laughed all the time. He worked a lot it seemed, David, but they were always talking about him, the things they'd do when Daddy got there."

He thinks for a moment.

"She seemed happy."

• • •

Gus is on the Long Island Expressway when the calls comes. The flight recorder is fixed. There is some degradation, they tell him, but it's in the quality of sound, not the content of the recording. His team is about to listen back and does Gus want them to wait for him?

"No," he says, "we need to know. Just put the phone up to the speaker."

They hurry to comply. He sits in his brown government vehicle in stop-and-go traffic. He is mid-island, past LaGuardia, not yet to Kennedy. Through the car's speakers he can hear hurried activity as they prepare to review the tape. It is a record of another time, like a jar that holds the last breath of a dying man. The actions and voices of the tape are secret still, but in moments they will be out. The last unknown thing will become known. And then everything that can be clear, will be clear. Any other mysteries are there for the ages.

Gus breathes recycled air. Rain dots his windshield.

The tape begins.

It starts with two voices from within the cockpit. The captain, James Melody, has a British accent. Charles Busch, the copilot, has a Texas drawl.

"Checklist, brakes," says Melody.

"Are checked," responds Busch after a moment.

"Flaps."

"Ten, ten, green."

"Yaw damper."

"Checked."

"Little crosswind here," says Melody. "Let's keep that in mind. Flight instrument and annunciator panels?"

"Uh, yeah. No warnings."

"Okay then. Checklist complete."

Traffic lightens ahead of Gus. He gets the Ford up to twenty-six mph then slows again as the line of cars ahead of him constricts. He would pull over to the side of the road and listen, except he's in the center lane with no exits in sight.

The next voice is Melody's.

"Vineyard flight control, this is GullWing Six Thirteen. Ready for takeoff."

A pause, and then a filtered voice comes through their radio.

"GullWing Six Thirteen, cleared for takeoff."

"Thrust SRS. Runway," Melody tells Busch.

He hears mechanical sounds from the tape. The phone relay makes them hard to identify, but he knows that techs in the lab are already making guesses about which ones are yoke movement and which are increases in engine rpm.

"Eighty knots." *Busch?*

More sounds from the tape as the plane leaves the ground.

"Positive rate," says Melody. "Gear up, please."

ATC comes over their radio.

"GullWing Six Thirteen, I see you. Turn left. Fly the Bridge. Climb. Contact Teterboro departure. Good night."

"GullWing Six Thirteen, thanks much," says Melody.

"Gear up," says Busch.

The plane is in the air now, on its way to New Jersey. Under normal conditions it is a twenty-nine-minute flight. Less than a short hop. There will be a six-minute lull before they are in range of Teterboro ATC.

A knock.

"Captain." A female voice comes in. The flight attendant, Emma Lightner. "Can I bring you anything?"

"No," says Melody.

"What about me?" asks the copilot.

A pause. What was happening? What looks were being exchanged?

"He's fine," says Melody. "It's a short flight. Let's stay focused."

. . .

Bill Cunningham leans forward in his seat. They are on a set designed to be seen from a single direction. This means that the walls behind him are unpainted on the backside, like a set built for an episode of *Twilight Zone*, where an injured man slowly realizes that what he thinks is real is actually theater.

"And on the flight," says Bill. "Describe what happened."

Scott nods. He doesn't know why, but he's surprised that the interview is unfolding in this way, as an actual interview about the crash, what happened. He assumed they'd be trading body blows by now.

"Well," he says, "I was late. The cab never came, so I had to take the bus. Until we reached the runway, I assumed I'd missed it, that I'd get there just in time to see the taillights lifting off into the sky. But I didn't. They waited. Or not waited—they were folding in the door when I—but they didn't leave. So I—got on—and everyone was already—some people were in their seats—Maggie and the kids, Mrs. Kipling. David and Mr. Kipling were still on their feet, I think. And the flight attendant gave me a glass of wine. I'd never been on a private jet before. And then the captain said, *Take your seats*, so we did."

His eyes have moved off Bill's by now, and he finds himself staring directly into one of the lights, remembering.

"There was a baseball game on, Boston. It was the seventh inning, I think. And the sound of that, the announcer's voice, was going the whole time. And I remember Mrs. Kipling was next to me and we were talking a little. And the boy, JJ, was asleep. Rachel was on her iPhone, maybe choosing songs. She had headphones on. And then we were up."

. . .

Gus snails past LaGuardia, incoming and outgoing flights roaring past overhead. He has the windows up and the air off so he can hear better, even though it's ninety degrees out. He sweats as he listens, tendrils running down his sides and back, but he doesn't notice. He hears James Melody's voice.

"I've got a yellow light."

A pause. Gus can hear what sounds like tapping. Then Melody again.

"Did you hear me? I've got a yellow light."

"Oh," says Busch. "Let me—that's got it. I think it's the bulb."

"Make a note for maintenance," says Melody. Then a series of unidentifiable sounds, and then Melody exclaims, "*Merde*. Hold on. I've got a—"

"Captain?"

"Take over. I've got a goddamn nosebleed again. I'm gonna—let me get cleaned up."

Sounds from the cockpit that Gus assumes are the captain getting up and going to the door. As this happens, Busch says:

"Copy. Taking control."

The door opens and closes. And now Busch is alone in the cockpit.

. . .

Scott listens to the sound of his own voice as he speaks, both in the moment and outside of it.

"And I was looking out the window and thinking the whole time how unreal it felt—the way you sometimes feel like a stranger when you find yourself outside the limits of your experience, doing something that feels like the actions of another person, as if you've teleported somehow into someone else's life."

"And what was the first sign that something was wrong?" says Bill. "In your mind."

Scott takes a breath, trying to make logical sense of it all.

"It's hard, because there was cheering and then there was screaming."

"Cheering?"

"For the game. It was David and Kipling, they were—something

361

was happening onscreen that had them—Dworkin and the longest at-bat—and their seat belts were off by that point, and I remember they both stood up, and then—I don't know—the plane—*dropped*—and they had to scramble to get back in their seats."

"And you've said before, in your interview with investigators that *your* seat belt was off."

"Yeah. That was—it was stupid really. I had a notebook. A sketch-book. And when the plane pitched down my pencil flew out of my hands and I—unbuckled and went after it."

"Which saved your life."

"Yeah. I guess that's true. But in the moment—people were screaming and there was this—*banging*. And then—"

Scott shrugs, as if to say, *That's all I really remember.*

Across from him Bill nods.

"So, that's your story," he says.

"My story?"

"Your version of events."

"That's my memory."

"You dropped your pencil and unbuckled to grab it, and that's why you survived."

"I have no idea *why* I survived, if that's even—if there is a why, and not just, you know, the laws of physics."

"Physics."

"Yes. You know, physical forces that picked me up and threw me from the plane and somehow let the boy survive, but not—you know—anyone else."

Bill pauses, as if to say, *I could go deeper, but I'm choosing not to.*

"Let's talk about your paintings."

• • •

There is a moment in every horror movie that hinges on silence. A character leaves a room, and rather than go with him, the camera remains in place, focused on nothing—an innocuous doorway perhaps, or a child's bed. The viewer sits and watches the empty space, listening to the silence, and the very fact that the room is empty and the fact that it is silent convey a dawning sense of dread. *Why are we here, waiting? What's going to happen? What will we see?* And so, with a creeping fear, we begin to search the room for something unusual, to strain against the silence for whatever whispers live beneath the ordinary. It is the room's very unremarkableness that adds to its potential for horror, what Sigmund Freud called the Uncanny. True horror, you see, comes not from the savagery of the unexpected, but from the corruption of everyday objects, spaces. To take a thing we see every day, a thing we take for granted as normal—a child's bedroom—and transform it into something sinister, untrustworthy—is to undermine the very fabric of life.

And so we stare into the normal, the camera motionless, unwavering, and in the tension of that unblinking stare, our imagination produces a feeling of fear that has no logical explanation.

It is this feeling that comes over Gus Franklin as he sits in his car on the LIE, surrounded by commuters on their way to points east, men driving home from work, families heading home from school or to the beach for a late-afternoon adventure. The silence in his car has a crackle to it, a hiss that fills the recycled air. It is machine noise, impenetrable, but unignorable.

Gus reaches over and turns up the volume, the hiss becoming deafening.

And then he hears whispering, a single word, whispered over and over again.

Bitch.

. . .

"Let's not talk about my paintings," says Scott.

"Why? What are you hiding?"

"I'm not—they're paintings. By definition everything relevant about them is there for the eye to see."

"Except you're keeping them secret."

"The fact that I haven't shown them yet is not the same as me keeping them secret. The FBI has them now. I have slides at home. A few people have seen them, people I trust. But the truth is, my paintings are literally irrelevant."

"Let me get this straight—a man who paints disaster scenes, literal plane crashes, is in a plane crash and we're supposed to think, what? That it's just a coincidence?"

"I don't know. The universe is filled with things that don't make sense. Random coincidences. There's a statistical model somewhere that could work out the odds of me being in a plane crash or a ferry accident or a train derailment. These things happen every day, and none of us is immune. My number came up is all."

"I spoke to an art dealer," says Bill, "who said your work is now worth hundreds of thousands of dollars."

"Nothing's been sold. That's theoretical money. Last time I checked I had six hundred dollars in the bank."

"Is that why you've moved in with Eleanor and her nephew?"

"Is what why I've moved in with Eleanor and her nephew?"

"Money. The fact that the boy is now worth close to a hundred million dollars?"

Scott looks at him.

"Is that a real question?" he says.

"You bet your ass."

"First of all, I haven't moved in."

"That's not what the woman's husband told me. In fact, she threw him out of the house."

"Just because two things happen in sequence, doesn't mean there's a causal relationship."

"I didn't go to an Ivy League school, so you're gonna have to explain that one."

"I'm saying the fact that Eleanor and Doug have separated—if that's what happened—has nothing to do with the fact that I came to visit."

Bill pulls himself up to his full height.

"Let me tell you what I see," he says. "I see a failed painter, a drunk, who's floating along ten years past his prime and then life hands him an opportunity."

"A plane crashed. People are dead."

"He finds himself in the spotlight, a hero, and suddenly everyone wants a piece of him—he starts banging a twenty-something-year-old heiress. His paintings are hot shit all of a sudden—"

"Nobody's banging—"

"And then, I don't know, maybe he gets greedy and thinks, Hey, I've got a good thing going with this kid, who's suddenly worth a fortune, and who has a beautiful, a very attractive, aunt and a kind of loser uncle—so I can come in like the hot shit I am, and take over. Get a piece of that."

Scott nods, amazed.

"Wow," he says. "What an ugly world you live in."

"It's called the real world."

"Okay. Well, there's maybe a dozen mistakes in what you just said. Do you want me to go through them in order, or—"

"So you deny you've been sleeping with Layla Mueller."

"Am I having sex with her? No. She let me stay in an unused apartment."

"And then she took off her clothes and got in bed with you."

Scott stares at Bill. How does he know that? Is it a guess?

"I haven't had sex with anyone in five years," he says.

"That's not what I asked. I asked if she got naked and jumped in the sack with you."

Scott sighs. He has nobody to blame but himself for being in this position.

"I just don't understand why it matters."

"Answer the question."

"No," he says, "tell me why it matters that an adult woman is interested in me. Tell me why it's worth outing her in public for something she did when she was under her own roof that she would probably want to keep quiet."

"So you admit it?"

"No. I'm saying, what possible difference does it make? Does it tell us why the plane crashed? Does it help us process our grief? Or is it something you want to know because you want to know it."

"I'm just trying to figure out how big a liar you are."

"About average, I'd say," says Scott. "But not about things that matter. That's part of my sobriety, a vow I took, to try and live as honestly as possible."

"So answer the question."

"No, because it's none of your business. I'm not trying to be an asshole here. I'm literally asking what possible difference it makes. And if you can convince me that my personal life after the crash has any relevance to the events leading up to the crash and isn't just this kind of parasitical vulture exploitation, then I'll tell you everything I am, happily."

Bill studies Scott for a long moment, a bemused look on his face.

And then he plays the tape.

. . .

Bitch.

That fucking bitch.

Gus realizes he's holding his breath. The copilot, Charles Busch is alone in the cockpit, and he is muttering these words under his breath.

And then, louder, he says:

No.

And switches off the autopilot.

CHARLES BUSCH

DECEMBER 31, 1984–AUGUST 26, 2015

HE WAS SOMEBODY'S nephew. That was the way people talked behind his back. As if he never would have gotten the job any other way. As if he was a bum, some kind of hack. Born in the final minutes of New Year's Eve 1984, Charlie Busch had never been able to escape the feeling that he had missed something vital by inches. In the case of his birth what he missed was the future. He started life as last year's news, and it never got much better.

As a boy he loved to play. He wasn't a good student. He liked math okay, but bore zero love for reading or science. Growing up in Odessa, Texas, Charlie shared the same dream as all the other boys. He wanted to be Roger Staubach, but he would have settled for Nolan Ryan. There was a pureness to high school sports, the knuckle slider and the backfield flea flicker, that got into your soul. Wind sprints and alligator drills. The low-shoulder kamikaze into heavy blocking sleds. The football field, where boys are hammered into men by pattern and repetition. Steve Hammond and Billy Rascal. Scab Dunaway and that big Mexican with hands the size of rib eyes. *What was his name?* A fly ball shagged on a cloud-free spring day. Pads and helmets shrugged on in jockstrap locker rooms, stinking of heat and the fight-or-fuck pheromones of hot teen musk. The oiled mitt between your mattress and box spring, and how you always slept better with it under there, hardball wrapped in a web of leather thumbs. Boys on the verge of what comes next, grappling in the dirt, using their heads to open alleys. And how it felt to run forever and never get tired, to stand in a dusty dugout trash-talking relief pitchers, your buddy Chris Hardwick lowing like a cow. The coffin corner and the crackback block. The primal monkey joy of picking dirt from your cleats with any old stick, a bunch of boys on a bench spitting sunflower shells and digging deep down in the rubber. The in-between hop and the lefty switch. Hope. Always hope. And how when you're young every game you play feels like the reason the world exists. The pickoff and the squeeze play. And the heat. Always the heat, like a knee in your back, a boot on your neck. Drinking Gatorade by the gallon and chewing ice chips like a mental patient, bent at the knee sucking wind in the midday sun. The feel of a perfect spiral as it reaches your hands. Boys in shower stalls laughing at each other's dicks, bell-curving the cheerleaders, and pissing on the next guy's feet. The beanball and the brushback, and how it feels to round first base and dig for second, eyes on the center fielder, sliding headfirst, already safe in your mind. The panic of getting caught in a pickle, and how white chalk lines when they're fresh gleam like lightning against the grass, itself a deep, impossible green. Heaven is that color. And the bright lights of Friday night, those perfect alabaster lights, and the roar of the crowd. The simplicity of the game, always forward, never back. You throw the ball. You hit the ball. You catch the ball. And how after graduation nothing would ever that simple again.

He was somebody's nephew. Uncle Logan, his mother's brother. Logan Birch, a six-term US senator from the great state of Texas, friend to oil and cattle, longtime chairman of the Ways and Means Committee. Charlie knew him mostly as a rye drinker with sculpted hair. Uncle Logan was the reason Charlie's mother pulled out the fancy plates. Every Christmas they drove out to his mansion in Dallas. Charlie remembered the family all dressed in matching Christmas sweaters. Uncle Logan would tell Charlie to make a muscle, then squeeze his arm hard.

"Gotta toughen this boy up," he told Charlie's mother. Charlie's father had died a few years earlier, when Charlie was six. Coming home from work one night an eighteen-wheeler sideswiped him. His car flipped six times. They had a closed-casket funeral and buried Charlie's father in the nice cemetery. Uncle Logan paid for everything.

Even in high school, being Logan Birch's nephew helped him. He played right field for the varsity team, even though he couldn't hit as well as the other boys, couldn't steal a base to save his life. It was unspoken, this special treatment. In fact, for the first thirteen years of his life, Charlie had no idea he was being elevated above his station. He thought the coaches liked his hustle. But that changed in high school. It was the locker room that woke him up to this conspiracy of nepotism, the wolf pack mentality of boys in jockstraps surrounding him in the shower. Sports is a meritocracy, after all. You start because you can hit, because you can run and throw and catch. In Odessa, the football team was notorious for its speed and precision. Every year veterans of the baseball team got a free ride to good colleges. West Texas sports were competitive. You put up lawn signs. Businesses closed early on game days. People took this shit seriously. And so a player like Charlie, mediocre in all things, stood out like a sore thumb.

The first time they came for him, he was fifteen, a skinny freshman who'd scored the starting kicker spot after shanking a thirty-six-yard field goal. Six hulking ranch thugs, stripped down and sweaty, shoved him into a shower stall.

"Watch your shit," they told him.

Cowering in the corner, Charlie could smell their sweat, the musky funk of half a dozen teenage linebackers, not one under 250 pounds, who'd just spent three hours steam-cooking in the August sun. He bent and vomited onto their feet. They beat him good for that, slapping him around with their cocks for good measure.

In the end, huddled on the floor, he flinched when Levon Davies bent and hissed in his ear.

"Tell a fucking soul and you're dead."

It was Uncle Logan who pulled the strings to get Charlie into the flight training program of the National Guard. It turned out he wasn't a bad pilot, though he tended to freeze in sudden emergencies. And after the National Guard, when Charlie was kicking around Texas unable to hold down a job, it was Logan who spoke to a friend at GullWing and landed Charlie an interview. And though he had yet to find anything in life he was truly good at, Charlie Busch did have a certain sparkle in his eye, and a certain cowboy swagger that worked with the ladies. He could charm a room and he looked good in a suit, and so when he sat down with the HR director of the airline he seemed like the perfect addition to GullWing's fast-growing stable of young, attractive flight personnel.

They started him as a copilot. This was September 2013. He loved the luxury jets, loved the clients he served—billionaires and heads of state. It made him feel important. But what he really loved was the grade-A, top-shelf pussy working the main cabin. Goddamn, he thought the first time he saw the flight crew he'd be working with. Four beauties from around the world, each more fuckable than the next.

"Ladies," he said, lowering his aviators and giving them his best Texas grin. The girls didn't even blink. Turns out they didn't sleep with copilots. Sure, the company had a policy, but it was more than that. These women were international sophisticates. Many spoke five languages. They were angels that mortal men could look at, but never touch.

Flight after flight, Charlie made his play. And flight after flight he was rebuffed. Turns out, not even his uncle could get him into the pants of a GullWing flight attendant.

He had been at the company for eight months when he met Emma. Right away he could tell she was different from the others, more down to earth. And she had that slight gap between her front teeth. Sometimes during a flight he'd catch her in the galley humming to herself. She would blush when she realized he was standing there.

She wasn't the hottest girl in the fleet, he thought, but she seemed attainable. He was a lion stalking a herd of antelope, waiting for the weakest one to wander off.

Emma told him her father had flown for the air force, so Charlie inflated his experience in the National Guard, telling her he spent a year in Iraq flying F-16s. He could tell she was a daddy's girl. Charlie was twenty-nine years old. His own father died when he was six. The only real role model he'd had for how to be a man was a rye drinker with fancy hair who told Charlie to make a muscle every time they met. He knew he wasn't as smart as the other guys or as skilled. But being less talented meant he'd had to develop ways of passing. You didn't have to be confident, he realized early on. You just had to seem confident. He was never a great fastball hitter, so he learned how get on base by walking. He couldn't deliver the monster punt so he mastered the onside kick. In classroom situations he'd learned to deflect hard questions by making a joke. He learned how to talk shit on the baseball field and how to swagger in the National Guard. Wearing the uniform made you a player, he reasoned. Just like carrying a weapon made you a soldier. It may have been nepotism that got him in, but there was no denying now that his résumé was real.

And yet who had ever really loved Charles Nathaniel Busch for who he was? He was somebody's nephew, a pretender, the varsity athlete who'd become a pilot. It looked, for all intents and purposes, like an American success story, so that's what he called it. But deep down inside he knew the truth. He was a fraud. And knowing this made him bitter. It made him mean.

. . .

He caught a ride from Heathrow on a GullWing charter, landing in New York at three p.m. on Sunday August 26. It had been six months since Emma broke up with him, since she told him to stop calling her, stop going by her place and trying to get on her flights. She was scheduled to do a milk run to Martha's Vineyard and back, and Charlie had it in his head that if he could just get a few minutes alone with her he could make her understand. How much he loved her. How much he needed her. And how sorry he was about what had happened. Everything, basically. The way he'd treated her. The things he'd said. If he could just explain. If she could only see that deep down he wasn't a bad guy. Not really. He was just someone who'd been faking his way through the world for so long, he had become consumed by the fear of being found out. And all of it, the cockiness, the jealousy, the pettiness, was a by-product of that. *You* try pretending to be someone you're not for twenty years, see how it changes you. But my God, he didn't want to be afraid anymore. Not with Emma. He wanted her to see him. The real him. To know him. Because didn't he deserve that for once in his life? To be loved for who he was, not who he pretended to be?

He thought about London, seeing Emma again, like a snakebite, poison spreading through his veins, and how his instinct when he felt out of his depth was to attack, close the distance between himself and his—what? Opponent? Prey? He didn't know. It was just a feeling, a kind of panicked advance, that had him put on airs, had him hike up his pants and slip on his best cowboy swagger. The only thing you can do, he had long ago decided, when you care too much, is to act like you could give two shits—about school, about work, about love.

It had worked often enough that the behavior had calcified inside of him, and so when he saw Emma, when his heart jumped into his throat and he felt vulnerable and exposed, this is what he did. Turned up his nose. Insulted her weight. Then spent the rest of the night following her around like a puppy.

Peter Gaston had been happy to give Charlie the Vineyard flight, get a couple more days of R&R in London. They'd bonded Friday night, drinking until dawn in Soho, bouncing from bar to night-club—vodka, rum, ecstasy, a little coke. Their next scheduled drug test wasn't for two weeks, and Peter knew a guy who could get them clean piss. So they threw caution to the wind. Charlie was trying to get his courage up. Every time he looked at Emma, he felt like his heart was splitting in two. She was so beautiful. So sweet. And he'd fucked it up so royally. Why had he said that to her before, about putting on a few pounds? Why did he have to be such an asshole all the time? When she came out of the bathroom in a towel, all he'd wanted to do was hold her, to kiss her eyelids the way she used to kiss his, to feel the pulse of her against him, to breathe her in. But instead he made some bullshit wisecrack.

He thought about the look on her face that night when he put his hands around her throat and squeezed. How the initial thrill of sexual experimentation turned first to shock, then horror. Did he really think she would like it? That she was *that kind of girl*? He had met them before, the tattooed kamikazes who liked to be punished for who they were, who liked the scrapes and bruises of reckless animal collision. But Emma wasn't like that. You could see it in her eyes, the way she carried herself. She was normal, a civilian, unblemished by the trench warfare of a fucked-up childhood. Which was what made her such a good choice for him, such a healthy move. She was the Madonna. Not the whore. A woman he could marry. A woman who could save him. So why had he done it? Why had he choked her? Except maybe to bring her down to his level. To let her know that the world she lived in wasn't the safe, gilded theme park she thought it was.

He'd had some dark times after that night, after she left him and stopped answering his calls. Days he lay in bed from sunrise to sundown, filled with dread and loathing. He kept it together at work, riding the second chair through takeoffs and landings. Years of covering his weaknesses had taught him to pass, no matter how he felt inside. But there was an animal attraction inside him on those flights, a live wire sparking in his heart that wanted him to push the yoke nose-down, to roll the plane into oblivion. Sometimes it got so bad he had to fake a shit and hide out in the washroom, breathing through the blackness.

Emma. Like a unicorn, the mythic key to happiness.

He sat in that bar in London and watched her eyes, the corner of her mouth. He could feel her deliberately not looking at him, could feel the muscles in her back tensing whenever his voice got too loud at the bar, trading jokes with Gaston. She hated him, he thought, but isn't hate just the thing we do to love when the pain becomes unbearable?

He could fix that, he thought, turn it back, explain the hate away with the right words, the right feelings. He would have one more drink and then he would go over. He would take her hand softly and ask her to come outside for a cigarette and they would talk. He could see every word in his head, every move, how first it would be just him. How he would lay it all out, the History of Charlie, and how she would have her arms folded across her chest in the beginning, defensive, but as he went deeper, as he told her about his father's death, being raised by a single mom, and how somehow he ended up a ward of his uncle, how, unbeknownst to him, his uncle paved the way for Charlie to coast through life. But how it was never what he wanted. How all Charlie wanted to be judged on his own merits, but how, as time went on, he got scared that his best wasn't good enough. So he surrendered and let it happen. But that was all over now. Because Charlie Busch was ready to be his own man. And he wanted Emma to be his woman. And as he talked she would lower her arms. She would move closer. And in the end she would hold him tight and they would kiss.

He had another seven-and-seven, a beer back. And then, at some point when he was in the bathroom with Peter doing another line, Emma disappeared. He came out of the john wiping his nose and she was gone. Charlie made a beeline for the other girls, feeling jittery and spooked.

"Hey," he said, "uh, so Emma, did she split?"

The girls laughed at him. They looked at him with their fucking haughty model eyes, and barked their disdain.

"Sweetie," said Chelsea, "do you really think you're in the same league?"

"Just, fucking, is she gone?"

"Whatever. She said she was tired. She went back to the flat."

Charlie threw some cash on the bar, ran out onto the street. The booze and the drugs had him feeling turned around, which was why he walked ten blocks in the wrong direction before finally figuring it out. *Fuck. Fuck.* And by the time he got back to the apartment she was gone. Her stuff was gone.

She had vanished.

And the next day, when Peter groaned and said he had to get to New York for a job and that Emma would be on it, Charlie offered to take the gig. He lied and told Peter he would clear it with the company, but it wasn't until he showed up at Teterboro Airport in New Jersey that anyone knew that Charlie was taking Peter's place. And at that point it was too late to do anything.

Riding a jump seat in the cockpit of a 737 across the Atlantic, Charlie drank coffee after coffee, trying to sober up, to get his shit together. He'd startled Emma, showing up like that in London. He could see that now. He wanted to apologize, but she'd changed her phone number, had stopped responding to his emails. So what choice did he have? How else could he fix this, except to track her down once more, to plead his case, throw himself on her mercy?

Teterboro was a private airport twelve miles outside Manhattan. GullWing kept a hangar there, its corporate logo—two hands crossed at the thumb, fingers spread like wings—was emblazoned in gray on the flat tan siding. The hangar office was closed on Sunday, except for a skeleton crew. Charlie took a cab from JFK, bypassing the city to the north and coming in on the George Washington Bridge. He tried not to look at the meter as the fare rose. He had a Platinum Amex card, and besides, he told himself it didn't matter what it cost. This was for love. Peter had given him the flight's itinerary. Scheduled time of departure from New Jersey was seven p.m. The plane was an

OSPRY 45XR. They'd take the short hop to the Vineyard sans passengers, board their charter, and head right back. They wouldn't even need to refuel. Charlie figured that gave him at least five hours to find a private moment with Emma, to pull her aside and touch her cheek and talk the way they used to, to take her hand and say *I am so sorry*. To say *I love you. I know that now. I was an idiot. Please forgive me.*

And she would, because how could she not? What they'd had was special. The first time they'd made love she'd cried, for God's sake. Cried at the beauty of it. And he'd fucked it up, but it wasn't too late. Charlie had seen all the romantic comedies these chicks swooned over. He knew that perseverance was the key. Emma was testing him. That was all. Putting him through his paces. It was Female 101. She loved him, but he needed to prove himself. To show her he could be steady, reliable, to show her that this time it was storybook. She was the fairy princess and he was the knight on the horse. And he would. He was hers, now and forever, and he would never give up. And when she saw that she would fall into his arms and they'd be together again.

He showed his pilot's license at the Teterboro security gate. The guard waved them in. Charlie felt the nerves in his stomach, rubbed his face with his hand. He wished he'd remembered to shave, worried that he looked sallow, tired.

"It's the white hangar," he told the cabbie.

"Two sixty-six," the guy told him after they came to a stop.

Charlie ran his card, climbed out, taking his silver roller bag. The OSPRY was parked on the tarmac just outside the hangar. Floodlights from the building made the fuselage glow. He never got tired of the sight, a precision aircraft, like a gleaming thoroughbred, all thrust and lift under the hood, but smooth as butter on the inside. A three-member ground crew was gassing her up, a catering truck parked near the nose. A hundred and four years ago two brothers built the first airplane and flew it on a North Carolina beach. Now there were fleets of fighters, hundreds of commercial airliners, cargo planes, and private jets. Flying had become routine. But not for

Charlie. He still loved the feeling as the wheels left the ground, as the plane surged into the stratosphere. But that didn't surprise him. He was a romantic, after all.

Charlie scanned the area for Emma, but didn't see her. He had changed into his pilot's uniform in the bathroom at JFK. Seeing himself in the crisp whites steadied him. Who was he if not Richard Gere in *Officer and a Gentlemen*? Wearing it now, he wheeled his roller bag into the hangar, heels clicking on the asphalt. His heart was in his throat and he was sweating like he was back in fucking high school, angling to ask Cindy Becker to prom.

Jesus, he thought. *What is this chick doing to you? Pull it together, Busch.*

He felt a flash of anger, the rage of an animal against its cage, but he ignored it.

Squelch that shit, Busch, he told himself. *Stay on mission.*

He saw Melody first, the captain on the flight. James. Older guy, not much fun, but competent. Extremely. British ponce, thought he was the boss of everything. But Charlie knew how to kowtow. It was part of passing.

"Afternoon, Captain," he said.

Melody recognized him, frowned.

"What happened to Gaston?" he said.

"You got me," said Charlie. "Stomach thing, I think. All I know is I got a call."

The captain shrugged. It was the front office's problem.

"Well, you're late. I was just about to do a walk-around. Stow your bag and let's go."

Charlie spotted Emma in the second-floor office. His heart rate multiplied.

"Just, uh, give me a minute," he said.

He left his bag and hurried past the captain, gone before he could say anything. The office was a catwalk overlook built into the hangar. Staff only. Clients never even entered the hangar. They were ferried directly to the plane by limousine. It was the strict written policy of the company that employees keep the behind-the-scenes process of GullWing Air invisible, nothing that would burst the bubble of the traveler's luxury experience.

To reach the office you had to climb an exterior flight of metal stairs. Putting a hand on the grip railing, Charlie felt his mouth go dry. On impulse, he reached up and adjusted his hat, giving it a slight cock. Should he put on the aviators? No. This was about connection, about eye contact. His hands felt like wild animals, fingers twitching, so he shoved them in his pockets, focusing on each stair, on lifting his feet and putting them down. He had thought about this moment for the last sixteen hours, seeing Emma, how he would smile warmly and show her he could be calm, gentle. And yet he felt anything but calm. It had been three days since he'd slept more than two hours straight. Cocaine and vodka was what was keeping him smooth, keeping him moving. He went over it again in his head. He would reach the landing, open the door. Emma would turn and see him and he would stop and stand very still. He would open himself to her, show her with his body and his eyes that he was here, that he'd gotten her message. He was here and he wasn't going anywhere.

Except it didn't happen that way. Instead, as he reached the landing, he found Emma was already looking his way, and when she saw him she went white. Her face. And her eyes went giant, like saucers. Worse, when he saw her see him, he froze, literally, with his right foot hovering in midair, and gave a little...wave. *A wave?* Like what kind of idiot gives a faggy little wave to the girl of his dreams? And in that moment she turned and fled deeper into the office.

Fuck, he thought, *fuckity, fuck fuck*.

He exhaled and finished climbing. Stanhope was in the office, the coordinator who'd be working tonight. She was an older woman with zero lips, just an angry slash under her nose.

"I'm, uh, here to work Six Thirteen," he said. "Checking in."

"You're not Gaston," she said, looking at her logbook.

"Stellar fucking observation," he told her, eyes searching the inner offices, visible through the glass wall, for Emma.

"Excuse me?"

"Nothing. Sorry. I just—Gaston is sick. He called me."

"Well, he should have called me. We can't just have personnel swapping shifts. It's screws up the whole..."

"Absolutely. I'm just doing the guy a...did you see where Emma..."

He peered through the glass, looking for his dream girl, feeling a little frantic. His mind was racing, auditioning scenarios, working double time to figure out how to rectify this whole disaster.

She ran, he thought. *She fucking turned tail and... what the hell was that about?*

Captain Melody came into the office.

"Jenny," he said. "I'm sorry, but we—it's almost liftoff time. Can we figure out the paperwork when we come back?"

The woman nodded.

"Okay. We'll deal with this after the flight."

She turned to Charlie.

"Check in with me when you land, okay? We have these protocols for a reason."

"Yeah," said Charlie. "Sure. Sorry for the—I don't know why Gaston didn't call."

He followed Melody back to the plane, casting around for Emma. He climbed the steps and was surprised to find her in the galley, breaking up ice.

"Hey," he said. "Where did you—I was looking for you."

She turned away, pretending not to hear.

The captain opened the cockpit door.

"Okay," he said. "Let's run the systems."

Reluctantly, Charlie followed Melody into the cockpit, stowing his bag. Powering up the system and running diagnostics, Charlie told himself that he'd handled things well, maybe not perfectly, but... She was just playing hard to get. The next six hours would go like fucking clockwork. Textbook takeoff. Textbook landing. There and back in five hours and then he'd be the one changing his phone number, and when she came to her senses and realized what she'd lost, well, she'd be the one begging him for forgiveness.

Cycling the engines, he heard the cockpit door open. Emma stormed into the main cabin.

"Keep him away from me," she told Melody, pointing at Charlie, then stalked back to the galley.

The captain looked over at his copilot.

"You got me," said Charlie. "Must be her time of the month."

They finished their pre-flight run-through and closed the hatch. At six fifty-nine p.m. they taxied to the runway and lifted off without incident, moving away from the setting sun. A few minutes later, Captain Melody banked to starboard and pointed them toward the coast.

For the rest of the flight to Martha's Vineyard, Charlie stared out at the ocean, slumping visibly in his seat. As the rage left him, the serious lightning nerves that had been fueling him, he felt exhausted, deflated. The truth was, he hadn't slept, really, in maybe thirty-six hours. A few minutes on the flight from London, but mostly he'd been too amped up. A lingering effect of the coke, possibly, or the vodka/Red Bulls he'd been drinking. Whatever it was, now that his mission had failed, had epically imploded, he felt destroyed.

Fifteen minutes from the Vineyard, the captain stood, put a hand on Charlie's shoulder. Charlie jumped in his seat, startled.

"She's all yours," said Melody. "I'm gonna grab a coffee."

Charlie nodded, straightening. The plane was on autopilot, gliding effortlessly over the open blue. As the captain exited the cockpit, he closed the door (which had been open) behind him. It took Charlie a few moments to register that. That the captain had closed the door. And why? Why would he do that? It had been open for takeoff. Why close it now?

Except for privacy.

Charlie felt a hot flush go through him. That was it. Melody wanted privacy so he could talk to Emma.

About me.

A new burst of adrenaline hit Charlie's bloodstream. He needed to focus. He slapped himself in the face a couple of times.

What should I do?

He ran through his options. His first instinct was to storm out and confront them, to tell the pilot that this shit was none of his business. *Go back to your seat, old man.* But that was non-rational. He could be fired for that probably.

No. He should do nothing. He was a professional. She was the drama queen, the one who brought their private business in to work. He would fly the plane (okay, watch the autopilot fly the plane) and be the grounded adult.

And yet he had to admit that it was killing him. The closed door. Not knowing what was going on out there. What she was saying. Against his better judgment he stood, then sat, then stood again. Just as he was reaching for the door it opened, and the captain came back with his coffee.

"Everything okay?" he asked, closing the door behind him.

Charlie turned at the waist and did a kind of upper-body stretch.

"Absolutely," he said. "Just...got a cramp in my side. Trying to stretch it out."

The sun was starting to set as they made their final approach into Martha's Vineyard. On the ground, Melody taxied past ground control and parked. Charlie stood as soon as the engines were off.

"Where are you going?" the captain asked.

"Cigarette," said Charlie.

The captain stood.

"Later," he said. "I want you to run a full diagnostic on the flight controls. The stick felt tight on landing."

"Just a quick cigarette?" Charlie said. "We've got, like, an hour before takeoff."

The captain opened the cockpit door. Behind him Charlie could see Emma in the galley. Sensing the cockpit door open, she looked over, saw Charlie, and looked away fast. The captain shifted his hip to block Charlie's view.

"Run the diagnostic," he said, and exited, closing the door behind him.

Fucking petty bullshit, thought Charlie, turning to the computer. He sighed, once, twice. He stood. He sat. He rubbed his hands together until they felt hot, then pressed them against his eyes. He'd flown the plane for fifteen minutes before landing. The stick felt fine. But Charlie was a professional, Mr. Professional, so he did what he was asked. That had always been his strategy. When you spend your life playing a role you learn how to make it look good. File your paperwork on time. Be the first on the field for grass sprints. Keep the uniform pressed and clean, your hair trimmed, your face shaved. Stand up straight. Be the part.

To calm himself he pulled out his headphones and put on some Jack Johnson. Melody wanted him to run diagnostics? Fine. He wouldn't just do what he was asked. He would spit-polish this thing. He started in on the diagnostic, soft guitars strumming in his ears. Outside the last sliver of sun dipped behind the trees and the sky took on a midnight hue.

The captain found Charlie in his seat thirty minutes later, fast asleep. He shook his head and dropped into his chair. Charlie shot up, heart jackhammering, disoriented.

"What?" he said.

"Did you run the diagnostic?" Melody asked.

"Uh, yeah," said Charlie, flicking switches. "It's . . . everything looks good."

The captain looked at him for a beat, then nodded.

"Okay. The first client is here. I want to be ready for wheels-up at twenty-two hundred hours."

"Sure," said Charlie, gesturing. "Can I . . . I gotta piss."

The captain nodded.

"Come right back."

Charlie nodded.

"Yes, sir," he said, managing to keep all but a hint of sarcasm out of his voice.

He stepped out of the cockpit. The crew bathroom was right next to the cockpit. He could see Emma standing in the open doorway, waiting to greet the first guests as they arrived. On the tarmac, Charlie could see what looked like a family of five, illuminated in the headlights of a Range Rover. He studied the back of Emma's neck. Her hair was up in a bun, and there was a loose wisp of auburn arced across her jaw. The sight of it made him dizzy, the overwhelming urge he had to fall to his knees and press his face into her lap, an act of penance and devotion, the gesture of a lover, but also that of a son to a mother, for what he wanted was not the sensual pleasure of her naked flesh, but the maternal feeling of her hands on his head, the unconditional acceptance, the feel of her fingers in his hair, the motherly stroking. It had been so long since anyone had just stroked his hair, had rubbed his back until he fell asleep. And he was so tired, so profoundly tired.

In the bathroom he stared at himself in the mirror. His eyes were bloodshot, his cheeks dark with stubble. This was not who he wanted to be. A loser. How had he let himself fall this far? How did he ever let this girl break him down? When they were dating he found her affection stifling, the way she would hold his hand in public, the way she put her head on his shoulder. As if she were marking him. She was so into him he felt it had to be an act. As a lifelong role player, he was certain he could spot another bullshitter from a mile away. So he went cold on her. He pushed her away to see if she would come back. And she did. It made him mad. *I'm on to you*, he thought. *I know you're fucking faking. The con is up. So drop the act.* But she just seemed hurt, confused. And finally, one night, when he was fucking her and she reached up and stroked his cheek and said *I love you*, something inside him snapped. He grabbed her by the throat, at first just to shut her up, but then, seeing the fear in her eyes, the way her face turned red, he found himself squeezing harder, and his orgasm was like a white bolt of lightning from his balls to his brain.

Now, staring at himself in the mirror, he tells himself he was right all along. She was faking. She had been playing him, and now that she was done she'd just thrown him away.

He washes his face, dries his hand on a towel. The plane is vibrating as passengers climb the stairs. He can hear voices, the sound of laughter. He runs his hand through his hair, straightens his tie.

Professional, he thinks. And then, just before he opens the door and reenters the cockpit.

Bitch.

FLIGHT

ON THE TAPE, Gus hears an automated voice.

"Autopilot disengaged."

This is it, he thinks. *The beginning of the end.*

He hears the sound of the engines, an increase in rpm that he knows from the data recorder was the copilot putting the plane into a turn and powering up.

You like that? he hears Busch mutter. *Is that what you want?*

It's just a matter of time now. The plane will impact the water in less than two minutes.

And now he hears pounding on the door, and hears Melody's voice.

Jesus, let me in. Let me in. What's going on? Let me in.

But now the copilot is silent. Whatever thoughts he has in the last moments of his life he keeps to himself. All that remains, under the sound of the pilot's desperation, are the sounds of a plane spiraling to its death.

Gus reaches over and turns up the volume, straining to hear something, anything. Because it's a digital signal, there is no tape hiss, just the silence of the cockpit, peppered with low mechanical noise and the thrum of the jets. And then—gunshots. He jumps, swerving the car into the left-hand lane. Around him, car horns blare. Swearing, he corrects back into his own lane, losing count of the number of shots

385

in the process. At least six, each like a cannon on the otherwise silent tape. And under them the sound of a whispered mantra.

Shit, shit, shit, shit.

Bang, bang, bang, bang.

And now a surge in rpms as Busch leans on the throttle, the plane spinning like a leaf circling down a drain.

And even though he knows the outcome, Gus finds himself praying that the captain and the Israeli security man will get the door open, that they'll overcome Busch and the captain will take his seat and find some miracle solution to right the plane. And, as if in sympathy with his own held breath, the gunshots are replaced by the sound of a body slamming into the metal cockpit door. Later, technicians will re-create the sounds, determining which is a shoulder and which is a kick, but for now they are just the urgent sounds of survival.

Please, please, please, thinks Gus, even as the rational part of his brain knows they're doomed.

And then, in the split second before the crash, a single syllable:

Oh.

Then—impact—a cacophony of such size and finality that Gus closes his eyes. It continues for four seconds, primary and secondary impacts, the sounds of the wing shearing off, the fuselage breaking up. Busch will have been killed immediately. The others may have lasted a second or two, killed not by the impact, but by flying debris. None, thankfully, lived long enough to drown as the plane sank to the bottom. This they know from the autopsy.

And yet somewhere in the chaos, a man and a boy survived. Hearing the crash on tape turns the fact of this into a full-blown miracle.

"Boss?" comes Mayberry's voice.

"Yeah. I'm—"

"He did it. He just—it was about the girl. The flight attendant."

Gus doesn't respond. He is trying to comprehend the tragedy, to kill all those people, a child, for what? A lunatic's broken heart?

"I want a full analysis of all the mechanics," he says. "Every sound."

"Yessir."

"I'll be there in twenty minutes."

Gus hangs up. He wonders how many more years he can do this job, how many more tragedies he can stomach. He is an engineer who is beginning to believe that the world is fundamentally broken.

He sees his exit approaching, moves to the right lane. Life is a series of decisions and reactions. It is the things you do and the things that are done to you.

And then it's over.

. . .

The first voice Scott hears on the tape is his.

What's going on? he asks. *In your mind. With us.*

The recording quality is distant, a layer of mechanical hiss over the top. It sounds like a phone call, which is what Scott realizes it is, in the instant he recognizes his own voice.

Let's go to Greece, he hears Layla say. *There's a little house on a cliff I own through, like, six shell companies. Nobody knows a thing. Complete mystery. We could lie in the sun and eat oysters. Dance after dark. Wait till the dust clears. I know I should be coy with you, but I've never met anyone whose attention is harder to get. Even when we're together it's like we're in the same place, but different years.*

"Where did you—" Scott asks.

Bill looks at him and raises his eyebrows with a kind of triumph.

"You still think we should believe nothing happened?"

Scott stares at him.

"Did you—how did you—"

Bill holds up a finger—*Wait for it.*

The tape plays again.

How's the boy?

It's Gus's voice. Scott doesn't have to hear the next voice to know that it will be his.

He's not—talking, really, but he seems to like that I'm here. So maybe that's therapeutic. Eleanor's really—strong.

And the husband?

He left this morning with luggage.

A long pause.

I don't have to tell you how that's going to look, says Gus.

Scott finds himself mouthing his next words along with the tape.

Since when does how a thing looks matter more than what it is?

Two thousand twelve, I think, says Gus. *Especially after—your hideout in the city. How that made the news. The heiress, which—I said find some-*place to hide, *not shack up in a tabloid story.*

Nothing happened. I mean, yeah, she took off her clothes and climbed into bed with me, but I didn't—

We're not talking about what did or didn't happen, says Gus. *We're talk-ing about what it looks like.*

The tape ends. Bill sits forward.

"So you see," he says. "Lies. From the very beginning you've been telling nothing but lies."

Scott nods, his mind putting the piece together.

"You recorded us," he says. "Eleanor's phone. That's how you knew—when I called her from Layla's house—that's how you knew where I was. You traced the call. And then—did you have Gus's phone too? The FBI? Is that how—all those leaks—is that how you got the memo?"

Scott can see Bill's producer waving frantically from off camera. She looks panicked. Scott leans forward.

"You bugged their phones. A plane crashed. People died, and you bugged the phones of the victims, their relatives."

"People have a right to know," says Bill. "This was a great man. David Bateman. A giant. We deserve the truth."

"Yeah, but—do you know how illegal it is? What you did? Not to mention—*immoral.* And we're sitting here, and you're worried about what—that I had a consensual relationship with a woman?"

Scott leans forward.

"And meanwhile, you have no idea what actually happened, how the copilot locked the captain out of the cockpit, how he switched off the autopilot and put the plane into a dive. How six shots were fired into the door—gunshots—probably by the Batemans' security guard, trying to get it open, trying to regain control of the plane. But they couldn't, so they all died."

He looks at Bill, who—for once in his life—is speechless.

"People died. People with families, with children. They were murdered, and you're sitting here asking me about my sex life. Shame on you."

Bill gets to his feet. He looms over Scott. Scott stands himself, facing off, unflinching.

"Shame on you," he repeats, this time quietly, just to Bill.

For a minute it seems Bill will hit him. His fists are balled. And then two cameramen are grabbing him, and Krista is there.

"Bill," she yells. "Bill. Calm down."

"Get off me," yells Bill, struggling, but they hold him firm.

Scott stands. He turns to Krista.

"Okay," he says. "I'm done."

He walks away, allowing the anger and struggle behind him to fade. He finds a hallway and follows it to an elevator. Feeling like a man waking from a dream he presses the button, then waits for the doors to open. He thinks about the floating wing, and how it was on fire, thinks about the boy's voice calling in the dark. He thinks about his sister, and how he waited on his bike in the growing darkness. He thinks about every drink he ever took, and what it feels like to hear the starting gun and dive into chlorinated blue.

Somewhere the boy is waiting, playing trucks in the driveway, coloring outside the lines. There is a lazy river and the sound of the leaves blowing in the wind.

He will get his paintings back. He will reschedule those gallery meetings, and any others that present themselves. He will find a pool and teach the boy to swim. He has waited long enough. It's time to press PLAY, to let the game finish, see what happens. And if it's going to be a disaster, then that's what it's going to be. He has survived worse. He is a survivor. It's time he started acting like one.

And then the doors open, and he gets on.